If you are ten years old, you have seen ghost. They live under the bed or in the shadows of your darkened room. I've seen them and I'm not ashamed to admit it. All the way from *Jack-in-the-Box Clown*, who haunts a child's room, to soldiers coming to the rescue, the disappearing, and on to the terrifying *Demon Eyes* creature that inhabits the dark, dank corners of the swampy woods, these tales will dredge up memories that you had hidden away, or you thought were hidden. Follow the animal trails through the thick underbrush to discover who the real murderer was in Traders Hill. This spellbinding book will keep you up at night, either reading it or afraid to go to sleep.

~Dave Tuttle, author of *Pirates, Gamblers, and Scalawags,*
and the *Lt. Wilson* series co-written by Cara Curtain

Ron Miller has put together an amazing collection of spellbinding stories sure to captivate writers and readers alike. Hang on to your hat and let Miller take you for a readable read.

~Dickie Anderson, *From the Porch* columnist and author of her
From the Porch book Collection

Reviews for
Callie Kinser of Brush Creek

With *Callie Kinser of Brush Creek*, Ron Miller has penned a dark and complex novel of good and evil set in the mountainous country of east Tennessee in the 1940s, a tale of simple joy and complex sadness played out by unforgettable characters of a bygone era. With incisive writing and sharp character development, the author draws the reader into the twists and turns of his plot: of innocence and sin, abiding love and loathsome deeds, vile acts and ultimate redemption. An excellent read.

~ William Rawlings, author of *A Killing on Ring Jaw Bluff*

Ron is a wonderful writer. *Callie Kinser of Brush Creek* is at times uplifting, tense, and tearful making it a wondrous yet heart-aching adventure. The characters are vivid, compelling, and sometimes far too real for comfort. Ron Miller is a masterful storyteller.

~T. A. Ridgell, author of *Operation: Stiletto*,
When Opportunity Knocks, and *Fractured Souls*

It is at the end of WWII that we find the beginning of Ron Miller's debut novel entitled *Callie*. It is the story of two families, each moving in different directions that eventually will collide as the summer of 1945 unfolds. Callie Kinser, a teenager is angry at the world in a way most young girls are as they fight the coming of adulthood. She battles her younger sister, Maggie, a musical prodigy whose talent with a banjo will lead her to never before dreamed of possibilities. But before such dreams can come true, darkness will invade McMinn County, Tennessee as Willow Branch arrives and slowly reveals the evil that resides with her father, Moss. Ron Miller has written a novel that will draw you into a simpler time before suddenly shifting expectations of story toward a darker study of rural Tennessee at a moment when the country was poised on the brink of post-war recovery. It is a stark reminder of where evil resides and how human compassion and love will in the end triumph. It is a novel to be read, if you are willing to look at life as whole cloth.

~ Jack Riggs, author of *When the Finch Rises* and *The Fireman's Wife*

Reviews for
*Horse Bones – 12 Tales of Secrets,
Ghosts, and Legends*

<u>For Middle Readers</u>

In this fine collection of "tales of the unlikely" Ron Miller spins a web of scary and richly atmospheric stories. Who knew that the piney woods, the boggy wetlands, and the abandoned railroad spurs of North Florida were stalked and haunted by spooks, specters, and vibrating balls of light?
With a sure command of character and place Ron Miller will scare and intrigue his readers. His character, Jimmy Redmon, temporary president of the Five Points Spook Club, may cringe as he always says, "I don't like spooky places!" But for those of you who do, *Horse Bones* is a great read.

~Adrian Fogelin, author of *Crossing Jordan,
Summer on the Moon,* and other young adult novels

I was hooked from page one by Ron Miller's ghosts. I even glanced over my shoulder a time or two to see if there was anything behind me. *Horse Bones* is a must read!

~Shannon Greenland, author of the award winning
Middle Grade spy series, *The Specialist*

Ron Miller writes with flair and imagination. His *12 tales* takes us back to a childhood where anything is possible, including a belief in the supernatural. Prepare yourself for a shiver-producing collection filled with strange happening and uneasy pleasures, yet filled with the camaraderie and good humor of its youthful cast of characters. *Horse Bones* is good fun.

~Vic DiGenti, author of the *Windrusher* and the *Francis Parker*
series. Vic is also a 35 year veteran in public broadcasting

CALLIE KINSER OF BRUSH CREEK

Copyright © 2014 Ron Miller

Ron Miller -
Callie Kinser of Brush Creek

Library of Congress Control Number: 2014936002
ISBN: 978-0-9860596-0-5

SOUTHERN FICTION: Coming of Age / Sibling Rivalry / Child
Abuse / Rape / Murder / Mystery / Friendship

Published by
Antebellum Press
86164 Vegas Blvd.
Yulee, FL 32097

Text Layout and Cover Design by Caroline Blochlinger -
www.cbAdvertising.com

FIRST EDITION

Acknowledgements

No author can bring a book to life without help. It has to be read by people who will give you an honest critique. It has to be edited by someone who is not afraid to tell you to throw away 10,000 words, or to rewrite the first five chapters. It takes good people who are willing to give you information when you are doing research. It takes a lot of patience from family members when you are holed up in your favorite writing place for hours and hours. The list goes on.

My first vote of thanks goes out to my long time friends who shared some great times for seven years critiquing each other's work; Sandy Callahan, Debi Kopach, Terri Wright, and for a while, Tom Silverio, my sincere gratitude for your help, and most of all for the fond memories. I wouldn't trade them for anything. Terri, a seasoned author of three novels and a novella offered a lot of stark advice and even more encouragement over and beyond our critique sessions. I was the only male in the room. You wouldn't believe what my ears had to endure. They had no shame, these three women. I learned more about "women stuff" than I cared to know. Aside from that, I am proud to call them my friends, and I love them.

Thanks Emily Carmine, of Noteworthy editing, for your outstanding job cutting and slicing "Callie"—and to Molli Nickell for helping me with the mechanics of writing. A special thank you to Chuck Barrett, author of *Absolute Power* and two other Jake Pendleton thrillers for helping me with the business side of publishing.

For those who were kind enough to read my work and offer praise, a simple thank you is not enough. Writers need other writers to succeed.

My wife, Linda, took it on the chin many times when I opened up my laptop and hid away to empty my mind of the words swirling around inside. She also took some great pictures of me for the Bio page and website. I love you.

My graphic designer, Caroline Blochlinger, of CB Advertising Services, Inc., did a fantastic job of conversion/layout, designing the book's cover and my imprint logo. Jason Foote, of Web Designs by Jason, did a wonderful job creating my web site. Thanks to the both of you.

Thank you Ricky Beebe for giving me your mother's favorite sayings; Maggie was lucky to have you and Sandy to take care of her in her later years.

My oldest living brother, Allen, took me around the hills of Tennessee introducing me to Sligers that I had never met and showing me places I had never seen. Those were great times.

Maggie's cat poem was written many, many years ago by my good friend Keith Dampier. It fits Maggie perfectly. I still laugh when I think about it.

Of course I would not have written this book in the first place without Callie, Corbit, and Maggie. You are an inspiration to me and my family of Millers and Sligers.

This book is dedicated to the three people who inspired it: Callie Sliger Miller, Corbit Sliger, and Maggie Sliger Beebe.

Your lives remain an inspiration to me.

In memory of Eric Miller
You left us to wonder what you might have become

Into each life some rain must fall.
-Henry Wadsworth Longfellow-

CALLIE KINSER
OF
BRUSH CREEK

RON MILLER

Chapter 1
The Hill

Standing behind a tree on the back side of the hill overlooking Brush Creek, a girl with auburn hair and somber eyes watched as Corbit and Callie Kinser ran to the top laughing and teasing. She ached to have a taste of what they had — something she had never known in her sixteen years. The pretty dress she wore represented everything she hated, and nothing she wanted.

The man she despised stalked her, watching her every move. The plug of Days Work wallowed in his mouth. Streaks of brown spittle channeled through three-day whiskers and ran down his neck. What she had belonged only to him, and he intended for it to stay that way.

❧

It had to be magic! What else could it be, this first day of summer? It awakened with a shower of sunlight inundating the landscape from forest to grassy hills and deep hollows. Clear rays of morning spread as far as the eye could see… or imagine. The iron clay soil had shaken off the doldrums of winter, replacing the drabness with lush blades of green and a blazing brilliance of warmth and joy. Every blade and leaf sparkled with early morning dew.

"This is it! I thought this day would never get here!" Corbit pumped his bony fist in the air. "Yes!"

"I'll be John Brown if I didn't, either!" Callie pulled her skinny knees up to her chin as she sat on the moist earth. "Look at the spider webs on the grass. They look like tents made for angels to live in instead of creepy spiders."

"Looks like something you'd live in," Corbit said.

She threw her head back and extended her arms, flapping them like wings. "I do look like an angel, don't I?"

"Don't flatter yourself. I meant you looked like a creepy spider."

"I'll be dad-blamed if you can make me mad this morning, Corbit *Ettis* Kinser. I've been looking forward to the first day of summer vacation all year."

"Yeah, me too… and don't call me that name!"

Callie's and Corbit's minds danced, giddy and alive with wonder and excitement as only the first day of summer vacation could bring… or a Saturday morning. It happened to be both.

The first day ranked high along with Fourth of July fireworks in town square, or Christmas morning gathered around the tree with the aroma of pine pitch crackling in the fireplace, or the first strawberry picking.

"Hot diggity dog!" Corbit cried, looking over the dewy hillside. The condensed droplets made everything seem fresh, a new creation unsullied from the footsteps of man, preserved only for forest creatures, innocent and pure.

As far back as the beginning of time, as old as the rocks, trees, and hollows, the Hill, as Callie and Corbit called it, had stood here. The highest point on the Kinser family's small farm, it overlooked the forest, lorded over the farmland, watching, and waiting. It had become a tradition, this climb to the top of the Hill on the first morning of summer vacation. Here, they celebrated the beginning, or was it the ending?

"How many years has it been, you think, since we started coming here on the first morning of summer vacation?" Callie yawned as she gazed at the pink-streaked clouds garnishing the azure sky. Shoulder-length black hair touched moist grass and a skinny shadow as she leaned back on her elbows.

"Let's see..." Corbit put three fingers on his forehead, tapping it with his index finger. "I'm fourteen and you're twelve, so... umm... about five years now, I guess."

"Five years! That long? Wow — that's forever."

"Yeah, we were young then." Corbit sighed and flopped down on the moist ground among the wildflowers wrapping him in a delicious scent. Corbit picked one and stuck it to his nose. "Ummm. These flowers smell good enough to eat."

"And look at the different flavors to pick from. I like the yellow, red, and blue ones with white eyes. They look so yummy," Callie said, looking over the carpet of blossoms.

"Eyes? Yuck! Who wants to eat eyes? I'll just stick to weeds and dirt. I like the earthy taste."

Callie looked downhill toward Brush Creek, or The Brush as the locals called it. The meandering water sparkled as it reflected the sun's early rays. "What about the creek?"

"What about it?" Molasses-slow laziness oozed from Corbit's voice as he yawned long and loud. The display of energy deficiency went straight to Callie's mouth, too, as she responded with a similar yawn.

"You know, where does it come from? It has to start somewhere, you know?"

"Come from?" Corbit took on the look of a professor while tapping his chin with his finger. "I suppose it could start in some far off place, like Egypt, or Rome, or Atlanta."

"No way, that's too far from Tenn'see. It couldn't come from those places." Callie yawned again. Corbit followed suit.

Corbit locked his hands around knobby knees and rocked back and forth as wet bare feet glistened from morning rays. With his big toe he idly brushed away specks of red clay from his other foot. "Well, how about Chat'nugga or Knoxville, then?"

"Hmmm. I don't know… maybe." Callie put her finger on her lips with the tip touching her nose and spoke with certainty. "Nooo, I don't think so."

Corbit snapped his fingers. "Hey, I got it!"

"Yeah?"

"What if nobody knows where it comes from? Maybe it just flows from yesterday."

Callie wrinkled her brow. "I'll be John Brown. That's it! How'd you figure that out?"

Unlocking his fingers from crunched-up knees and stretching one leg out in front of the other, he said, "Oh, that's plumb easy. Today it's here, right?"

"Uh huh."

"And yesterday, somewhere else, you see?"

Callie lit up. "Hey, yeah, of course. I think you got it! So,what about tomorrow?"

He opened his arms wide. "Why, the future of course. Where else?"

"Oh, wow, why didn't I think of that?" Callie could always count on her brother to come up with the right answer. She nodded, completely satisfied with his revelation.

"Do you think we should've brought Maggie with us?" Corbit asked.

Callie frowned. "Nah, we'd just have to listen to that ol' banjo of hers. It'd ruin everything. Besides, she'd be a dumb Dora, saying stupid things, and all."

"Yeah, I suppose… maybe. But I don't think her being here and strumming her banjo would be so bad."

Callie rolled her eyes. "That'd be awful — absolutely awful! I hate that thing — and her, too!"

☙❧

The girl listened intently. Everything sounded so perfect to her, except for the thing about Maggie. *I don't understand why she doesn't want her sister to be with them here.* She gazed at the two siblings with longing. *I'd love to be on this hill with my brother and sister. That'd be wonderful!* She couldn't help but dream, to imagine a life without guilt or fear. She envisioned a family, together, full of love and laughter, something she had never known except in her visions, her castles in the sky.

❧

Callie thought of something else. "Do you think things will ever change?"

"Change? Like how?" Corbit asked.

"You know, we stop swimming in the creek, or cutting cane poles, or going fishing and such. You know, grow up and move away. Things like that?"

He thought for a second. "Yeah, I guess so. At least one day it will."

Callie pushed off her elbows and sat straight up. "Oh, that's an awful thing to say!"

Brush Creek snaked along, replete with ancient rocks, long-dead trees and endless Indian summers. It held the laughs and shouts of rope-swinging revelers as far back as the first row of corn. It flowed with memories, meandering, lazy and content. The Brush had coursed perpetually through the East Tennessee hills and hollows ages before pioneers had settled the community of Brush Creek. It had graciously provided enough fish to fill scores of empty dinner plates, sustaining the community even during the hungry days of the Great Depression and many days before.

"Look at our house." Callie pointed down the hill. "It looks old and worn out. I remember when the paint looked like white clouds, or at least that's how I imagined it."

"Yeah, the paint's turned a rotten kind of gray. It kinda looks dead. But I still like it."

"Me too. It looks… well, like home."

The worn and swaying steps led up to a tired, wrap-around porch where a swing hung from rusty, squeaky chains. White cane-back chairs adorning the porch offered rest and conversation for Sunday company, or peace and silence at the end of each day. The outside looked old and fading, but inside their home was not dead, or dying, but alive with young and not so young, growing up and growing older.

A mix of rich and poor farmers with stately antebellum mansions and modest homes standing next to each other defined the community of Brush Creek. A place, too, where shacks run-down by poverty, dotted the hills and hollows of the Smoky Mountain foothills. The rich and scrub-poor worked, lived, and died together in this peaceful Corner of the world.

The Brush, as Corbit imagined, ran from yesterday's cool hazy mountains carving its way through the woods and fields of the countryside all the way to tomorrow… and the next day. The old-timers compared Brush Creek to a patchwork quilt stitching the community together through good times and bad — a guarding moat separating and protecting everyone from the outside world.

Callie picked up a twig and snapped it in two. "I sure am glad Whirl War II is over and Deddy's back home."

"Yeah, so am I." Corbit, pushing himself off the ground, stretched high on tiptoes and drew in a slow, deep breath, "I smell bisquits…"

"And bacon," Callie joined in. "Ummm."

"And coffee, too. Plurp, plurp, plurp."

"Race ya!" Callie hopped up like a rabbit and took off down the hill.

"Hey, no fair! Wait for me!"

Feet challenged, stumbled, recovered, and pounded the earth. Brown dead leaves crunched. Pine saplings bent and swooshed as the siblings swept down the Hill in a cyclone of new energy.

In a dead heat they smashed through the last shrubs and undergrowth of the forest into the open yard. The smell of fresh-plowed earth from newly planted fields mixed with succulent wood smoke from the blackened brick chimney.

Callie and Corbit stopped short of the house, stood there, inhaled slowly and deeply. "That sure is a nice smell," Callie said.

"Yeah, for sure."

They trotted the last few yards toward breakfast and summer.

Little did Callie and Corbit know that, like the creek flowing to tomorrow, the summer of 1945 would define their future. Change would come. The Kinser children would experience a metamorphosis, shed their innocence where they would hang from their cocoon for a moment, and then, like butterflies, float off to a different stage of life.

As Callie and Corbit joined their family for breakfast, a huge man stepped from the morning shadows, grabbed the sad-eyed girl, slapped her, threw her to the ground and kicked her in the ribs.

"I done tole you not to be nosin' around," he sneered and unbuckled his overalls. "Looks like you need sumpin' I got."

Chapter 2
Maggie the Opry Star

I can't wait to go to the revival preachin' tonight," Maggie gushed. "Julie McCracken says a gospel quartet from Chat'nugga is gonna sang tonight. They call themselves the Chicken-mauga Soldiers of Christ."

"No, Maggie," her mother gently corrected, "Chick-a-mau-ga, not chicken-mauga, silly." Ellie's brown eyes crinkled with love as she brushed back short black hair with wisps of gray from her face. A little plump and a tad over five feet tall, she watched over her brood with a stern but gentle hand.

Maggie, tall for a ten-year old, loved music more than food, or breathing; she drew nourishment and life-sustaining oxygen from the timbre of swirling notes no magician could replicate. She'd come to be regarded as the family expert, except by Callie, who only considered her lazy.

Maggie had begged for a banjo since the age of five, having seen one in a Montgomery Ward catalog, and developed a love for the crisp sound by listening to the Grand Ole Opry on the Philco radio prominately displayed in the living room and watching performers make music on the back of a flatbed truck in downtown Athens.

Bud, Maggie's father, surprised her with a used banjo

two years ago, on her eighth birthday. The frets were worn and the varnish scratched, but it had a tight leather head and five brand new strings. When Bud pulled it out of a feed sack and presented it to her, Maggie couldn't speak. Tears welled up in her large brown eyes as shaky hands reached for the instrument. She pulled it to her bosom with reverence. A natural for music, it didn't take long before she could strum "Turkey in the Straw," "Tweedle-o-twill," and a couple of gospel tune as well. The more advanced picking and rolls would come later with hours of practice.

Callie and Corbit considered farm chores work. Maggie avoided chores altogether. Her work, according to her, consisted of learning to play the banjo. Corbit didn't care. He took pride in Maggie's newfound talent. Callie, though, had resented it from the beginning.

"You strumming that ol' thing again?" Callie had said — more than once — with gooey sarcasm.

Maggie always responded without missing a beat. "I've gotta practice if I'm gonna be a Grand Ole Opry star."

"You *already* think you're a star. All you want to do is sit and fram on that old piece of wood and cowhide, especially at chore time."

Callie had her own talent. She could sew anything out of feed and flour sacks, or mill ends from Chattanooga cotton mills, most of the time without using a pattern. She could imagine what it would look like, whether a dress or a pillow case, and it would always turn out right.

Her parents, and even Corbit, fussed more over Maggie and her banjo than they did over the things she sewed. She'd noticed it right away. The banjo became her sworn enemy. Maggie became the object of her resentment.

Today, Maggie announced, "Julie's brother, Wilton, is gonna sang ah ca pelican. That means he's gonna sang without music." She threw her head back proud as a peacock for knowing something so sophisticated.

Maggie may have been the music expert, but Callie didn't know any better either, until their mother turned from the stove and said with a smile, "No, Maggie, it's pronounced *a capella*, not ah-ca-pelican."

"See! You don't know everything," Callie snapped in a high-pitched mocking tone.

"That's enough, Callie. Maggie knew what it meant even though she didn't say it right." Momma looked at Callie with her "don't-say-another-word" eyes before turning to check on the biscuits browning in the oven.

Corbit loped into the kitchen and slumped into a chair. "I don't want to go hear no stupid preacher a-blabberin' his mouth off about me being a sinner and all."

Like a fired rifle Ellie shot straight over to Corbit, who leaned back comfortably on the hind legs of a chair. "Sounds like you need to be preached to more than anybody else in this family, or maybe Brush Creek as the matter goes. Fact is, it might do you good to have your blabber, sin-filled mouth worshed out with soap."

"But, Momma, I…"

"Shush! I've heard enough of your belly-aching about revival. You're going tonight with the rest of the family and I don't want to hear any more about it. Understood?"

Corbit's mouth clamped shut like a rat trap. He was licked, and he knew it.

After a hearty breakfast with plates sopped clean, everyone, except for Maggie, helped clear the table. She continued to prepare for stardom on the Opry stage.

Ellie snapped her fingers. "All right, younguns get to your morning chores, and no lollygagging around, that is if you want to go swimmin' later on."

"Come on, *Ettis*. Let's scat." Callie grinned at her brother and scampered out the back door.

A slap in the face, a cold bucket of water over his back, being stabbed, beheaded, or called a dirty rotten yellow dog sounded better than being called Ettis, Corbit's middle name. He hated it. He never could understand why his parents would give him a "pickin' fight" name, as he called it.

Callie taunted him with the hated moniker when she wanted to get under his skin or get back at him for some perceived injustice, but in most cases, just for the fun of it.

He knew better than to smack his sister when his mother had already sentenced him to a Saturday night on the chain gang, or church, which to him meant the same thing. So he stormed out to the woodpile and placed Callie's imaginary head up on the splitting block. He pretended to be an executioner for King Henry the Eighth. He donned his black hood, ran his finger over the blade to test the sharpness so as to ensure the job could be done with one whack. No bone, no sinew, nothing, just a clean, smooth cut so Anne Callie Boleyn's head would roll free, right into the basket. *Plunk!*

Whack! "There, it's done! That'll teach you to call me that confounded name!"

Corbit snatched around and glared at Callie standing across the yard. She grabbed her neck and winced, stuck her tongue out, smirked, and flipped him the finger. The bird flew hard, fast, and right to the roost. She grinned, having the assurance of safety because of Corbit's previous slight of the Lord's anointed, and Momma's subsequent indignation.

She skipped over to the chicken yard wrapped in small meshed wire holding the yard birds prisoner. There they labored day after day, laying golden eggs just to have their treasure plundered and devoured.

Maggie, the egg thief's derelict accomplice, wasn't there. It was Maggie's job to spread corn on the ground while the head thief checked the nests for fresh-laid eggs, or cackle berries, as their daddy called them.

Callie turned at the sound of strumming. "That Old Gray Mare Is Back Where She Used To Be" didn't set well with her ears.

She boiled hot, steam rolled from both ears, and a whistle sounded in her head. Thoroughly annoyed, she stormed through the prison yard. Frenzied, cackling chickens, sounding like gossipy old ladies, scattered as the egg thief rumbled through.

Callie yanked the gate open and slammed it behind her, not bothering to latch it. The chicken-prisoners seemed to sense it not to be a good time to escape.

Callie transformed from an egg thief to a freight train going downhill with a full head of steam. Her wheels gripped, turned, faster and faster.

The Grand Ole Opry star stood on the chair-stage singing and strumming. The imaginary crowd went wild, begging for more. The star gladly obliged her fans by giving them what they paid for.

"There you are!" Callie snatched the banjo out of Maggie's hands. "I'm gonna shove this thing in the cook stove and burn it." She puffed toward the kitchen.

Maggie hollered, "Maaa… maaa! Callie's gonna burn my ban …jerrr! Help meee! Maaa… maaa!" She grabbed at the banjo like someone possessed by demons.

Callie pushed her away. Maggie came back, scratching, clawing at the coveted instrument. Callie pulled open the firebox. Maggie shoved it shut again; her screams were louder than her adoring fans' accolades. Again, Callie pushed her away and raised the latch. The gateway to hell yawned open.

The hungry flames licked at the air for a taste of the prized food, the same food that, just a moment ago, had fed the famished fans enjoying the delightful meal of music and song.

The banjo touched the fire.

Ellie's hand reached out, grabbing Callie's arm, shoving the firebox shut as she did. The fire retreated. The cavalry had arrived in the nick of time.

"What in tarnation do you think you're doing, Callie, huh? Answer me!"

"I'm gonna burn this confounded banjo, that's what!" Captured, but not defeated, she held on to the contraband.

"No, you're not," Ellie said, holding Callie's arm in a vise grip. With her free hand she reached for the banjo. "Now give it here!"

The banjo slipped from Callie's grasp. Maggie lunged, snatched it away from her mother, and hugged it like a baby. The instrument, once again in the arms of its doting mother, seemed safe and secure, at least for the time being.

"But Maggie won't help me!"

"No matter, that's no reason to destroy her banjo."

Maggie climbed back onto the stage and resumed the show.

"See?" Callie said, pointing to the would-be Opry star. "That's all she ever does and nobody never says a thing to her. Not never!"

"Go back to your chores," her mother said, softening her voice. "I'll handle Maggie." She looked at Callie and added, "I'll handle *you* later."

Callie joined the cackling inmates behind the wire mesh fence. Not one had dared to escape through the partially open gate, probably sensing from past experience that the pen was the most likely place to get breakfast.

Ellie understood how Maggie felt. She once had big dreams, too. Hers, like those of most poor country girls, had been put aside by realities of life.

Maggie got it honest. She can't help herself... dreaming is part of her life, just like for me at her age. Ellie remembered how her family lived on hope. They hoped spring rains would come to sustain their crops, hoped their cow would give milk for another year before going dry, and hoped that their only plow mule wouldn't die or go lame. A family with greater means wouldn't think twice about such things, but for Ellie's family it would have meant hardship and even hunger.

While Ellie's parents had lived on hope, she, like Maggie, had lived on dreams. Those dreams, however, faded in the real world where survival meant working from sun up to sun down. Ellie had a better life now, easier, more promising. Still, her dreams had eroded away like a windswept plain, day to day, month to month, until the years had passed her by.

That wouldn't happen to her children, she thought. Hope for them would be something realized, eternal, enduring, and dreams would be truth fulfilled.

Do it, Maggie. Don't ever give up. Keep dreaming, and never lose hope. Memories of her youth and what could have been hurried through her mind. A tinge of regret struck her heart like a wayward arrow. "Oh," she murmured aloud.

Ellie walked over to the front of the makeshift stage. The spotlight clicked off and the house lights came on, illuminating the concert hall as she touched her daughter's hand. Maggie's fingers stopped on the bottom string. The show was over. A star would be born… tomorrow. The Grand Ole Opry would have to wait. Gently Ellie crooked her finger in the come-here sign. With banjo around her neck, Maggie left the stage.

"Go feed the chickens and help with the chores," Ellie said with sympathy in her voice.

Chapter 3
Whirl War II Soldiers

The way Corbit saw it, squirming in church was a waste of time. *I could be building a rabbit trap, or taking something apart to see how it works, or weeding the garden.* He stopped and gave a second thought to the weeding.

He shook his head with resolve. *Even weeding's better than church. Shoot, ain't it enough I have to go to that dad-blamed schoolhouse ever' durned day when school's in? Now I have to go back at night during the summer to listen to some loud-mouthed preacher. Blast it and confound it all to hell!* He puffed out his cheeks, cleared his lungs with a loud swoosh, and placed the preacher's head on the chopping block, too. He now had a nice pile of heads for the cook stove.

Corbit's flat feet, stringy body, and lanky arms hauled water from the well, swilled the pigs, and shoveled manure, all the while trying to figure out a way to get out of going to the revival.

He and Callie, with Maggie mostly dawdling and dreaming, finished their chores early.

"Okay, younguns," Ellie called from the porch, "you can go down to the creek for awhile and cool off."

"Hot diggity dog!" Corbit shouted, running to change into his cut-offs.

Ellie let out a sigh. "That is, while there's still some water left in the creek." She looked skyward. It hadn't rained in four months. The young crops were thirsty, having been denied suckle from the breast of Mother Earth. Cloudy white monsters, bears and unicorns that once lived in the deep blue sky now hid in some far-off place, held captive in a hazy prison void of imagination.

Famished corn and weepy vines would not fill the horn of plenty. Thirsty tobacco would not survive to satisfy the cravings of Prince Albert rollers and Days Work spitters. The lowering water table would dry up wells. Ponds used for irrigation, for those who were lucky enough to have it, would soon be too low to pump anything but mud. Blue skies were not needed nor wanted. A firmament covered with a black blanket and producing earthshaking thunder is what the people of Brush Creek desired. They wanted to see lightning pitchforking through the heavens, bursting open the clouds, and the liquid, life-giving sustenance falling to earth.

"And watch out for snakes," Ellie cautioned. "They'll be crawlin'."

Corbit, Callie, and Maggie with her banjo headed down the trail toward the Brush. The sweet smell of clover permeated the warm, muggy air.

"I just love these partridge berries. Their red and white flowers and dark green leaves remind me of a rainbow. Why, I could just play a tune that sounds like they look," Maggie said in a reverent, almost whispering voice.

Callie turned and faced her. Walking backward she sneered, "I don't know why you're even coming with us, Maggie — you didn't do nothing except throw out a handful of corn to the chickens and carry in a half-bucket of water. Just stop your dreaming. That's all you're good for."

Maggie looked down at her feet and kept on walking.

"Wait up!" Fred Plank hollered from the top of the hill.

He waved before charging down the rise.

Tommie Sue Elder cried, "Wait for me, you old skeercrow." She quickly caught up, her brown pigtails bouncing in an uneven cadence.

"Howdy," Fred said, slapping Corbit on the shoulder.

"Hi-de-ho," Corbit said, slapping him back.

"Hi, Tommie Sue, how come you're running late?" Callie asked her best friend.

"I didn't empty the pee pots this morning like I was s'posed to, so Momma made me do some extra chores."

"I don't blame you, Tommie Sue, I wouldn't empty no stinkin' pee pots neither," Maggie said. "Pee gets all over your hands and splashes on your feet and legs and all."

"Since when have *you* emptied pee pots or done *anything* but fram on that stupid thing tied around your neck?" Callie slapped at the banjo. Maggie recoiled and retreated a few steps.

"Let's go, I'm hot." Fred flipped carrot-colored hair off his forehead, repositioned the ever-present straw in his mouth and started down the path toward the creek. The rest of the gang fell in behind him.

"Hey, lookit," Callie said. "We look like them Whirl War II soldiers a-marchin'."

"Yeah," Tommie Sue agreed. "Just like in the newsreel at the pitcher show."

A rusty barbed-wire fence held in place by gray, cracked posts kept the cows penned in the south pasture where they munched on drought-short grass supplemented by peanut hay. The make-believe troops marched along with an eye single to the task at hand — the cool waters of Brush Creek.

Fred and Corbit, armed with a combination of flat and round stones, dangled their slingshot weapons from back pockets of faded overalls. An occasional bellow from the herd of heifers led by a lone bull drifted across the field.

Corbit kicked a rock and watched it rattle down the

hill. "Gotta go to that durn revival tonight!"

"Yeah, me too." Fred took the straw out of his mouth and slung it to the ground. "Blamed ol' stupid preacher!"

"Yeah, blamed ol' stupid preacher!" Corbit aped.

"I can't wait," Maggie spoke up. "I wonder if them chicken-mauga fellers'll have banjers and git-tars?"

Tommie Sue hugged her skinny frame. "Yeah, and a pickle-o. I always wanted to play a pickle-o."

"Why, I ain't never heard of no pickle-o b'fore." Maggie looked dreamy as she slipped into her private "real" world. "But I bet it sounds purty." She shifted the banjo from her back, repositioned the strap over her shoulder and began to strum "Turkey in the Straw." The column of weary soldiers began to sing, except Callie, who just rolled her eyes at Maggie. She soon relented, though, and joined in.

> *As I was a goin*
> *On down the road*
> *With a tired team*
> *And a heavy load,*
> *I cracked my whip*
> *And the leader sprung.*
> *I says day-day*
> *To the wagon tongue.*

"If they'd sing this at church instead of them danged ol' hymns I might not mind going so much," Corbit interrupted. They all laughed and Maggie played on.

> *Turkey in the straw,*
> *Turkey in the straw,*
> *Roll 'em up and twist 'em up*
> *A thick tuck a haw,*
> *And hit 'em up a tune called*
> *Turkey in the straw.*

They marched into a thick stand of fir. Callie had managed to set herself up as the platoon sergeant leading with great fanfare. With straight shoulders and arms as rigid as if in splints, she pushed her flat chest out, and her skinny legs and hill-bred feet high-stepped to the rhythm of the music.

The marching legion followed the straight, narrow path through grove of Christmas-scented cedars, finally halting on the banks of Brush Creek. The mountain-cold creek flowed serene and lazy as it always had, a little bit of yesterday mixed with the present. Water whooshed and gurgled pleasantly as it ambled over a partially submerged log. A limp, frayed rope, used by revelers to swing out over the stream and then drop with a festive whoop, hung from a gnarled limb of Old Man Oak.

The Old Man had stood there for decades, perhaps centuries, watching time drift by. He had observed, listened to, and sheltered hordes of children as they washed away field dirt and sweat from brown, sun-drenched bodies. The roots, now bare and ropy where red clay and green grass had been trampled away, fanned out like knotty, grasping fingers clinging to what little earth remained. There it stood calling up old memories and storing away new ones.

"Dismissed," the platoon sergeant snapped.

Fred stuck his foot in the water, jerked it back. "Ouch! Damn, it's cold!"

"You stop cussin', Fred Plank," Tommie Sue scolded, "or I'm gonna tell your momma!"

"Aw, I ain't cussin'. I just said damn, thet's all. Damn ain't a cuss word. Right, Corbit?"

"Damn right it ain't." Corbit caught the rope, pushed off, swung far and high until reaching its peak, hesitated, fell back and let go. *Splash!* Water sprayed in every direction. The cold seized him instantly, chasing away sweltering heat of a summer sun.

He spat water and called out, "Last one in is a stinkin' polecat." No person with respect wanted to be called a skunk. In they jumped, Tommie Sue, Fred, Callie… everybody, but Maggie.

"Maggie's a polecat," they all hollered at once, laughing.

"I ain't gettin' my banjer wet," Maggie proclaimed. It would never have crossed her mind to let it out of her grasp, let alone out of sight. She would never think of setting her banjo on a bed of grass any more than she would of tearing her arm off and hanging it from a limb.

"Polecat! Polecat!" they sang.

Unperturbed, she said, "I'll play while you swim." So she strummed a few chords and they took up where they left off at the end of the march—everyone, of course, except Callie, who crossed her arms and pursed her lips.

> *Went out to milk*
> *And I didn't know how,*
> *I milked the goat*
> *Instead of the cow,*
> *A monkey sittin'*
> *On a pile of straw*
> *A winkin' at*
> *His mother-in-law.*

Corbit churned out of the water and climbed the bank to the swing rope for another jump. Shaggy strands of hair lay plastered over his ears like glue. With both hands on the rope he pulled back, back, back until it was taut and creak, creak, creaking on the limb. His toes barely touched the knotty roots. He immediately transformed into the legendary Buck Rogers of the   twenty-first Century. He lifted his foot ready to launch into outer space. He leaned back. The rope labored a final creak, and then with one last glance around, he shoved off.

Something caught his eye.

"Aaahhh!" Buck let go of the rope, stumbled, and rolled head over heels, landing at the edge of the creek. He jumped like a cat to his feet and bellowed, "Didja see it?"

"See what?" Fred asked.

"That ghost over yonder by that tree." Corbit's once-bronze face resembled a sack of Martha White Flour.

"Yep, you've gone crazy as Cooter Brown," Fred said, shaking his head.

Corbit pointed upstream toward another oak as big and old as the rope tree. "I done saw a ghost over yonder by that big ol' oak, I tell you. I saw a ghost standing right over yonder!"

Chapter 4
Minner

Hearing the word *ghost*, Maggie's finger froze on a sour note. "Well, I swanny. You don't say!"

"Where'd he go, you reckon?" Corbit asked, throwing back a shock of wet hair.

"Where'd *who* go?" The gang, except for Maggie, questioned in harmony.

"Well, shoot fire in the morning! The ghost boy standing over yonder, like I said." Corbit pointed again at the oak tree standing along a narrow foot path on the edge of the creek. "That's the skinniest ghost I ever did see. More of a skeleton than a ghost, I'd say. It looked like he'd starved to death."

Maggie's eyes grew wider. "You mean you've seen other ghosts?"

All five examined, from a distance, the empty trail with eager eyes searching through the rippled sunlight of approaching dusk.

"Aw, cut it out, you're always trying to skeer us." Tommie Sue scooped up a handful of water and slung it in Corbit's direction.

"No, I ain't, neither," he gruffed. "I did see a spooky-eyed ghost boy standing over yonder by that ol' tree, and I know it."

Corbit's Martha White complexion soon returned to a

baked brown. "If that weren't a ghost my name ain't Buck Rogers — er, I mean, Corbit Kinser."

Callie egged him on. "Well, I guess it ain't Corbit, then, it's *Ettis*!"

"Shut up, you booger—"

"Tell us more about the ghost boy," Maggie said, strumming a C chord.

Corbit thought of something. His eyes narrowed. His voice, low and deliberate, said, "Maybe it's the ghost of the boy they pulled out of the creek a few years back."

"Aw, hush up," Tommie Sue scolded. "You've cooked up something with Fred to try and skeer us, that's all."

"No, really. A few days ago I heard Mr. Ford tell Deddy how he pulled the dead boy out of the creek."

"Shut up, *Ettis*!" Callie crossed her arms and glared at the two boys. "Don't listen to them, Tommie Sue, they're just dumb."

Corbit shot back like a rifle. "You'd better shut up, you ol' skinny fence rail, before I—"

"Go on, tell us," Maggie pleaded, cutting him off. Callie and Tommie Sue stood in knee-deep water with their arms crossed.

"Yeah, finish telling us," Fred encouraged. "Don't pay no attention to those little sissies." The two girls glared at Fred with dart-throwing eyes.

"Well, all right," Corbit hissed. "But ol' skinny flat-chest had better keep her mouth shut and quit calling me Ettis!"

"Or what?" Callie snapped.

"You'll find out all right—"

"What's his name? The ghost, I mean," Maggie asked, strumming another C chord.

Corbit glared at Callie, "As I was about to say before being interrupted by fence rail over there... the ghost, uh, the boy's name was Minner. They called him Minner because he was so small. You know, like a little fish. His last name was Jenkins and he lived with his folks over on Fox Hill in the old shack at the top." Corbit looked around for effect before continuing. "They were down here at the creek early one evening fishing when Minner decided to go find himself a better spot on down the creek a bit.

"Time went on and no one had heard anything from him in a good while. His folks got worried and started calling his name. When Minner didn't answer, they went looking." Corbit paused to rake dripping hair away from his eyes. He leaned forward for effect. "They found something awful. He had fallen into the creek right into a nest of cottonmouth moccasins. They were latched onto him like barbed wire. He was dead, all swolled up, black and blue from the poison."

"Oooh! Awful!" Maggie wrapped her arms around her banjo to protect it from the terrible vision.

Corbit cleared his throat. "As I was saying, Mr. Ford, who was fishing yonder ways up the creek, heard Minner's folks hollering and carrying on. He ran to see what was wrong. Old man Jenkins was in the water trying to get Minner out. He was jerking snakes off Minner's body and throwing them ever' which way. Mr. Ford helped haul them both out, snakes and all. One of the cottonmouths had latched onto Mr. Jenkins, but he paid it no attention. He was only thinking about his dead boy."

Callie, Maggie, and Tommie Sue shivered, and Fred stared at Corbit with Moon-Pie eyes.

"Anyhow, they moved away shortly after the boy died. Mr. Jenkins got real sick from the snake bite, but folks said he mourned so over Minner's death that that's what made him sick, not the poison from the moccasin."

"What about Mr. Ford?" Fred asked. "Did he get bit?"

"No, but he said the dead boy and those wailing parents were the most pitiful thing he ever did see." Corbit lowered his voice, "Said he'd never forget it as long as he lived."

"Oh, shaw." Tommie Sue brushed the air with the palm of her hand. "Ain't no boy drownt and you know it!"

"He ain't drownt. He got snake bit," Maggie said, then added, "Me and Fred believe you. Don't we, Fred?"

"You'd believe anything," Callie barked.

Corbit skimmed the water's surface with his hand—a thin sheet of water fantailed and sizzled across the creek. "I *ain't* lying. The reason Mr. Ford brought it up in the first place was because of what happened the other day."

No one said a word. Everyone watched and waited. Corbit moved his head slowly staring at each face individually. The rest of his body stayed straight and unmoving.

Finally his eyes settled on Callie. "Huh," she said, "You gonna tell us or just stand there like a big bupkis?"

"So you wanna know, huh?"

"Blah! I'll be dad-blamed if I care if you tell us or not!"

"Uh huh, sure you don't. Anyway, about two days ago Mr. Ford was fishing at the exact spot where Minner died. He started feeling funny all over, like he was being watched, he said. Then ice cold chills ran up and down his body — said it was almost unbearable."

Corbit stopped again. He enjoyed being the center of attention and liked watching their expressions as he kept his audience waiting.

Callie couldn't stand it. "Are you going to stand there all day looking goofy, or are you going to tell us?"

"It ain't none of it true anyhow," Tommie Sue said curtly.

"You just shut up, Callie! And it is so the truth, Tommie Sue! Just ask Mr. Ford. Deddy'll tell you too. Anyway, Mr. Ford looked right at Minner. When he did, Minner ducked behind a tree and disappeared into the woods, just vanished, like a ghost, he said."

Fred's eyes bugged out, "It had to be Minner you saw, or I'll be a monkey's uncle."

"No, you're the monkey, and a big ugly one, too," Callie mocked.

Tommie Sue laughed. "Who ever heard of a red-headed monkey?"

"You done saw a ghost, Corbit," Maggie cried with awe.

"You're a lying *Ettis* rat," Callie spat. "You and Fred both."

Corbit sloshed toward Callie with the fire of doom in his eyes. He lifted his hand.

"I believe you," Maggie blurted.

"Me too," Fred joined in. "And I ain't no liar, and I ain't a monkey, neither."

Corbit stopped one foot away from sending Callie to the twenty-first century along with Buck. "Durn skinny bed rail!" he snipped, slapping the water. Dozens of tiny droplets sprayed up and plopped back into the cool stream.

"Then how come Deddy didn't know about it?" Callie asked.

"Because he was off fighting the war, that's why!"

"Whatever!" Callie smirked. "Besides, we'd better get back, Deddy'll be home soon." She always had to be the one to break up the fun. "Supper will be ready by the time we get back."

Some ah-shoots, aw-shucks and durn-it-alls came from the rest, except Maggie, who said, "Yeah, it'll soon be time for revival meetin'."

Maggie's reminder brought some damns and other lurid remarks from Fred and Corbit.

"I'm going to tell your mommas about you cussing," Tommie Sue threatened. "You'll get your mouths worshed out with soap. The devil's gonna gitcha, too, and that's a natural fact."

"Oh, shaw," Fred said. "You're just an old duddy-fuddy."

"It's fuddy-duddy, you dumb ol' red-headed nigger," Callie said sticking her tongue out.

Fred came back, "I'd rather be a red-headed nigger than a scrawny little chigger like you."

All the sweat, field dirt, and cow manure odors from Corbit, Callie, Fred, and Tommie Sue — Maggie didn't have the aromas of work — had been absorbed into the cool waters of the creek. They were refreshed as they started back up the trail. Maggie positioned her banjo and began to strum again. They continued more verses of "Turkey in the Straw" their boistious voices carrying through the bush, the briars, and over the pastures serenading the cows and the parched crops.

Arms swayed and heads bobbed as feet skipped to the beat of another tune called "Shoo Fly Shoo." Callie brought up the rear, choosing not to share in the revelry.

A mixture of soft, rippled clouds painted with varied hues of sunset became a fresco covering the late evening sky. Old Man Oak, his younger siblings, and coniferous cousins cast long shadows of dusk-dark. This was Callie's favorite time of day, calming and reassuring.

Usually.

A strange sensation slowly crept over her body.

She glanced back.

There, in the encroaching shadows of the evening, stood not a ghost but a boy, rail thin, his clothes loose and ragged.

Chapter 5
Willow

W here's Willer!" Moss Branch bellowed, towering over his submissive wife, a jug of whisky in his hand and a cut of Days Work tobacco wallowing in his mouth. "Where is she, I said!"

"I don't reckon I know…"

He back-handed her. She back-stepped half way across the room, wobbled, and fell prone on the floor. Rose's blurred eyes could see dirt through the cracks of the rough pine boards. She wished she could slip through the crevice like a roach and live in the darkness of the foul-smelling soil beneath the house.

"You don't *reckon* you know? I tole you not to let thet gal outta your sight! I don't want her talking to nobody. I want her here when I want her, when I need her."

Rose pushed off the floor, propped against the bare wall, then backed up to a straight-back chair, and plopped down. Blood dripped from her split lip. "She's prob'ly with Thorny somewhere."

"I don't give a rat's ass about thet no-account boy or where he might be. As far as I'm concerned he can stay gone. I just want to know where Willer is, damn it all to hell!" He sucked in a mouth full of shine and swallowed it in one gulp, gurgling as it washed down his throat. "I'm goin' to finish settin' up my still. Won't be back 'til tomorrow. She'd better be here all purtied up in thet new dress waitin' for me when I git back. Understand?"

Rose sat there unable to utter another word or look at her drunkard husband for fear of a beating. She gave a slow nod.

Moss spat. Thick brown spittle ran down Rose's cheek and dripped in slow motion onto her thin rag of a dress.

❦❧

A gentle breeze fluttered through the trees, its air tempered by the cool water of the creek. The sun, having done its tour of duty, began its descent behind the western hills. The setting sun seemed to offer a reprieve from the harshness of drought. Hazy skies, thick with wavy heat, began to clear to make way for the Big Dipper and its celestial cousins. Birds sang lullabies to their nestlings, their music spreading contentment throughout the countryside.

Pied Piper Maggie, taking the place of General Callie, led the column of soldiers to the parting point. Fred and Tommie Sue, who lived next door to one another, took the path leading over to Snead's Ridge and home.

"Bye, Buck, I mean, Corbit," Fred said with a smile as he slapped him on the back. "See ya tonight, preacher boy."

Corbit frowned. "Aw, poot, you *had* to go and remind me of that again!"

Tommie Sue shook her finger at him. "The devil's gonna getcha if you don't stop saying those bad words. See you tonight, Callie. Bye, Maggie."

Maggie, residing in her own little world, happily strummed "I'll Fly Away" at the mention of revival. Corbit clouded his brain with dark thoughts of Brother Loudmouth pounding his fist on the oak pulpit, preaching everybody to hell for chewing tobacco and drinking hard cider. Both of which, Corbit felt certain, the preacher enjoyed himself while nobody looked.

The three Kinsers scurried up the hill toward home where supper waited, and revival imminent.

Then, out of nowhere appeared a magical fairy-dusted creature with hair the color of fall leaves flowing down to her shoulders. Butter-cream skin glowed like early morning sunshine.

Maggie saw her first and howled, "An angel done come to fetch us to revival." She dropped to her knees.

"Oh my!" The angel jumped and caught her breath. She backed up preparing to run.

"It's okay," Callie said. "We didn't mean to skeer you." The frightened angel, hands clasped over her mouth, kept edging backward. Callie noticed the angel's eyes right away. They were a dull green, full of fear and uncertainty, a stark contrast to her beauty.

"Don't run," Callie said gently. "We won't hurt you. Honest."

Callie watched her, drawn to her eyes. They revealed much more than a startled girl. They were sad, even old, an empty well.

Angel girl stopped, but said nothing as she looked down at her feet.

Corbit grew moon-pie eyes, transfixed to the angel's face. A rock turned his foot. He grappled for a hand-hold as he fell and slid downhill past Callie on the gravel and dirt.

The girl finally uttered, "H-howdy." Her voice, although shaky and small, carried a melodic quality. She looked down as she said it.

Not exactly what the tongue-tied, farm-bred, and totally hypnotized brood expected an immortal goddess to say.

"Howdy. My name's Callie."

Corbit's brown eyes turned puppy-dog warm. Slowly he pushed himself up from the rocky ground and stood there, speechless.

"I'm Willow and I'm new here." The angel's light, butterfly voice floated through the evening air.

Head still bowed, she lifted her eyes but would not look directly at them. "We just moved here a day or two ago," she pointed toward Fox Hill, "in that ol' house… well, more like a shack, I guess, on top of the hill yonder."

"Howdy-do," Maggie blurted. "I play a banjer. I bet you play a harp, I betcha." She stayed on her knees out of respect for the angel.

Callie swept her arm back without looking at Corbit and said, "This is my brother, Corbit. The one down on her knees is my dumb sister, Maggie. She don't like to work. She only plays that stupid banjo of hers."

Maggie ignored the remark. "You gonna go hear the Chicken mauga sangers at revival tonight?"

"Chick-a-mauga, stupid," Callie corrected. "Yeah, there's a revival at the schoolhouse tonight. You want to come?"

"You can sit by me if you want to," Corbit announced.

Shocked, Maggie and Callie turned to look at their brother. Nobody seemed more surprised than Corbit.

"Well, I ain't…" The princess-fairy-angel hesitated. "I — I ain't never been inside a church b'fore."

Never in the lives of the Kinser children had any of them ever known anyone who hadn't been to church, even if only at Easter or Christmas.

"Ain't *ever* been to church?" Callie's voice grew higher. "*Ever?*"

Willow lowered her eyes again. "No, I reckon I ain't."

"I do declare, I thought angels always went to church!" Maggie stared at the stranger.

Finally Willow raised her head. "Do you think they'll let me in?" Her forehead wrinkled. "And I ain't no angel."

"Why, sure they will," Callie assured her. "Why wouldn't they?"

Willow looked embarrassed. "You know, me being a heathen sinner, and all. There may be rules against it, or something."

"That's silly." Corbit surprised himself again. "Sinners go to church all the time. Why, I even know one."

The corners of Willow's mouth half turned into a smile. Corbit flushed beet-red.

"You *are* one," Callie spat. "And you can call him Ettis instead of Corbit. He just loves to be called Ettis."

He shot back, "Dag-nabbit, Callie, if you don't shut up, that mouthy preacher'll be preaching your funeral tonight instead of accusing everybody of being sinners."

Willow's shoulders dropped. She looked at Corbit and said in a low, shaky tone, "You ain't gonna kill 'er, are you?"

He looked surprised. "Why, heck no, I ain't."

"He just snaps his cap when I call him Ettis," Callie said. "It's nothing to worry about. He's all talk and no bite. Completely harmless, he is, like a toothless dog."

Corbit started to strike back but thought better of it. He paused, sensing something in Willow's demeanor. His harsh-sounding words had frightened her. Her body shook. He noticed something else, too. A pale red splotch garnished her left cheek. "Yeah, I didn't mean nothin'. I wouldn't really kill her — I mean, hurt her."

Callie glanced at her brother, hearing something unusual in his voice. She Looked at Willow and smiled. "Come on and go with us. Nobody cares if you ain't never been to church."

"The preacher man will. Why, he'll know who I am right off."

"Yeah, Preacher Roberts talks to angels all the time, him bein' a preacher, and all," Maggie assured her. "He won't have any problem knowing who *you* are."

"Shut up, Maggie!" Callie sneered. "And get off your knees. You ain't got a lick of sense!" Willow backed up a few steps. Immediately Callie felt bad for her outburst. "Anyway, we live in the house up yonder. See?" Callie pointed to their house partially hidden by a sweet gum tree.

"That's a funny name you got," Miss Manners Maggie said.

Willow looked at her feet. "It's because my last name's Branch and my no-account deddy named me that. My little sister's name is Olive, and my brother's name is Thorny. Of course that ain't his real name, but that's what he answers to. Deddy says he's a thorn in his side. My momma's name is Rose but folks call her Rosie, except for that no-account. He calls her… I mean… never mind. I'm sorry."

"For what?" Corbit asked. "And what about your deddy? Ain't he got a name?"

"No account, that's what! He ain't no good for nothin', except…"

"What?" Corbit pressed.

"Never mind that. Moss, Moss is his name."

"Willow's a purty name… purty, like you." Maggie strummed an open chord. "It sounds so musical, but a little sad too, like one of Bill Monroe's songs."

"I guess it's a perfect name for me, then."

"I like your name, too," Corbit said in a dreamy voice before he realized it. "I mean, for a girl and all." He dug his toe in the dirt and flicked it, showering dry leaves with bits of earth.

Willow's sad mouth slowly turned up into a dimpled smile.

She looks like a flower full of sweet nectar, Corbit thought. His musing turned to words before he realized it. "Boy, I bet you'd make good honey." He slapped a hand over his mouth.

Callie glared at Corbit's blazing red face. "What are you talking about?" She turned back to Willow. "Well, we've got to go and get worshed up for supper and see what's wrong with Corbit. I think he's sick."

"I ain't neither."

Callie had a thought. "We have to go right by your place this evening. We'd be glad to give you a ride."

"No! I mean… well, I like to walk, that's all. I'll come if I can."

"Okay. Well, it ain't far from your place—we walk there ever' day during school. It's just the other side of the hill, down in the holler. Hope to see you there," Callie said. "See ya."

"Bye. Maybe I'll see you later," Willow said as she turned toward the shack at the top of the hill.

"I'll be John Brown," all three said at the same time, and laughed.

"She sure had a pretty dress. I ain't never seen a farm girl wear a dress like that," Callie said.

Corbit nodded toward Fox Hill. "It doesn't make sense at all why anybody living in an old shack like that would have such a nice dress."

"It's because she's an angel," Maggie noted.

"She ain't no angel!" Callie snapped.

"Boy, I can't wait to go to church tonight." Corbit, realizing what he had said, jerked around to face his sisters. He spat, "Just shut up, you hear? Just shut up!"

"He's done gone crazy," Callie whispered.

Maggie's voice filled with wonder. "I'll say. He's done got saved and ain't been to revival yet."

❧❦

The hulking figure hiding behind a boulder disappeared into the woods. He spat, wiped his chin with the back of his hand and whispered, "I'll tend to you later, missy. I'll learn you a thing or two." He smiled at the thought.

Chapter 6
Blue Flowers and Gold Lace

D eddy's home," Corbit announced. Dust, still visible from the dry roadbed, announced his arrival.

Steam puffed from the radiator of the dented black Ford parked in front of the house. Bud Kinser had only been home a few months from the war in Europe. During his absence his family had struggled to make a living off their small farm. They had made it, somehow, and he felt grateful for their hard work and dedication. It had been tough for them, and they, like most families, had gone without. Out of need Bud had taken a job as a deputy for McMinn County Sheriff Joe Vaughn, a distant cousin.

Corbit, Callie, and Maggie scrambled into the house all talking at once about Willow. Bud placed his hat on the nail by the door. "She must be part of the new family up on Fox Hill."

"Yessir, I suppose," Callie said.

"Don't you think we should hurry and eat supper?" Corbit's voice held the excitement of Fourth of July and Christmas all rolled into one. "Ain't polite to be late for preachin', you know."

Bud's mouth flew open. Ellie walked in from the kitchen, staring at her converted son.

"Did you hear that?" Bud asked, not believing it came from his son.

"Well, I'll be!" Ellie's fingers flew to her chin, hands clasped in the sign of prayer, her eyes focused to the ceiling. "It's a miracle!"

Corbit trotted toward the back porch to get washed up.

Bud looked at Ellie standing stoically in prayer mode. He whispered, "I'll declare, somebody done stole our son."

Ellie, dropping her hands, turned and peeked around the door as Corbit lathered up the bar of lye soap and hummed to himself. With awe she said, "You reckon he's one of those space aliens like in those Buck Rogers serials at the pitcher show?"

"Ain't no doubt it," Bud agreed. "He's sure had us fooled."

"He ain't had me fooled. I tried to tell you he was spacey a long time ago," Callie said.

Her father chuckled. "Okay girls, I know you done traded your brother for the alien impostor on the back porch. Want to tell me what planet your *real* brother's on?"

"Oh, Deddy," Callie giggled. "I think Corbit's carrying a torch for that new girl."

"Yeah," Maggie strummed her banjo for effect. "She plays the harp, but her deddy ain't no good for nothing."

Callie retorted, "She don't play a harp, and I've heard enough of that blamed ol' banjo today!" Then, settling down she said, "But Willow did say her deddy was a no-account."

"Stop pestering your sister, Callie! And it's a strange thing for a youngun to say about her deddy," Ellie said with a look of concern. "What else did she say?"

"Nothin', except she's never been to church before."

Bud stroked his droopy mustache. "I don't know either, but our impostor son's right. We'd better hurry if we're to make it to church on time." He shooed the girls away. "Scat and get worshed up." He looked at the pile of lather on Corbit's face and arms. "If there's any soap left to worsh with."

"Maybe we should stop by and welcome them to Brush Creek," Ellie said.

Bud laughed, "And check them out to see if they're aliens from the twenty-first century? Anyhow, I had better see about the milking before I get worshed up. I assume Corbit hasn't done it since he's been ogling over that new girl, and all. Willow, is it?"

"I think, and no, he hasn't. I've already done the milking, though. The younguns have been working hard lately and I told them they could stay at the creek a little longer today."

The lines in Bud's face deepened. "Down there yesterday. The creek's down a couple of feet at least. We've got to have some rain or…"

"The rain'll come. We've got to have faith."

Corbit flung the screen door open and let it slam behind him. "Willow got scared when I told Callie I was gonna kill her for calling me *that* name."

"Well, no wonder," Bud admonished. "You ought not say things like that,"

After a supper of fried potatoes, squash, green beans, and side meat, everybody pitched in to clear the table.

A plate fell to the floor and shattered.

Ellie gasped. "No! Not my beautiful plate!" A plate with blue forget-me-nots and gold lace around the rim lay broken in fragmented pieces, the white jagged porcelain in stark contrast to the soft hue of the flowered front.

"Now look what you've done. Maggie," Bud scolded. "Put down the banjo. You can't carry dishes and it too." She slipped the strap from around her neck with one hand while holding the dishes between her other hand and the fold of her arm and placed the banjo on the table.

Callie volunteered, "Want me to break that ol' banjo and burn it in the cook stove, Deddy?"

Maggie flung down three more of her mother's prized dishes. Large and small pieces scattered over the floor, the stems and petals of forget-me-nots jumbled like a jigsaw puzzle.

"You ain't gonna burn my banjer!" In desperation she grabbed it off the table, fell to the floor and cradled it like a baby.

"Oh, my beautiful dishes," Ellie whimpered, fingers playing on her trembling lips. She dashed across the kitchen. "Martha... Caroline... Kinser, look what you've caused!"

"But—"

"Hush, you hear me?"

Callie started to protest again, and then stopped, thinking better of it.

Bud placed calming hands on Maggie's trembling shoulders. "There ain't nobody going to mess with your banjo. Come on now, get up off the floor and go get ready for church."

"She hates it... *skeenk*... Deddy." Maggie made disgusting sobbing sounds between words. "She's...*skeenk*... always try-i-ing to... *skeenk*... do something to my... *skeenk* ... banjer." Snot dripped from her nose, mixing with tears.

"Just look what you've caused, Callie!" Ellie looked with teary eyes at the shards of porcelain. "Oh my. Gracious me. Just look at my beautiful dishes."

"But, Momma, she—"

Ellie whirled around. "Why you have to constantly torture your poor sister about her banjo is beyond my understanding."

"But, I didn't—"

"Can't you just let her be? Don't you see how much she loves that thing?" Ellie dropped listless arms to her side, letting out a deep sigh. Callie watched silently as her mother turned to face the kitchen door, her body quivering.

"It's all *your* fault!" Callie screamed at her still sobbing sister.

Maggie wailed.

Ellie snapped around, started to say something, but clamped her mouth shut afraid at what she might say.

Bud stood, pulling Maggie to her feet. He handed Callie the broom. His eyes looked directly into hers. He didn't say anything; he didn't have to. Tight-mouthed and defiant, Callie grabbed the broom and began sweeping in broad strokes, clattering and clinking broken blue flowers and gold lace.

Chapter 7
Amazing Grace

Darkness, the official end of a work day, meant all of the night sounds would come alive throughout the countryside. Deep singing bullfrogs accompanied by soprano crickets and melodious birds rose to a crescendo of harmony.

The end of the work day, however, only offered a temporary reprieve, a diversion from the mundane and stark reality of the way things were, and, with few exceptions, the way things would always be. For most, quitting time would only come at death. Church, however, presented a chance for everyone to forget their problems for a few hours and to connect with neighbors and friends.

Maggie scrunched in the corner of the threadbare back seat of the old Ford holding on to her banjo and scowling at Callie. Corbit sat in the middle acting as a buffer. The battered Ford whined and jerked as Bud changed gears while turning onto the narrow dirt road leading to Fox Hill and to the schoolhouse, alias church, on the other side.

Most people used coal oil lanterns for light, but a few had the luxury of electricity provided by the Tennessee Valley Authority. A single light could be seen hanging from the ceiling of a few homes of the more affluent. For those who did have electricity, life became easier. Conveyor belts and belt-driven machinery made less work for the farmer. Electric stoves, refrigerators and wringer washing machines made life more tolerable for farm women who grew old before their time. For the majority of people, however, such luxuries were but a dream.

"We're gonna be late because of you, Callie," Corbit harped.

"Shut up, Ettis!"

"Momma, make her stop," Corbit whined.

"Callie, you've said enough for one day," her mother scolded with fire and brimstone. "I hope you'll talk to the Lord about your hard ways toward Maggie... and ask him to temper your mouth while you're at it."

Ellie waited, her patience wearing thin. "Callie?"

"Yessum."

"Yessum, what?"

"Yessum, I'll..." She didn't finish what she wanted to say, *I'll talk to the Lord about burning that durned ol' banjo in hell,* but she knew better.

Ellie looked over the seat at her rebellious child, "I'm waiting."

"I'll talk to the Lord... 'bout Maggie's banjo."

"Well... good. See that you do."

The Ford's rear end whined as it crawled up Fox Hill in second gear. In the meantime, the recently converted brother and imposter alien son reminded everyone, for the fourth time, who had made them late.

A dilapidated shack stood just off the road at the apex of the hill.

"There's Willow's house," Corbit said. "But I don't see her nowhere."

Maggie let go of her scowl long enough to say, "Maybe she's already at the church house with her harp."

"She ain't got..." Callie pursed her lips.

A wisp of a woman stood in the crack of a half-open

door, the light of a coal oil lantern revealing her features. Her dress had a rip at the bottom hem and a brown splotch just under the neckline. No more than thirty-five, she looked to be twice the age. Her sallow skin sagged. Worry lines crisscrossed her face.

Bud waved. Rose backed into the house without acknowledging his gesture.

"The poor woman looked to be half dead," Ellie said, shaking her head.

❧

Willow perked up at the news of Moss' departure. *Gone, the whole night.* She smiled at the thought. She whirled around, her skirt fanning out like a flamenco dancer.

She looked at her mother, pleading in her eyes. "Oh, go ahead and go," Rose said.

A smile radiated from her daughter's face. Willow hurried to get ready for her first taste of the Spirit.

❧

The school yard, turned parking lot, was littered with cars and trucks, but mostly wagons. Horses and mules stood hitched, stamping their feet and swishing their tails trying to shoo away flies and mosquitoes. The one-room schoolhouse looked to be already packed.

"Shoot," Corbit complained. "Looks like we're gonna have to sit on the back row because of Callie."

Callie's blazing eyes burnt a hole through his head, but she knew better than to say anything.

"I hope Willow's here so we can play the harp and banjer together," Maggie said in a dreamy voice.

"Maybe she saved us a seat," Corbit said. As the car rolled to a stop Bud gave his usual spiel. "Okay, younguns, go to the privy if you have to, because there ain't going to be no running in and out after the preaching starts unless it's absolutely necessary, and by necessary I mean it better be gurgling in your throat. It ain't respectful to be traipsin' back and forth while the word of God's being sermonized…and Corbit, comb your head, you look like a refugee.

They all rolled out of the car like ants. "Yep, looks like we'll have to sit on the last bench, or stand up," Ellie said just as they stepped onto the porch.

The desks had been replaced by benches made of rough pine and chairs of cowhide and hemp rope. They squeezed onto the back bench. Callie looked for Willow, and seeing she wasn't there, saved her a place.

Tommie Sue, sitting on the bench in front of them, turned with a smile. "Howdy, Callie, I hope them fellers brought a pickle-o."

"Howdy," Callie said. "They probably don't even know what a pickle-o is."

The room, lighted by coal oil lamps, shone with dim plainness over a gaggle of worshippers. Waffle-necked farmers with the smell of dirt ingrained into their skin, stood and talked with one another about the low price of corn and cotton, but mostly about the drought. Women with wrinkled hands capable of swinging a double-edged axe through a pine log, or chopping with a hoe through long rows of garden weeds, held babies tenderly while chatting with one another.

Doctor Theodore S. Morton, who delivered almost everyone in Brush Creek, sat on the "amen row." He wore a black crumpled suit with a crooked, checkered red-and-white bowtie. An unlit stogie pushed against his cheek. He was one of those men who had seemingly been born old. He claimed to have delivered Cain and Abel from the Mother of All Living. Everyone took it as a fact.

Preacher "Sonny Boy" Roberts bade everyone to take a seat and opened the meeting with a prayer, which sounded more like a sermon. Callie especially noticed his pleadings to the Lord. "Grab hold of these sinners, oh Lord, and bring them to salvation." A string of "Amens" and whispered "Yes, Lords" resonated from the front row. Callie wondered how they all knew about Momma's plates. With head bowed and one eye open, she kept a constant vigil for Willow.

"Well, folks," Preacher Roberts continued after the prayer-sermon, "before we get started on the spoken word with Evangelist Howard Goss, amen, we're gonna praise Jesus with congregation sangin'. After the sangin' we'll be blessed, praise His name, with a special number by one of our very own right here in Brush Creek, Brother Wilton McCracken."

"Amen!" someone shouted. Not to be outdone, a half dozen more "amens" followed even louder than the first.

Wilton, wearing an ear-to-ear smile and looking like a jackass eating briars, shared the make-shift stage with Preacher Sonny Boy and evangelist Goss. Dressed in his best pair of overalls, blue flannel shirt and freshly polished brogans, Wilton looked stiff sitting there with his dark brown hair parted down the middle, held in place by a dab of Murray's Pomade.

"After Brother Wilton sangs, brothers and sisters, a real treat," Sonny Boy continued, "Our special guests, the Chickamauga Soldiers of Christ, who come all the way up from Chat'nugga, praise the Lord, is going to play and sang for us."

Maggie popped to her feet bouncing on her toes to a scattering of competing amens.

A piano had been brought in just for the revival. The pianist, Sister Heidi Loudenslager, weighing in at two hundred and fifty pounds, looked like a big ball of butter with a dress on. She struck up "Give Me That Old Time Religion" on the out of tune piano. Every ounce of butter fat shook as she pounded away, rocking back and forth, and from side to side. The legs on the piano bench wobbled and groaned under the load. The Holy Ghost clearly had a hold of Sister Heidi.

The bench legs miraculously held on to life as she continued with "Count Your Blessings," "Rock of Ages," "Saved by the Blood," and "Standing on the Promises." Her head bobbed every which way as she pounded out the first verse of "I'll Fly Away" while singing at the same time and trying to outdo everyone there. The louder she sang the harder she pounded the yellowed ivory.

Willow walked through the door.

Lucas Ward, the animated music leader with horn-rimmed glasses, suddenly stopped flicking his hand; his wrist, bent and lifeless extended droopy fingers toward the cracks in the floor. His jaw went slack. Sister Loudenslager froze on a high note allowing it to resonate throughout the packed room. Her butter shook for another ten seconds.

The congregation turned and stared. No one moved, as if a wayward comet had flash-frozen them in time. Centuries later, probing archeologists would no doubt proclaim this place to be an ancient ceremonial site, and for once would be right.

Willow stood within a few feet of the doorway looking every bit the angel from heaven. A ruffled grass-green silky dress wrapped around her perfect body like a Christmas present. Shiny hair the color of autumn leaves plunged to her shoulders like a waterfall and her skin shone creamy pale.

Alarmed at the abrupt pause, she took a step backward.

"Oh," she squeaked, as fingers flew to her open mouth as though to stem the rising panic. She took another step backward toward the open door. She turned to run.

A hand reached out, grabbing her by the arm. She jumped and pulled away. "Oh my," she whimpered.

"Howdy, Willow. It's okay, come and sit with us." Callie put her arm around the frightened girl's shoulders, pulling her toward the empty space on the bench.

"Oh, Callie, they hate me, 'cause I'm a no-good-for-nothin' sinner."

"No, they don't," Callie assured her. "It's just, well, everybody here's just plain folks and they've never seen anybody so beautiful before, that's all." She led Willow to the bench, squeezing the reluctant worshipper between her and Corbit.

"H-howdy, Willow, you sure are pretty," Corbit blurted. Immediately his face turned fever red. Willow gave a weak smile, looked at Corbit, and scooted closer to Callie. Corbit wondered why. Everyone in the room tried to get a peek at the new girl. Men smiled, women scowled, and children giggled.

The novice churchgoer clasped her hands together in a death grip and gazed down at the cracks in the rough planked floor.

"Howdy, young lady," a calming voice said. "Welcome to the revival. I'm Bud Kinser and this is my wife, Ellie."

Ellie smiled sweetly as she reached over Maggie and Corbit, and patted Willow gently on her hands. "I'm glad you could come. The children said they'd met you today on the way up from the creek."

"Yessum," Willow said in soft, quivery voice.

"Where's your harp?" Maggie asked. "You should've brung it. I brung my banjer… see?" Maggie held it up and smiled.

Willow returned the smile. "Why, I ain't got no harp."

Maggie, stunned, plopped against the rail-back bench, her face looking anguished at an angel in church without a harp.

∾∾

Outside in the dark at the edge of the woods a man crouched behind tall bushes. He peered through the open window, eyes narrowed, breathing hard, trying to control a murderous temper. The watcher seethed with anger. His temples throbbed. His nose flared. He crouched low and thought about what he would do next. A gun lay in the fold of his arm.

❧◦❧

Wilton McCracken's ears fanned out from his head resembling two wings attached to a smile. His brown eyes ogled the heavenly vision in the back of the room. The wider his smile, the more his ears flickered, giving the impression he was warming up for take-off.

"Welcome, young lady," Brother Ward finally boomed. "Glad you could join us." He nodded at Sister Butterball and flicked his wrist. The congregation thawed from its sudden deep-freeze and continued with the second verse of "I'll Fly Away," seemingly appropriate considering an angel had flown into their midst.

The song ended, sending Sonny Boy bouncing to the pulpit in a spiritual frenzy. "Amen!" he shouted, striking his fist on the pulpit.

Willow jumped. "Oh my," she said, and buried her face in Callie's shoulder. Her foot touched Corbit's leg. Afraid to move, he stared straight ahead for fear she would move her foot from the precious spot. Out of the corner of his eye he watched as Willow cowered in fear. Her weakness made him feel like a prince in a fairy tale, or a shining knight with his biggest conquest. He felt indomitable, even immortal, as a waft of light perfume touched his nose and haloed around his head. She moved her foot. Corbit felt the magic wane.

"It — it's okay, Willow, it's just the preacher's way of keeping everybody awake — he don't mean nothing by it." She raised her head and smiled.

Still watching her with a furtive eye, he wanted to say, *No, the preacher is mad, even crazy, so keep your foot on my leg so I can protect you from his evil onslaughts.* But he didn't. With the foot gone he felt as though he had been robbed of his most treasured possession.

"Do you feel God's spirit here this evenin'?" Sonny Boy shouted loud enough for every sinner within ten miles to hear.

Scattered "amens," not quite together, but equally as loud resounded throughout the room. One person always seemed intent on having the last amen as if the congregate affirmation wasn't complete without it.

"Somebody," Sonny Boy continued, "praise His name and shout… a-men!"

"Amen!" The affirmation resounded again with the same person getting in the last "so be it."

Corbit imitated a rigid washboard. His nerves jiggled like low-voltage energy traveling through his body.

"Why, you're shaking," Willow leaned over and whispered. "The preacher man done skeered you too?" He only offered a weak smile.

Sonny Boy announced the local boy with praise and fanfare. Wilton stood, shoved his hands deep into his overall pockets, and shuffled over to the podium. He flashed a shy smile. His ears wiggled, his face flushed a deep red, and his freckles wrinkled up on his perfectly straight nose.

"Howdy, folks," he whispered, pulling his hands from his pockets and placing his thumbs through his overall straps. The Murray's pomade made his reddish-brown hair look darker than it actually was. He closed his eyes and began to rock gently back and forth on his heels.

Silence fell over the cramped room. Not a word was uttered, nor a baby's whimper, nor a movement of any kind. Then, as if directly from the halls of heaven, a remarkable voice flowed from Wilton's mouth.

Amazing Grace, the anthem of the Christian world, wafted through the air wringing tears from all those the harmonious notes touched as it reminded them of God's eternal love and Christ the Savior's redeeming grace. Rich or poor, they were believers.

Wilton, no longer the tall skinny farm boy, a field laborer wearing shaggy and faded overalls, had been transformed into something eloquent. And the worshipers were changed right along with him. Strong, field-working men were humbled. Restless children were suddenly attentive and everyone, rich, poor, and poorer, became one. His velvety baritone gifted them with something no instrument alone could have offered. It went way beyond mere music or the power of speech. It was his soul, bare, laid out, testifying of something considerably greater than he.

Wilton gloried in two more verses and then ended with the same stanza he had started off with. His thumbs slipped from behind overall straps, his strong hands again sank deep into his pockets, and he sat down amidst sobs and sniffles. Not a dry eye remained in the house. Craggy work-hardened old men, weather-beaten women, and gangly teenagers succumbed to his spiritual power.

Even Corbit's eyes were damp with tears of thanksgiving and joy. Maggie, leaning against her mother's arm, blotted the corners of her eyes with the sleeve of her mother's dress of white and red checks. Callie, repentant, at least for the moment, gazed at her parents through moist eyes. Bud and Ellie smiled at their wayward daughter approvingly.

Willow cried too. She didn't know why. She had felt something stir within her, something she had never experienced before. At that moment she knew what had been missing all of her young life. The angel-princess had submitted to someone other than her father.

Chapter 8
Sweet Chariot

Outside the air was stagnant. The watcher swatted at mosquitoes as they buzzed and drew blood. The figure impatiently skulked around trees like a ghost around tombstones. The muted light of the schoolroom reflected amity to anyone passing by, but to the silent stalker in the bush, the light seemed cold and threatening.

❧❧

The ping of tobacco spit hitting spittoons brought the crowd back.

"Glory to God," someone shouted. The "amen" row, not to be outdone, joined together in refrains of praises and shouts.

As the voices died down and folks regained composure, the gravelly sound of lids being screwed off Mason jars could be heard around the room. *Spa-tooo* sounds followed as churchgoers released the pent-up contents of their mouths. Having been seized by the spirit during Wilton's a capella a spit would have been considered sacrilegious. For those without a jar or spittoon, the paneless window or a crack in the floor would suffice.

Maggie leaned over and whispered to Willow, "Wilton sang 'Amazing Grace' ah-ca-pelican. That means he sang without git-tars, harp, and banjers." She cocked her head and smiled, proud to be sharing intimate knowledge with a harp musician.

"Why, you sure know a lot about music and all," Willow whispered back. "I ain't ever heard anybody sing ah-ca-pelican b'fore. It sure was pretty."

Clamoring footsteps assaulted the front porch of the school house. Lottie Finch burst through the door shouting at the top of her voice. "Hallelujah! Glory to Jesus!" Hopscotching around chairs, Lottie, flailing arms over her head, shouted, "There's fire dancin' on the rooftop! The Holy Ghost done got a-holt of the schoolhouse!"

Willow sat straight up, grabbing Corbit and Callie by the arms. Callie winced. "Ouch," she exclaimed, forgetting to whisper. Corbit didn't seem to mind.

"The schoolhouse is on fire!" Willow blurted. "We're gonna burn up!"

Everyone turned and looked at the neophyte worshipper. "We're gonna burn up," she cried again. She jumped to her feet and stomped on Corbit's feet as she scrambled for the door.

She tripped, and Callie grabbed her arm preventing her from tumbling to the floor. "It's all right, Willow. There ain't nothing on fire. You ain't gonna burn up. Why, it's just Sister Finch saying she done seen the Holy Ghost on the rooftop."

Willow glanced at the ceiling and shrieked, "They's a ghost on the roof, too?"

"No, silly, come on, sit down, it's not the spooky kind of ghost. I'll tell you about it later. Come on now, don't be afraid. Sit back down, okay?" Callie pulled her back to the bench and tugged her down.

"Yeah, it's okay, I'll protect you," Corbit blurted. Realizing what he'd said, his eyes again acquired the Moon Pie look as his hand slapped across his mouth.

Willow looked at him, mistrust in her eyes. "You will?"

Corbit blushed. Callie rolled her eyes.

"Is there a problem, Miss?" Preacher Sonny Boy asked between Sister Finch's whooping and dancing.

"No, sir," Callie spoke up. "Willow thought the Holy Ghost was gonna set her on fire." Scattered chuckles came from the congregation.

"Well, I surely hope he does," Sonny Boy said with a chuckle. The worshippers laughed.

Willow stood and readied herself to escape, not knowing what to think about the laughter, and not being totally reconciled with the fire and ghost on the roof, especially since the preacher seemed to give permission to burn her up. With further coaxing from Callie she sat back down.

Ellie reached over, patted her on the arm and whispered, "There's nothing to worry about at all. Sister Finch is just getting carried away with things. You just relax now, and enjoy the service. I'll explain it all later."

Willow sat, but not totally convinced she was safe.

Lottie, dancing and flailing her arms, kept repeating, "Jesus! Sweet Jesus!" She turned in circles, her body swaying and head bobbing. Gibberish about fire on the roof and the Holy Ghost having taken over the schoolhouse continued, until someone put arms around her and calmed her down.

Willow leaned in front of Callie and said to Ellie, "I ain't never heard of no ghost in a church house before. But I ain't never been inside a church before. Maybe that's why there's fire and a ghost on the roof."

Her silky hair brushed Corbit's face as she turned. He closed his eyes taking in her fragrance, feeling the smoothness of her hair against his skin. Something new stirred within him. He leaned forward, taking a deep whiff as he did. His lips were close enough to touch her check with just a pucker. *I could kiss her*, he thought. He wished he could, but remembered he had never kissed a girl before, and didn't quite know how to go about it anyway.

Without realizing it he still held his mouth in a pucker.

Willow drew her head back brushing his lips along her cheek.. She stopped and half turned, as Corbit's pucker rested at the corner of her mouth. "Why, Corbit, you done kissed me," she whispered. Being kissed by a man had only meant one thing to her. She drew back and scooted against Callie.

"Ain't done it!" Corbit snapped and leaned back against the bench, embarrassed. "Well, I ain't," he said. Willow glared looking a little uncertain.

The Chickamauga Soldiers of Christ stood with their guitars, mandolin, fiddle and "doghouse" bass. They lined up and began to play and sing "Great Camp Meeting in the Promised Land." Maggie jumped to her feet, her banjo hanging from its leather strap around her neck. She bounced on the balls of her feet with her arms whirling over her head. Her body twisted with the pounding of each note. She had fire in her eyes and joy in her heart.

None of the windows in the school had glass, only open shutters latched against the outside walls. Not one hint of a breeze existed. Almost every man, woman, and child waved a hand-held fan that read "Carter's Funeral Home" on the front. The increased excitement of music worship made it even hotter. Women fanned and breastfed their babies at the same time.

The next song the Soldiers sang, "Shout All Over God's Heaven," started out in the valley, the deep voice, melodic and powerful, started a slow, steady ascent to the top of the mountain. The three other singers joined in, blending their voices to create a harmony that brought shouts of "glory to God" and "praise Jesus" from the congregation.

Maggie worked herself into a frenzy beating on the drum hide of her banjo. Her mother reached out and gently patted her arm. "Now, Maggie, calm down before you bust wide open."

"Ain't them Soldier fellers wonderful, Momma?"

"Yes, they are, Maggie." Ellie pulled her down and hugged her close. "Just like you, baby, just like you." Maggie smiled and then sprang to her feet again to resume worshipping the way she knew best.

Callie looked at her and frowned. She whispered to Willow, "Maggie is so dumb."

Willow gave her a surprised look. "How come? Ain't she supposed to be happy? I thought the ghost was just burning her like the preacher said."

"I feel the Holy Ghost here tonight, folks," one of the musicians shouted. "Hallelujah to God in hedges! Hallelujahs echoed throughout the room in reply.

After a few minutes, when the shouting and praising subsided, the mandolin player said, "Now's the time when we take request from you folks."

Alice Sykes, a girl about Callie's age, jumped up and hollered, "Man, sing 'Casey Jones'!" A hush fell over the congregation. The gospel singers stood speechless.

"Honey," the mandolin player finally said, "That's a real good song and all, but I guess we'd better save that one for another time."

All the kids burst out laughing. Pops could be heard around the room as parents slapped arms and boxed ears. Alice plopped down and slumped over, hands covering her face. Then somebody suggested they sing "Swing Low, Sweet Chariot."

"Well now, that's a goodun," the gospel singer said. The tenor started it off. His voice spread across the room creating a peaceful atmosphere—a baby, restless and whinny, seemed to quiet down after hearing the soothing notes. Then, the rest of the quartet joined in.

The lead singer motioned for everyone to sing along. Lucas Ward stood to lead the congregation.

Lucas' head snapped back and exploded. The song leader crumpled to the floor a few feet away from where the quartet stood. Blood and brains splattered all over the stage.

Sonny Boy's tie and shirt had become two-toned with streaks of crimson.

The singing stopped.

Sister Ward, sitting in the front row, screamed and immediately passed out, her face and dress covered with blotches of red. Shrieks bounced off the walls. The room erupted in chaos. Parishioners pushed and shoved their way toward the narrow door. Parents hovered over their children. Folks poured out of windows like water over a dam.

Sister Loudenslager rolled off the piano bench, threw her arms high over her head and shouted, "Lord, Jesus! Lord, Jesus! Lord, Jesus!" She took short hops around Lucas, her corpulent body quivering. Dog-ear breasts flapped against her stomach. Her thighs shimmied like ripples in a pond.

Sheriff Vaughn rushed over to Lucas. Seeing nothing could be done, he bolted for the window hoping to catch the shooter before he escaped into the dark woods. Bud glanced at the window where the bullet had entered. He pushed people out of the way and pressed toward the opening, also hoping to see the shooter before he vanished.

Sister Ward opened her eyes and sat up. Several worshipers gathered around her to try and block her vision, but she managed to push a small woman away enough to glimpse the ghastly scene. She shrieked and passed out again. Two men carried her out. The smell of blood and death spread throughout the building.

Willow shrieked, "The ghost done kilt him and it's my fault! I caused the ghost on the roof to kill the singin' man." Tears poured from her eyes.

"No, it ain't!" Callie said over the noise. Everything seemed surreal, like a good dream turned nightmare.

"Yes, it is," Willow sobbed. "It's because I'm a no-good sinner. I'm dirt filthy, and I caused it!"

Callie held her by both arms to steady her. Looking

her in the face she said in a firm voice, "It… ain't… your… fault. Honest. Not going to church before ain't got nothing to do with it. God's proud you came."

Willow wasn't listening. "No! I done it! I done it! I shouldn't have come here! All of them babies — you just don't know how sinful I am. It's my fault the ghost jumped on the roof to start with, and because of me it kilt the song man!" She screamed, falling to the floor between the benches, floundering around like she had gone mad while people, eager to get away, stepped over her.

Those not escaping out of the windows or doors lay on the floor with arms over their heads. Mothers lay atop their children, and husbands atop their wives. Oppressing odors of blood, sweat, and tobacco saturated the stale air.

"Come on, honey, it's okay. It ain't your fault," Ellie said, kneeling beside Willow. "Come now. Let's get up off the floor before you get trampled on."

"I *knowed* there was sumpin' about this gal the minute I laid eyes on her," Elvira Clancy sneered, leaning over and wagging her finger in Willow's face. "I knowed it. She's a Jezebel, a pure-dee harlot. Why, she done brought the judgment of the Lord down on all of us righteous folk!"

"Elvira Clancy!" Ellie scolded with a killing glare while trying to calm the frightened child.

"A witch's spell," Elvira shouted for all to hear. "She's done put a witch's spell on Brother Ward!" She nodded and stared at Willow. "You're a witch. You done it all right. You kilt him!"

"She ain't neither, you old goat!" Callie grabbed Elvira's wrinkly arm, snatching her around. "You shut your mouth, you gossipy ol' hen!"

"Callie!" Ellie scolded. "Stop it!"

Corbit jumped in, "You mean ol' bitch!"

Ellie's hand flew to her mouth. "Corbit Kinser!"

"She ain't no witch, you are," Corbit shouted, shaking

his finger in Elvira's face.

"My word!" Ellie gasped, surprised at her children, her eyes darting from one to the other.

"Huh!" Elvira sniffed, turning up her nose. "I ain't never been talked to like that by no younguns!" She pushed toward the door. "Just ain't raised proper!"

Ellie glared at Elvira, then turned and looked at her children, but didn't say a word. Gently she lifted Willow, cradling her in her arms as the confused girl sobbed softly. "Don't pay no attention to any of that, honey, nobody's blaming you."

The building finally emptied out, except for the dead song leader. The sweet chariot, without a doubt, had swung low and carried Brother Ward home.

❧

The crouching figure fell to the ground, his rifle landing in the dirt and leaves. He lay there not quite sure what to do, afraid to move, afraid to even breathe. The man was dead. Even from his hiding place in the woods, and the poor lighting of the church, the watcher could see the side of Lucas Ward's head burst like a watermelon. After a few indecisive seconds he raised his head and cautiously looked around. He jumped to his feet, scooped up his rifle and scurried off through the woods.

❧

"I've got the dogs comin', Bud," Sheriff Vaughn said, tamping Granger tobacco into his pipe and lighting it. Off duty deputies, already there for the revival, were busy combing the area for the shooter. The sheriff asked, "Got any idea who'd want Lucas dead?"

Bud looked back toward the empty school. "About to ask you the same thing. No… no idea at all. Lucas didn't have any enemies, none I'm aware of, anyhow."

"I guess it was possible a stray shot from a fire hunter

found its way to Lucas's head," the sheriff mused. "But it's not likely considering the damage done. I'd say the shooter would have to be fairly close."

"Yep, I agree with you, Joe. More like two hunnert feet, I'd guess."

The sheriff took a draw from his pipe, took it out of his mouth, and pointed it at Bud. "I've asked everybody to stick around so I can ask them a few questions. Why don't you round up the folks out here in the yard. The sooner we get them in one place the sooner they can go home."

"Okay, Joe, I'll get started."

Not long after a call from the sheriff's patrol car radio, a fender-rattling GMC pickup squeaked to a halt at the side of the road. Deputy Jimbo Honeycutt shoved open a door with McMinn County Sheriff painted in bold letters on the side. He slid off the seat. Bloodhounds fenced in by wooden rails barked and whined in anticipation of the hunt.

"Get the dogs, Jimbo, and come with me," Vaughn ordered. The tailgate dropped and the bloodhounds jumped down, with Jimbo holding on to the leather leash strapped to their necks, their noses instinctively touching the ground. Jimbo could barely rein them in.

"You reckon it could've been a stray bullet from somebody fire hunting?" Jimbo offered.

"Thought of it, but I don't think so. Too much damage to Lucas's head." Jimbo held on to the eager dogs and followed the sheriff into the brush.

Sheriff Vaughn stopped and said, "Look at this." He held a lantern where the weeds had been trampled down next to an ancient oak. "Looks like the killer stood right about here." Signs of tobacco spit covered leaves and bare ground around the trampled spot.

Jimbo turned, his sight following a straight path to the window where Lucas had stood. "Uh, huh, looks like he had a straight shot. And looks like he had a wad of 'baccer in his mouth, too, from the looks of the brown stuff everywhere."

"Exactly! Take the dogs and see what you can turn up." Vaughn turned to two other deputies who had come with Jimbo and the dogs. "Take Omer and Walter with you — and Jimbo, watch out that you don't get shot. The killer could be anywhere in these woods." The hounds were baying as they sniffed the patch of ground where the shooter had been.

Vaughn walked back to the school yard where everyone waited impatiently, especially the women with babies. "Bud, why don't you start asking these folks what they saw, and what they might know about any enemy Lucas might've had. I'll be back in a few minutes."

The county coroner, who happened to be Doc Morton, had retrieved his camera and medical kit, and busied himself taking pictures with his Brownie 6-20 Flash. He looked up as the sheriff walked in. "Looks like a 30-aught-6 to me, Sheriff."

"From the size of the chunk it took outta Brother Lucas's head, I'd agree, Doc." Vaughn noticed the splintered wall opposite where Lucas Ward had stood. He walked over, opened his Uncle Henry Schrade and dug out a slug. "Yep, looks like a 30-aught-6 all right."

"Any idea who might've done it, Joe?"

"No, not yet, got the dogs out runnin' though." Another bulb exploded. "Doc, you always carry your camera with you?" The sheriff asked, pointing his pipe at the camera as it flashed one more time.

"Yep, never know when a body might turn up."

Ellie finally calmed Willow down. "You can ride home with us. We'll leave just as soon as the sheriff says we can."

"Yes, ma'am, thank you, ma'am." Willow twisted her hair and pulled at her dress as tears continued to seep from the corners of her eyes.. Anguish distorted her face.

"Now listen here, young lady, and you listen good."

Ellie lifted the girl's chin and looked into her troubled eyes. "I'm going to tell you again, you didn't cause nobody to die just because you came to church, so you just get that out of your head, you hear me? God don't work that way."

"Yes'm." Willow let her chin drop and a tear fell on Ellie's hand.

Someone hollered, "Hey, Sheriff, somebody's comin' down the road."

"I better get out there, Doc. You'll get with me first thing in the morning with the pictures and any other findings?"

"You betcha… first thing." The coroner went down on his right knee at yet another angle and ignited his last bulb.

A shadowy figure carrying a coal oil lantern, swinging with each step, made its way toward the school. Light from the globe had an eerie effect with one-half of a massive frame in its light and the other in the dark.

"Who is it, Bud? Can you tell?" asked the sheriff after pushing his way through the crowd.

"No, but I'll go see." He clicked on a flashlight and started walking toward the approaching figure. "Might be just a neighbor checking to see what all the screaming and shouting's about." Bud met the shadow as it came within 500 feet of the church. With a possible murder, and the shooter still loose, no chances could be taken. Bud had retrieved his county-issued revolver and holster from underneath the car seat and pinned on his badge.

"You'll have to stop right there, mister." Bud placed the palm of his right hand on his Smith & Wesson Victory .38 Special.

The shadow stopped. "I aim to git my gal outta thet damned church house."

"What girl would that be, and who are you, anyhow?" Bud stepped closer to the lantern.

The man responded. "The purty gal, the one ever'body was a lookin' at like starvin' dogs."

"I'm guessing you're talking about Willow."

"Exact! Ain't hard to figger out."

"How come you to know she was being looked at like 'starvin' dogs,' as you put it?" Bud stepped closer.

"Well, it's what happened, ain't it? What always happens, and I don't like it. She ain't got no biz'ness in no church meetin', anyhow. Just a bunch of do-gooders there thinkin' they's better than I am, filling my gal's head full of lies."

"Your daughter's all right, Mister Branch, and nobody's said they're better than you are. Besides, your daughter enjoyed herself, at least until the — well anyway, she's all right. Follow me."

Shoving past Bud, Moss tramped the remaining distance to the church, swinging the lantern like a conductor signaling his engineer. He didn't slow down as he reached the mob of people looking on. Pushing through the crowd, he bellowed, "Where's my gal?" Tobacco spittle sprayed from his mouth and ran down his gray-whiskered chin. A single strap held up one side of faded overalls; the other side of the bib flopped over revealing a dirty red and green flannel shirt.

Willow cowered when he walked up.

"I gather this is the girl you're talking about," Sheriff Vaughn said.

Moss spat. "Thet's the little whelp, all right."

"Deddy," Willow's frail voice could hardly be heard. "I —"

"Shat up!" Moss glared at her. His body shook with rage. "Git out here, gal, and let's go!"

Ellie held her back, "Willow attended the church service with my children, Mr. Branch — that's your name, ain't it? Anyhow, she wasn't harmed."

"Yeah, she didn't git shot or nothing," Maggie piped up. "She was just listenin' to the sangin'… and you need to buy her a harp!"

Moss just looked at Maggie and furrowed his brow. "She ain't got no biz'ness in no church meetin' listenin' to no mealy-mouthed preacher puttin' foolish notions in her head about God, do-goodin' and other such nonsense!"

"But, Deddy, I didn't mean no harm—"

"I said to shat up b'fore I show you what for!" Moss reached out and grabbed Willow's arm, snatching her away from Ellie. "Come on, let's git!"

"Now see here," the sheriff said, blocking Moss's path. "You don't have to get rough with the girl just because she came to church." He looked dead into the man's eyes without flinching. "Now get your hands off her before I take them off, and throw you in jail to boot."

Moss continued to hold on to Willow, his mouth working the tobacco. He spat, and then without saying a word, let go of her arm, stepped around the sheriff, and pushed through the crowd.

Willow, with bowed head and eyes staring at the ground, followed silently, her arms hanging loose and unmoving. The feeling of love and acceptance she had experienced for the first time had vanished — the feeling of hope in a higher power evaporated with the death of a good man and the appearance of an evil one.

"I tole you she was no good, just like her old man!" Elvira spouted. "Trash. Both of them. Just pure-dee-trash!"

Moss lumbered down the road with Willow slinking behind. A shadow in the form of a spooky-eyed boy watched from the cover of darkness. Another shadow, slight and just as tormented, wove through the shrub and trees of Brush Creek

Chapter 9
Books, Cloth, and Marbles

The sun ascended over the hills and treetops and the first rays of light revealed an empty sky as vast as a desert. No rain clouds were in sight, assuring the continuation of the drought for another day. The crops, stunted and droopy, barely hung to life in earth thirsting for liquid nourishment.

The brightness of the new day contrasted starkly with the dark sadness of the night before, when a bullet had secured the fate of a man who would never see sunlight again in mortality. Another light, infinite and eternal, would now brighten his days in another world where droughts and uncertainty would not exist. Brother Ward left behind parched earth and days of insecurity for a land of milk and honey, and a well flowing with living water.

Callie, lethargic from lack of sleep, dragged down the stairs one forced step at a time. Corbit, already in the kitchen and slumped down in a chair, had one arm hanging over the slatted back, and his head leaning on his shoulder. Maggie sat on the opposite side of the table staring into space. The night had been sleepless for everyone in the Kinser household.

"Good morning, Callie. Breakfast will be ready in a few minutes," Ellie said with a yawn. Her face seemed haggard and much older than her thirty-two years.

"Where's Deddy?" Callie mumbled.

"He ain't come home yet. I guess they're still looking for the man that killed Brother Ward." Ellie slowly sifted flour into hot bacon grease and stirred until it turned a golden brown. She added milk and stirred some more for a thick gravy. Biscuits baking in the oven would soon fill the breakfast table along with bacon and oatmeal.

"Poor Brother Ward," Corbit said. "He's all I could think of all night long. Just doing the milkin' seemed awful hard this morning — even forgot to put sweet feed in Betsy's trough."

Ellie pulled the sheet of biscuits from the oven and said, "It can be expected, Corbit. I forgot to start the fire in the stove until I had the biscuits rolled and cut. And I suppose we all had a restless night."

"And Willow — I'm worried about her and what her deddy might do, or has already done," Callie said. "He seemed awful mean to her, and she looked real scared. I hope he didn't whup her."

Ellie wiped her hands on her apron. "I'm worried about her, too. And some of the things she said… about the babies. I don't understand it at all."

"Me neither. And she kept saying how she's sinful and filthy, and all. And she really believes it's her fault Brother Ward died."

"And she seemed to be scared of me, or didn't trust me, or something," Corbit said. "Anyway she didn't like it when I sat too close to her."

"But you liked being close to her, didn't ya?" Callie wiggled her middle finger. "Woo whoo!"

"Shut up!"

Ellie half smiled. "Now, now, you two. Behave. But yes, you're both right. I noticed and heard the same things you did."

"Poor Willow," Maggie whined. "I don't know why her

deddy was mean to her last night, and it's a shame he don't buy her a harp."

"Shut up, Maggie!" Callie barked. "You're so dumb!"

Ellie sat down. "I think it best you keep your mouth shut this morning, especially after your stunt yesterday with my beautiful wedding dishes. Now, apologize to your sister."

Callie stared at Maggie with hardness in her eyes.

"Well, Callie, I'm waiting."

"I'm sorry!" *That you're so dumb*, she wanted to say.

Her curt apology didn't go unnoticed by her mother, but Ellie held her tongue as though she'd just remembered what the children had seen the night before.

"After breakfast you can do the dishes."

"But it's Maggie's job," Callie protested.

"Not for the next month it ain't. Not only are you going to do the dishes, but all of Maggie's chores as well. It's your punishment for you helping Maggie break my dishes."

"You mean, Maggie don't have to do nothing the *whole* month? It ain't fair!" Callie slumped down in her chair, planted hands on her cheeks and pouted.

"Ain't nothing new," Corbit jumped in, "Maggie don't do nothing anyhow."

Ellie pointed a gravy ladle at him. "Maybe *you'd* like a month of extra chores, smarty pants."

"I wouldn't," he said without hesitation.

"Then I suggest you hush your mouth. Enough's happened in the last few hours to frazzle all of our nerves. You and Callie don't need to be adding to it. Now eat!"

"Where's the oatmeal, Momma?" Corbit asked.

"My mind just ain't with me this morning. It's on the stove."

Corbit and Callie glanced over at Maggie, who had a briar-eating grin on her face. Her tongue popped in and out like a snake's. Corbit's face turned a deep red. Callie gritted her teeth, "Asshole!" she snapped.

Ellie dropped the pot of oatmeal she had just picked up. It clattered on the stove top. Oatmeal splattered and sizzled as it hit the hot iron. "Now it's two months! You want to say anything else?"

"No!" Callie said curtly.

Ellie pointed to the back porch. "You know where the soap is, now get to it."

Corbit flashed a wicked grin. "Probably go good with a biscuit."

Callie shot from the chair and stomped across the floor. The screen door slammed and tap, tap, tapped as she stepped onto the porch where a fresh bar of soap waited to be lathered.

"Ought to make you worsh your mouth out, too, after what you said last night." She breathed deeply and let out a slow sigh. "After you finish breakfast go let Kate out to pasture and clean the stall."

"But, Momma," Corbit whined, "that ol' mule hates me."

"He hates everybody, but he still needs to be let out to pasture."

"Deddy's the only one that ol' pointy-eared devil won't bite and kick. Can't it wait until he gets home?" The misery in Corbit's voice didn't sway his mother.

"I don't know when that'll be, but I know you'll find a way to get it done."

"Can Callie help me?" he pleaded.

"I suppose, as long as it don't take too long. She's got a pile of chores of her own to do."

Callie stepped into the kitchen just in time to hear the conversation. Between the taste of soap and facing the Pointy-Eared Devil, she felt the pain and anger surging inside her. "It ain't fair, Momma. Why do I have to help put that ol' mule out?"

Ellie dropped her arms in exasperation. "For heaven's sake, Callie, it won't kill you!"

"Who says? That ol' mule's more ornery than a stepped-on rattlesnake. Why can't Maggie help, she ain't doing nothin'. I got her chores to do — and mine."

Maggie fell prostrate on the floor and put on a performance to make every star in Hollywood jealous. "Oh, Momma, *boo hoo hoo*. Callie's always picking on me, *boo hoo hoo*. I have to do ever'thing. Make her leave me alone, *boo hoo hoo*."

"Why don't you shut up, you big faker!" Callie shouted.

"Oh, Momma, *boo hoo hoo*!" Maggie's wails grew louder.

Ellie dropped her arms to her side and let out a sigh. "Oh, for heaven's sake, don't start again, Callie, unless you want another month of chores and a fresh bar of soap. Good God in heaven, have mercy!"

Callie stomped toward the door. "Come on, Ettis, let's go before prissy pants fakes her death!"

"Momma, tell her to stop calling me Ettis. I hate that name!"

Ellie rolled her eyes, "I declare, Corbit, just…get… the mule… out…of… the barn… and be done with it! Okay? And for land's sake, Maggie — please, will you just be quiet and go somewhere out of the way?" The Oscar winner smiled as she bounded off the floor, slipped the banjo's strap around her neck and headed for the front porch.

Everyone caught the familiar sound of Bud's 1936 Ford as it hurried up the long drive in a cloud of dust.

"Here comes Deddy," Maggie announced.

Everyone went out to meet him hoping for some news.

"Your deddy's had a rough night, so let him be with the complaining, you hear? And, Lordy mercy, look at that dust. If it don't rain soon the crops are gonna dry up and blow away. What's it all coming to?"

The Ford squeaked to a stop. Bud pushed the door open and stepped out looking tired and haggard. His mustache, surrounded by day-old whiskers, seemed to droop a little more than usual and his six foot five frame stooped with fatigue.

Maggie turned into a magpie. "Didja catch 'im, Deddy? Is the murderer in jail? Do we know 'im? When are they gonna hang 'im? Can I watch?"

"Maggie!" Ellie scolded. "Stop those infernal questions, and nobody's gonna hang nobody." Ellie cleared her throat. "Well, did you?"

"Hang anybody? "

"Oh, stop it. You know what I mean — catch the killer."

"No, no luck at all. Whoever done it got away. I've got to hand it to him, though. He's smart enough to know a bitch in heat can throw a bloodhound off track. The dogs were hot on the trail, but after about twenty minutes they were sniffing the hind end of a bluetick hound tied to a tree down by the creek."

Ellie looked worried. "So he could still be around here?"

"Could be, but more than likely not. I'd say he's probably over in Meigs County by now, or in the mountains for that matter. Anyway, just to be sure, I want you younguns to stay close to home." Bud took his hat off and slapped it across his leg dislodging a storm of dust. "I'm ready for a biscuit and a nap."

"You get worshed up and I'll make you some fresh bacon and gravy to go with the biscuits. Oh, and Corbit's going to let Kate out to pasture." Ellie took Bud by the arm and led him toward the house.

Corbit pleaded, "Can't you do it, Deddy? Kate hates me."

"Kate's as tame as a cat, son."

"Yeah, a wildcat!"

"You're deddy's tired. Just do as you're told."

"Oh, I almost forgot." Bud shuffled back to the car and took out a cardboard box. "Got something for you here, Maggie."

Maggie drew in a deep breath and crossed her chest with both arms. "For *meee*?"

"Yep, banjo-playin' music books. They mark where to put your fingers." Maggie had learned how to strum claw hammer style like Grandpa Jones, and had gotten very good at it. She didn't know, however, how to use three picks to do rolls. The books had diagrams with instructions on how to pick a five-string banjo. "If you plan to play on the Grand Ole Opry, I figured you needed to learn how to pick like that Scrubbs feller."

"Oh, Deddy," she wailed, then threw her arms around him and bawled like a baby. "I ain't never had such a good present b'fore." With arms loaded with music books and banjo strapped around her neck, Maggie skipped to her room to prepare for Nashville and the Opry.

"And this's for you," Bud said, handing Callie a box full of cloth. "Mostly flour sacks I guess. Went over to check on Sister Ward this morning and she wanted you to have it. She knows how you like to sew. Sent some thread, too." He held up two spools, one white and one red. "She remembered the shirt you made for Brother Ward, said he wore it until it fell apart, said he really loved it."

"Oh, thank you Deddy… and I'll be sure and thank Sister Ward, and I'll make her some piller cases with lace all around them, too."

"Here you go, son. I didn't forget about you." Bud reached into his pocket and pulled out a small cloth sack. "Marbles, cat-eyes and solids mixed."

"Thank you, Deddy." Corbit's mouth spread into a wide smile.

"You're welcome. It's the least I can do since you're gonna let Kate out to pasture." The smile vanished.

Leading her husband toward the kitchen, Ellie asked, "How is the poor soul doing this morning?" She paused and sighed. Pulling up her apron she twisted the bottom into a pretzel, drew in a quick breath, and sighed, "Well, I do declare, what a silly question. Of course she's not doing well, after seeing her husband killed and all."

"She's doing as well as can be expected, I guess. Her sister's there and her brother's on the way in from Nashville. Ought to be here in an hour or two. The kids are on their way from Jacksonville and Mobile. She wants to wait until they get here before making funeral arrangements."

"I'll bake a ham and take it over this afternoon and see if I can lend a hand at getting the house ready for the wake. Airy Mae Plank's picking me up. I'm sure the other church ladies'll be there, too."

"It's like a thundercloud's settled over the whole area," Bud said in a low mournful voice. "I can feel the sorrow in the whole town, but especially the folks around Brush Creek."

"I'm afraid seeing it all happen, and Lucas dying in such a horrible way will have a long-lasting effect on the children. They've been trying hard to act normal, but I know it's really bothering them. Last night was hard. I heard Callie crying and Maggie talking in her sleep, and Corbit, well, he just sat on the porch most of the night."

"I knew it'd be hard on them. I wish I could've been here. And I know it's weighed heavily on your mind, too."

"I have to say it has. But what about that poor girl? The first time she's been to church and she sees a murder, and thinks it's her fault to boot. And then her horrible, good-for-nothing thing of a deddy… well, you were there." Ellie looked up at the hazy sky. "And speaking of a thundercloud, I don't know what we're going to do without the rain.

Bud gazed at the empty heavens. "If only thunderclouds covered the sky instead of the community. I think the good Lord's stopped making rain, at least for the folks here in Tenn'see."

৯৵৶

Callie liked to sew on the back porch during warm weather when she had cloth, and now she had enough to keep her busy for as long as she could hold a needle. She thought of all the things she could make, and who she would make them for. *Let me see. I'll sew a dress for Tommy Sue and something real special for Momma, and for Maggie, a big sack for her to hide that confounded banjo in.*

Then she felt a little guilty knowing where the cloth came from and what had happened to Sister Ward's husband. *Well, maybe a plain sack dress for Maggie. But first I'll sew for Sister Ward. I'll make her some piller cases with fancy stitching with the thread she gave me. I'll add some blue and green, too.* With plans made, at least for the moment, Callie dropped the box of cloth on the smooth worn work surface of an old table she used to cut out patterns and to sew on. She started rummaging through the box when she heard the crunching of leaves.

Willow stood at the edge of the yard in the shadows of a hackberry tree. She looked gaunt, tired. Worse. She looked like the walking dead, like she had just climbed out of her grave after molding for a week.

"Willow?" Callie sensed something wrong. The girl's eyes, dark and lifeless, looked as if they were hiding deep in a cave. Without saying a word, she turned and ran off through the woods.

"Willow — wait up!" Callie sprang off the edge of the porch. She called again. "Wait for me! What's wrong?" She hit her stride as she plunged into the forest in hard pursuit.

Willow's auburn hair, though matted and tangled, glistened in the sunlight as she faded in and out of the shadows of loblolly pine, and cedar. She staggered, almost fell, grabbing onto a pine sapling to steady herself. The trees grew thicker. As she ran, her shape wobbled in and out of light and shadow creating the effect of jerky images from a silent movie projector.

"Ouch! Durn briars!" Stickers latched on to Callie's cotton dress, then *pluck, pluck, plucked* as they pulled away. Blood oozed from small punctures resembling stitches on her arms and legs. "Willow, Please wait for me."

The fleeing girl disappeared into a thicket of shortleaf pines and heavy, knee-high brush, seemingly unaware of Callie's pursuit and persistent pleas to stop. Undeterred, Callie followed her into the thicket, but lost her. She paused to look around and listen. "Willow?" she said softly. "Where are you, girl?" No answer.

Soft, haunting, almost indistinguishable sobs seemed to float through the air from beyond the pine thicket. Callie didn't say one word for fear her new friend would flee. She moved deliberately, watching for twigs or loose pine burrs that could snap or scatter with an inadvertent step or kick that might alert the sobbing girl.

Her furtiveness soon paid off. Peeking from behind a tree she observed a disheveled girl she hardly recognized. The angel-princess, the very one that stopped a church service by simply walking through the door, the same beauty that, just yesterday, had Corbit the preacher-hater, converted to a pious saint, now looked as scruffy as an empty broken-up pecan shell that had been gnawed by a hungry squirrel. Willow sat on a mound of straw on the edge of a gully filled with rotting logs, bush, and tall weeds. A mixture of old dried-out and new prickly green pine burrs lay scattered on the ground around her.

Slumped over with arms resting on her knees and hands covering her face, she continued to sob. Sobs turned to wails and her delicate body shook uncontrollably.

"I ain't no good," she moaned, her voice quivering. She brought both fists down on her knees. "I… ain't… no… good!" Gut-wrenching laments poured from a soul that seemed overflowing with torment. "I'm just an awful, no good sinner. No good! No good! No good! Oh, God!" The tears flowed unencumbered.

Callie watched for a moment, behind the cover of a forest steeped in sepia shadows. Then, as if nudged by an invisible hand, she stepped from her hiding place and moved softly toward Willow.

"It's all my fault, Callie," Willow said, never looking up, but somehow sensing she was there. "It's me who's to blame, ain't nobody but me." She wiped her hope-void eyes and gazed up at her newfound friend.

Callie sat down beside her. "It ain't your fault, Brother Ward dying, I mean. And you are good." Willow laid her head against Callie's shoulder. Callie's arm stretched and pulled her close. "It'll be okay, honest it will. You can tell me anything. I'm your friend. I'll understand." Willow raised her head. "No, you won't… you can't… and it ain't just the song man … it's ever'thing!"

"I can, too, honest I can. You can trust me. So, why don't you tell me what's bothering you, and why you look like you fought a bull and lost."

"I don't know why I'm no good for nothin'. I try to be good, I really do. Momma says it's me, that I cause it all, because the devil made me pretty. She said it had to be the devil, that ever'thing happened because I'm pretty, and that's what makes Deddy crazy, and makes him do the things he does."

"Why, that's silly. God made you pretty, not the devil. And what's it got to do with anything, anyhow… and what does he do to you, besides beat you? Those bruises on your face, arms, and legs look awful."

"I can't tell you. It's too horrible."

A stream of tears rolled down Willow's cheek. "You'd hate me if you knew how bad I am. Why, I'm so bad God hates me."

"No, I wouldn't. And you ain't bad, neither, and God doesn't hate you. He loves you."

"Loves me? Then why don't he help my momma, and Thorny, and Olive… and me? Well, them anyway. I know he can't ever love me because of what I done to those babies."

"What babies? What'd you do?"

Willow cried as though her heart would break. Her body shook. "Oh, Callie, I can't stand it no more!"

"Come home with me."

"No! I… I can't." She grabbed Callie's hands. "Promise me you won't tell your folks about any of this."

"Why?"

"Those babies, and… never mind, you don't wanna know. Just promise. You have to, for me. Okay?"

"I don't know—"

"But you said I could trust you, that you're my friend, and all."

"You can, and I am your friend, but…"

"Please?"

"Well, okay, I won't say anything if that's what you want."

A twig snapped.

Callie jerked around, scanned the trees and bushes.

"Is somebody there?"

"Leave her be. I'll take care of her." A strong but quiet voice penetrated the foliage and drifted off through the forest. It felt, to Callie's ears, like an arrow shot from a taut bow.

Gaining her composure, Callie said, "Who in John Brown are you?"

"Ain't none of your concern," the voice said from somewhere amidst the trees and bush.

Callie stood. "Why don't you go away and mind your own business!"

"It's okay. He's my brother, Thorny." Willow wiped her eyes with the sleeve of her ripped stepsister looking dress, which contrasted the Cinderella gown she had worn on the trail yesterday and to revival later in the evening.

"He's a little shy." Willow dabbed at her moist nose with the back of her hand. "He won't come out while you're here. You'd better go, okay? And remember, don't tell nobody about this, okay?" She pleaded with her vacant eyes as much as with her voice. Desolation showed in both.

"I promise," Callie said. But it bothered her to make such a promise. It felt as though she was hiding something dark and disturbing from her parents.

Willow threw her arms around her neck and whispered, "Thank you."

"Let's go," the sonorous voice from the bushes ordered. "We got to get home."

"Go on home, Callie, and I'll see you later. Okay? I'll be all right directly."

Callie gave her a weak smile, turned and walked toward home. Then she noticed the stinging. Small splotches of blood oozed out of the stitch holes in her legs and arms where the briars had bitten while running after Willow. Funny she hadn't noticed it before, she thought. An empty feeling swept over her. She felt as though her soul had been sucked out of her body, leaving an empty shell. She felt frightened, not for herself, but for Willow.

Chapter 10
Corbit and the Corn Field

With each passing day of continuing drought it looked more and more like a long bleak winter ahead. With most people depending on their crops to stave off starvation, even in good times, this year's meager yield would surely make for a bitter cold deeper than a winter's chill.

Bud walked in from the field and plopped down in a chair. It groaned underneath his weight. "Damn it, Ellie, I don't know what we'll do if it don't rain soon. No point in hoeing, it's so damn dry the weeds are dying on their own."

Ellie wrinkled her brow. "Swearing won't help. It won't bring the rain. More'n likely keeps it away longer."

"Well, prayers ain't worked, that's for damn — uh, that's for sure. The corn's twisted and everything else is stunted and droopy as hound ears. We'll be lucky to have enough corn to grind into meal and flour, let alone have something to put up till next year's harvest, if there is a harvest. And what about the livestock, how are we going to feed them? I expect market prices for beef and pork'll be in a drought, too, to make it even worse."

"Now, Bud, where's your faith?"

"Well."

"It'll work out, you'll see. I've enough faith for the both of us."

She handed him a glass of tea. He took a long drink. "I hope so. I surely hope so. One thing's for sure, Lucas won't have to worry about it. Puts a mighty burden on his widow, though."

Ellie refilled the glass. "The funeral went nicely, don't you think?"

"I'd say so. Preacher Roberts did a good job of saving Lucas. Sister Ward and their younguns ought to feel proud. To hear Sonny Boy tell it, Lucas done took the Lord Jesus's place on the right hand of God and wrassled the trumpet away from Gabriel. They'll have to change the Bible to read, The Father, Lucas, and The Holy Ghost."

"Oh, Bud, it weren't *that* bad. Well, maybe he did go a little overboard on the praising. Made the family feel good though, that's the important thing. And Lucas was a good man."

"Well, I reckon he was, and better than most, I'd say."

Ice clattered against the glass as Ellie held it to her cheek. "We're better off than most people, too."

"I suppose so, and I ought to be thankful we have St. Lucas watching over us. And yes, he was a good man, one of the best, but he had his faults like all of us. Sometimes I think preachers go too far with the praising where it sounds almost phony. Ought to be pointed out that Lucas had his ups and downs, but dealt with them in a Christian way… most of the time. I guess Sonny Boy maybe felt a little guilty because Lucas died in such a terrible way, right there in his revival meeting at that." Bud shook his head. "Some revival, huh?"

The three Kinser kids ambled into the kitchen from different directions. "Dry as heck fire, ain't it?" Corbit said, flopping down in a chair and rearing back on its hind legs.

"What did I tell you about leaning back in the chair?" Ellie scolded. Corbit leaned forward letting the chair free-fall. The front legs hammered the pine floor and scooted to a screeching halt. Exasperated, Ellie threw up her hands and sighed.

"Think it'll rain before summer's out, Deddy?" Corbit asked.

"I'll be John Brown if I know, son. Don't look promising."

Maggie perked up. "I've got an idea how to make it rain. Wanna hear it, Deddy?"

Callie bumped her head with an open hand. "Oh, horsefeathers! Here we go!"

"Callie!" Ellie warned with a glare to match.

"Why, sure I do, little Maggie. Shoot!"

"I'll play the banjer while Corbit and Callie do a rain dance."

"If that ain't the dumbest thing I ever heard!"

Another stern glance, her eyes narrowed. "Callie, I ain't gonna put up with it."

"Yessum."

Bud chuckled, reached over and tugged Maggie's ear. "Well, little Maggie, at least you're thinking, I'll give you that."

Something clicked in Corbit's brain. His mind raced through time and space blocking out everything around him. A smile spread across his face and the look in his eyes said, *I have an idea*, and not just an idea, but a history-making idea. Callie noticed, gave him a wry look, but said nothing.

"Guess what, Deddy? I can pick like Earl Scruggs, or a little bit anyway." Maggie shook all over with excitement. "Wanna hear?"

"Already?" Ellie sounded equally excited. "Why, you just got the books a few days ago."

"It's all she's done; she ought to be able to play ever' dad burn thing in them!"

"Callie," Bud admonished. "You should be proud of your little sister for working so hard."

"Working!"

"Yeah, Callie, I worked hard," Maggie said. Callie rolled her eyes.

"Say, ain't Earl Scrubbs—"

"Scruggs," Maggie corrected. "His name's Earl Scruggs."

"Yeah, him. Ain't he the feller who plays with Lost John Miller on Dubya NOX radio over in Knoxville?"

"Yep, it's him all right. He's the bestest banjer picker in the whole world. I got a pitcher of him holding a Gibson Mastertone banjer. It's what I want more than anything, Deddy. This here Montgomery Ward's a goodun an all, but it don't hold a light to a Gibson."

"Pleease," Callie muttered with a look of total disgust.

"Well," Bud said, "You just keep practicing like you've been doing and I'll be sure you get one of those fancy banjos one day."

"Really? Oh, Deddy, you promise? I'll really get one if I practice hard?"

"You can count on it," Bud tweaked her nose and laughed. Maggie giggled. "Now let's hear what you've learned."

The Earl Scruggs imitator placed three picks on the fingers and thumb of her right hand. In an instant the house filled with the spirited "Sally Goodin'." Her fingers rolled with precision, all three picks working in unison. Her left hand fretted the strings with ease, gently touching them with accuracy to compliment the lightning speed of her right hand. Not one time did she look to see where her fingers were on the strings and frets. Her face showed no signs of concentration, only the unmistakable expression of joy radiating from her eyes like sun rays cutting through a clear morning sky. Maggie appeared to be a natural, like Babe Ruth to baseball, or Charles Lindbergh to aviation.

Everyone stared in wonderment and respect, everyone but Callie. The more Maggie played the madder she got. *I hope she makes a mistake. Show them she's not perfect. I hope a string breaks and pops her in the eye. That'd shut her up!*

She played it perfectly. Maggie finished the tune, and then without the least bit of hesitation jumped into "Hook and Line," singing as she played. Everyone, except Callie, clapped, nodded and stomped to the rhythm. Callie quietly seethed and wished for bad things to happen.

After the performance Bud whistled, Ellie clapped, and Corbit stomped his feet to show their approval. The Grand Ole Opry was alive and well in the Kinsers' kitchen. Maggie took a quick bow and threw kisses to her adoring audience.

Corbit noticed Callie's lack of enthusiasm. "Hey, Callie, ain't you gonna clap? Didn't you think she was good? I sure did!"

"I reckon. Hey, Deddy, look at what I sewed." Callie pulled pillow cases from her basket. "See? I made these piller cases for Sister Ward. And I made this for you, Momma." She held up a flour sack dress with blue and yellow flowers. "You like it, Momma?"

"Why yes, it's beautiful. Thank you, you're so sweet. I've been needing a new house dress, and, well, it's so pretty. And the piller cases are very pretty, and thoughtful. I'm sure Sister Ward will love them." Ellie took the dress and held it up for everyone to see. "Ain't it pretty, Bud?"

"Uh huh, sure is. You done real good, Callie." Bud added, "What do you think of your sister's banjo picking ? Ain't you proud of her?"

Callie ignored the question. "Do you think I could have this new Singer sewing machine, Deddy? See, here it is, right here in the new Sears & Roebuck catalog." She opened the catalog and laid it on the table in front of him. A picture of a 1039 Singer 221 Lightweight stared up at him. In 1940 the Singer Company had started manufacturing pistols, artillery, and bomb sights for the war effort. The company started making sewing machines again after the war.

"Look, it doesn't have a foot treadle like ours. It has attachments, needles, a carrying case and a 'lectric foot pedal. See? Why, it even has an oil can. Can I have it, Deddy? Can I?"

"Well, we've got a good sewing machine. I suppose it'll have to do for now, being the way things are, and all. Besides, we don't have 'lectricity."

Callie's shoulders slumped, her countenance dropped. She stood there, arms limp at her side, staring at the floor.

"Yessir, a Grand Ole Opry star, that's what we have here," Bud gushed. "Why, I bet you'll be pickin' as good as that Scrubbs feller before you know it."

Callie bolted from the room.

"I think you're a good sewer, Callie!' Maggie called after her. "Momma's new dress sure is pretty, too!"

The screen door meowed open, then slapped closed with a bang.

"Well, I'll say! I wonder what's wrong with her?" The chair groaned as Bud stood. "Better worsh some of this dust off and get a nap, I guess. The sheriff wants me to work the evening shift. It's a good thing I have a job; at least it'll keep us in staples this winter."

❦

"Whatcha doing standing out here?" Corbit asked.

"Nothing!" Callie snapped. She stood at the corner of the house, arms crossed and tapping her foot looking like a pot ready to boil over.

"I think you're jeal-ous," Corbit sang.

"I am not!"

"Are too."

"Am not! Everybody thinks she's *so* great!"

"Aw, forget it. I don't know why Maggie makes you snap your cap all the time," Corbit said, putting his thumbs in his overall straps and rocking back and forth on his heels.

"Anyhow, I have an idea that's gonna save our crops."

"Really? I knew it! I saw the *I got it* look on your face when dumb Maggie was talking about us doing a stupid rain dance."

Corbit hooted, "Yeah, I guess that was a dumb idea. Can you imagine Maggie playing while we jump around whooping and hollering like Indians?" Callie unwound and joined Corbit in a round of hoots and knee slapping.

Callie wiped tears from her eyes. "So, what's the big idea you have to save us from starvation?"

"You'll see. Come on, let's go to the barn." They took off in a run.

"Cor-bit… Cal-lie… wait up!" Fred shouted, waving his arms. His red mop of hair glowed like fire in the early afternoon sun.

"Yeah, wait for us," Tommie Sue joined in.

The two runners slowed to a trot, turned around, but continued to walk backward. Flicking his wrist Corbit shouted back, "Come on to the barn!"

As soon as Fred and Tommie Sue entered the barn, Corbit extended his arm. "Here's a shovel for you, and one for you, too, Tommie Sue, and—"

"What's this for?" Fred demanded, his ever-present straw twitching in his mouth.

"To dig a trench with." Corbit handed the last shovel to Callie and picked up a hoe. "I'll use this."

"Holy mackerel! Are you outta your mind? It's been a week since Brother Ward bought the farm. Tommie Sue and me ain't been allowed more 'an hollering distance from the house. We want to go swimmin', so I ain't diggin' no trench. 'Sides, it's too damn hot."

"You better stop cussin', Fred Plank." Tommie Sue scolded.

"Dang-nabbit, Tommie Sue! I told you, damn ain't cussin', is it, Corbit?"

"Hell no, ol' boy, damn ain't cussin,' for sure."

"I'm gonna tell Preacher Roberts on the both of you," Tommie Sue barked, stomping her foot for emphasis.

Just then a shadow darkened the doorway.

"Hey, you all, whatcha doing?" Maggie asked as she walked up to the others, her shadow blending with those in the barn.

"Oh, hey, Maggie," Tommie Sue sing-songed.

"Hi-de-ho," Fred said.

"Howdy, Tommie Sue, howdy, Fred. You come to go swimmin'?"

"We got shovels in our hands, you Dumb Dora," Callie sneered. "Does it look like we're about to go swimmin'?" Fred and Tommie Sue stared at Callie, surprised at her tone of voice.

"We're going swimmin' later," Corbit said quickly, hoping to temper Callie's remarks. "First we're going to dig a trench."

"*You're* gonna dig a trench," Fred harped. "*I'm* going swimmin'."

"Okay, little sissy," Corbit said in a whiny voice. "Give your shovel to Maggie, then."

Horrified, Maggie took a step back, "I can't use no shovel. Why I might mess my hands up and I couldn't play my banjer."

"You lazy prissy pants!" Callie hissed, lunging for the hated instrument. "I ought to use that stupid thing to dig a hole with, and then bury it."

Maggie fell to the straw. "Nooooo! Mom-maaa!"

"Shut up!" Callie snarled.

Corbit grabbed Callie's arm pulling her back. "Aw, why don't you quit snapping your cap and leave her alone."

"Git your hands off me, Ettis," she growled, slapping his hand away.

"Like I said, you're just jealous because Maggie can pick

so good, that's all it is."

"It is not!"

"is too!"

"No, I ain't! Besides, everybody just says she can play that stupid thing so they won't hurt her feelings. Everybody knows she really can't play all *that* good!"

Maggie pushed herself up from the straw-covered floor and stood dead still, her head down, not saying a word. Tears formed in the corners of her eyes. They clung for a moment like a dying leaf to a branch before finally whispering down her cheek and dripping onto her bare feet.

"You shut your mouth, it ain't true and you know it!" Corbit turned to his little sister. "It's okay, Maggie, don't listen to her. She's just jealous because she ain't got no talent."

"I have too got talent. I can sew!"

Maggie, in an attempt to stave off her sister's anger, said, "I know I can't play near as good as you can sew. Why, everybody says you're the best sewer in Brush Creek — everybody!"

"Yeah," Tommie Sue interjected. "You're the best. My momma says so, too." Callie's anger seemed to subside somewhat with the praise.

Tommie Sue brightened up. "Hey, Maggie, I know what, why don't you play while we dig. It'll make it funner."

"Gosh, Tommie Sue," Fred cut in "You got a dumb way of having fun."

Callie rolled her eyes and snapped, "Let's go."

"Swimm-in?" Fred held the first syllable trying to sound hopeful.

"Later, Plank, first we have to save the crops." Corbitt waved everybody out the door. "Follow me to the corn field."

Arid soil barely supported the roots of the twisted and bent corn stalks. Four pair of feet kicked up dust as their owners trudged along, dragging, instead of carrying their shovels. Maggie, shovel-less, tuned her banjo as she walked.

The sky, a hazy blue, suspended patches of puffy clouds offering no sign of rain.

"Okay, here's the plan." Corbitt stood on the outer parameter of the parched field and pointing toward the pasture. "We're gonna dig a trench about two feet deep and about three feet wide all the way to there."

"What? You been drinking giggle water, or something? Why that's more'n a hunnert yards!" Fred agonized.

Corbit rubbed his chin and said, "More like fifty, I'd guess. The soil's loose until we get to the pasture, then it'll be a little harder because it ain't been plowed."

"By the way," Maggie asked, "why're we digging a ditch anyhow?"

Callie rebuked, "Did you say *we*?"

"Can't tell you, it's a surprise," Corbit interrupted before his sharp-tongued sister could say more. "Okay, let's get to digging."

Without another complaint, to Corbit's surprise, everyone lined up and began digging in the direction of the barbed-wire fence. Maggie positioned her banjo and started in on "Hook and Line." Immediately everyone picked up their pace.

One reason everyone agreed to dig so quickly, except for Fred, was because they knew if Corbit said he had an idea to save the crops, it was as good as done. They all recognized him as a thinker, a planner, and above all, a doer. They were intrigued and Corbit knew it. That's why he kept them guessing so they would keep up their enthusiasm, and, he knew, they liked to be surprised. Callie had perceived his idea would work when she saw "The Look," earlier, in the kitchen.

Maggie kept them in stride with the spirited "Oh, Susanna" and other lively tunes.

"Wow, Maggie," Tommie Sue marveled, "you're good, ain'tcha?" Callie's face tensed but she kept quiet. Before long the trench had been extended all the way to the fence.

"How do we get past this ol' fence?" Fred asked, his freckled face a ruddy red from the heat.

Corbit rolled his eyes. "We dig *under* it?"

Fred flipped his hair to one side revealing more freckles. "Well, laws, you think of ever'thing."

"Yeah," Tommie Sue said. "You sure are smart, and Maggie sure can play the banjo, too." Callie gave Tommie Sue a hard look. Tommie Sue hunched her shoulders. "What'd I say?"

Maggie stopped playing and said, "But Callie can sew *even* better."

They threw their shovels over the fence before squeezing between the rusty wire strands. Corbit climbed through first. Fred held the strands apart so the girls could climb through without getting snagged. All but Maggie, who looked at the pointy barbs with anxiety.

"Well?" Fred asked. "Are you comin' or not?"

"What if I scratch my banjer?"

Callie stuck her hand through the stretched fence. "Oh, for pity's sake, hand it here."

"No!" Horror-stricken, she jerked back. "Let Tommie Sue hold it!"

Tommie Sue said in a sweet, trustful voice, "Hand it here, I'll hold it while you go through the fence." Disgusted, Callie picked up her shovel and stomped off.

With shovels and hoe in hand the four laborers resumed digging. Maggie, with banjo safely around her neck again, let loose with "Comical Coons" followed by other equally brisk tunes. With clothes sweat-drenched and dirty with red clay, the excavators worked with renewed vigor. "Well, here we are at the spring," Corbit said with finality.

Fred roared, "Don't tell me we have to dig under thet?"

"Boy, Fred, you're a real flat tire," Corbit teased.

A narrow, mild-running spring hidden by tall grass

gurgled as it meandered its way through the pasture and all the way to Brush Creek where it emptied. Upstream, cows stood in the once knee-deep water swishing their tails. The drought had lowered the water table to the point where the spring did not flow as fast as it once did. A bellow greeted the bedraggled kids' arrival. Everyone gave Corbit, resident genius, a quizzical look.

Then, as if someone had lit a lantern, everyone sang, "Oooh, I get it!"

Except for Fred who said, "I still don't know how we're gonna dig under thet water."

Totally wordless, everyone stared at the red-headed boy wonder. Even Maggie shook her head. Boy Wonder looked back at the corn field and then back at the spring. His face turned crimson. "Aw shucks, I knowed what we were doin' all along." Everyone had a good laugh. Fred picked a fresh piece of straw and stuck it in his mouth. "Well, I did."

A pile of rocks that had been removed from the fields years earlier were loosely stacked in a pile a few yards down the fence line. Corbit hitched up his britches and said, "Come on, let's build a dam."

"I ain't gonna help if you're gonna cuss," Tommie Sue said curtly.

Fred rolled his eyes. "D… A…M, not D… A…M… N. Hell, I'm even smarter than thet."

The two boys, arms stretched to their knees with bowed backs, and squinting eyes, took staccato steps as they bore their heavy load. Callie and Tommie Sue shared the burden of one small rock. Maggie, of course, encouraged them along with her flawless five-stringed picking. Corbit, the engineer, gave instructions where to place each rock until they were stacked about four feet over the water line and extended several feet over the shallow bank on both sides.

"I think that'll do it," he said.

The small stream, held back by the rock dam, slowly

ascended to the top of its banks. Corbit jabbed the shovel into the top of the earthen barrier separating the spring from the man made canal. The cool water rushed into the trench, drenching Corbit's claycoated feet and pants legs.

"Hot diggity dog," he shouted, jumping to dry ground. The rushing water quickly filled the new channel, pushing its way toward the withered corn. To keep time with the racing stream Maggie cut loose with "Banjo Sam" while Corbit, Callie, Fred and Tommie Sue danced, jumped and whooped while running beside the new water course.

Before they'd even started digging the trench to the spring, they had cut a shallow furrow horizontally to a few of the corn rows, with shorter trenches resembling a pitch fork cut down the middle. The water hit the furrows, coursed down the pitchforked rows, then spread throughout the field.

That's when it happened. Maggie stopped picking. All five stood with gaping mouths spellbound at what they were seeing and hearing. As water made contact with the twisted, withered stalks, they straightened like soldiers coming to attention, popping and crackling, sounding like pistol shots.

"Wow," everyone breathed at once.

After watching the miracle play out Callie asked, "What made you think of this?"

"Well, remember how we used to stand by the spring when it rained and tried to count the raindrops as they hit the water?"

"Yep," Callie said. "Sure do. Like to have drove us bonkers trying to count them all."

"It did drive you bonkers," Corbit teased. "You never recovered."

"You were already bonkers," Callie said. "It's why you insisted on counting raindrops to start with."

"Well, anyway, to let you know how my genius mind works, when Maggie mentioned us doing a rain dance, I just naturally thought of the spring and how I could get some of that water over to the fields." Corbit snapped his fingers, "Zap! Boom! And that's how I came up with the idea."

"It just goes to show that you're bonkers, and not a genius like you think you are." Callie made a wide swath with her hand. "Only crazy people would think of things like building dams. We sane people would never think of that."

"I guess it means Fred here is a damn Einstein," Corbit said tapping Fred on the shoulder.

"You'd better stop your cussing, Corbit Kinser," Tommie Sue warned.

"Gee whillikers, thet's good thinking, Corbit boy … and damn, Tommie Sue, damn ain't cussing, neither."

Water spread from the corn field, then extended to the peas, and pole beans, the squash, the okra, and watermelons. Like a church full of sinners the crops were baptized and reborn.

Ellie ran from the house and stood at the edge of the porch. She watched in awe as the corn stalks unbent, crackling like thawing ice on a pond.

"My God, it's a miracle," she muttered. One hand slapped over her mouth, then the other. She uttered a muffled, "Oh!" and then, gasping a short breath, said, "I've just seen a sure enough miracle!" She bounced down the steps, spread-out fingers covering her mouth.

Then she spotted the miracle workers in the pasture and the dirt piled up along the trench. "Lord, have mercy!" she offered, her hands wrapped around the ever-present apron. "What in the world have those kids been up to now?" She hurried toward the pasture, watching as the parched fields soaked up the precious liquid.

"Momma, over here!" Maggie yelled, waving her arms. "Come see what *we* done!" Of course Callie noticed the "we" part, but said nothing, too elated at the sight of the crops springing back to life.

Ellie made her way across the pasture, arriving in time to see the dam being dismantled, the fields having been sufficiently watered. The four saviors, redeemers of crops, had already removed enough of the rocks for the water to drop below the banks and the fresh-dug canal opening, allowing the spring to flow over the remaining rocks to its proper course.

"I wish your deddy could've seen this. He had to go to work, but he'll have a dandy of a surprise when he comes home."

Chapter 11

Don't I Buy You Purty Dresses?

Moss Branch slouched on the porch in a slat-back chair thinking about Willow. He leaned forward, spat tobacco spittle off the edge of the porch. It splattered on hard clay creating tortuous designs.

A warm night, a full moon, and shine whiskey stirred thoughts of the pleasure awaiting him in the back bedroom. He stood, spat again, and stumbled toward the ripped screen door. The spring, stretched and frazzled, barely twanged as he flung the door open. He grabbed the door jamb to catch his balance, swayed back and forth, and then staggered through the house clutching a package wrapped in white paper.

Rose Branch, in bed in the broken-down shack's front bedroom, could not sleep. Olive, who just turned four, lay beside her. Moss's thorn-in-the-side son had taken to the woods earlier in the evening with rifle, his Blue Tick hound named "Bones", and a head lantern, the kind coal and copper miners use deep in the mines.

The door creaked open. Moss's shadow completely covered the entrance. He stepped in. Willow sat scrunched in the corner. She heard the vault door slam shut.

"It's me, girl. Come to your deddy." He dropped the package on the floor beside the bed.

With her slender feet, Willow shoved herself against the wall as hard as she could. Her knees met her chin. She sucked on two fingers like a child. She closed her eyes wishing with all her heart she could disappear into one of the cracks. *A roach*, she thought, *I wish I'd been born a roach.*

"Come to your deddy," Moss spoke softly. "Your deddy needs pleasurin'."

"Oh," she whimpered, releasing fingers from her mouth. She knew what was coming, felt bile build in her throat. Her legs, covered with chills of fear and shame, trembled. Her arms cradled her knees and her body rocked back and forth. A tiny shivering voice tried to plead, wanted to, but instead all that came out were quivery, garbled whimpers. One word, however, made it out of her tight throat, the word "please." The only word Moss heard.

"I like to hear ya beg, it's pleasin' to know ya want it. I see you're shakin' with 'citement." He crouched over his victim. His eyes could have been borrowed from the devil.

Willow pulled her knees closer to her body. Moss reached out and grabbed them. He dragged her across the room still in a sitting position, her arms still locked around her knees. Her whimpering became louder, more frantic, and the only word to escape her lips, the only one Moss seemed capable of hearing, "please," resonated in his ears like an invitation.

He yanked her off the floor and flung her on the bed.

"You like to be manhandled, like your ma does, like all women do."

Willow closed her eyes, craning her head toward the wall as far as she could making no effort to do his biding.

Moss laughed. Willow bleated like a scared lamb. He laughed again, not a light moment of merriment, but daunting jeers, contemptuous, evil, deep, and abiding,

The expression on his face suddenly changed, as he paused beside the bed as if in a trance, gazing, traveling into another world, distant, known only to him. There in his private mirrored world he beheld his father's twisted face, saw the hate, the anger, the pure meanness in his eyes. The old man looked through Moss' mind's eye and grinned. His childhood remembrances opened up like the pages of a horror book, unfolding like a nightmare. It all rushed back to his miserable, worthless upbringing.

Moss's father had allowed him to live after birth for two reasons: to work and to be beaten for nothing but pleasure. If he had been a girl, as his father had hoped, it would have been all pleasure. He grew up in a world of little hope and wanted those around him to have even less than he had. Cruelty had been normal in his life, expected, given, received, and passed on.

So why shouldn't he have his little pleasures, his few things, just a few — his whiskey, a little satisfaction from an ungrateful daughter, his dominance over a wife and useless son whose only reason to exist was to do his bidding, to serve his needs as a good boy should. After all, hadn't he himself been a good boy to his daddy?

The mirror closed, the unpleasant journey of childhood had ended. He thought of Olive, sweet little Olive. He smiled. Soon, he thought, soon.

His eyes focused once again on the pleasure awaiting him on the sagging bed.

A gallus hung loose from faded, dirty overalls. Grinning, he unlatched the other one allowing the overalls to fall from his shoulders and come to rest around his ankles. He stepped one foot out and with the other flung them against the wall.

The girl's eyes faded to empty.

He climbed onto the lumpy feather bed, pulled her from the wall and forced his daughter's legs apart.

She resisted. She had to. Snatching her legs from his grasp she fought to roll off the bed.

He flew into a blind rage, grabbed her by the hair and

pulled her back. "Little bitch!" A sickening thud echoed off the walls as a thick hand battered her cheek. The delicate body slackened. A red welt swelled up like yeast underneath her right eye.

He leered at her through hard eyes, chewing on his Days Work. It rolled slobbery and disgusting in his jaw. Dark spit oozed from the corners of his grinning mouth, channeled through his whiskers, over his chin, and down his neck leaving dark brown runnels of stain.

Tears rolled out of her eyes like a summer storm as he did the unthinkable.

∿∿

In the other room, Rose pulled a pillow over her head so she couldn't hear the steady squeak of the worn springs, her daughter's haunting silence. Moss knew what his wife would be thinking. He liked it. He took immense satisfaction in knowing she couldn't stop him. She had tried before and he had knocked her out cold for her effort. He thought about his other little girl lying beside her momma. *It won't be long. It won't do you no good holdin' on to her.*

The tears dried up. Willow's mind hardened. Her mind carried her away to some far off place — a place of sunshine where fields of aromatic flowers filled her nostrils with delight, where a serene stream meandering through expansive fields parted the flora dividing it into colorful bouquets. That's how she kept from going insane.

Willow endured, empty, unfeeling and broken — she wanted to die. The image of Mr. Ward drifted into her mind. *If only the bullet would've hit me instead of you.* But it hadn't. She ached for death. *At least I'd be safe in the ground.*

She knew from the times before that it was almost over. He gave a loud sigh and held his breath. Holding still with his full force against her, he threw his head back. It was done at last.

Having spent all of his energy Moss sank down on top of her. She could smell the tobacco and whiskey mixed with putrid body odor. His whiskers stuck her face and neck. She thought she would heave right on his neck. After a few agonizing seconds he rolled off her, picked up his dirty overalls and pulled them on.

Willow lay still as death, staring blankly at the bare unpainted wall. A roach squeezing from a crack stopped to stare, its feelers twitching. Then it scampered away as if there was something in the room dirtier that it. *I don't blame you. I wouldn't stay in a room with anyone as filthy as me, either.*

"There, now, don't I buy you purty dresses?" Moss said, throwing a package on the bed. "Wear it tomorrow." The door creaked open and he walked out with a satisfied grin on his face.

Once again she drew shaky knees to her chest. *Die*, she willed. But she didn't.

⁕

Moss heard the gun cock. "I'm gonna kill you, you filthy bastard!"

Moss twisted around and grabbed the gun by the barrel. It fired as Thorny's finger slipped from the hair-pin trigger. The bullet landed next to Moss's foot tearing a ragged hole in the floor. He grabbed the rifle from the boy's hand and flung it against the far wall. Before Thorny could recover Moss slapped him with his bear-like hand. He hit the floor with a thud.

"I'll teach ya to point a gun at me you little Idjit!" he screamed while reaching down to pluck Thorny off the floor. With one hand he braced the bone-skinny boy against the wall and beat him unmercifully with the other.

Thorny sank into a dark, barren world not unlike the one he lived in. The only real difference in the waking world and this one where he resided on the other side of consciousness, in this world he had peace.

Rose pushed the door open tentatively.

Moss stopped, his fist drawn back for another punishing blow. He whipped his head toward his wife —his eyes followed her gaze.

She stared at the gun. Every ounce of her slender, battered body wanted to run for it.

He let out a wicked laugh. "Go ahead, git it!" he howled. "I'd jest like to see you try." His arm remained cocked ready to throw another deadening punch.

The defeated woman dropped her gaze toward the floor, backed into her room, and closed the door. She heard the fist land one final, sickening blow.

Moss let go of the limp boy. "That'll teach you, you little good-fer-nothin'." Thorny fell in a heap onto the bare, splintered planks. Moss, satisfied, staggered out to the porch, and plopped down.

Chapter 12
Family Funnies

"We are the family funnies," said Corbit, Callie, and Maggie in unison while standing on their heads. "We are the family funnies," they repeated and then fell to the floor on their backs. "Here are our shoes," they continued after placing hands inside their shoes. Squatting down, the three entertainers held their shoes, soles up, making it appear as if they were standing on their heads. "We are … the family funnies," they repeated. Ellie and Bud applauded and whistled.

Every Saturday night after chores and supper, the Kinser household gathered for family time. The children would take turns making up skits or doing the "Family Funnies" out of the *Play Books*. Bud would tell jokes or pantomime. Ellie would tell stories about her childhood and would bake cookies or a cake for a treat. They played games, too, games like Battle of the Oranges, Blow-Ball or Clothespins in a Bottle.

Maggie jumped up and down with excitement. "My turn! My turn! I choose Clothespins in a Bottle."

"What a surprise!" Callie frowned.

"Not now, Callie," Bud warned.

"But it's all she ever picks—"

"I said, that's enough, hear me?" He cocked his head and raised an eyebrow. One corner of his mouth turned down causing his mustache to droop below his chin. "Now, don't ruin it for everybody."

"Okay, let's get started," Ellie said after clearing her throat. "Here's the milk jug. Everybody count out ten clothespins apiece. You all know the rule."

We should, Callie thought. *It's all dumb Dora knows how to do.*

"Whoever drops the most clothespins in the bottle wins," Maggie sang.

Callie seethed. *Yeah, like we don't know.*

Corbit won the first round, Maggie the second and third. Callie won the fourth, and she even found herself having fun. Everyone clapped and yelled, egging each player on. Ellie and Bud played, too, but somehow always managed to lose.

The sweet smell of cookie dough baking filled the kitchen. Mouths watered, stomachs growled and noses lifted high in the air. The aroma meant much more than a snack. It meant family, togetherness, a feeling of safety, and a home filled with love. The Bible was also taught in the Kinser home, not only on family night, but every night. Not only did they read the Word, but lived it by example, by both parents. They practiced its precepts with the same pervasiveness as taking a bath at the end of the day. Faith seemed to be in Ellie's genes. Bud, although doubting at times, held a moral authority never to be questioned. Family night always closed with a verse from the Bible, with the family members taking turns choosing a scripture.

Corbit already had his scripture planned. He smiled at the short and sweet verse he had picked out.

"Okay, son, are you ready with the closing scripture?" Ellie asked.

"'Jesus wept,' Luke 6:26," Corbit said with a jack-o'-

lantern grin. Bud and Callie tried to hold back snickers.

"Why did Jesus weep?" Maggie asked, genuinely wanting to know.

Ellie glared at Corbit and said, "Probably because your brother feels the need to make light of the Bible. Since you made your scripture a short one, I'm sure you won't mind reading a longer one at next week's family night. Right?"

"No, ma'am," Corbit said, knowing not to push it, even though he only meant it to be a lighthearted moment. He knew, though, his mother took every word of the Good Book as hallowed down to the last amen.

"Good." Ellie walked over to the oven, pulled down the door and reached in. Hot sugar cookies emerged from a blast of heat waves. Taking a metal spatula she scraped them from the pan and laid them on a rack to cool. When they had firmed up, she moved them to a plate, then to the table. Watching Methuselah grow old would have been easier for the four watchers.

"Okay," Ellie announced. "Get 'em while they're still warm. Callie, go fetch the milk out of the icebox, and, Corbit, you can get the glasses." Nobody argued.

Bud stood and raised a cookie over his head. "Before we eat this golden morsel, I'd like to thank Corbit, again, for saving our crops" Everyone cheered as they tapped each other's cookies.

They stuffed the warm treat into their mouths and washed them down with milk. After the cookies were properly taken care of Bud asked, "Callie, I believe you have a poem to read?"

"Yessir-ree, I sure do. Made it up myself."

"Can't wait." Bud popped the last bit of cookie into his mouth.

She started off : "My poem's called 'The Cat,' by Callie Kinser."

> *Twiddlee, twiddlee dee,*
> *The cat climbed up a tree,*
> *He looked around,*
> *Fell down,*
> *And broke his nose.*
> *The end*

At first everyone stared. Then, realizing how flat a cat's nose is, they all smiled, then snickered, then burst out laughing. Corbit fell to the floor with tear-filled eyes and pounded it with his fist. Ellie and Bud lay their heads on the oilcloth and slapped the table with both hands. Callie joined in. When everyone quieted down Maggie said, "I don't get it." Another round of fist-pounding and table-slapping ensued.

Maggie still looked perplexed.

Perking up she said, "Oh, I have one, too." She jumped up and down. "Can I say it, can I, can I?"

"Why, sure you can, Maggie," Bud said. "Let's have it."

She stood up straight, rose up on tiptoes, and cleared her throat.

"Oh, for the love of —"

"Now, Callie, don't interrupt, Bud said gently. "She has to get into character. Whenever you're ready, Maggie."

With another round of throat clearing she began:

> *My nose itches,*
> *I smell peaches,*
> *Here comes Johnny*
> *With a hole in his britches.*

Wild applause erupted. Callie, looking aggravated, scarcely touched her hands together.

Then Maggie said, "I wanna play a new song I learnt on my banjer."

"Does she have to play that ol' thing?"Callie whined.

"Now, Callie," Bud reproved. "You gave a right funny poem, and all, so I think we should let Maggie play us a tune."

"But she said a poem, too."

"Cal-lie," Ellie gently warned with a little firmness in her voice.

"Yeah, Callie," Corbit chimed in. "Don't be such a Gloomy Gus."

"Shut up, Ettis!"

"You shut up or I'll—"

"Children!" Bud admonished, lifting an eyebrow. "Go ahead and play, Maggie."

"This's a song I learnt from listenin' to the radio." Maggie sliipped picks on two of her fingers and thumb of her right hand. "It's called 'Old Dan Tucker,' by The Skillet Lickers. This's s'posed to be a good dancin' tune."

"You don't say," Bud smiled at Ellie. "Let's show 'em how the Hucklebuck's done."

"Oh, Bud, no. Not in front of the children."

"Come on now, don't be an old fuddy-duddy," he grabbed her hand and pulled her to the middle of the kitchen floor. "We'll do the mild version."

Using a piece of stove wood for a foot prop, Maggie lit into a boisterous intro. Immediately Bud lined up behind Ellie, put his right hand on her waist and his left on her shoulder. They gyrated from side to side, hip to hip in unison.

Callie's eyes grew wider and wider. Corbit's mouth dropped open. They looked at each other and drawled, "Well, I'll say," and started giggling.

Ellie traded places with Bud and they gyrated slowly across the floor. Maggie hit the chorus. Bud grabbed Ellie's hand and swung her to the front. Putting his arm around her waist he pulled her close, put his cheek against hers, and gyrated hip to hip backward across the floor. They faced each other, placed hands on their hips, and thrust at each other.

Callie's eyes grew saucer size, her hand slapped over her mouth. She exclaimed in a lilted voice, "Deddy?"

"Momma?" Corbit drawled, his mouth forming an O. He whispered in Callie's ear, "I'm sure glad Tommie Sue ain't seeing this, she'd tell Preacher Sonny Boy and they'd be preached straight to hell next Sunday morning."

"Yeah, for sure!"

Ellie, seeing the shocked look on her children's faces, broke loose and scampered over to the stove. Not knowing what else to do, she opened the firebox and stuffed in another piece of wood.

Maggie finished "Old Dan Tucker" with flair and took a bow. Bud looked around for Ellie and said, winking at the children, "Ain't it hot enough in here without adding to the fire?"

"Well, I'll say it is!" Ellie quipped. Callie and Corbit burst out laughing. Bud joined in. Ellie's red face broke into a sheepish smile. She tried to hold back, but couldn't. She exploded into uncontrollable laughter. Table-slapping, belly-grabbing and fist-pounding followed.

Maggie looked from one to the other. "I don't get it."

Callie rolled her eyes.

"Can we have just *one* more cookie?" Corbit pleaded.

Everyone waited. Ellie smiled. "Okay, just one more."

They each smiled and scooped up the treat, savoring it to the last crumb.

∞

On the back porch, crouched behind neatly stacked stove wood, Willow peeped through the window screen mesmerized. She looked on in awe at children and parents together, playing, laughing, and having a good time. *I'd give anything for that. If I could have a normal family, to have parents, and brothers, and sisters that loved each other the way the Kinser family does. Why, it'd really be somethin'.* The yearning for such a life made her feel disembodied, like her soul had taken flight leaving behind an empty shell. Stark reality stared back cold and hard. She knew it could never be. She felt alone, hopeless, and most of all worthless.

"I'm useless," she mumbled. "A big bupkis, that's all I am." She sat and faced away from the happy scene inside. With a far-off gaze into the clear night she wondered, again, why God didn't love her, Thorny, and Olive, and even her mother, as much as the Kinser family. Her heart felt like winter as she rested against the pile of wood. Out of despair she thumped her head against a knotted pine log, strainds of hair stuck to the resin yanking it from her scalp.

"Oh, Olive." Tears dripped like a leak in a dam right before the breach. The thought of her little sister in the iron grip of her tormenter sent waves of anguish through her. She felt a cold, sharp blade sliding through her body, twisting and turning through bone, marrow, and sinew, slicing every nerve in two until her entire body felt dismembered, carved up like a butchered hog. How long would it be before he preyed on her? She knew the answer.

Not long!

Willow knew her mother had been a victim, too. She pictured Thorny's battered, emaciated body as he fought to protect her. Tears fell in a stream now, widening the hole a little more. The rip enlarged, and then the dam breached, with a torrent of silent despair. The family inside the Kinser kitchen would never be hers.

A clump of hair stuck to the resin as she pulled her head from the lighter knot. With the pain in her heart at the threshold she hardly noticed. The clean smell of turpentine and woodsy odor of pine bark tickled her nose as she leaned forward to peep through the window again. *Why does God hate me?* she asked in the confines of her mind. But no answer came.

The sun climbed over the horizon furnace-hot as the drought continued across the land of the Brush. Bud shared Corbit's idea with neighbors lucky enough to have a spring or branch close to their fields. A Saturday morning at the livestock market brought Corbit slaps on the back and comments like, "You really cooked with gas on that one." He had become the local hero. For the less fortunate, though, the drought continued to take its toll.

"I really had fun last night, didn't you, Momma?" Callie asked as she plopped down in front of a plate of gravy and biscuits.

"I sure did, honey, and I loved your poem about the cat," she laughed quietly, recalling the cat's broken nose. "I think you might be a poet as well as a talented seamstress." Ellie whirled around in her outfit. "And I love my new dress." Callie responded with a beaming smile.

Maggie sauntered in and plunked down across from Callie. "Didja like my banjer tune, Momma, and my poem?"

"I'll say I did, little Maggie, your tune and poem was killer diller. *Everybody* enjoyed it, didn't we, Callie?"

Callie put on her Gloomy Gus face and said a little too harshly, "I reckon."

Ellie looked at Callie, then at Maggie who looked back with apprehension. "We're so proud of the both of you."

Maggie brightened and said, "That sure is a purty dress you made for Momma, and I really liked your poem about the cat."

"You didn't even understand it," Callie snapped. The brightness immediately faded from Maggie's eyes.

Ellie started to scold Callie when a foot-stomping barrage shook the back porch as the two Kinser men knocked dirt from their brogans. Bud had worked a double shift filling in for Jimbo, who had called in sick. Though tired, chores still had to be done, so he roused Corbit and together they took care of the milking and other before-breakfast chores

The screen door screeched open. "I'm ready for a biscuit," Bud boomed.

"I'm ready for a whole sheet of biscuits," Corbit said a little louder.

"Fresh out of the oven," Ellie said, then gave them a long look. Bud and Corbit looked at Ellie, and then at each other. "Well, do you plan on eating cow manure for breakfast? And take those brogan stompers off before you come in the house."

Corbit frowned. "Cow manure? Why, heck no!"

"Wash your hands?"

"Oh," they echoed and promptly backed out the door.

"Any new leads on the killer?" Ellie asked after everyone had settled in at the table.

"Well," Bud said, pausing to take a sip of coffee.

Collective breaths caught.

"No, not yet, or at least we don't have anything solid. Just a hunch for now." He took another sip and removed a coffee ground from his tongue with his index finger. "All I can say is to be careful. He could, well, he could be a neighbor."

Ellie's hand rushed to her heart. "Heaven forbid, you don't say!"

Maggie's eyes bugged out. "Is he gonna murder us, Deddy?"

"Maggie! Of course not!" Ellie said, but her eyes held worry.

Bud pointed out, "Now we don't know for sure, but evidence, what little we have anyway, points to it."

"To murder us?" Maggie blurted.

"No, Maggie, I didn't mean the evidence pointed to him murdering us. I meant he could be somebody from around here." Bud poured the grounds left in the bottom of his cup into his saucer. "Any more coffee left in the pot?"

"Can I go see Willow this afternoon after my chores?" Callie asked.

"No! I don't want you anywhere near that ossified man. You hear?" Ellie ordered. "He gives me the heebie-jeebies."

Bud agreed. "Your momma's right. I don't want you near that place. Drunk or not, the man's mean and dangerous. No tellin' what he might do."

"Is he the murderer, or is it somebody we might know?" Callie asked in a whisper as if the murderer sat at the table.

"It could be anybody, and no, not personally. All I can say is keep an eye out and don't stray far. I wish I could say more, but I can't give a name just yet. Anyhow, you kids get to your chores and mind your Momma. Oh, and Corbit, check the trot lines this afternoon. Ought to have a mess of cats hooked for supper."

"Cats?" Maggie looked horrified. "We're going to eat *cats* for supper?"

"Yep, if there's still water enough in the creek for a cat to live in," Bud said.

"Well, I declare," Maggie drawled. "I thought cats didn't like water. And I ain't eatin' no cat, neither!"

"That's okay," Corbit said as seriously as he could. "We'll eat the cats. I'll catch you a fish."

Callie snickered and even Bud and Ellie smiled.

"Now, Corbit, don't mock your sister," Bud half-scolded with a smile accentuating his cheek bones while lifting his mustache almost to his ears. He turned to Ellie. "Better get busy, got to go in early today. I'm only working half a shift, though, but I'll probably be late for supper, so don't wait on me. In the meantime I'll get cleaned up and take me a three- or four-hour nap."

"I declare, Bud, you're working too much, you're going to wear yourself out." Ellie looked defeated, knowing they needed the extra money. "Well, anyway, I'll fry your fish when you get home so it'll be hot when you eat it."

"Lordy," Maggie went on. "I thought Deddy said he wanted to eat cats instead of fish."

Callie couldn't stand it any longer. "A cat *fish*, stupid, not a house cat. You're such a dumb Dora."

"I ain't neither a dumb Dora!" Maggie retorted. "I knowed they were talking about fish. I was only doing a Family Funny, that's all."

"Yeah, right," Callie scoffed.

"We know you were only making a joke," her father said gently. "Why, anybody that can make music the way you can ain't dumb at all. Fact is, I think you're smart, little Maggie, and don't let nobody tell you different." A beaming Maggie stuck her chin out and held her head high.

"Enough about cats and fish," Ellie said. "You're all gonna drive me to the hollerin' house before it's over with. Lord help me! Now, finish your breakfast and get to your chores."

"Maggie doesn't *have* any chores, remember?" Callie said with an imperious tone.

"And do you remember *why* she doesn't have any chores, hmm?"

Callie's look would have made the devil hide.

"Well, do you?"

"Yessum," she snapped, and to avoid a prolonged sentence of extra chores she decided to only *think* what she wanted to say out loud.

"You'd do well to remind yourself from time to time, and maybe, just maybe, your mouth wouldn't get ahead of your brain."

⊱⊰

In the Branch household, there was no such thing as bickering among children and admonishing by parents.

A temporary lack of judgment was unforgivable, the punishment harsh. A drunken, evil man leaned close to a frightened girl and demanded, "Where'd you sneak off to last night after I left your bed?" Tobacco spittle sprayed in Willow's face.

She flinched. "Nowhere."

A bear-like hand smashed into her face. She fell to the floor. A red welt appeared, blemishing her smooth skin. "Don't lie to me or I'll—"

"She was with me," Thorny said, venom in his voice. He had bruises all over his face and arms from the beating the night before. His lips, cracked and swollen, made him sound like he was talking through a window pane.

"Shat yore sorry mouth, boy, I ain't talkin' to you! Didn't you git enough of me last night, or do you want more of the same?" Moss drew his hand back. Thorny didn't blink, just held out a bucket full of skinned catfish and cleaned brim.

Thorny lied without showing a fragment of fear, "Went moon fishin' and took her with me."

After the beating, Moss had passed out in his chair on the porch, the whisky hammering his brain When Thorny recovered from the beating enough to stand up, he'd grabbed the rifle from the floor where Moss had flung it, intending to finish the job he had started out to do. His mother had stepped in front of him, placed a gentle hand on his shoulder and pleaded with cheerless, anxious eyes.

"Don't do it. The law'll put you in prison. He ain't worth it." Thorny had leaned the firearm against the wall and staggered out the back door, the beating leaving him weak and hurting. He grabbed his cane pole, whistled for his dog, and together they disappeared into the woods.

"It's true," Rose lied. "I tried to wake you up but the shine had you under."

She had watched as her daughter stumbled out of her room to the back door with disheveled hair, a bruised face, and an empty soul. Willow had opened the door, turned and gazed at her mother with questioning eyes, then stepped out into darkness. *I hope she runs and never comes back*, Rose remembered thinking. Shame vexed her soul for not having the courage at least to have tried to protect her daughter.

She repeated the lie again, "I tried to wake you."

Moss looked toward his clearly frightened wife, then back to the fish. "You'd better be tellin' the truth, the both of ya, or you'll be sorry."

Rose looked down and shuffled toward the kitchen. "Breakfast's on the table," she muttered.

"Mind what I say," Moss said, looking directly at Thorny, then at Willow. He swaggered to the table, pulled a chair back, screeching it across the bare floor. He nodded his shaggy head in finality and then flopped down. "Put them brim and cats down, boy, me and Olive'll have 'em for dinner. Won't we, little girl?" Olive hid behind Rose's bony legs.

Moss winked at Willow. "Now, you come and eat. Gotta keep you in shape for pleasin'." He smiled at Olive. "Come and sit in daddy's lap, gotta git you growed right for later on." Rose nudged Olive toward Moss. He picked up two pieces of fat bacon and threw them on the table. "Here, old woman. This is fer you and thet sorry boy over yonder."

"I don't need nothin' from you!" Thorny spat, slamming the door as he stormed out. *I'm gonna kill the slimy bastard! I'm gonna cut his damn throat the next time he gets liquored up, prison or no prison.* He kicked a rock and disappeared into the woods.

❧

"Come on, Willow, honey, drink this," her mother said, handing her a cup. "I know it tastes bad, but it'll… well, you know."

Willow drank the bitter tea of cotton root bark as she screwed up her face in displeasure.. Rose had gotten up early and boiled three ounces of the dried bark in a quart of water, strained, and poured it into empty cane syrup bottles. Willow had to drink the whole quart in a day's time to prevent or interrupt pregnancy. It had become routine. She drank without complaint.

❧

The morning sky with patches of trailing clouds prepared to send rays of sweltering heat toward a parched earth. The scent of pine sap and wild flowers hung weighty in the still air, and twittering birds filled the trees, their songs pleasant.

"Oh, don't have a hissy fit," Corbit said. "You only have another three weeks left of your sentence."

"Just shut up, okay?"

"Hey, I'm just sayin'."

"Huh," Callie sniffed, "go ahead and take Maggie's side like you always do."

"I don't do no such thing. Besides, you could be nice to her every now and again instead of being a stinky piss pot all the time."

Callie's ears turned red. "You ain't nothing but a stinking *Ettis* pee bucket yourself!"

Corbit morphed into a ripe beet. His voice smoldered. "Oh, yeah?" He reared back with a full bucket of well water. "I'll show you!" He let it go.

Callie ran, arching her back to escape the deluge. *Floof!* Water hit the dirt and splattered on her heels and ankles as she disappeared around the corner of the house.

"Nobody's on my side," Callie muttered as she gathered eggs. "It's Maggie this, and Maggie that, and oh, Maggie's *so* smart, she's *so* talented. Well, phooey on her!" After a few minutes of self-pity her wandering gaze spotted Fox Hill. Her thoughts quickly turned to Willow.

I wonder why I ain't seen her lately? she mused. *Hmmm*

— I know, I'll go see her. Yep, by golly, I'll do it, right after I finish my chores. Nobody'll ever know. She completed them in record time, avoiding Corbit as she worked. She didn't want to take a chance with another blow-up and didn't want him to find out about her planned trip to Fox Hill.

Instead of walking up the hill by road, an obvious giveaway, she decided to cut across the corn field and follow the foot path leading to the top of Fox Hill, where she would eventually come out behind Willow's shack. Hidden by the straight stalks of tasseled corn and later by trees foresting the hillside, Callie would not be seen. The path curved around trees and rocks, taking twisty turns up and down for short distances. Callie, young and strong, took the climb in stride trotting at a steady pace. Cheerful flowers sprinkled the open spaces along the ridge. Although the blooming season was almost over, a few patches of mountain laurel, resembling white umbrellas with red dots, still lingered.

The air exploded! Callie yapped and fell to the ground. She rolled, caught hold of a sapling, jumped to her feet, and scurried behind a dogwood tree. She couldn't breathe. Her heart pounded like a kettle drum.

Surprised, a flock of ruffled grouse thundered into the air breaking the silence of the summer day. Callie wilted against the dogwood and slid to the ground, her body shaking from fright. After a few heart-pounding seconds, her heart slowed to a normal pace. After pushing to her feet she stepped back onto the trail and continued her hike to the top. She following the path for another ten minutes and worked her way through a copse of red maple.

There, in the shadows of the trees stood the shack. She shrank at the sight.

The back porch, slumping and buckled, looked to be on the verge of collapse. A tin roof completely covered with rust and dotted with holes, hung over walls with loose, split boards, the paint long gone except for a few gray flecks.

A grimy film completely covered the lone window at the back porch. The dilapidated dwelling exuded loneliness and despair… and something else, something Callie had never felt so deeply in her life. Why she would have bad feelings about a place where such a gentle heart lived, a sweet girl with a sweet name did not make sense to her still tender mind.

Deep down, though, she knew why, and it didn't have anything to do with Willow living there. If Willow dwelled there alone, the shack would be a castle, a magical fairyland, home of a princess. Maggie, Callie thought, would have been right.

Evil and pain, not magic, oozed out of the walls as if it were a living entity. Callie pushed against a red maple as if it would hide her from the awful feeling.

But it didn't. She shoved off from the tree, wanting to get as far away from the shack as possible. She bolted down the trail, but stopped after a few yards. She stood there, seething. "I won't run away," she whispered through gritted teeth. "Willow's my friend. Why should I?"

She turned like a soldier snapping to attention and faced the shack. She paused. Her resolved slackened just a little. The old place had never looked so spooky, she thought, at least not from the front. But her resolve soon returned. *I'll sneak around the corner and take a quick look around. Willow might be there and I can get her attention.*

Moving like a cat to the side of the shack, Callie plastered her body against the rotting boards and slid along the wall feeling as if her back was against a nest of spiders. Her chest heaved as if there were two hearts inside running a race. Fear treaded in every footfall.

A rifle shot echoed through the woods. Terror exploded through her brain. She wanted to run. Her head ordered shaky legs to move, but they wouldn't budge. Finally lifting her foot to turn, she noticed the broken tree branch underneath her foot and realized it had not been a gunshot she'd heard. Her fear had amplified the sound of the limb snapping in two.

A growl, like some wild animal, came from the front of the house. Callie's legs crumpled, flinging her to the ground. She laid still, arms wrapped around her head. The growling grew louder, more intense.

Then she recognized the sound. Her body relaxed. It was only somebody snoring, she thought. Pulling up, she flattened against the shack, scooted to the corner, and lingered there for what seemed like an eternity, but in reality only seconds. Trying to gather courage to look, she turned to face the wall, her arms pasted to her sides. Cautiously she peeped around the corner with one eye half-closed, afraid at what she might see, or rather what might see her. She gasped and ducked back behind the wall.

Slumped over in a slat-back rocking chair with the bottom two slats missing, sat Moss Branch. Flies buzzed around his head. A whiskey jug sat next to his drooping arm. *Empty, no doubt*, Callie thought. After a morning at his still he had returned to try out his fresh brew.

Not quiet brave enough to risk the porch, Callie turned to leave.

Someone grabbed her arm.

"Ahhhh —" A hand plastered over Callie's mouth, squelching the scream.

"Shush," Willow whispered. "What're you doing here?" She removed her hand from Callie's still open mouth.

Callie's eyes scanned Willow's swollen eye. "What happened to your eye?" she asked in a muted voice.

Without answering Willow said, "Come on, follow me." Callie, still shaking, trailed her into the thicket of maple. Willow turned to face her while walking backward. She whispered, "I've got a special place I go when I want to think or to just be alone. I was about to go there when I saw you going around the corner of the house."

Callie stopped. "How did you get that bruise on your cheek?" Willow's mother had soaked the sapphire bruise in vinegar trying to fade it as much as possible. "And that knot's as big as hen fruit."

Her eyes turned from Callie. "Oh, I got up during the night to go to the john and run into the door. It ain't nothing."

"Gosh, you look like a flag — red, white and blue."

Willow half smiled. "It ain't nothing, be okay in a day or two. Come on, it ain't far to my secret place."

They followed the path down and around Fox Hill deep into the woods until they came to an outcropping of rock and a lone oak. Through an opening in the forest they could see the Kinser farm and the treeline of Brush Creek below the pasture. Cows loitered in the field chewing their cuds of hay and grass.

"This way," Willow motioned. Callie followed her down a zig-zagging path to the base of the rocky outcropping. Deep lush grass carpeted a narrow arroyo where a small spring not more than three feet wide gave reason for the verdant ground. The spring emerged from a shallow cave in the rock, the water running fifty yards before once again disappearing into the earth where a small pool had formed against another cluster of rocks.

Callie looked around, amazed, "Oh, wow! How did you find this place? It's beautiful here."

"The day after the song man got shot, I took off through the woods to sort of get away from ever'body, you know, to think about what I'd done—"

"You ain't done not one thing!" Callie interrupted, a little annoyed. "I… everybody told you it ain't your fault."

"You don't know what a sinner I am. God got mad when I walked into the church house 'cause of all the stuff I'd done before."

Callie looked mystified. "What in the world could you've done to be such a bad sinner?"

"I just am. All those babies and…

"Babies? It's the third time you've mentioned babies. What babies?"

"Nothin'. I didn't mean nothin' by it. I'm just talking, that's all."

"I'm your friend. You can tell me anything."

"I know, but some things are best left alone."

"But—"

"Please?"

Willow looked over her miniature valley and extended her arms. "I happened upon this place. It's kind of, you know, like a church, except nobody gets shot here."

"I see what you mean, it is sorta like a church," Callie said with reverence. She changed her tone, "And it still ain't your fault."

"You wouldn't understand, Callie, believe me, you just wouldn't." Making her way to the stream Willow put both feet in the cool water and sat down on the low bank. Callie waded to the other side and sat facing her and the outcrop.

"Well, you're wrong, I just know it. And I would, too, understand." Callie glanced around. A feeling of peace overcame her. "And I sure wouldn't mind a place like this to come to so I could get away from Maggie and her dad-blamed banjo pickin'. It's the awfulest thing ever!"

"Why'd you want to get away from that?" Willow recalled the first time she had heard Callie mention the banjo on the hill at the beginning of summer. In her world she could not conceive how such a silly thing would matter.

"Well, Maggie, mostly, I guess. You don't know what I go through. It's awful what I have to put up with. Just awful! Everybody thinks she's *so* great, *so* talented. Why, I even have to do her chores because I said something about that stupid banjo and she got upset and dropped Momma's favorite dishes. Maggie don't do a thing, nothing at all! She's made my life plum miserable, that's what!"

Willow wrinkled her brow. A bewildered look crossed her face. "Is *that* all? It looked like fun…" She started to say something about the night she watched Callie's family from the back porch, but caught herself.

"Is that all? Ain't it enough? What would you think if you were in my place?"

"I'd be happy. Why, I'd be the most happiest person in the whole wide world if that's all I had to worry about."

"Huh? You mean you'd be—" Callie choked on her words.

Willow registered the alarm in Callie's eyes and followed her gaze. A jagged pain tore at her stomach.

On the edge of the precipice staring down stood Moss Branch.

Chapter 13
The Trot Lines

Corrr-bit!" Ellie's voice started low and ended in a drawled-out high pitch. "Corrr-bit! Time to come ho-ome!"

Corbit and Fred popped around the corner of the house. "Aw, it ain't time to come in. It ain't dark yet." Corbit hated to give up one minute of freedom to the close of day.

"No, but it's time to check the trot lines down at the creek, though. Remember what your deddy said?"

"Oh yeah, forgot. Me and Fred'll tend to it."

"Yeah, me and Corbit'll tend to it," Fred parroted."

"You two be careful down there. It's getting late. Check the lines, bait 'em up and come right back. I don't want you lollygaggin' down there after dark. No telling what you might run into, the killer, or…" The words already in the back of Ellie's mind rushed to her tongue like a flash flood. "Moss Branch!"

"What?" Fred screwed his face up, and then unscrewed it. "Aw, we ain't skeerd of no murderer, or Moss Branch neither, are we, Corbit?"

"Why, heck no!" Corbit said with bravado. "Ain't nobody gonna mess with us."

"Yeah, well, never mind, he ain't skeered of you either. Hurry up now and get on back before it gets dark. No lollygagging, you hear?"

Corbit grabbed a couple of stringer lines for the fish and a bucket of fresh chicken guts Ellie had saved to replenish the hooks. Bud had a fried chicken dinner before going off to pull his shift and a couple of extra pieces to take with him. Ellie had promised him a plate of catfish when he returned home from work.

The two boys, pockets stuffed with marbles as usual, scurried across the yard and down the hill. The unconcerned world of childhood filled the young men with bravery and an adventurous spirit no adult could possibly have, and could only remember, if they were lucky. They talked back and forth as they ambled down the footpath. A bird fluttered from its perch to escape the approaching storm of excited chatter. A distant bellow of a cow carried across pastures of stunted, parched grass. A warm breeze carried with it the scent of honeysuckle.

"What if the murderer really is hiding out down by the creek?" said Fred, eyes steady on the trail.

"Gee whillikers." Corbit wiped sweat from his brow. "Ain't no murderer hiding around here. Anyhow, if he is, we'd teach him a thing or two."

Fred pulled the straw out of his mouth and spat. "Yeah, we'd show him not to mess with us. Whup him good, we would."

A rabbit hopped from the bushes.

"Ahhhh!" Fred skidded to a stop, his arms gyrating to keep from falling.

"Ahhhh!" Corbit slid to the ground, his feet whacking Fred's legs out from under him—landing on Corbit's outstretched body. "Ouch! Dang it, Plank, get off me!"

Fred rolled off of him onto the dirt. "Well, gee whiz, Kinser, whatcha yellin' at me for? You put me here!"

"Well, you didn't have to land so hard. I think you broke my ribs." Then he started laughing, in spite of the pain. "We're really gonna whup that killer good." Corbit held on to his side. "We're gonna… throw a rabbit at 'im!"

Fred, sprawled out beside Corbit and joined in. "Yeah, thet mean rabbit'll skeer 'im to death." He threw both arms over his head and laughed himself to tears. "We'll show thet killer what for!" The boys, a little less brave than before, slapped the ground, hooted and snorted until completely out of breath.

"I'll tell you what we'll do." Corbit snickered through his words. "If we come upon that murderer, you get his attention by jumping up and down and hollering as loud as you can. While you're doing that, I'll come from behind and hit 'im in the head with the rabbit." They howled and rolled some more.

"Then," Fred said, "We'll tie him up and take him to your house and hand him over to your deddy."

Corbit wiped tears with the back of his hand. "Yeah, then we'll eat the rabbit for supper." After their hooting session ended, the two boys trotted on down the hill.

❧❦

Moss looked like a wild animal ready to pounce, and Callie could sense hatred in his dark eyes. She hurdled the narrow spring, tearing off through the trees, briars and bushes.

"You'd better git!" Moss bellowed. He stumbled down the embankment.

Willow tried to explain. "We were just talking —"

He slapped her. "Shat up! You been tellin' thet little whelp my bidness, ain'tcha?"

Willow cowered. "Don't hit me again… please, I ain't told her nothin'."

He drew his giant hand back. Willow slumped, throwing her arms around her head. "I ortta skin you alive, what I ortta do. Why, I even sold some shine to buy you a purty dress with, and this is what I git for my trouble? Now, git on home before I slap yore head off!"

He kicked her with his worn, scarred brogan as she started to run. She stumbled and fell to her knees. He kicked her again. "I said to git!"

❧❦

Recovering from their rabbit adventure Corbit and Fred continued their hike to Brush Creek. On each side of the trail an array of flowers decked out in multi-colored bonnets stirred in the warm June breeze. A dash of gold here and there reflected the evening's molten rays dazzling the landscape, dripping with beauty in spite of the drought.

"Hey, Kinser boy, that was close," Fred said.

"Yeah, close."

"Gotta be more careful about skeering rabbits thataway, ain't good for 'em."

"That's right, for sure, Freddy boy. It'll cause them to dream about hawks…"

"And panthers…"

"And humans," Corbit concluded with a light chuckle. The boys jogged down the trail, their shaggy mops of hair, one brown, one red, mussed and tangled, bouncing with each stride.

They could smell the water, a combination of trees, rotted logs, ground vegetation and fish. The ancient sentinel oak stood guard over the dwindling watercourse. The recurrent lapping of water against the creek's bank, submerged logs and hanging low limbs gave the boys comfort in its familiarity.

"I could live down here," Corbit mused with a soft, slow sigh.

"Yeah, me too. Forever," Fred agreed.

"We have all we need… plenty of fish to eat, plenty of water, wood for fire…"

"And trees to build a cabin." Fred pointed to the building site. "Right over there amongst those cedars."

"That's it. Perfect!"

"Yeah, perfect." Fred reveled in his dream a few minutes longer.

Corbit broke the spell. "Better check the trot lines."

Fred's brow wrinkled like an accordion as his daydreams merged with reality. "Yeah, trot lines, sure."

Following a worn path downstream they reached a foot log spanning the width of the creek. "I'll go over to the other side and untie the line." Corbit scampered over the hickory log bridge while Fred stayed on the other side. "You can undo your end, Freddie boy, while I undo this end."

Fred fell to his knees. "Okay, ready?" Reaching over the bank, he grabbed the line tied securely to a sturdy low-hanging limb, held it with one hand and untied it with the other. He felt a tug.

Corbit untied and hauled his end out of the water, then backed away stretching the line out as he did. Eighteen snoods, or leaders, hung from the weighted line. Yellow bullhead cats dangled and thrashed struggling to get free, their mouths opening and closing sounding like mad cussing sailors as they grunted and made crackling sounds.

"Nice catch," Corbit said.

"Holy mackerel — I mean, holy catfish, I reckon so." Fred eyed the fish, imagining them in a frying pan of hot sizzling lard.

Corbit knew the look. "Wanna eat supper with us?"

"Boy, do I!" He could almost taste the floured, golden fried sweet meat. "Your momma won't mind?"

"Why, heck no." Corbit stepped up on the log bridge. "Back up and stretch the line while I cross." Scurrying across without so much as looking down, Corbit stretched out his end of the trot line and laid it on a bed of pine straw. They each unhooked a catfish from a snood, then slid the nail through the gill, and pushed the fish down to the looped end. To secure the fish from falling off, they ran the cord back through the loop. With that done, the rest of the flopping, cursing cats were slid onto the stringers.

Fred eyed the two strings of catfish as they held them up by the nail. "Man, this supper sure looks good." The supper seemed to cuss louder. "Hey, know what? Tommie Sue wouldn't eat them she'd take them to church to be preached at for cussin' so much."

"I'll be a yellow dog if she wouldn't," Corbit agreed. Both boys snickered at the thought.

Suddenly the air felt strange, hair prickled on their necks. A spooky, frightening sensation chilled them to the bone.

They snatched around.

Someone stood blocking the trail holding a rifle with both hands, finger on the trigger.

❦❧

Callie plunged through brush, dodging trees and rocks. She finally made it down the hill without glancing back for fear Moss might be one step away from grabbing her. Tired and out of breath, she made her way back to familiar surroundings.

At last she felt safe. Sitting on a dried-out stump behind the corn crib, she thought about the day as the lowering sun scattered thin, serrated clouds with shades of purple and red. The evening silence settled on the countryside preparing to end the day. *Almost dark. How long was I with Willow at the secret spring?*

The interlude with Willow had lasted much longer than Callie had realized. Without an inkling of passing time they had talked for two hours with arms wrapped around their knees rocking back and forth as they chattered. They had lain on their backs staring at puffy clouds as they shaped into camels, monsters, and castles while the soothing sounds of the gurgling spring and chirping birds added to their imagination. Willow's smile, Callie had noticed, while wide, and her laughter quick at times, still held a sense of melancholy. Her eyes, Callie thought, had a sad hardness, deep and seemingly impenetrable.

"There you are!"

Callie jumped, caught her breath and waited for Moss to grab her neck.

"Woops, I didn't mean to skeer you," Ellie said, looking Callie over. "What in tarnation have you been up to? Why, you've got scratches all over your arms and legs. Mercy!"

"Oh, nothing," she lied. "Just playing in the woods in back of the corn field. I stumbled and fell into some blackberry bushes."

"Had me worried to death, and you were told not to go off."

"I didn't think it'd hurt, being that close to home, and all."

"Well, that's what you get for thinking, and you must've wallowed in the briars. Now skedaddle and get cleaned up, and put some salve on those scratches." Watkins Salve, a mainstay in every Brush Creek home was dabbed on everything from a scratch to a snake bite. Ellie started for the house, then stopped and turned around. "Seen Corbit anywhere?"

"Not since we finished our chores."

"Oh," Ellie said. Worry lines appeared on her face.

"Everything all right, Momma?"

"I reckon… I suppose it is." Ellie relaxed her worry lines a little as she and Callie stepped onto the back porch. As they entered the kitchen Ellie said, "But they've been gone an awful long time — Fred and Corbit, I mean."

"You know how it is when Corbit and Fred get together, especially if they've got a pocket full of marbles. Why, they'd rather play marbles than eat. Well, Corbit, anyway. Fred now, he'd even eat the marbles if they had molasses on them."

Ellie smiled. "I know, but I told them to check the lines and come right back, and that's been two hours ago, as long as you've been gone. In fact, I thought you might have been with them." Ellie eased over and cracked open the screen door stepping halfway out onto the porch. "Where *is* that boy?"

Callie walked up behind her and said, "Be dark soon."

"I declare, it sure will, and I ain't started supper yet since I planned on having those catfish to fry up." Ellie stepped back inside letting the screen door gently tap closed. She stood with a worried look.

"What's the matter, Momma?"

Ellie untied her apron and hung it over a chair. "I'd better go see what's been keeping them so long."

"Can I go watch you whup him?"

"Right after I whup you. Don't forget, you went plundering around in the woods after you were told not to."

"Oh," Callie said with a sheepish grin. Then she said, "Reckon Corbit and Fred got kilt by that murderer?"

"You don't say!" Maggie blurted, eyes growing wide as she stepped into the room.

A wave of fear rushed through Ellie, worry lines grew into craters. "You and Maggie stay here. Your deddy'll be home soon. Tell him where I've gone." The screen door's spring twanged as she pushed it open and stepped out onto the porch. She paused long enough to grab the coal oil lantern that always hung on the rusty nail just outside of the door. With a hurried gait she clattered down the steps toward the foot path, the door tapping shut behind her.

Coming up the quarter-mile drive from the county road, an old gray beat-up Ford truck with black fenders machine-gunned over hard washboard ripples, rattling, squeaking and shaking.

"Ain't that the Plank's truck, Momma?" Callie called out through the screen door.

Ellie shaded her forehead with a hand. "Yeah, that's it all right." Seconds later the clattering pickup squeaked to a stop. Dust settled around it like a cloud. "Airy Mae, is ever'thing alright?" Ellie asked with apprehension in her voice.

"Howdy, Ellie, and I don't know. Have you seen Fred? S'posed to of been home an hour ago to do the milkin' and other chores. His deddy ain't too happy."

"Fred went with Corbit to check on the trot lines down at the Brush. He was told plain to go down and come right back—that's been two hours ago. That's where I'm headed now."

"Hold on and I'll go too. Got an extra lantern?" Airy Mae shoved on the pickup's caved-in door forcing it open with a loud pop, then slid off the ripped mohair seat, dragging a 12-gauge shotgun with her. "Double-aught buckshot," she said, in a matter-of-fact tone. "Just in case."

The two worried mothers hurried down the trail. Airy Mae, wearing a faded flour sack dress unraveling at the hems, tucked the ancient Iver Johnson's scarred butt under her arm with the barrels broken down for safety. "Gone git dark on us," she said. "If that boy ain't kilt I'm gonna whup 'im 'till his britches fall off for making Elsie suffer."

"Who's Elsie?" Ellie asked. "And they ain't nobody kilt."

"My milk cow. Her sack almost busted. Teats stuck out like porky-pine quivers, they were swolled so much. And I hope nobody's kilt, but them boys ain't where theys s'posed to be, neither. I told Fred he could go and play around with Corbit, but to go and come straight home. He'd been cooped up pretty much since Lucas up and got his head blowed off. Didn't think it was safe, but I let 'im talk me into it."

With lanterns swinging and gun pointed toward the ground, the two hard-raised farm women continued at a steady pace in strained silence. They were friends and neighbors who had stuck together through some hard times.

That had always been the way of the people of Brush Creek. If something happened to one, it happened to all of them, good or bad. They celebrated, mourned, and sang praises together. They built barns, helped each other harvest their crops, took care of each other's children, and tended to the sick and the dead. Their doors stayed unlocked just in case someone needed a place to stay, or needed to borrow a cup of sugar, or just wanted to drop in and pass the time of day.

It was not unusual to walk into the kitchen and find a fresh-baked loaf of bread, a blackberry pie, or a whole meal if needed. The neighbors plowed and put in crops if anyone happened to be down and couldn't manage it on their own. If a child misbehaved, it was as likely to have a switch stripe its butt by a neighbor as by its parents, and then the neighbor would get thanked for it.

The sun sank a little lower. "Laws, I hope them boys is just up to tomfoolery," Airy Mae said. Ellie knew exactly what she meant. If they were into what she called tomfoolery, they were into boy mischief, and they were probably okay.

Then they heard it. A commotion of stampeding feet rushing downhill. Airy Mae stopped in mid-stride, swung around, and shouldered the Ivers, the barrels clicking into place.

"Momma, Momma!" Callie and Maggie called in harmony, "Wait up!"

Then they saw what looked like a cannon trained on them, hard eyes looking down the barrel. Callie slid to a stop, eyes so big they almost became her whole face. She threw her arms up and shrieked, "Don't shoot!"

"Lordy mercy," Airy Mae cried, dropping the barrel. "I almost kilt you."

Ellie staggered, almost fainting. Maggie scrambled back up the trail as fast as her legs could carry her.

"Maggie," Ellie called. "It's all right, you can come back!"

Callie had to run her down. "Come on," she said, grabbing her arm and jerking her to a stop.

"No! Miz Plank's gonna shoot me. Let go!"

"No, she ain't, now come on." Callie yanked her around. When they started back down the path she said, "She's just gonna shoot your banjo."

Maggie froze, wrapped her arms around it, fell to the ground and squealed, "Noooo!"

"Shush your mouth, Maggie, I was kidding!" Callie, knowing what she had done, couldn't resist doing, tried to reassure her without success. Maggie held her banjo in a death grip, her sobs getting louder and louder.

"Oh, lordy," Callie muttered.

Ellie huffed up the trail, "Callie, I declare, your brother might be hurt, or worse, and here you are carping about that banjo. I've had enough, and didn't I tell you to stay put at the house? Don't you ever listen? Why, you could've got shot, the both of you."

Callie looked at her feet. She knew she had stepped over the line. Then it registered that Corbit really could be hurt. "I'm sorry, Momma, I wasn't thinking, it's that, well, we got the wollyboogers being by ourselves and all."

The truth was Moss Branch had been on her mind since seeing him glare down at her from the overhang earlier that day. His bulky frame, dirty and disheveled, had appeared menacing, his voice hateful. Just seeing and hearing him had made her stomach feel like a brewing storm preparing to do irreparable destruction. Then she remembered how shocked and fearful Willow had looked and recalled the scars and bruises on her arms and legs the day she chased her through the woods, and the flag bruise on her cheek, and how Willow had always dismissed it with what sounded like weak excuses.

"Come along then," Ellie said. "But stay close, and don't you say another word to your sister. I ain't in the mood to put up with your nonsense." She turned toward Airy Mae and frowned.

"I'll break it down," Airy Mae said. The barrels opened, exposing the two double-aughts.

They walked on in silence. Maggie held on to her momma just in case Airy Mae changed her mind and decided to blow her banjo to kingdom come.

The ragged, thin clouds blazed with glory set afire by a slumping sun. An owl greeted the shadows as an old friend, echoing the familiar hoots throughout the forest.

They walked on. Callie noticed the nervousness in her mother's steps, the taut features on her face. Airy Mae's cadence seemed forced, stiff, determined, but unsure.

Callie felt a stirring sensation, an emotion she could not at first understand, a feeling so new, so foreign, like an alien language bouncing around in her head. Slowly, however, she began to comprehend, to put it all together, and then, as if an interrupter had translated her emotions, she suddenly knew. This could be real, unchangeable, like the last shovel full of dirt over a grave.

Her heart sank. Corbit could really be hurt and Fred too, or — she refused to allow her mind to think the word. She breathed deeply — released it. A sadness she'd never known enveloped her like darkness in a cave, smothering and desperate. The shooting at the church had disturbed her, but that wasn't as personal. Lucas wasn't family. Her hand reached out and latched on to her mother's other hand, which also held the unlit lantern.

The little band of searchers stepped out into the open from the copse of cedar at the trail's end, the trees' Christmas smell lingering in the sultry air. The frazzled swinging rope hung loose from the stout oak limb. The creek spoke its own language as it flowed slow and easy along its diminished banks. They looked to the left, started to call the boys by name, and then decided against it.

Then Ellie saw them. She screamed.

Corbit and Fred lay sprawled on the ground, legs wide and feet facing each other, a tall frame towering over them.

Airy Mae snapped the barrels closed.

The gun swung to her shoulder.

She touched the trigger.

Chapter 14
Shotgun and a Porch Swing

D on't shoot," Corbit shouted.
Blam!
Corbit's body jerked. Fred rolled.

The barrel swung upward just in time, twigs and bark ripped from tree trunks and branches. Shredded leaves rained down like ash from a volcano.

The tall figure dived behind a tree, then ran, stumbled, recovered and scurried through tall weeds and blackberry bushes, disappearing into the darkening woods.

"Minner," Callie yelled.

"A ghost," Maggie gasped.

Ellie's hand, still grasping the hot gun barrel, glared at Airy Mae. "You're gonna kill somebody yet with that blamed scatter gun of yourn." Airy Mae stood in shock at what almost happened. Letting go of the gun barrel Ellie stepped forward. "Are you boys all right?" She looked from one wide-eyed boy to the other. "Why were you two on the ground and who was that boy standing over you?"

"That ain't no boy," Maggie said. "That's a ghost that got snake bit in the creek."

Ellie looked perplexed. "What?"

"It *is* a boy," Fred said, propping up on his elbows. "And he ain't snake bit."

Corbit rose to a sitting position. "And he ain't Minner, either. His name's Thorny Branch, Willow's brother."

"I'll say this," Airy Mae cried. "He shore enough *like* to of become a ghost and that's a fact." She looked at the boys. "And you two got some explainin' to do."

The boys stood, brushed dirt and leaves off of their overalls and looked at each other.

"Well?" Ellie said, hands on her hips. She tried to look firm, in control, but her whole body shook from built-up tension, and its sudden release.

"We were playing marbles, that's all." Corbit said in his easygoing voice.

"Yeah," Fred interjected, "And Thorny's the best marble shooter in the whole world.

"Marbles!" Ellie felt a surge of anger, but then her eyes softened and so did her heart. Relief saturated her mind, her body relaxed, and the world seemed right again. "You mean to tell me you've been down here all this time playing marbles? You like to of worried us to the grave."

"Grave," Airy Mae muttered, looking at the Ivers. She realized how close she had come to shooting and maybe killing that boy, or maybe all three. The acrid smell of gunpowder still hung in the air.

"Marbles? Really, Corbit? Really? Would you mind telling us what *marbles* has got to do with you and Fred lying spread-addled on the ground?"

"Why, that's easy," Fred said, as if everyone should know the answer. "Thorny bet us he could throw his cat-eye up in the air and it'd land smack dab in the middle between our feet, and he done just that."

"Yeah, he done that all right," Corbit said. The boys looked around at everyone expecting them to be amazed.

Callie gave them the *so what* look and said, "So?" And then it clicked , her brow furrowed, "Did you say *Thorny?*"

"Sooo?" Corbit dropped his arms as if to say, *Why isn't*

everyone totally astounded. "And yeah, Thorny."

"Yeah, and that's not all," Fred looked for a reaction before continuing, "We played dropsies and he hit the marble ever'time—"

"And *chase*," Corbit threw in with the excitement of Christmas. "And when we rolled to see who could get the closest to the line we drew in the dirt, Thorny'd land on it everytime."

"Ever'time, with his eyes closed," Fred drawled for emphasis.

"Well, that ain't nothin'," Maggie offered. "All ghosts can do that!"

"He ain't a—"

"How did you get Thorny to talk to you?" Callie interrupted Fred. She thought about the encounter in the woods, remembered his voice. "Willow said he didn't like to be around people."

"We saw him standing right over there," Corbit pointed to the spot, "with a rifle in his hands—"

"Lordy," Ellie said. "Everybody's totin' guns. Somebody's gonna get kilt before the day's out."

"Huntin' rabbits, that's all," Fred said. "We surprised him and he surprised us. When he ran off I hollered at him to stop. Told him we were just fishin' and why didn't he come back and shoot some marbles. Well, that stopped him dead. That's when we learned he was Willow's brother and that he's the best marble shooter in the whole world. Said he ain't had anybody to shoot marbles with since he moved here."

"The *whole* world," Corbit said. "So we put the stringers in the creek, tied them off, and played and played until he won ever dad-blamed marble that me and Fred had, except our shooters, that is." He held up a green cat-eye.

"Put-near dark," Airy Mae said. "We'd better be headin' back."

Fred grinned at her. "Boy, I sure am glad you almost kilt

Thorny — and us, Momma."

Airy Mae's face froze and her voice was barely a whisper. "What?"

"You know… almost."

She hung her head. "Oh, okay. Yeah, me, too."

Ellie glanced at the shotgun. "You best breach that scatter gun."

Without a word Airy Mae pushed the release. The barrels looked at the ground as if in shame. One barrel held a spent shell while the other still held a loaded double-aught.

The purple sky disappeared as the sun sank to the horizon. With the surrounding forest blocking the remaining light, they lit the two lanterns and began the walk back. Corbit and Fred carried their supper on the two stringers. The catfish, still alive, grunted and crackled.

They walked in silence as darkness enveloped the forest. The dim light of the lanterns, preceded by shadowy outlines, illuminated the ground just a few steps ahead of their feet. Airy Mae led the way, her shotgun lying across one arm and a lantern swinging from the other. Ellie, holding a lantern with a stretched-out arm, guarded the rear.

Crickets and frogs talking and singing in their own language resonated throughout the woods. Night birds and bats invaded the nocturnal sky. An owl hooted. To the superstitious, just one of the three meant bad luck. Airy Mae noted all three. "Lordy, Lordy," she whispered with a slow shake of her head. "We're headed for somethin' awful."

As soon as she uttered the words a light appeared on the path farther up the hill. It was now totally dark.

Airy Mae stopped, put down the lantern. Everyone behind her halted.

A silhouette followed an erratic light. It came fast.

Footsteps pounded the earth, not in a steady cadence, but disjointed, as though running downhill trying to keep from slipping down.

Clack! The Ivers-Johnson snapped shut.

The pounding footsteps stopped. The light went out. The silhouette disappeared, folding into darkness.

From up the trail came a *"ca-lick!*

Fear gripped the children. Maggie fell to the ground, wrapping her arms around her head, banjo tucked underneath her body. Fred slipped into the brush. Corbit kneeled down, reached out, pushed the side-lift lever on the Victor lantern Airy Mae had placed on the ground, and blew out the orange flame. Ellie puffed hers out.

Silence.

Everyone's breathing became shallow.

More silence.

Although dark had fallen, a shadow of a man could be seen now, his proximity to the horizon making the area where he stood a little lighter.

The shadow disappeared. Airy Mae was the first to notice. Ellie pulled Maggie from the ground hugging her close; Corbit and Callie gathered around like chicks around a mother hen.

"Where's Fred?" Airy Mae whispered with alarm.

A deep voice commanded, "Hold it *right* there."

Airy Mae shouldered the gun, swung toward the voice, pulled the trigger.

Click!

"It's me, Bud." He stepped from the brush onto the path.

"Bud! Oh my Lord!" Ellie grabbed her heart. "You like to of been kilt!"

Airy Mae dropped the gun and fell to her knees. "Thank God," she uttered and wept. If she had remembered to reload the empty chamber, Bud would have been dead. She would have pulled the trigger on the second barrel if Bud had not spoken. She lamented, "That's three times today I like to of kilt somebody."

Fred stepped from the brush with a limb in his hand. Airy Mae gasped, horror twisted her face, hands slapped over her mouth, she prostrated herself on the ground and sobbed, her body shaking. A sobering splash of cold reality revealed that Fred, too, would have been killed if the barrel had not been empty. Fred, sneaking up from behind, had planned to hit the would-be murderer of the Kinser and Plank family with the sturdy limb he clutched in his hands.

Ellie, recognizing her friend's sorrow, kneeled beside her to give her comfort. Fred dropped the limb and ran to his mother.

"Oh, Momma," he said. "Don't cry — it's okay." Airy Mae turned to one side, held out her arm and pulled her son close.

They all had been affected, Callie, Corbit, Maggie and Fred. They had never known fear, not real fear. They had been frightened by ghost stories and spooked by shadows on the wall cast by a dimly lit moon or flickering coal oil lantern. Every boy and girl at some point during childhood experienced it. This type of fear, mild, even fun, something to laugh over, was completely different from what they had experienced this specter filled evening. Childhood phobia should be what it is, irrational. But today fear gained a new meaning… dark, menacing, and dangerous… the kind that whispers death.

"Why did you come down here, Bud?" Ellie asked, her heart beat almost back to normal.

"I heard the shotgun blast, saw Airy Mae's truck and nobody at home. When I saw the lanterns go out I didn't know what to think, so I sneaked down the side of the trail."

"Yeah, and Fred like to of put a knot on your head, too," Corbit reminded.

"I'm glad you were thinking, Fred," Bud said with a firm grip on his shoulder. "You did good. And I'm double glad you didn't clobber me with that tree you were holding."

That broke the tension and everyone laughed. Together they walked home with newly lit lanterns to guide the way.

Fred held up the stringer of cats. "Can I stay at Corbit's and eat this dinner we're holding?"

"That's a good idea. Airy, why don't you both stay?" Ellie pointed to the stringers, "Got plenty."

"Thanks, Ellie, but me and Fred better get on home. Why, if we stayed I might wind up blowin' somebody's head off."

"Oh, shoot!" Fred said.

Everyone looked at Fred and laughed. Airy Mae put her arm around her son and said, "Poor choice of words, son."

❧

"Corbit, there's no excuse for what you did today, scaring your mother and all. You're old enough to know better."

Son and father spent the next hour skinning and gutting catfish while talking about responsibility, rather, father talked and son listened. Corbit knew he deserved it, but he'd much rather have taken the sting of a hickory switch than endure a lecture. A whipping would be over in just a few seconds, with only the prickling of the switch lasting a little longer. The switch was better, even preferred, to an hour-long sermon.

Ellie, having stoked the fire in the stove for a late supper, came out to see how they were doing. "I declare, Bud, Airy Mae and that confounded scattergun, it's a true miracle she didn't kill somebody today."

"I know," Bud said. "Maybe she learnt her lesson seeing how close she came to killing me."

"And Thorny and Corbit," Ellie added to the list.

"And Fred. Twice," Corbit said as a stark reminder.

"That's where that first shotgun blast you heard came from, Bud," Ellie said. She explained what happened.

Bud closed his eyes and shook his head. "Lord have mercy!"

"He did, if you asked me," Ellie said. "And I don't know about that Branch boy, if he's anything like his deddy—"

"He ain't," Corbit snapped. "He's nice. Had some bruises on his face and arms, though."

Ellie and Bud looked at Corbit, sudden concern on their faces. Bud asked, "Did he say how he got them?"

Corbit hunched his shoulders. "Said he slipped and fell."

"Humm, well, he looked mighty puny to me, what little I saw of him, that is. They must be starvin' him half to death, or ..." Ellie started to say, *or beating him half to death*, but decided against it. "Maybe they just don't have enough to eat."

Bud handed Ellie the pan of fish. "I ain't seen him yet, but Willow sure looked well fed. That don't mean they ain't hungry though. I'll check on them tomorrow and let the boy know everything's all right, that he's not in trouble. Need to introduce myself to Mrs. Branch anyway, let her know who her neighbors are."

Ellie took the fresh cleaned fish and headed for the kitchen. Her cast iron Estate stove, born in 1914, had been an anchor in the Kinser kitchen for twenty years. Bought used at Rockholt's Hardware store in the neighboring town of Decatur, it had been paid for on time for five dollars a month. The cooking surface, large enough for six pots and skillets, made frying the fish a quick chore. Cornbread hot out of the oven sat in the warmer located over the cooking surface along with a pot of black-eyed peas. The water reservoir located underneath the firebox would provide warm water for washing dishes after the meal. They ate with little talk, choosing instead to enjoy the comfort of good food and a soothing feeling of their family together, safe and secure.

Everyone joined in to clean the kitchen, everyone except Maggie, that is. She played lively tunes that seemed to hurry the work along. Afterwards the well fed and content family turned in for the night.

Callie lay in bed looking at the starry heaven through an open window. She gazed in wonder at the night sky, its vastness, which, until tonight, she had not really noticed before. The sounds of night creatures she had somehow taken for granted, perhaps because of their familiarity, filled her ears with a new awareness. The varying scents of the land stirred her soul. The world had grown larger. Before, it had been a cozy place, established, safe, a world of hard work, and plenty of fun to make up for it. The tight-knit community of Brush Creek had expanded beyond its boundary.

She wondered why she hadn't felt that way when Lucas Ward had been killed. Maybe, she reasoned as she had earlier, because this time it had been personal, her family had felt threatened, she had experienced a feeling of dread accompanied by deep fear that someone she loved might have been dead and gone forever.

The bedroom door creaked open. Corbit joined Callie by the open window, both on their knees, arms on the window sill looking out into the infinite darkness of space. The bed sagged as a new set of knees joined the others. Maggie squeezed in between them, but Callie didn't seem to mind. Treetops silhouetted against the horizon and the fragrance of honeysuckle gave the siblings a feeling of peace. But they now knew with a certainty that, along with the familiar, creeps in the unfamiliar. The known, sooner or later, is replaced by the unknown in everything.

Or almost everything.

Ellie and Bud, deciding to wind down before retiring, sat on the front porch gently swinging, their feet pushing in rhythm, the rusty chains squeaking and mingling with their soothing voices talking over the day's events. Callie, Corbit and Maggie listened, not quite making out the words, but they didn't have to; their parents' tender laughter seemed to be enough. They knew, the three of them, that their love would always be there, never changing except to grow stronger with the flow of years.

No one said a word as they propped against the window sill listening as the voices downstairs faded with the tap, tap, tapping of the screen door. Their parents, finally relaxed enough from the day's events, had retired for the evening.

To Maggie's musical ear, listening to her parents' gentle voices and soft laughter meant something special. She broke the silence. "Oh, that sounded like a song."

∾∾

The orange lamp light flickered out from the downstairs bedroom. A shadow emerged from the woods, stood and listened. Satisfied that everyone was in bed, the dark form crept across the yard and up the steps to the back porch. He crouched behind the stack of stove wood to listen. With the stealth of a cat, he eased open the door and slipped into the house.

Chapter 15
Fish, Peas and Sweet Milk

omebody must've got hungry during the night," Ellie said. "Even ate the bowl." All of the leftovers from last night's feast had disappeared. Not even a crumb of cornbread had been left.

Maggie's eyes opened wide, the sleep suddenly gone. "Well, I'll say. How did you swaller that bowl, Corbit?"

"In little pieces," he said.

"You ain't done it!" Maggie chirped, utterly amazed.

"Yep," Callie joined in. "I helped him. "He ate half and I ate the other."

Maggie recognized the devilish look in their eyes. "That ain't no ways true. You're just funnin' me."

"Well, I ain't funnin'," Ellie said, frowning at Corbit. "Did you leave the bowl in your room… and how in creation did you eat so much after all you ate at supper?"

"I didn't," he said.

"Didn't what?" Ellie asked.

"Eat the bowl, I mean, leave it in my room. Must've been somebody else besides me, I was too stuffed to eat any more."

"Who ate a bowl?" Bud asked, scooting his chair up to the table.

"There ain't *nobody* ate a bowl," Ellie said. "Now stop it! I don't care who ate all the fish, peas and cornbread, like a starvin' dog, I just want my bowl back."

"Weren't me," Bud said. "I had plenty at supper." He stared with amusement at his three children. "Well?"

They shook their heads. "Weren't me," they sang in harmony.

"Maybe that ghost boy, Minner, ate it," Maggie offered.

Corbit rolled his eyes. "He *ain't* no ghost and his name ain't…" He paused, a light of understanding crossing his face. "Betcha that murderer ate it!"

"Well I'll say!" Maggie's eyes opened wide as sunflowers.

"I'll be a yellow dog," Callie twanged. "A murderer right here in our house."

"Oh, now," Bud said. "Let's not jump to conclusions. We don't know that, probably just somebody hungry. Some people around here don't have much, you know. I'd say that's the case."

"They're welcome to the food, but not my bowl," Ellie insisted.

"Maybe they'll bring it back when they come for seconds," Callie said.

"Well, I hope they do." Ellie motioned to Callie. "Go get the sweet milk out of the icebox."

The chair screeched as it slid back. She pulled the door open. "Milk's gone," she said.

"Got more in the spring house," Bud said. "At least he didn't get the cow. Corbit milked her a little while ago."

"Might be feeding everybody in Brush Creek this time next year," Ellie said. "Looks like we're only one of a few having any kind of a crop thanks to our brilliant son here." Corbit glowed.

"Speaking of," Bud said, looking at Corbit. "Better dam the spring again, crops looking a little thirsty."

Bud reached over and tapped Corbit on the head.

"The good Lord put a brain in your noggin', Corbit Kinser. Anyway, everybody with a spring close to their field's built a dam. You're the hero of Brush Creek, I'd say."

After breakfast the mundane chores were completed. Callie continued to do Maggie's part, which, as it turned out, wasn't that much. The thought still made her angry. "It ain't fair that I don't have that many more chores to do!"

Corbit looked perplexed. "Say that again?"

"What I mean is… well, you know, Maggie didn't have that many chores to begin with, so I don't have that many more to do."

"So? That's what I've been saying all along."

"So, it ain't fair, that's what!"

"Look at it this way," Corbit reasoned. "Momma's doing you a favor by punishing you with Maggie's chores."

With a startled look, she said, "Hey, I never thought of it that way. Boy, you're right."

Corbit slipped his thumbs underneath his overall straps and stood on his toes. "Yep, I know."

"You don't have to be so smug about it."

"I ain't smug. I can't help it if I'm right all the time. Why, being right just comes natural, like Maggie playing the banjo, and you sewing piller cases and dresses, and stuff."

"I guess so," Callie admitted. "But you still don't have to be so smug. Besides, you're not right about *everything*, you know."

"Oh yeah? Just what am I wrong about?"

"Maggie, that's what. About being talented and all. She ain't, you know. She just thinks she is. Everybody makes a fuss over her because she's so dumb and they don't want to hurt her feelings, and such."

"That ain't no ways true, and you know it. Why can't you admit Maggie's good at making music? And why're you so jealous anyhow?"

"It *is* so — and I *ain't* jealous!" Callie stormed off to sulk.

❧

"See you tonight," Bud said to his wife while donning his hat. The old Ford ground into first gear and rattled down the long dusty driveway.

The engine labored in second as it climbed the slow incline toward the Branch place at the top. As the car turned into the yard, a hulking form stepped off the slumping porch and vanished ghostlike into the woods. The car squeaked to a stop and the emergency brake growled as he pulled the lever back. Bud stepped out and leaned on the open door. He started to call after Moss, and then remembered his belligerent behavior the night of Lucas Ward's murder. He knew Moss had seen him as he drove up.

Pushing the door shut, Bud walked across the yard and stepped onto the porch. "Mrs. Branch, it's Bud Ward, is anybody home?" he called while knocking on the door. After a few seconds a silent figure approached. With a combination of morning light and indoor shade, he could only partially see through the dingy screen. A woman of slight build in a worn-out sack dress approached the door with caution.

"Moss ain't home." Her small voice held a tinge of nervousness.

"I know, ma'am, I just saw him go into the woods, didn't catch him in time." Bud pulled off his hat. "My name's Bud Kinser, I live on the farm down below you. Just thought I'd stop and introduce myself. Already know Willow, met her at church. Callie, Corbit, and Maggie are my younguns. You might've heard Willow talk about them."

Rose, her face lined with worry, pushed the door slightly open. Her eyes were blank of emotion and her pallid skin, although still relatively young, looked wrinkled and dry. Her eyes widened when she saw the badge on Bud's shirt. Rose snatched the door shut and backed away from the door. "You come to take my Willow, ain'tcha?"

Bud looked down at the badge. "Why, no, Mrs. Branch, what made you think that? Is there something wrong?"

Rose heaved a sigh of relief. "Oh, uh, no, nothin's wrong."

Bud hardened his eyes. "Are you sure?"

"Everything's all right, Mr. Kinser." Willow stepped into the living room, but stayed back in the shadows so her swollen face couldn't be seen. "Howdy, Mr. Kinser. Tell Callie, Corbit, and Maggie that I'll see them soon."

Bud shaded his face with a hand to his forehead and narrowed his eyes trying to get a better look at the girl, but could only see her outline. The sun in its early morning brightness reflected light from the rusty and dirt-caked screen. "I'm sure they're looking forward to it, Willow." Bud turned to Rose. "I need to speak with Minner, I mean, Thorny."

Rose drew in a quick breath. "Thorny! Is he in some kind of trouble?" She cracked open the screen door revealing one side of her face.

"Oh, no ma'am, he ain't in no trouble, I just wanted to talk to him about last evening. I'm sure he told you about what happened down at the creek … and how'd you bust your mouth?"

"Accident, and he ain't told me nothin'," Turning to Willow still hidden in the shadows. "Thorny told you anything?"

"Said somebody shot at him with a shotgun."

Rose's hand flew to her mouth. "Shot!" Her voice rose to a high-pitched whine. "Lordy mercy, is he hurt?"

"No," Bud and Willow said at once.

Bud continued. "No, ma'am, he ain't hurt. The shot went into the trees. You see, Airy Mae Plank, that's the one who done the shooting, well, she thought Thorny was the man that killed Lucas Ward—"

"He ain't kilt nobody," Rose said, her voice deepening.

"Yes, ma'am, I know he didn't."

Then Rose asked, "Got any notion who might've done it?"

"We have our suspicions, that's about all. We really don't know for sure."

Rose backed up, making the door opening a little smaller. "The sheriff came out the other day, talked to Moss, asked him a bunch of questions, and all, like he'd done it, or something."

"He's asked a lot of people questions, ma'am. But, anyhow, tell Thorny everything's all right and that my boy Corbit, and his friend, Fred, were impressed with his marble-shooting ability." Bud explained everything that had happened the night before, including Ellie's quick thinking that had sent the buckshot into the trees.

"Thank you for coming out and checking on Thorny," Rose said. "I'll be sure and tell him what you said." She cleared her throat. "And thank your boy and his friend for taking up time with my boy."

Willow said from the shadows. "Thorny told me about their marble playing. He really likes Corbit and Fred."

"They like him, too. Tell him to come around anytime."

"I will," Willow answered.

Putting his hat back on, Bud turned and stepped off the porch. "Have a good day, ma'am, you too, Willow." Pulling the car door shut, he pushed the clutch and worried the engine until it started with a pop sounding like a gunshot.

Rose closed the door and disappeared into the house.

Something's not right. Bud's alert mind had sensed Rose and Willow were trying to hide something, and that both were afraid. *Just what are they afraid of?* Grinding the gear into reverse, Bud backed out of the narrow drive and pointed the Ford toward town.

❦

Moss vanished into the woods for his daily visit to his lover that lay hidden in the mouth of a cave surrounded by a canopy of trees. The outcrop and closeness of the trees dispersed the smoke from the cooking fire of the still, making it difficult for anyone to spot. Despite his dirty, sloppy nature, he distilled a pure moonshine, making it desirable and highly sought after by his customers. He demanded and received the highest price for his illegal elixir.

That's the way it had been in Blount County, too, until the sheriff busted up his still for the second time. Moss had not been there either time, but that was his sign to get out of the county and to stay out. Not that the sheriff minded the still, he just wanted a share of the profit, and Moss had not been willing to share.

Moss made a good living from his illegal trade, but the money he acquired was strictly for his pleasure and entertainment. He gambled, paid for prostitutes, ate prime pork and beef, and bought pretty dresses — but not for his wife. He provided barely enough food for his family to stay alive. If not for Thorny fishing and hunting for meat and selling hides for staples, they would have very little. At best they stayed on the edge of starvation.

When Moss was home he allowed Thorny only a small portion of food and kept track of every crumb. Every wedge of bread, every chunk of bacon, and every pea had to be accounted for. If not, Rose, and especially Thorny, would face the consequences of his rage. Willow, for his own personal reasons was allowed, or rather made, to eat more while everyone watched. With bowed head and spilled tears, shame filled her being. She could not bear to see the hungry look in her little sister's eyes, eyes that did not understand why she had to be hungry while her daddy and big sister were not. Rose's eyes held pity, while Thorny's were filled with rage.

"Why does Willow get to eat more?" Olive once asked.

"Shat up," Moss had barked his favorite expression. "You'll git yore turn soon enough."

Willow remembered the evil in his eyes, could still see the wicked grin and the dark yellowed, tobacco-stained teeth that reminded her of a troll.

He had laughed and said, "Now, you be a good little girl so you can be good for yore deddy." His dark eyes drilled holes into Olive, and then he laughed again. "Yore time will be here b'fore you can say 'scat,' little girl." Willow had shuddered. She noticed that lately he had been giving Olive a little more to eat. Maybe her time was almost here.

With Moss gone to check on his still, Willow could escape hell for a few hours. This she could count on, rain or shine, hot or freezing cold, his lover would never go without his tender touch. The only thing Moss truly loved came in the form of steel, copper, and sour mash, only because of the money and pleasure it gave him.

Willow screeched open the back door and stepped out onto the rotted porch. "Can I come too?" a small voice pleaded. Willow turned to gaze into the innocent face of her little sister who had just turned four. Like her big sister, Olive had a fair complexion and auburn hair that could be shiny-beautiful with proper care, but instead appeared flat and limp. Her liquid green eyes caused Willow's heart to flutter, to hurt. She had no doubts as to what Olive's future held.

"I'll be back soon and we'll play a game. Okay?"

Olive's countenance fell, but she seemed to understand, even at her young age, that Willow needed to be alone. Willow knew her baby sister had seen her father dole out beatings, felt his rage, and comprehended the unhappiness of her family. The youngest child knew no peace, had never known any, and as long as she remained under the iron rule of a drunken, cruel man she knew as her father, she never would.

"Okay," Olive agreed. "Promise?"

Willow fell to her knees and Olive ran to her open arms. Her delicate body folded into her sister's loving embrace. Willow kissed her. "I promise a thousand times."

Rose watched her two daughters embrace from the doorway of the bedroom. Her heart had splintered years ago. She no longer felt it beat, and no longer desired for it to. Still, she loved her children regardless of her weakness that kept her from showing it the way a mother should. The desire to protect them had always been there, but her fear had been greater. She knew that a mother should protect her children even at the expense of her own life. But she hadn't, and guilt consumed her. Death was preferred, but at least if she were alive she might be able to offer some measure of protection and comfort. That's how she rationalized her weakness.

Olive ran from the porch back into the kitchen where she joined her mother. Leaning over, Rose scooped the little girl up into her skeletal arms, placed her head over her shoulder, pressed her face against her neck and tried to hide the tears. She walked to the window with part of the pane missing and watched as her oldest daughter disappeared into the forest. Rose knew the beautiful dress her daughter wore, required to wear by her tormentor only covered her body, not the ugliness she felt within.

"I am free," Willow sang as she whirled about, her imagination winging her away. "I'm so happy. Everything's so perfect." Those thoughts carried the flight of her dreams, lifting her into a fanciful world and the yearnings within her soul. The trees were alive with birds warbling their secret language. Were they all happy words? Willow wondered. Or were they also expressing fears, concern for their young, or just discussing the order of the day? A deer wandered into her path, stopped, and looked at the girl in the pretty dress. The big buck, seemingly sensing no danger, simply walked away.

A little startled at first, Willow stopped her fantasizing long enough to watch the beautiful animal walk off into the lingering early morning shadows. The buck stopped, turned his ten points to face the girl, blew through flared nostrils, and then leaped over a dead-fall disappearing into his realm.

Willow wanted to follow, to run, to leap, to frolic, to be as free as the deer, even if only for a little while. This little piece of sanity was all she had that she could truly call hers and hers alone. She determined not to allow the "real world" enter into her thoughts, to let truth belie her world of dreams. Not now, not here.

But it did. The truth always won out in the end. She touched her swollen face, felt the tenderness around her eye. "Tenderness," she whispered. "How odd." She fell to her knees and wept.

❧

Thorny, bruised and stiff, sat on a boulder overlooking the fields below. The forest offered a backdrop to a panoramic view of the land and a deep blue sky. The early morning held a tinge of coolness. That coolness would soon be boiled away by the drought-bearing sun that, as the day progressed, would cast a haze over the countryside. The cattle in their own uncomplicated world grazed and drank from the Kinser' spring in the field below. *Even the cows have a better life than I do*, he mused.

He thought about his name and how he came to have it, not his real God-given name his mother had given him, but the one he loathed, the one given to him by the devil. *Maybe Thorny's a perfect name for me. It describes my life … full of thorns.*

Robert Daniel Branch had entered the world on a bitter-cold January morning in 1929. The midwife came, not because his father cared for his wife or for his soon-to-be-born child, but because, and only because, he didn't want to be bothered with the details of birth or death, whichever one occurred.

Rose went into labor at five o'clock in the morning. A foot of snow lay on the ground with more flurrying down. "It's time," Rose said, arousing Moss out of a liquor-induced sleep. "I need Fanny, the baby's coming."

He threw the covers off and pushed himself up, then stumbled over to the window. Howling wind drove the snow in blinding sheets and cold air pushed through the cracks of the hovel, whistling like banshees. Moss, infuriated, staggered to the bed, jerked Rose up and slapped her.

"You picked a helluva time to have a youngun!" he bellowed. "I can already tell this little shithead's gonna be a thorn in my side!" He threw on his coat and galoshes, and then turned as he opened the door, "At least if it's a girl youngun I'll git my due." He pushed out into the storm leaving the door open behind him.

This afternoon, Thorny thought of Willow and how he had let her down… again. "I *hate* him!" he yelled. Rage sliced through his brain like a Gillett Blue Blade. His fist pounded the rock. Blood oozed from torn flesh, but he didn't notice. He was used to pain, expected it. But why Willow? Why his mother? And why would God, if there was one, allow Olive to be subject to the same fate? He shook his head when no answer came.

A hand touched his shoulder. He jerked away, cringed and covered his face.

Startled, Willow snatched her hand back. "I'm sorry. I didn't mean to skeer you."

Thorny relaxed but could only offer a lopsided smile because of the swelling and bruises his father had inflicted.

Willow sat down beside him. "Are you hurt bad?"

"He can't do nothin' to hurt me."

Willow smiled in return. "Thank you for trying to protect me and for the food you brought to Momma and

Olive." Then she realized that tenderness did exist in her life. "You're all I have," she whispered, looking down at her feet.

"It ain't much."

"It's ever'thing."

"I'm sorry I let you down. But that ain't nothin' new. Right?"

Willow shook her head. "Don't say that. You could never let me down — not never!"

Thorny balled up his fist and jammed it into the palm of his other hand. "I'm gonna kill the bastard, that's what! Should've done it the other night when I had the chance. Would've too, if it hadn't been for Momma."

Willow touched his arm. "No! Don't let him make you into a killer. You'll get away from him one day—make a life for yourself, and a good one too. Just wait and see."

"What about you and Olive? How will you two get away? He's gonna do the same thing to her as he does to you." Willow closed her eyes as shame flooded over her. "And look at Momma, she might as well be dead, her body, I mean, her soul's already dead. There might be a heaven waiting on her when she's gone, but right now she's in hellfire. Her punishment's already done."

They sat in the comfort of each other's company, felt the pain, not for themselves, but for each other and wondered when it would end.

Chapter 16
Dishpan Water

Ever trying to perfect her music, Maggie sat on the back porch doing finger exercises to increase her picking speed. The fingers on her left hand slid from one fret to the other as if slick with grease while the fingers on her right hand plucked the five strings with lightning speed.

Callie stood at the kitchen counter washing dishes while water sloshed over the rim of the dish pan leaving a wet line across the front of her apron. Each note felt like a pin sticking her ear drums. Her nerves were as tight as the plucking banjo strings.

Then Maggie cut loose with "Banjo Sam" and sang along with the lively tune. She did a banjo run full of energy, her foot stomped, her head bobbed, her fingers moved with the precision of a sewing machine. She sang with equal passion.

After each refrain Maggie would do a banjo run with each note hitting like cylinders firing in perfect order.

Callie roiled with resentment. Her mind whirled, her teeth clamped together so hard her jaw ached. Like a brittle twig between two taut fingers, she snapped. Water splashed all over her apron, wetting her dress as she snatched up the pan. That made her even madder. She backed into the door pushing it open.

Dirty dishwater soaked Maggie. "Shut up, shut up," Callie screamed. The pan landed with a hollow clankity-clank on the solid pine boards of the porch. "You ol' lazy thing! You ain't no good for nothing, you hear! Good… for… nothing! I hate you, you hear me? I haaate you!"

Like a sudden heart attack, the happy music died. Maggie didn't move, didn't even flinch. She stared at the floor, eyes unblinking. Water dripped from drenched hair, ran down her face and trickled from her chin. Tears mixed with greasy water formed a stream of sorrow.

Callie looked around to see if their mother or Corbit had witnessed her disgusting deed. No eyewitnesses were found. She wasn't sorry for what she had done. She just didn't want the punishment it would bring. It would be worse than a few extra chores, she knew, or a mouth full of soap. She eyed the thin branch of a young hickory tree, thought about how the supple limb would easily conform to her backside and legs. She cringed. Still, her eyes hardened to a steely glare, her mouth clenched shut like a bear trap. She gritted her teeth and her body quivered with rage. She didn't care about a switch, or a belt, or more chores, or a mouth full of soap, either. Not then anyway.

Without saying a word Maggie got up from the slat-back chair and stepped off the porch.

"I guess you're gonna go and tattle-tell," Callie sneered. "Well, all right then, I don't care!"

The print sack dress stuck to Maggie's skin, the patterned roses looked wilted, her black hair glistened as rays of sun danced about her now greasy hair. The leather hide on the banjo's head turned dark from the drenching. She held it in her right hand, arm extended toward the ground as if dragging it, only it didn't quite touch the dirt, and for the first time she didn't care if it did.

"That'll teach you what for!" Callie picked up the dish pan, turned on the balls of her feet, stuck her chin out in a show of defiance, and thundered back into the kitchen.

Tears continued to fall as Maggie walked toward the corn field with the intent of hiding among the stalks for the solitude she now desperately craved.

"What in tarnation happened to you?" Ellie stepped from the smokehouse with a shank of beef and touched Maggie's arm.

Maggie didn't look at her, just said, "Ain't nothin'."

"Nothin'? You're soaking wet! How in the world…" Ellie stepped back and lifted Maggie's chin with her fingers. "Look at me. Did Callie do this to you?" Maggie just stood there, water dripping. "And did I hear loud talk?"

"No. It's all my fault. I carried the dishwater out for Callie and I tripped and fell against the porch post. The pan turned up and poured water out all over me." She hated to lie, it wasn't in her nature, and until now she had never felt the need to. She turned her eyes so she wouldn't have to look directly at her mother.

"Don't turn your eyes. Look at me." Maggie turned her head but didn't gaze directly into her mother's eyes. "Are you telling me the God's honest truth?"

Maggie flinched at the word "God" and the judgment that would surely come to her for telling a lie. She took a deep breath. "Yessum."

Exasperated, Ellie exhaled a lung full of air and untied her apron. "Here, take this and dry yourself off."

"Yessum." She took the apron and walked off, but dried her banjo instead.

Callie watched the episode through an open window above the kitchen washstand while standing inconspicuously to one side. She couldn't believe what she had heard, although she only heard snippets of words here and there, Maggie had lied to cover up for her, to keep her from getting a switching. And no doubt a switching it would have been, and more besides. Not only would she have gotten a limber switch across her rump and legs from her mother, but one from her father as well, plus a long, stern talking to. And that would have been the first part of the sentence. The second part she didn't want to think about at all.

That made her even madder. She muttered through clinched jaws. "I don't *need* her taking up for me!"

Ellie steamed toward the kitchen huffing like a locomotive late for a scheduled stop, her walk brisk and her face as taut as a piano cord. She noticed the wet porch, and the post that wasn't, and the slat-back chair that was. Callie jerked her head back and busied herself drying the dishes. The screen door meowed open, straining as it neared its limit. Ellie released it. The door slapped against the door jamb sounding like leather on a naked butt. Callie flinched.

Furious, Ellie stopped short of the dining table and stood there, staring. Callie dried the same dish for a good minute. Realizing what she was doing, she reached up and placed it on the shelf with a clatter and then grabbed a glass. It slipped out of her hand, hit the floor, exploded. Her body became an inflexible knot.

Turning abruptly, her mother marched into the living room. Short breaths puffed from her nostrils like an angry bull. She knew, and Callie knew that she knew. Ellie never uttered a word, but her point had been well made.

∾∾

Maggie wandered into the corn field, her head bowed, eyes fixed on the fertile ground. It didn't register where she was. She didn't see the rows of corn, straight and green, or smell the sweet fragrance of silk hanging from tightly wrapped ears. Her bare feet trod the red dirt but felt nothing. A heavy heart and warm tears were her only companions. Even though no rain fell from the sky, and the day wasn't overcast from dark clouds, and thunder did not rumble from horizon to horizon, her mind and her heart believed otherwise.

Her beloved banjo fell to the ground as she released her grip. A string plucked as it landed face down. She dropped to her knees and wept. Tears fell softly at first, and then they poured, heavy, drenching, heart-wrenching sobs.

❧❧

Corbit placed a rock on top of the dam, preparing to raise the water level so the thirsty fields could irrigate. Upstream two starlings fluttered in the cool spring washing off dust and heat. The drought had worsened, requiring the fields to be watered every two days instead of the previous four. He looked up from his labor into the open rows of corn and watched as Maggie fell to her knees. When her beloved instrument fell to the ground without her snatching it up, he knew something to be terribly wrong.

Leaving the rocks where they lay piled next to the stream, he walked the several yards to where Maggie knelt spilling her tears. Her sobs came in rushes making her thin body shake.

Corbit walked up behind her and gently, almost reverently, touched her shoulder. He dropped to his knees, also in prayer fashion, to join his sister. "What is it, Maggie? What's wrong?"

"She… she ha-hates me!"

"Who?"

She answered in jerky sobs. "Ca-ca-ca- Cal-lie. She — she ha-hates me, and I-I don't know why."

"That ain't no ways true, Maggie."

"It is t-too. She ca-can't stand m-me. She hates my ban-banjer. She hates ever'thing about m- me. Ever'thing!"

Corbit noted her wet, clingy dress and hair. "Did Callie do that to you?"

Maggie wiped her nose with the back of her hand, but said nothing.

"Did she?"

Her sobs softened to sniffles. "Yea-yeah, but don't tell M-Momma!"

"Why not? She deserves a good whuppin'."

"No! Promise not to tell." Maggie grabbed Corbit's arm. "You gotta promise. Okay?"

"But why not? I don't understand."

"I don't want her to get a whuppin'. She'll hate me even worse."

"Well, then, I'll give her a whuppin' myself! I'll whomp her good, I will. And she doesn't hate you, neither. She just thinks she does."

Maggie looked up and wiped her eyes. "If she don't hate me, then why does she act the way she does toward me, and why did she tell me she does?"

"Because she's jealous."

"Jealous — of me? Why, that ain't so. Callie's so smart, and she can sew better than anybody in Brush Creek. Why would she be jealous of me? I can't do nothin'. I'm dumb, even you say so."

"Can't do nothin'! You're kidding, right? Why, you're the best banjo picker around. Besides that, you learned on your own. Nobody showed you a thing. Callie's jealous because she thinks Momma and Deddy pay more attention to you than to her, that's all. And you ain't dumb. You just act like it sometimes. Anyhow, Callie looks at sewing as work, and banjo pickin' as fun. She's just mad because she can't play and you're having all that fun. Besides, she knows you're good. She wouldn't care so much about it if you weren't. And that's the God's honest truth."

Maggie collected her instrument and brushed it off. "I just won't play it no more. That way she won't be mad and she'll like me again."

"You ain't gonna do no such thing, why…" Corbit paused. An idea popped into his brain. "But I know what you *can* do."

Maggie's face brightened. "What? Tell me what, and I'll do it."

"You can help her with chores."

"Chores?"

"You know, clear the table and worsh dishes without saying anything, sweep the floor, things like that."

"But I hate doin' dishes and —" Corbit's face grew stern. Maggie, embarrassed, looked down at her feet. "Okay then, I'll do it."

"Good. She'll come around, just you wait and see." He stood and brushed the dirt off his pants, then reached for Maggie's hand and pulled her up. "Now come with me. You can help dam the spring."

Maggie placed the banjo's strap over her shoulder. "I'll play while you build the dam." And so she did. Maggie spent the rest of the day with her understanding brother, playing lively tunes while he worked. The perfect combination, she thought.

∾∾

Dust cast a sweltering haze over the land. The air rippled with heat as the sun bore down in relentless waves. The fresh scent of clover growing around the spring wafted through the sultry air, hanging on like perfume. Rain seemed to be a thing of the past in Brush Creek, something that only invoked fond memories of an accompanying cool breeze and the soothing music the drops composed against tin roofs. The wind, the swaying trees, and the cool, damp air were things everyone missed and longed for as if they were forbidden fruit in Adam's garden.

The worst drought in twenty years had taken its toll on the hard-working farmers as they labored from dawn till dusk, seemingly for nothing and with no end in sight. Hand pumps became increasingly harder to prime, and ropes were lengthened so buckets could reach the receding water in the stone-lined wells. The Brush was at its lowest point since the last dry spell two decades earlier.

That evening Callie piled the supper scraps onto a plate and took them to the swill bucket hanging from a nail on the back porch. She lingered there listening to the evening settle in. A bobwhite called and another answered. In the meantime, inside the kitchen two unaccustomed hands were preparing warm dishwater from the stove's water reservoir. Maggie slipped into the living room just a second before Callie re-entered the kitchen. Plates, glasses, forks and spoons stood stacked ready to be washed and dried. Callie, thinking the dishbpan to be empty, grabbed it with one hand. It slammed against her leg and dropped to the floor with a clang. Water drenched her legs and feet, then coursed over the floor until finding cracks to disappear into. She stood there, seething.

"Corr-bit!" she shouted, snatching open the screen door. "I'm gonna get you good for that! I know you done it, so quit hiding and come on out! I'm gonna whup your butt, you stupid little *Ettis* thing! You hear me?"

Corbit rounded the corner of the house. "Whup me? What for?" You're the one that needs whuppin'!"

"You know what for!" Callie shouted raising her fist for the blow. "You're gonna get it!"

Corbit dodged the first strike but caught a fist square on the shoulder with the second one. He grabbed both wrists and held them tight. "What in tarnation's got into you? And how did you get so wet?" He grinned and snickered. "The dish pan done got mad at you, or something?"

"Let go of me, you stinking little *Ettis* turd head! And you know what's wrong since you're the one that did it!" Callie struggled to get loose. Corbit tightened his grip.

"I didn't do noth —" She kicked him on the shin. "Ohwee! Ouch!"

"Let go, I said!" Callie screamed while straining to get her hands free.

"No! And you better not kick me again."

She kicked him on the other shinbone.

"Ohwee! Durn it, Callie, you'd better stop!" Corbit clutched both wrists with a deadly grip and jumped back. Both legs were at an angle and his arms extended as he struggled to get out of the way of the staccato kicks.

"I'll teach you to put water in my dishpan, you — you stupid, dumb *Ettis*."

That was more than Corbit could take. "I'm gonna whup you for calling me that, and for what you done to Maggie!"

Corbit rammed a defiant Callie with his head, knocking her down. He dove and landed on her sprawled body. She kicked and scratched but couldn't budge her heavier sibling. Corbit reared back, prepared to put a knot on his sister's head.

"Corbit! Stop it this instant!" The sound of his mother's stern voice arrested his fist as if it had hit a wall. "Get off of her — now!"

"But she called me—"

"I don't care, and I don't want to hear your excuses. Now get up!"

Corbit slung her arms down against the dirt and applied as much pressure as he could get away with while pushing up.

"Want to tell me what's going on? I could hear the screaming in the barn."

They both stood looking at each other with fiery darts. Dirt clung to Callie's wet dress. "He put water in the dish pan without me knowing it, knowing I would pick it up. When I did, I dropped it—"

"I did not, you liar! Momma, she's lying, I didn't do no such thing!"

"Did too, you lying Ettis!"

Corbit got louder. "Did not, and you stop calling me that!"

"Did too! See, Momma? He caused me to get water all over me and the kitchen floor." Callie clamped her hands on her hips and shot a defiant stare at the accused.

"And so you went after him. Is that right?" Callie glared and patted her foot. Ellie waited. "Well?"

"Yessum," Callie said, crossing her arms in defiance.

"And she called me—"

"Shut your mouth! I don't care what she called you! The both of you should've come to me, or better yet, tried to of worked out your differences without fighting." Ellie turned to Corbit. "Well, did you put water in the dish pan without her knowing it, hoping she'd spill it?"

"No!"

"Then who did, can you answer that?"

Corbit blurted. "Maggie done it!"

Ellie had doubt written all over her scrunched-up forehead. "Maggie? Are you saying Maggie intentionally put water in the dish pan so Callie'd spill it?"

"He's lying," Callie snapped. Then she thought about this morning's drenching on the porch.

"No, I'm not! But it's my fault it happened." He looked at Callie. "I told Maggie to help you with the chores. She thinks you hate her, you know. She just wants you to like her, that's all."

Callie shot back. "I don't need her help!"

Ellie asked, "But why would you tell her that? You already know Callie's doing her chores. Want to be a little clearer?"

"Like I said, she thinks Callie hates her, but I said she was only jealous—"

"I ain't jealous!"

"Shut up! And, yes, you are jealous." Ellie's eyes sent

steel waves at her daughter. "You're plumb scared to death Maggie might be able to do something better than you. Now, ain't that right?"

Callie bowed her head and gave a tepid response. "No, it ain't."

"Anyway," Corbit looked at his reproved sister and continued to explain, "I told Maggie if she'd help with chores that you'd feel better toward her. Besides, you ought not to of poured dishwater on her like you did — oh, shit!"

"What did you say?" Ellie grabbed his arm.

He turned red. "I promised Maggie I wouldn't tell about the dishwater."

Ellie glowered at Callie. "Now, see what you've caused with your constant nitpicking? You should feel ashamed." She thought of Maggie dripping with greasy water. "And I think you deserved what you got. In fact, you deserve worse for what you did to that little girl… your sister. You should be ashamed to tears!"

"Yeah, sure, blame it on me. Maggie's always right no matter what she does. She's perfect!" Callie folded her arms and tapped her foot.

"That's enough from you. If I hear or see one more incident involving your sister, you'll be confined to this yard the rest of the summer. Do you understand me?"

The fire in Callie's eyes could have burnt down every house and barn in Brush Creek.

"Well?"

"Yessum."

Ellie wasn't satisfied with Callie's tepid response, and warned, "I mean it. I've had it with your sorry attitude. Is that clear?"

Callie shook with anger but dared not say anything except "Yessum."

"Now, go and cut a switch — a good limber one." Ellie turned to face Corbit. "And as for you, if I ever see you laying a hand on your sister again you'll get a whuppin' you'll not soon forget. Do you have a problem understanding that?"

"Yessum. I mean, no'm."

"Good. Now come with me. I've got a fresh bar of soap to clean out that nasty mouth of yours." As she led Corbit to his fate she mumbled, "Lordy, you two could drive a wooden woman crazy!"

Corbit cleaned his mouth with the new bar of soap his mother had lathered up. It tasted terrible, but he didn't care. He found comfort that a hickory switch hadn't been used to take the first layer of skin off of him.

"Are you telling the truth?" Callie asked as she joined Corbit in the barn. She grabbed a cup and scooped it full of sweet feed, then sifted it into the trough for the cow. Corbit sat on the stool and placed a shiny galvanized bucket underneath the full udder, clutched a teat with each hand, then squeezed. The warm milk sizzled into the bucket with perfect rhythm.

Callie insisted. "Well, are you?"

"What? You think I'm lying? I suppose calling me by that name I hate so much ain't enough. You've got to call me a liar, too. And it'll take a week to get that soap taste out of my mouth that you helped put in."

"Shut up! You're gonna get us in trouble sure as 'John Brown's Baby had a cold upon his chest.' And it'll take a week for these welts to go away. I don't need anymore."

"And you're gonna get clobbered sure as 'John Brown had a little Indian' if you call me that name again."

"Well," Callie retorted, "you're gonna get the pee knocked out of you sure as 'John Brown's body lies a mouldering in the grave.'"

They looked at each other and laughed over their silliness, finally breaking the tension. They could have gone on and on forever about the famed Harper's Ferry hero. Since the Civil War, John Brown had been a popular moniker to use in short songs and poems, and as a term for approval or disappointment.

"Maggie really does think you hate her, you know," Corbit said.

"I don't care what that lazy ol' thing thinks. She ain't no good for nothing anyhow."

"I declare, Callie. You're head's harder than a granite rock. Think about it. Maggie's ten years old and plays the banjo like a Grand Ole Opry star. Nobody taught her, either. She learned it all on her own."

"Yeah, well, that's all she does. She never does anything to help out around here, and she's as dumb as a turkey. And I don't want her doing anything for me, and you can tell her so. And I do hate her!" Callie turned, stormed back to the feed sack and scooped out another cup of feed. Kate brayed and kicked the stall.

Callie jumped.

"See," Corbit insisted. "Even ol' Kate thinks you've got a hard head."

Callie Kinser, young, self-absorbed with youthful superiority and stubbornness, had not been aware of the green-eyed monster following her like a twin. With a silent voice it had fed her envy, shadowed her every move as a stalker does its prey. She had yet to learn, as Ralph Waldo Emerson wrote in *Self Reliance*, "There is a time in every man's education when he arrives at the conviction that envy is ignorance."

❧

"I knew she hated me," Maggie said in a broken whisper. She had been standing in the shadow of the barn door listening to Callie and Corbit talk. She hurried back to the house.

Callie returned to the kitchen to finish the dishes. The floor, still wet from the spilled water, had been cleaned up.

Probably Momma, she thought as she replenished the pan from the stove's reservoir.

Finishing up, Callie leaned over the green plaid oilcloth wiping it with a damp dish cloth, which amounted to a piece of left-over cotton flour sack doubled and stitched, one that she had made.

Maggie stopped in the doorway. "I'm sorry I made you get wet, and all."

Callie's hand stopped in mid-motion. She looked up. "Just shut up you dumb ol' thing." She groused in a gruff whisper no one else could hear but Maggie, "Get away from me. I hate you!"

With downcast eyes Maggie crept out the door to the back yard. The sun blazed over the western horizon turning the sky's scattered and fluffy clouds a crimson red. The day sourroundings transformed to a peaceful sienna as shadows deepened, sounds of dusk suffused the air. Birds were migrating to their roosts. Insects and creatures, both big and small, were settling down transforming the noisy day-world to a realm of nocturnal calm.

It would be dusk dark in less than an hour, but Maggie decided to go down to the creek so she could sit and think, something she had been doing a lot lately. No one knew of her excursions. She would get into trouble if her parents found out about her going alone, but she didn't care. Not now. Besides, with the solitude of the woods as her companion she felt certain she could figure out something to do to make her sister like her. Picking up her long-necked banjo, Maggie made her way down the stairs toward the kitchen

She didn't care about a murderer, or darkness. She felt dead anyway and darkness shrouded her soul already. Down the trail she wandered in search of calm assurance.

Callie watched through the screen door as Maggie took to the trail and disappeared into nature. The banjo strapped around Maggie's neck caught her attention. She threw the wet dish rag in the direction of the pan full of dirty water. It missed hitting the wall with a *splat*. She stood, staring and seething resentment. She couldn't stand it any longer.

"Horsefeathers!" she said with resolve. "I'll fix that lazy thing." She thundered out the door and down the trail.

The familiarity of the surroundings offered comfort to the late evening troubadour as she made her way through groves of sweet gum and red maple, the mixed leaves creating an intoxicating fragrance. Finally she emerged from the copse of fir at the end of the trail. The rope hung from the oak as usual. The creek flowed, although with less water on its journey to tomorrow, making water music as it sloshed against its banks and rippled over and around the rocks. The felled tree that once lay partially submerged now stuck out of the water by a good three feet with only the tip of one end underwater.

Maggie found a place underneath the shelter of the guardian oak and sat on a ropy, bald root that had lost its dirt to erosion and rope-swinging feet. After a few silent moments in thought, the forest and the hushed movements of its inhabitants began working its soothing effects on her. A squirrel scampered up a tree stopping halfway to turn and look at the intruder while swishing its tail in jerky motions.

Maggie's toes touched the water, its cooling effect traveling from her feet and up throughout her body pushing out the summer heat and pent-up emotions. "How can I make Callie like me?" she contemplated out loud as though Mother Nature would tell her what to do. The squirrel chattered as if answering and a whippoorwill whistled its name. With a sigh Maggie turned to the one thing that might give her the repose she sought—her banjo.

Swinging it around her shoulder and grasping the long neck in her left hand, she positioned the three picks on the long fingers and thumb of her right hand. She started out playing one of her favorite mountain ballads, the mournful

"Black Jack Davy." That made her even sadder, so she decided to play something a lot more spirited than she felt. She took off on "Froggy Went a Courtin'." The melody seemed to evaporate the gloominess hovering over her as finger picks lightly touched the taut strings.

A hard tug pulled her head to one side, and the strap stung her neck as it slid up and over her head. The picks skimmed across the strings as the banjo jerked from her hands, the melody crashing into a jumble of sour notes.

Callie stood over her, arms raised high over her head with Maggie's very life clutched in her hands. "I'll show you," she screamed.

Maggie's heart seemed to stop beating. She tried to speak, but words froze in her throat. Hands with spread fingers opened and closed, reaching out for her best friend, her true love, her very existence.

The banjo smashed against the big oak. The long neck dangled from loose strings, its frets the only thing holding it to its round body. Callie flung it into the creek. The water took it away. Maggie plunged in after her precious instrument. Immediately her mouth filled with water. Strangling, she turned onto her back, coughed, sputtered and gasped for air. She rolled and slapped the water with open hands attempting to swim after the banjo's remains. The current took her.

She couldn't swim. The banjo bobbed to and fro. Maggie hit a submerged rock with a thud throwing her into the branches of the once-submerged tree. The breath went out of her. She managed to grasp a limb and wrap an arm around it. The current pulled her under as her arm slid around the slippery limb. Pain tore through her body as a snag ripped a gash down the side of her arm. She let go.

"Maggie!" Callie screamed. Rage turned to terror as she watched her sister drift away. She ran along the bank. Blackberry vines festooned with fishhook briars hindered her movement. Trees blocked her sight. The approaching darkness made it even harder for her to focus. She reached the log just as Maggie let go. Blood streamed after her.

"Maggie!" Callie screamed again. Reality hit her like a closed fist against her cheek. Fear like she had never felt welled up inside her. "Oh, God, no," she whimpered.

Another large rock sat half submerged in the middle of the creek. Maggie hit it with a sickening thwack. The current swirled her around, then flung her into a bed of smaller rocks. Her leg sliced open. Blood wisped through the water like a thin red cloud at sunset. She caught on to one of the slimmer rocks and struggled to hang on. Mustering the last remaining strength she had, Maggie pulled herself up onto the bed of stones. She tried to stand, slipped, fell on her side. Her ribs cracked, her arm snapped, her head bounced off the slick rocks. She slipped back into the now dark, swift moving stream face down.

Callie jumped into the swirling water and grabbed for her sister. Fingers touched Maggie's face as she drifted away into darkness.

Chapter 17
The Long Walk Home

Maggie! Oh, God, no! I've killed her! What've I done?"

Callie's mind swirled like eddies in her head. She felt as if she were being sucked under by a vortex, her breath pushed from her lungs by the weight of the churning mass of water. Panic, regret, shame and fear gripped her all at once like a vise, squeezing, squeezing. Darkness swallowed up the dusk. Only a quarter-moon glowed in the heavens, barely visible over the horizon, its beams glistening off the dark water that had taken Maggie away.

"Help," Callie shouted. "Oh, help me!"

Not knowing what else to do, having completely lost sight of Maggie, Callie ran for home. With a double shot of adrenalin shooting through her body she hit the trail at full stride. Her arms pumped, ramping up her heartbeat. She made her way through the copse of cedar. The trail suddenly turned. It threw her off course. She stumbled. Her feet slipped. She hit the ground hard. Her breath left her lungs. She rolled on her back and gasped for air. She clamored to get up. Not quite having her breath back, but too scared to care, she tore up the trail.

Callie could see her sister's face as she heard herself spew, "I hate you!" Maggie's sad brown eyes haunted her.

How could I've been so cruel? Thoughts ran through her mind like a time machine going backwards. In an instant all the terrible things she had said to her sister flooded her mind like a burst dam. Her heart flooded with pains of regret.

The image of Maggie floating on her stomach into darkness kicked in another dose of adrenalin. She ran as if the wind was pushing her. She couldn't feel herself breathing any more. The sensation of movement was gone as though she were in a vacuum, screaming without being heard.

Callie caught sight of the house. "Help, somebody help," she managed to scream between pants. "Momma — Deddy — help me!"   The closer she got the more her strength ebbed. She struggled to stay upright.

Bud drove up just as Callie topped the hill, the brakes squeaking as the car drifted to a stop.

Coal oil lanterns throwing light from the house windows, once a comforting sight now meant dread and hopelessness because Maggie was not there. Callie stumbled the last few feet and fell against the car. She held onto the mirror to keep from falling. "Deddy! Deddy! It's Maggie!"

The door popped as Bud shoved it open. He ran to the other side of the car, grabbing Callie as she fell into his arms. "What about Maggie? What's wrong?" A sudden sense of dread smothered him.

"Maggie drowned."

The words slammed into his ears with a hard jolt.

Bud grabbed her by both arms. "Where is she?" Callie tried to talk between sobs. He bent down, his face almost touching hers. "Tell me!" He grabbed her, shook her. "Where!"

"She's in the creek!"

"Where in the creek, damn it Callie. Tell me!" Panic riddled his body.

"Past the swing… by the big rock." Bud let go. Callie fell to her knees, weeping.

"Ellie," he shouted. "Get out here!"

The door burst open.

"What's wrong?" The panic in his voice summoned a sense of dread. "What? What is it?"

"It's Maggie! She's in the creek!"

Ellie sucked in a quick breath, hands rushed to cover her mouth. She whimpered, "My God." It was more of a plea than a statement. Ellie ran toward the creek, disappearing down the dark trail.

Corbit heard the commotion and the screen door zinged open and then slammed shut as he ran out.

"Get a lantern," Bud shouted while taking to the trail.

"What's wrong?" Corbit asked, but didn't want to know. He knew it had to be bad.

"Maggie's in the creek," Callie cried. "She's drownt!"

Corbit glanced at Callie with a hard look, ran back into the house and grabbed the lantern sitting on the table, then rushed for the door. He hit it with full force, slamming it against the outside wall. Again he glanced at Callie still on her knees bawling her eyes out.

"What did you do?" he roared, and ran for the trail.

"Oh, Maggie," Ellie whimpered, running and stumbling down the hill. Her disturbed mind recalled a scripture from the Gospel of John that always gave her strength. *And whatsoever ye ask in my name, that will I do, that the Father may be glorified in the Son.* Her heart leapt as she recalled the next verse. *If ye shall ask anything in my name, I will do it.* Her sobs mingled with earnest prayer, giving her hope as she pleaded with God. She ran blind, barely making out the trail in front of her. She willed her legs to move faster.

Corbit's lanky legs soon caught up to Ellie. He shot around her, the lantern's light flickering.

Bud rounded the bend ahead of Corbit and raced downstream; his lungs burned, his breath came in quick bursts, his side heaved, his body called out, *stop, rest, I'm at my limit*, but his mind said, *go, go, faster, faster!*

The stoic oak's long drooping limb appeared to point the way. The faint light of the stunted moon, now well over the horizon, threw little light amongst the trees and shrubs.

His mind whirled. *The big rock? Which one? What does it matter! She's probably way downstream by now.* His mind roiled like a turbulent sea, a gathering storm of foreboding emotions rising to the brink of insanity. "She can't be dead!" he muttered. Frustration and terror shrouded his mind and darkened his soul as he thought about Maggie floating, lifeless.

Ellie, not far behind her husband and son, kept trying to summon courage by constantly recalling the word of God and his holy prophets, doing everything she could to show she indeed believed. *No! Not believe! Not good enough… faith… yes, faith, I must have faith.* "I do! I do!" she cried. But, somehow the words seemed hollow, contrived and full of doubt.

Corbit stabbed at the air with a clenched fist and berated himself. "I should've done more — spent more time with her — been her friend — her brother." The rope swing hanging slack from the limb made him think of Maggie lying in the creek, limp and still.

✂❧

The pain in Callie's heart seemed more than she could bear. Her body quaked with anguish, threatening to explode into a million pieces. "Oh, God," she moaned. "What've I done?"

The tears were as bitter as her words had been to Maggie. She never imagined such sorrow existed in the world. Her knees gave way. The ground caught her prone body. The earth absorbed her tears. Her world had changed in a few seconds, altering forever every fantasy of childhood, every sentiment of security that ever existed. Today the moat that had protected her from the world had been breached.

❧❧❧

Bud fought his way around protruding limbs and vines, grabbing, snatching, and pulling. Then the path opened up. Something stood in the way. An outline, a dark figure against the hushed moonlight, bent over a dark blob in the trail.

The figure rose up like an animal protecting its prey. It turned, bolted, disappearing into the forest.

"Wait! I need help!" Bud shouted. His eyes tried to focus on the form before him.

His pulse quickened. Dread filled his trembling body.

Three quick steps and he fell to his knees.

"Maggie!" He lifted her head, cradled her in his arms and sobbed.

Corbit drew up, trying to focus on the two forms before him. Ellie passed him, stopped, and fell to her knees. "Oh, God, no — not that." Her ragged breathing and sobs mingled in a pitiful sound. "Maggie… Maggie… Maggie, oh, Maggie!"

Corbit watched his weeping parents and the limp form they held in their arms. The lantern fell from his hand. In a trembling childlike voice he said, "Deddy… is she…"

❧❧❧

Callie could not accept what had happened, that her sister was dead, that she was responsible. Her mind kept pushing it away, but reality kept thrusting back with the truth. "It's not real!" she screamed. She needed to get that thought out of her head. She needed something to hang on to, she needed hope. "I'll go look in her room. Maggie'll be there, I know she will … she has to be."

Wet eyes looked up toward the room she and Maggie shared. The window pane stared back. It looked cold and uninviting. The numbing truth tumbled down and buried her.

A soft light appeared at the top of the hill. The flame flickered in the lantern as it swayed back and forth. Corbit appeared first leading the way. Callie heard someone sobbing. She stood and wobbled. Another sharp pain of grief shot through her heart. She felt sick. High pitched mewing sounds mixed with "I'm sorry, Maggie… I'm sorry" squeezed from her throat.

The light grew closer. Behind Corbit two forms appeared as silhouettes in the moonlight, two shadows scrunched together walking as one, shoulder to arm. The larger form held a small body, legs hanging limp, one arm dangling. It had been a long walk home.

The lamplight grew brighter. Corbit's face, now visible, held a puzzling look, frightened, sad, and more, something strange, something very different. Scorn? Hate?

"I didn't mean to kill her," Callie lamented through heart-wrenching sobs. "I didn't mean it."

No one looked her way. Her father said, "Come on inside, Callie."

No one else spoke. They just turned and walked toward the porch. The door wheezed open and then shut with a final tap. Then a tiny voice said, "My banjer, Deddy. My banjer."

Chapter 18
Repentance

Both breaks are clean, but the cast will be on her arm for at least eight weeks," Doc Morton explained, peering over the top of his glasses. "I taped up her cracked ribs and popped the dislocated shoulder back into place. The cut on her arm's not real bad. Didn't need stitches. There's no other damage that I can see, but she'll be plenty sore for a few days."

"What about the cut on her leg, and her other cuts, Doc?" Bud asked.

"Oh, yeah, that. Had to put ten stitches in it. Sliced it pretty good, on a rock probably. The other cuts are only superficial, though, and they should heal just fine. Going to leave a scar on her leg, I'd say. Keep it cleaned and dressed and I'll check back in a couple of days. I've given her something for pain and to make her sleep the rest of the night. Keep a close eye out and monitor her for a fever. Don't want it to get too high. Just give her some Anacin and keep a cool wet cloth on her forehead. Send word if you need me and I'll get here as soon as I can."

Ellie sat on the side of the bed holding Maggie's hand, her brow wrinkled with worry. She looked up at the doctor and asked in halted words, "What about brain damage, do you think she…"

"Now, now, Ellie," the doctor gently admonished, "Don't go getting yourself all worked up. I think she'll be fine. After all she seemed to be lucid enough to talk about the boy that pulled her out, a Minner, or something or other. Only Minner I ever heard of hereabouts that I can recall was the Jenkins boy that died a few years back of snake bites. The family lived in that old shack on Fox Hill if I remember right. The one that Branch family lives in now. Pronounced the boy dead myself."

He shook his head. "I felt so sorry for that family. Good people, too." The old doctor closed his worn leather bag and turned to leave. "Well, she's a mighty lucky girl. All I can say is the Man upstairs had a hand in it. If that boy hadn't pulled her out of the creek when he did, it would've probably been a different story all together. Do you know who this Minner might be?"

Bud remembered something. "You know come to think of it, Minner's what Maggie called the Branch boy that Corbit and Fred played marbles with down at the creek the other day. That right, Ellie?"

"Well, I'll be John Brown if Maggie didn't call him Minner, and Callie talked about him, too."

Bud interrupted, "Anyhow, Minner or not, he jumped up and high-tailed it like a skeered rabbit soon as we walked up. I was just too upset to think about anything but Maggie. Don't understand why he ran off, though."

"Oh, and that bump on her head, probably from a rock, might have knocked her out, and if that boy hadn't come along when he did she would've surly drowned. I'm assuming he pulled her out, of course. No other way to explain it." Doc placed his hand on Bud's shoulder. "Better put a little extra in the collection plate next Sunday."

The worry lines relaxed and tears rolled gently down Ellie's face. "Praise God," she said as her lips moved in a whispered prayer of gratitude.

"I ain't prayed in a while, but I sure made up for it tonight — before and after," Bud admitted with a soberness of a new convert. "Matter of fact, we all did."

"Thank the Lord with every breath," Ellie praised. "And every thought."

Doc Morton with bag in hand turned to leave. "Like I said, I'll be back to check on her in a couple of days, but send for me or come get me if the need arises."

Bud extended his hand. "We will, Doc, and thank you for coming out."

"Yes," Ellie reiterated. "Thank you, and say hello to Martha."

Doc Morton winked. "I will. Good night, now."

Bud and Ellie stood on the porch, arm in arm, as the door of the old black Cadillac slammed shut and the engine jumped to life. Gravel popped and crackled underneath the weight of the tires as the Cadillac backed up and turned around. With a wave of his hand Doc Morton headed back to Athens with the hope of being able to eat supper without being interrupted with another emergency.

"Where's Callie?" Ellie suddenly realized she hadn't been seen since Maggie's return home. "I've been so busy seeing about Maggie I totally forgot about her."

"She's been on the back porch behind the woodpile," Bud said. "I ain't said nothing to her, just left her there to think about things. I don't know what happened at the creek between the two of them, but what Corbit and you've told me about their little feud —"

"You mean Callie's feud. Maggie's simply being picked on because she's good at making music, and it makes Callie jealous to think Maggie can do something she can't."

"I hope this changes her thinking." The lines in Bud's face showed a combination of optimism and sadness.

"Lord, have mercy! Does she still think her sister's dead — that she caused it?" Ellie turned and headed for the door..

Bud grabbed her arm.

"She knows. Corbit's been out there talking to her, so she's aware of everything. I think it best we wait 'til morning to talk to her, give her some time to think about her role in all of this, and what almost happened."

They walked up the stairs, stepping softly on the hard pine steps trying not to make too much noise. As they approached the bedroom where Maggie lay, they heard a voice mixed with agonizing sobs. Stopping short of the door they peered inside. Callie was kneeling at the bedside, tears rolling down her face, pleading with God, pouring out her heart like a true repentant sinner. Only this time it wasn't a preacher standing in front of the pulpit extending a call to accept Jesus while the congregation sang "Just As I Am." Nor did she express sorrow or regret for getting caught in some unfortunate act. It was more than that.

Her heart, full of godly sorrow, expressed personal pain, displayed suffering as one with a broken heart and contrite spirit. As Preacher Roberts said in a recent sermon, "If a person hasn't suffered, he hasn't repented." Callie's heart, without any doubt, had been broken, and she indeed suffered her repentance.

Bud and Ellie backed away a few feet from the door, still within earshot.

"God, please don't let Maggie die," Callie pleaded, her sobs so great that every word came out in broken syllables.

"Please, make her well. I promise to never do anything to hurt her again. I'm sorry for what I done, for breaking Maggie's banjo and throwing it in the creek. I didn't mean for her to get hurt, honest I didn't." A rainstorm of tears washed her face as her prayer continued in fractured words between sniffles and sobs.

"I'm sorry for being jealous because you gave Maggie so much talent. But I won't be jealous no more and I won't mind if Momma and Deddy like her more than me, I promise. Just make her well. Please?"

Callie gently placed her arms over Maggie's legs, careful not to touch the cut, then laid her head against the side of the bed and cried, "I'm sorry, Maggie, for making you get hurt and for breaking your banjo. I am so sorry, please forgive me."

The appreciative parents looked at each other and smiled as they made their way quietly down the stairs.

"I guess that explains everything," Bud said. "Callie really does think we love Maggie more than her." He remembered clearly his promise to Maggie for a new banjo and snuffing off Callie's request for a new electric sewing machine.

Ellie added, "And we're always praising Maggie about her music, too."

Bud shook his head and sighed, "Yeah, I reckon that's true and all, but still, that's no excuse for what she's done."

"I know, but maybe this has taught her a lesson, at least it appears it has." Ellie gave her husband a little shove. "You get some rest, I'll check on Maggie later. Now go!"

The rocking chair creaked like a soft familiar lullaby as Ellie sat and prayed, giving thanks for sparing Maggie's life and for Callie's change of heart toward her sister. A whisper joined the creaking rocking chair, as she said, "You do work in mysterious ways, don't you, Lord?"

Even though a lot had happened over the past few hours to cause her grief and unimaginable pain, she nodded off to a peaceful sleep with the comforting knowledge that her family was still together.

Upstairs Callie crawled into bed beside her sister and stared into her face by the dim light of the lamp that had been tamped down to its lowest flame. Her eyelids soon grew heavy and she slept.

Ellie woke with a start and shot out of the chair, leaving the rocker to rock on its own as if a ghost had taken over the job. She remembered the doctor's words to watch for a fever and hoped she hadn't slept too long. Taking the stairs two at a time she arrived at the room to find a wet cloth draped across Maggie's forehead and Callie lying beside her, asleep. Removing the cloth she felt for a fever and found none. Wetting it again with cool water from the pan, she folded and placed it back across Maggie's forehead.

She reached out and touched Callie's hair, then went back downstairs to the now still rocking chair. The creaking of the rockers soon lulled her again into a land of peaceful dreams.

Chapter 19
A Scarecrow and Apple Pie

Bud and Corbit clattered up the porch steps and filled two wash pans, lathered up their arms and face, then rinsed. Bud stretched and yawned. "Now that we've got the milking and feeding done, I'm ready for a biscuit and a cup of Maxwell House." The fragrance of baking bread and perking coffee waffled through the screen door.

"Yeah, me too, well, the biscuit anyway." Corbit let the screen door bang shut behind him as he asked his mother, "Has Maggie woke yet?"

"Still sleeping when I looked in on her about fifteen minutes ago," Ellie said.

"Callie?" Bud asked.

"She's still in bed with Maggie, sound asleep."

"Callie in bed with Maggie?" Corbit couldn't believe it. "I'll be John Brown if that ain't something."

Ellie warned, "Don't say nothing to her about it, you hear me? Not one word!"

Bud took a sip of Maxwell House and leaned back in his chair. "Good coffee. I checked on her before we went to the barn. No fever, at least in no wise a high one. She felt just a tad warm, though."

Corbit poured cane syrup over a buttered biscuit with a few drops running down the neck of the bottle as he turned it up and replaced the cork stopper. He swiped it with his finger and licked it. "Want me to cut a switch for Callie?"

"Let me worry about that," Bud said. "You pull a stunt like you did the other day off playing marbles and whatnot, and you'll be cutting one for yourself — which reminds me. Did you say that Branch boy's name is Minner?"

"Why, heck no," Corbit said, wiping his mouth with the back of his hand. "His name's Thorny. Minner's what Maggie calls him. She thinks he's a ghost on account of Minner Jenkins getting snake bit when he fell in the creek. I heard you and Mr. Ford talking about it one day, and I told the story to Fred and everybody while down at the creek swimming."

"I guess that explains it." Bud pushed the chair back and stood. "I'm going for a walk down by the creek and I'll check the trot lines while I'm there. Be back in a bit."

☙❧

The Brush whispered good morning as Bud emerged from the cedar, the peaceful swirling and lapping of the water belying its treachery from the night before. He sat on a rock near the bank for a moment watching daybreak over the treetops, their outlines glowing like haloes. He observed the peaceful opulence as the crimson sky transformed to a soft yellow, and then to a bright white. The mixed scent of cedar and pine needles made him feel alive and exuberant. He bowed his head and gave thanks in a way he had not done for a long time.

The new sun crowded its way through narrow passages of branches clothed with verdant leaves and pine needles, displacing morning shadows with each shooting ray. Bud's spirits were high despite the drought. Maggie had been hurt, but lived, and she would recover without any permanent damage. Nothing, he thought, could be more important than that.

He stood and stretched, felt the warm rays penetrate his tired body. Walking along the worn path parallel to the creek, he found himself standing next to the island of rocks where, according to Maggie's description, she had fallen. He stared at the rocks and imagined Maggie slipping, battering her body on its inflexible surface, then falling into the water, its current dragging her away. He shook his head dismissing the horrible image.

Then he saw it. Beyond the rock just up the trail the steel of a gun barrel ricocheting light. A 30-aught-6 Springfield leaned against a tree. He walked over and picked it up. The barrel's bluing, mostly gone, had allowed pits of rust to form. The stock, scarred and cracked down the middle, had the initials *TB* carved into it.

"Thorny Branch," Bud said under his breath. He thought of Lucas Ward, who, according to the county coroner, had been killed by a 30-aught-6 bullet. Tucking the stock under his arm he turned and retraced the trail, forgetting all about the trot lines.

Scattered puffs of clouds like tiny islands hung in the sea-blue sky. Fourth of July fireworks had passed and still the heavens had not granted rain. The land about Brush Creek remained parched, that is, except for those fortunate to have a spring to dam or mechanical irrigation. Corbit's creative thinking had turned their arid land into an oasis. The corn, adorned with crowns of golden tassel had produced ears full and plentiful. Peas and beans were putting forth fruit and watermelons were growing fat on meandering vines.

A quick movement caught Bud's eye. He stopped, looked around, but saw nothing. Starting his ascent again, he felt as if piercing eyes were boring into him. A curious bobcat, he thought. But somehow he knew better.

He saw it again; a flicker of movement hardly discernible.

He stood still and listened. "Who's there?"

A twig snapped.

"Is that you, Thorny?" Bud asked, playing on a hunch. Nothing.

Bud tried, "I want to thank you for saving Maggie. That's a wonderful thing you did, son."

"I need my rifle back," a strong voice acknowledged from behind a tree.

"Sure thing," Bud said. "Come on out, Thorny. It's all right."

"Just lay it down and I'll fetch it."

"I'd like to thank you face to face," Bud insisted. "You don't have anything to be afraid of, not of me, or anybody in my family. We all admire what you did."

"Ain't nec'ssary. Just pulled her from the crick, that's all."

Bud leaned the battered gun against a tree. "You need anything, anything at all, just get word to me and I'll do everything humanly possible to help. You understand?"

"Don't need nothin'."

"Well, in case you do, you know where I live." Bud walked away.

Thorny watched as the tall man disappeared around a bend into the grove of cedar.

The boy crossed the trail, bent over in stealth mode, eyes straight ahead fixed on the rifle like a cat stalking its prey. He grabbed the Springfield and fled like an escaping prisoner.

"My God in heaven!" Bud whispered. "What in the name of Cooter Brown happened to that boy?"

Once Bud had stepped out of sight into the copse of trees, he had hidden behind a thick cedar so he could see the mysterious person behind the big voice. What he saw shocked him. Thorny's threadbare overalls hung loose on his frail body making him look like a scarecrow with half the straw missing.

Then he thought of the missing food and whispered, "I'll be John Brown if that ain't where the missing food's going, or I hope it is." He made a mental note to have Ellie prepare a little extra for supper. The extra food had been left out since the first time they had disappeared. Bowls and plates were always brought back empty and clean. He had also noticed some pea and beanvines picked clean and ears of corn missing from time to time.

⮞⬥⬤

Maggie awakened and let out a groan. Callie's eyes popped open. "You okay? How do you feel?" A wave of guilt rushed over her. Suddenly she felt strange, out of place lying in Maggie's bed asking her such casual questions as if she had stumped her toe on the door jam.

Maggie stared at her and without saying a word turned her head to glare at the opposite wall. Her leg and arm hurt and her body ached all over. That's not what really hurt. What caused the most pain had been broken beyond repair. Tears slipped from her eyelashes onto the pillow forming a wet spot.

Callie stumbled for words, searching her brain for the right thing to say. The words *I'm sorry* seemed so trite, casual, so unremorseful, like a sinner asking for forgiveness before truly repenting. "Maggie, I…"

"My banjer." The bed shook as her body jerked with every sob. Without looking at Callie she asked, "Why did you do it, Callie? Why did you have to take it away from me?" The bed continued to shake, her body shuddered as if it were about to come apart. "I wish I'd drownt, then you'd be rid of me, and you'd be happy."

Callie rolled off the bed, ran to the other side and dropped to her knees. Her heart felt as if someone had taken a knife and split it in two. Sheets of tears covered her cheeks like rain sliding down a treeless mountain. "Oh, Maggie," she wailed. "Please don't hate me. I'm sorry I did what I did. I didn't mean for you to get hurt and I'm sorry for being selfish and for busting your banjo and everything."

"No, you ain't! You hate me and you're glad my banjer's gone." Maggie tried to rise up. "Ouch," she cried, falling back onto the pillow. She grabbed her arm. "It hurts so bad." She faced Callie. "It's all your fault I ain't got nothin' no more. I wish I'd drownt!"

Callie could not stand anymore. She ran from the room and down the stairs, her heart heavy with remorse. Without stopping she shoved the screen door with the palm of her hand slamming it against the outside wall. Bounding down the porch steps she ran to the barn, climbed to the loft and fell in the scattered hay. There, she wept and contemplated what she had done.

Kate, still in her stall, kicked and brayed, showing no sympathy for the distraught girl. "Maggie hates me even more than that stupid mule does," Callie muttered, and wept some more.

After a few minutes Kate greeted a tall mustachioed man with a nicker as he entered the barn. Bud could hear sobs coming from the loft as he climbed the ladder. He kneeled beside his daughter and gently placed his hand on her shoulder. "Callie, Maggie's gonna be all right."

"Oh, Deddy," she cried. "I'm sorry for what I did to Maggie. I didn't mean for her to get hurt, honest I didn't." Burying her head in his chest, the floodgates opened wide.

"Now, now, don't cry, I know you didn't mean to hurt your sister. But what's important is that she's going to be okay."

"But she hates me, Deddy. She can't stand the sight of me."

"Now, that ain't no ways true. She's upset, but she'll get over it in time. You'll see. Just be patient. You know the old saying, 'time heals all things.'"

Callie looked up at her father. "I know she'll get well from the broken arm and cuts, and all. That ain't what hurts her the most, it's not having her banjo to play. That's how I hurt her the most — and the fact that she thinks I hate her." She buried her head and sobbed, "Oh, Deddy, what can I do to make it up to her?"

"I think you can make things right by being kinder and more patient. I don't think you realize how much Maggie looks up to you. Why, she idolizes you. She's always wanted to be just like you."

Callie gazed up at her father with a stunned look on her tear-stained face. "Just like me? Really?"

"Uh huh. She thinks you cause the sun and moon to rise." Bud tapped her nose with his finger. "She brags about your sewing to everybody who'll listen."

"Really? My stars! She does that?"

"Uh huh, she sure does. She looks up to you, and Corbit, too."

Callie smiled and wiped her tears, and then said again with a little more emphisis, "*Well my stars*! I'll do better. I promise."

"I know you will. Just remember, Punkinhead, we all make mistakes, but the important thing is what we learn from those mistakes. Doing our best not to muddle it up and do it again is the important thing." He lifted her chin and kissed her forehead. "You just give Maggie time, she'll come around."

"Okay. Deddy, can I ask you something?"

"Shoot."

"Do you think you and Momma could ever like me as much as you do Maggie?"

"What? What makes you think —?"

"Because she plays the banjo so good and everything, and all I know how to do is sew old dresses and piller cases and stuff."

Bud's forehead creased with wrinkles. "Is that what you think, that we love Maggie more than you because she plays the banjo?" He remembered her prayer from Maggie's bedside and grimaced.

"That's what I always thought, but I don't mind anymore. It's okay if you do."

"Callie, look at me," he said gently. "Whether you can play a banjo or sew, or can't do nothing at all makes no difference to me and your momma. We love all three of you just the same. You all have talents and you're all special in your own way. And it's true what Maggie says, there really ain't nobody in Brush Creek can sew like you can. Every woman around here wishes they could turn a needle like you, and everybody says so all the time, too. So you have your talent, just like Corbit's good at fixing and figuring out things and Maggie at playing the banjo … and maybe being a little dramatic at times."

Callie cocked her head. "You mean Corbit being smart is a talent?"

"Why, sure it is. He can figure things out and fix most anything he puts his mind to."

"Yeah, he even fixed your pocket watch when it stopped working."

"That he did." Bud made the point a little more poignant. "And don't forget his idea about building the dam that saved our crops. That's a special talent called reasoning."

Callie's face lit up. "That's right, he did. I guess Corbit does have a natural way of thinking things out." She thought of Thorny. "And of course Thorny's talent is being the best marble player in the world."

"Yep, like Thorny being the best marble player in the world." Bud recalled the scarecrow boy and wondered what he could do to repay him for saving Maggie.

Callie said, "The way you and Momma, and even Corbit, always carries on when Maggie playes a song or wins a game at Family Funnies, well, you know, I just thought she was your and Momma's, and even Corbit's favorite."

"I can see how that looks and all, but like I said, that ain't the way it is. I guess Maggie being the baby sort of made us kowtow to her more."

"And when you promised her a new banjo and told me I couldn't have a new sewing machine, I just naturally thought you liked Maggie more, and that her wanting a new banjo was more important than me having a new sewing machine."

"I guess I did sort of brush off the sewing machine. But don't forget, we don't have 'lectricity, so I guess that's another reason I said what I did. Anyhow, your Momma and me do fuss over Maggie a lot, don't we? We didn't realize we were doing that, and for that I'm really sorry. Maybe it's because she does need a little extra help now and again... with, well, about everything, I guess."

Callie laughed. "Except the banjo, that is. She really is good at that." Her laugh turned to a frown when she remembered Maggie no longer had a banjo because of her. "I'll find some way of getting Maggie a new banjo. Not *just* a banjo, but that Gibson she wants. Wait and see if I don't."

Bud looked at his daughter and smiled. "You know, I believe you will at that."

"And I'll get it before summer is out, too!"

"No doubt you will, Callie. No doubt about it." Bud pushed his arms straight out, putting Callie in direct eye contact. "You know, Callie, everybody makes mistakes, and I am proud of you for owning up to yours. Your momma and I have made our share of mistakes, and that's a fact."

"Wow, Deddy, I didn't think you or Momma ever made mistakes — ever!"

"All the time, and we'll make more, now and again, but we'll try and do better, too. Okay?"

Bud squeezed his daughter and said, "A bushel and a peck and a hug around the neck."

Callie's smile brightened. Kate brayed and kicked the stall.

❧

The big rock overlooking the valley below became Thorny and Willow's special place where they could talk, encourage each other, and enjoy a moment of peace.

"I reckon Maggie didn't drown last night," Thorny said casually.

Willow looked at her brother with a profound look of respect. "No she didn't thanks to you. Mr. Kinser came by a while ago and told me and Momma what happened. Says you're a hero."

"I ani't a hero, just happened to be there, that's all. Anyhow, pulled her out of the crick yesterday evening a little past dusk dark. She would've drownt. I guess."

"What happened anyway? Mr. Kinser didn't say why Maggie was in the crick that late in the evening or how you happened to see her."

"Callie tried to drown her."

Willow's mouth dropped open. "She ain't done it!"

"Uh huh, but I don't think she meant to. I heard Callie yell at her and a minute later Maggie's banjo come a-floatin' by like a dead fish, all broke up. I'm s'posin' she jumped in after it." Thorny explained everything including his encounter with Bud Kinser the next morning.

"I'll be a Rusty Hen," Willow breathed. "Is she all right?"

"I reckon. Her deddy says so anyhow … and you ain't ugly, or a hen."

Willow looked skeptical, "*You* talked to her deddy? And I am too a Rusty Hen, at least ugly on the inside. Besides, you're a mellow man, you know, handsome, and a hero to boot."

"Yeah, right! Just look at me. I look like one of them Jew refugees Hitler like to of starved to death."

"You don't neither. You're handsome, a real mellow man, and I mean *man*, too. You ain't never been a boy."

Thorny blushed and then explained his early morning encounter with Bud at the creek. "Mr. Kinser said he was grateful. Nobody's ever said that to me b'fore. It kind of felt good."

"You should feel good, and I'm grateful all the time for what you do for me." Willow stood and looked out over the valley below. "I'm going down and see Maggie, make sure she's okay."

"If the old man finds out he'll beat us both, and Momma too, for lettin' you."

"He won't find out. I'll go right down and right back. 'Sides he's with his girlfriend, you know, Miss Sally Still. Ain't nothin' else on his mind but that."

Thorny laughed. "Yeah, I reckon."

"Want to come with me?"

"Goin' fishin' soon as I dig some wigglers. Might even play a game of dropsies or tag with Corbit and Fred, if they're at the crick, that is."

"You're gonna play marbles with Corbit and Fred... again?" Willow couldn't believe what she had heard from her standoffish brother.

"Yep, already did once... I guess you already know that. Anyhow, beat the tar out of 'em. The only marbles they had left were their shooters." Thorny stood, stuck both thumbs behind the bib of his overalls and said with pride. "Yep, beat 'em good. Showed those old boys how real marble playing is done. Anyhow, no matter, you'd better scoot down and scoot right back. No tellin' when that no-good devil might show up."

Willow started to leave, and then asked. "How did you know Maggie played the banjo?"

"I'd see her down at the crick practicing. I've never seen anybody work so hard at being good at something as she has. I'd find a place down crick, put my worm in the water, and just listen. Sometimes I'd stand behind a tree across the crick from her and watch."

Willow made her way down the hill around rocks and trees and through the sparse brush growing along the worn trail. As she approached the bottom, the aroma of fertile fields stuffed her nostrils. A gentle, warm breeze swayed the cornstalks just enough for the leaves to make a swishing sound as they rubbed against each other. A peaceful feeling settled over her.

She made her way through the cornfield to the last row and stepped out into the open.

A car door slammed.

Willow scampered back behind the tall stalks and hunkered down. Raising her head to peek out, she observed Mr. Kinser pull out of the yard and point the car down the long drive, leaving behind bellows of smoke and dust. It mingled together to form a dirty gray cloud that lingered long after the car had turned onto the main road to Athens.

A hand reached out and touched Willow's arm. She jumped and threw a hand over her heart. "Shoot fire, Corbit!"

"Hey, Willow. What're you doing out here in the cornfield?"

"For heaven's sake," Willow shrieked. "You like to of caused me to jump out of my skin."

"Sorry. I was hoeing weeds when I saw you. Didn't mean to skeer you though."

"Well, you did all right. But that's okay. You didn't skeer me much."

Corbit snickered, "Then why're you shaking so hard?"

Willow took a deep breath to try and calm down. "Oh, umm, I'm just worried about Maggie, that's all. Is she okay? I heard about what happened."

"Broke her arm and got some cuts and bruises, but

she'll be all right in a week or two, or maybe more. She didn't drown like we thought she had. Thorny saved her life, you know."

"I know, and I'm glad she didn't drown. Would your momma mind if I went in to see her?"

"Why, heck no, she won't mind one bit. Just go on up to the house and holler at the door."

Willow started to hug him, but backed off. Corbit's boyish face had suddenly become the evil face of Moss Branch. She backed away. "I'll just knock. See ya."

Corbit didn't know what to think. "Lordy, what'd I do?"

Ellie came to the door wiping her hands on her apron. She smiled and said, "Willow, what a nice surprise. It's so good to see you, young lady. Come on in, make yourself at home."

"Thank you, Miz Kinser. I heard that Maggie got hurt and almost drownt in the crick, so I come by to check on her."

"Glad you did. I'm sure she'll be thrilled to see you. I guess you heard your brother's the one that saved her."

"Yessum."

"You be sure to tell him how much we appreciate what he did. We'll never forget it."

"Yessum."

"She's upstairs. Come on, I'll take you up. And what a beautiful sundress you have on. It makes your eyes so green, and that perfume smells so good on you."

Willow lowered her head. "Yessum."

Each step squeaked and groaned under their weight. Willow's eyes scanned the walls decorated with family photographs. Everyone smiled as they posed, whether separate or together as a family. She noticed they had a certain look about them... happy and content.

She noticed, too, everything had a different look, a

different feel. The whole atmosphere felt unlike anything she had ever known. She took in the furniture and the old grandfather clock standing in the corner of the living room. Everything seemed clean, even the air smelled fresh as if it had blown down from the mountains.

Willow knew why. Yet it felt so strange, but wonderful. She knew love lived here; a love open and sacred. She knew her mother loved her, and she knew Olive and Thorny loved her, too, but somehow this seemed different.

Her imagination ferried her away to a dream world where she was a Kinser daughter playing Family Funnies with her brothers and sisters, eating cookies and drinking milk. She could hear the laughter in her head, the way it had been when she had peeped through the window and watched as Mr. and Mrs. Kinser did the Hucklebuck while Maggie picked the banjo. In her daydream Willow had joined Callie and Corbit, her brother and sister, clapping with the beat. Her heart ached for that, just a little of it, just a taste.

"Maggie, honey, guess who's here to see you?" Ellie said softly.

Pulled from her daydream back to reality, Willow said in a soft, almost apologetic voice, "Hi, Maggie, I hope I ain't bothering you or anything."

Maggie perked up and smiled. "Hey, Willow, I can't play the banjer with you when you get a harp. Callie broke it and throwed it in the creek." She tried to rise, but quickly gave up when pain flashed through her broken arm. "I'm too sore to sit up. I reckon you'll have to sit on the side of the bed."

"I'll leave you two alone to visit while I tend to my chores in the kitchen," Ellie said with a smile. "Stay as long as you will."

"Thank you, Miz Kinser," Willow answered as she sat beside Maggie on the soft feather mattress.

"Callie hates me, you know. She wanted me to drown so I wouldn't be a bother to her anymore."

Willow shifted on the bed. "I don't think she really meant to hurt you."

"She poured dirty dishwater on me, too."

"Oh, Maggie, I don't think she means to be unkind or anything. I bet she's sorrowful for what she done and all."

"No, she ain't! She says she is, but she ain't. She hates me, and I hate her!"

Willow sighed and whispered, "If you only knew…"

"Knew what?"

"How lucky you are — all of you are — you, Callie and Corbit. Why, you got everything a body could want."

"I ain't got a banjer."

"But you got everything else, and I ain't got nothin', not even a harp."

"Your deddy must be mean not to buy you a harp, but you got purty dresses, though. I ain't got no purty dresses like you wear all the time. Mine are just plain ol' flour and sugar sack dresses. I used to like them, but now I don't no more because Callie sewed them. But I like your princess dresses."

"You can have them all, Maggie. I *hate* them!" Willow looked down at the light yellow sundress. "This one, too. You can have them all far as I care!"

Maggie stared at her and said, "Well, why do you wear them if you hate them so much?"

Willow's voiced oozed with venom. "Because my ol' deddy makes me, that's why!"

Maggie couldn't understand. "But he must be a good deddy to buy you all those purty dresses."

"No, he ain't!" She stopped. Realizing how she must sound, she changed the subject. "Why, just look at you. You got a cast on your arm and everything. Can I spell my name on it?"

Maggie's smile filled her face. "Really? Well, okay then. You can spell it right by where Corbit spelled his."

"I'll get the pen and ink."

Willow jumped.

Ellie had been waiting outside the bedroom door when the conversation about Moss and the dresses came up. Curious at the odd things Willow was saying, and how she was saying them, she purposely waited outside the door hoping to hear more.

"Oh, Miz. Kinser, I didn't see you standing there."

Not sure what Ellie had heard, Willow looked down at the plank floor. "That's okay, ma'am. I guess I'd better be getting back."

Ellie insisted, "You have to write on Maggie's cast before you leave." The fragrance of apple pie wafted throughout the house. "Besides, I've something for you and it's still in the oven. Just hold still and I'll get the pen and ink. Be right back."

Feeling awkward, Willow looked down at her dress, clamped her hands together and said, "I'm sorry, Maggie, I shouldn't have talked thataways."

"I don't know why you don't like your deddy. I ain't never heard of nobody not liking their deddy before, especially when he buys purty dresses and all."

Again, Willow drifted away trying to imagine what it would be like to feel the way Maggie did, to know only the good in a father. She noticed the open closet, glimpsed the plain dresses arranged on wire clothes hangers from a bowed gray pole. She longed to wear cloths like that, something plain and simple, something made with love. She considered her princess dresses to be ugly, nothing but rags, and she yearned to be rid of them.

Maggie went on. "My deddy don't buy us fancy clothes like that. But I don't mind, because he does other things even better. He tells jokes and makes us laugh at Family

Funnies. Does your deddy tell jokes and make you laugh the way my deddy does?"

Every event, every description from Maggie became a wish—a dream conjured up in the mind of a girl with "pretty" dresses, dresses she hated.

"Deddy and Momma dances the Hucklebuck and does silly things at Family Funnies. Does your momma and deddy do that when you have Family Funnies at your house?"

As if in a trance Willow recalled the warm feeling she had while watching the Kinser family laugh and play games that night through the window. She recalled Bud and Ellie dancing and the way Callie, Corbit reacted to the risqué moves — a little surprised, but not embarrassed. Most of all she noticed the love and respect in their eyes and the glow of happiness on their faces. She wondered again why Callie thought her life to be terrible, and Maggie somehow responsible.

Then Willow thought about the feelings she had about her own life that night — the loneliness, the deep empty hole where her heart should be. Oh, how she had craved that kind of peace and security. But she had known, too, deep down, that it could not be.

And then the shame and horror of what had taken place after she had returned home flooded back. Darkness shrouded her mind. She felt the degradation again… and again… and again, for it never ended. *Even the maggots in the outhouse have a better life*, she thought. *At least they have a purpose.*

Maggie tapped Willow's arm. "You all right?"

Willow jumped again.

"You sure like to jump a lot," Maggie said.

"Uh, sorry."

"Here you are." Willow jumped again. "Oh my, I didn't mean to skeer you," Ellie said in her comforting, sing-song voice. "Write or draw whatever you're of a mind to."

Willow avoided looking into either her or Maggie's eyes. The visions in her head were so real, like a play before a live audience. It felt as though Ellie and Maggie had actually witnessed the shameful act as it had played out in her mind.

Maggie pointed to the spot and said, "Write something special. Okay?"

"Uh, sure, okay." She took the pen and dipped it into the inkwell and after a few seconds of thought wrote: *I hope yur arm mens real fast and it don't hurt much. You sure are lucky your daddy didn't brake it. Yur friend Willow Branch.*

"Oh, Willow, read to me what you wrote," Maggie pleaded. "I can't see it real good." Willow cleared her throat and read with a halting cadence everything she had written. Almost. When she got to the part about Maggie being lucky she had a daddy that didn't break her arm, she stopped and drew a line through it. She hadn't realized that she had written it that way. The thin line, however, didn't hide what she had written. Ellie leaned forward to get a better look. She furrowed her brow.

"I have to go now," Willow said meekly while backing toward the door. "Bye, hope you feel better, and I'm glad you didn't get drownt."

"Bye, Willow," Maggie said in the most pathetic voice she could muster. "I'm glad you came and all, and for writing on my cast." She added with sincerity, "I'm awful sorry I didn't have a banjer so I could play you a tune."

"We're so glad you came and — oh, I almost forgot. Come with me, I have something for you to take home."

Willow followed her down the stairs and into the kitchen. Grabbing two pot holders Ellie gently picked up a hot apple pie and placed it in an empty box. She handed it to the wide-eyed girl. "Here you go. I hope your family enjoys it. It should still be warm when you get home."

Willow looked from the pie and back to Ellie. "Oh, thank you, Miz Kinser. It looks so good. Olive, that's my baby sister, will be so happy. She — ah, we, don't get a lot of pies and such, because my deddy...," she stopped. Ellie furrowed her brow again.

"Is everything all right?" Ellie spoke quietly while reaching out and gently touching a slight blue spot on Willow's left cheekbone. The girl flinched. Then, Ellie noticed remnants of bruises on her arms and legs. "What happened, Willow? How did you —"

"It… it's nothing," Willow stammered while talking to her feet. "I — I just fell on some rocks last week and got bruised up a little bit, that's all. But I'm okay now. Thank you for the pie, Miz Kinser. I'll be sure to bring your pan back." The spring made little screechy sounds as she pushed the screen door open with her shoulder and squeezed through the small opening, while holding the box securely with both hands.

"Callie's in the barn cleaning Kate's stall if you want to see her before you leave."

"I'd better get back. Tell her I said hello."

Willow walked past the corn crib and smokehouse. She pulled the box up to her nose and took a deep whiff of apples and cinnamon. She stepped to the edge of the cornfield. Washboard ripples left behind by spring water running through the rows were still moist, a sign of Corbit's recent work. The stalks stood straight and green, and ears of corn poked out from underneath full leaves, with silver silk hanging from the tips. Willow leaned into an ear touching the silk with her nose, and with eyes closed inhaled deeply its earthy scent.

Willow thought of how sweet life was for Callie, Maggie, and Corbit and thought of their little problems as nothing more than love taps. Sadness enveloped her like a cocoon, only she would not wake up to be a beautiful butterfly fluttering from one place to another with no care or worry while spreading whimsical happiness to everyone that happened to see her. She would remain in her cocoon a prisoner without the possibility of parole.

I'm only a worm living in dirt. A mockingbird sat on a fence post fussing at the cows in the pasture. *Or maybe I'm just an old ugly buzzard living off of dead things.* Instead of walking through the corn, she chose to go around the edge of the field, following the watermarks where irrigation had flowed outside its boundaries. She weaved in and out leaving dainty footprints behind.

After leaving the cornfield behind Willow followed the slightly worn trail through the grass leading to the base of Fox Hill. Looking up she could see the outcrop of rock where she and Thorny had sat earlier that day discussing their lives. She had hoped to see Thorny, but he had already left.

The trail, lined with wildflowers on both sides, disappeared into a thicket of cedar, the warm sun causing its fragrance to permeate the still air.

"Where've you been, gal!"

Willows jumped and almost dropped the box.

Moss stepped in front of her blocking the path. Fear clouded her eyes. "I — I just went to check on Maggie, she—"

"Shat up!" His meaty arm crossed his chest, hand positioned for a back-hand slap. Willow cowed. "I know whare you been." He reached out and snatched the box from the frightened girl's hands. He took the pie from the box and said, "Well, lookie here," and then threw the box to the ground. He fished out his Barlow from a ripped pocket and sat down on a rock.

"Mighty nice of Miz Kinser to bake me a pie. I'll have to thank her personal." He cut a ragged wedge and wiped the blade on the leg of his overalls. He spat out his wad of tobacco. Scooping the pie wedge out of the pan with his dirty hand he shoved it into his mouth. Pie filling squeezed out of the corners of his mouth. He smacked his lips like a pig swigging swill from a trough. "Mighty good. Yessir, shore is mighty good." He grinned and said to his daughter. "You like apple pie?"

Willow nodded.

"That's good." Moss stood, scooped out a handful and placed the pan on the rock. Willow trembled as he approached. "Well then, have some." He jerked her head up, dug his fingers and thumb into her cheek and forced her mouth open. "Here, take a bite." He shoved it into her mouth. Warm pie smashed onto her face and pushed up her nostrils.

Willow gagged.

"Good, ain't it?" He grabbed her arm and dragged her over to the rock, scooped up another handful and shoved it into her face. "Shame to let such a good pie go to waste." He grinned, turned the pan over and watched as the remaining pie fell to the ground and splattered. He drew his hand back, pie dripping from his meaty fingers. He slapped her. She landed with a thud on the hard ground.

"What did I tell you about messin' 'round with those people, tellin' them about my bidness." She laid face up, pie covering her face, an apple slice clinging from her ruffled bangs.

Moss stood over her and unbuckled his worn overalls, a heinous grin spread across his unshaven face. "I got sompin' here better than pie." The dirty overalls fell, pilling up around his ankles. "Well, here it is, jest the way you like it."

Chapter 20
Arrowheads Along the Brush

Callie stayed in a state of gloom. The vision of Maggie floating face down was an image she could not get out of her head. The broken banjo haunted her, too. The mental image of the anguish on Maggie's face, the pitiful mewling, and her flailing arms as she tried to retrieve it from the creek, the current taking both away. Even in broad daylight the nightmare continued, a movie run over and over in her mind's eye. And even worse, Maggie hated her for destroying the thing she loved most. Callie now realized the banjo defined her, set her apart as a person. *She was willing to give her life for that banjo, and I destroyed it.*

"Aw, come on, Callie, come and go with us," Tommie Sue pleaded.

"Yeah, come with us," said Fred, his ever-present straw twitching. "You might find a nice arrowhead along the creek."

Corbit added his two cents worth of encouragement, "Quit being an ol' Gloomy Gus and come on. We won't get this chance again until the next drought. The best time to find arrowheads is when the water gets low."

With a little more cajoling they finally talked her into it, but dragged behind everyone else dreading to see the place where Maggie almost drowned. Brush Creek had become a monster, grotesque and menacing, waiting to pounce on the evil sister, to throw troves of unpleasant memories in her face.

"Hey, Callie, is this the place you like to of drownt Maggie the other night?" Fred asked pointing downstream. Everyone turned to stare, Callie bowed her head. Her arms hung limp by her side.

Fred kept on. "Where did you throw her banjo in at? Was thet the rock she fell off of down yonder and broke her arm?"

Callie didn't say a word, only staredat her feet, the chasm in her heart growing wider.

"Shut up, Fred!" Tommie Sue scolded. "Can't you see she feels bad about what happened? Ain't you got any sense at all between those big mule ears of yourn?"

Fred stuck his hands in his pockets. "Well, golly, Tommie Sue, I only asked."

Tommie Sue put her arm around Callie. "It's all right, we know you didn't mean to hurt Maggie, honest we do. And Maggie's gonna be all right in a week or two. Why, she'll be playing 'Comical Coons' on that ol' banjo in no time."

Callie flinched.

"Shut up, Tommie Sue! Ain't you got any brains between those big mule ears of yourn?" Fred said, grinning.

"Sorry, Callie, I forgot."

"Found one!" Corbit bent to pick up an arrowhead lying in plain sight.

"Nice one," Fred said. "Let me see it."

"I think it's a spear tip, though." Corbit explained, "See how big it is? Arrowheads are smaller."

Tommie Sue gushed, "You know everything, don'tcha, Corbit?"

The find piqued Callie's interest. The worst drought in ten years had dropped the water level lower than the four amateur archeologists had ever seen it. Digging in the damp earth they uncovered arrowheads fashioned by the Creek and Cherokee hundreds of years earlier.

"You know what? Indians always camped near water," Corbit instructed. "Just look anywhere near a creek, spring, or lake and you're bound to find an arrowhead or some kind of Indian stuff."

"You don't say!" Tommie Sue said, totally amazed. "How'd you know so much about arrowheads, Corbit?"

"Aw, everybody knows that," Fred said. "Why, me and Corbit's found pockets full of arrowheads around the spring running through their farm. Ain't we, Corbit?"

"Pockets full."

Finding arrowheads, spear tips, rock chisels, and other tools seemed almost a sure thing around any significant body of water in Tennessee. Even though the Brush had probably changed course many times over the ages, finding relics was a testament to its importance in the lives of the ancient as well as the more recent tribes that had camped along its banks.

"Gotta get back and do the milkin'," Fred announced. "Ol' Elsie's bag'll be so big she might drown before I get there."

Everyone stared at the red head. Except Callie, who again stood with her head bowed and shoulders hunched. The word "drown" had made the Gloomy Gus feeling return.

Tommie Sue scolded Fred for the second time. "Mercy, can't you shut that dad-blamed mouth of yourn? You're just a big ol' hunk of stupid!"

Fred shot back. "All I said was ol' Elsie might drown before — oh."

With pockets filled with arrowheads the four collectors headed for home, deciding to take the trail leading across the bottom of the ridge intersecting with the path leading to the Branch place.

The sun, capable of nearly melting a tin roof, bore down on the four friends. Something flashed as they rounded the curved trail.

"Look over yonder," Fred said pointing to a metal object reflecting sun rays.

Corbit bent to examine it. "Why, it's a pan of some sort."

"Why, it looks like Momma's pan," Callie said. She noticed pieces of crust and apple slices covered with ants. "I bet this is the pie, or what's left of it, Momma gave to Willow this morning."

"Sure enough," Corbit said. "Wonder why Momma's pie pan's up here on the ridge, and the pie scattered everywhere?"

"Maybe Willow et it," Fred reasoned.

"Et it?" Tommie Sue mocked, "The whole thing? She ain't done it!"

"Looks like most of it wound up in the dirt, anyway," Callie noted.

Corbit held the pan in his hand. Dried crust that hadn't been eaten by ants or pecked by birds still clung to the rim with remnants of dried apple slices stuck to the bottom. He shook the ants off. "Maybe Thorny helped her eat it."

"Thet's it. Betcha," Fred said. "Looks like they et too much and upchucked it."

"But it doesn't make sense, it being scattered about, and all. If Willow'd dropped it, it would've been all in one place," Corbit reasoned,

"And she would've taken the pan, too," said Tommie Sue.

Corbit agreed. "I think you're on the nose with it."

Fred held up a perfectly shaped arrowhead. "I'd of traded this for a bite of thet pie."

Corbit released the pan with a spin causing it to twirl high over his head. Reaching out he caught it. Dry crust broke off in small chunks and sprinkled his hair. A piece landed in his mouth. He spat. "Oh, poot! Yuck!" A lingering ant bit him on the finger. "Oowie! Double poot!"

Tommy Sue stomped her foot and leaned into his

face. "Dad-blame it, Corbit Kinser, don't start cussin' like a booger, or I'll tell your momma."

"Poot ain't cussin', Tommie Sue."

Tommie Sue turned to Callie. "Ain't it cussin'?"

Callie brightened up and smiled. "Yeah, Corbit, poot's a cuss word all right. Ain't that right, Fred? Don't you think poot's a cuss word?"

"Why, sure poot's a cuss word. Everybody knows poot's a cuss word." Fred looked at Corbit and grinned. "You'd better stop saying *poot* or you're gonna get your mouth worshed out with soap. We're gonna tell your momma, ain't we, Tommie Sue? We're gonna tell her right to her face how he said poot."

Corbit looked at the ground, stirred the dirt with his big toe and tried to look humble. "Dang-nabbit, Tommie Sue, I guess you're right. I suppose poot is a cuss word after all, so I won't say poot no more. Okay?"

She looked from one grinning face to the other not quite sure if they were teasing her or not. "Well, okay," she said. Fred snickered.

"Say, you're just funnin' me."

Corbit and Fred fell to the ground and rolled. Callie bent over, crossed her arms and held her ribs. Their laughter turned to muted clucks as their breath gave out.

"It ain't funny!" Tommie Sue leaned against a tree, crossed her arms and pooched her lips out. "Well, it ain't!"

Recovering, Callie wiped her eyes. "We're just having whoopee with you, Tommie Sue, ain't no need to snap your cap."

Corbit, still holding on to the pie pan, stood and pulled Fred to his feet. He turned serious again. "Better get on home, I guess."

"What we waitin' for?" Fred asked. "Come on let's go see if your momma's got another apple pie ready to eat." Fred trotted off.

"Hold on, you've got milking to do," Corbit called out. "No time for apple pie."

Fred rubbed his stomach. "Boy, would milk go good with apple pie."

Callie felt better after the light-hearted moment. She said seriously, "Maybe a bear got after her and Willow flung it and ran."

"Maybe, but I didn't see no bear tracks." Corbit spun the pan high in the air again, this time he missed, allowing it to hit the ground and bounce in short hops.

Fred caught it on the third hop. "No, but did you see those big ol' stomper prints all around here?"

Callie agreed. "Well, I'll be if there weren't, and a lot of them, too!" Immediately Moss popped to mind. Her forehead crinkled at the thought of the burly man, remembering how he looked, dirty and wicked, his gruff voice matching his looks. "I'm getting the heebie-jeebies. Let's go."

"Maybe she had to hurry because she had to poot." Corbit grabbed the pan from Fred and took off running.

"You'd better shut up, Corbit Kinser," Tommie Sue shouted, breaking into a run. Pockets jangled as they trotted the short distance to the Kinser house.

Arriving minutes later, the four bypassed the steps and leaped onto the porch sounding like stampeding cattle. The boys plopped down on the rough planks, backs resting against the wall while the girls fell into the swing, the chains groaning against their weight. Callie looked toward Fox Hill and could see an outline of the shack between the trees. She thought of Willow, and then Maggie. Sadness overwhelmed her again.

⌘

Callie's sorrow was little compared to the circumstances inside the crumbling hovel at the top of the hill. A pall of hopelessness shrouded every corner and crack. Unlike Longfellow's home, there was no laughing Allegra or merry eyes of two daughters plotting and planning together. No secret whispering plots to take their father by surprise in a plethora of merriment. And Henry's village smithy, a mighty man, a kindly man with brawny arms, bore no resemblance to Moss Branch who seemed to be more animal than man. He allowed no room for kindness from daughters, nor a son, nor a wife, whose golden hair had turned a dull gray long before its time. Willow lay on her bed in a comatose world not of her making, although she believed it was. For what purpose did she live and breathe, she wondered for the millionth time. Her mother, who had died inside years ago, had finally stopped asking that question when no miracle happened to relieve her suffering. Heaven's gate had seemingly slammed shut to her prayers and pleadings.

Thorny stood at the edge of the woods and watched Moss as he sat in his chair on the porch in a drunken stupor. He held his rifle in the cradle of his arm, his anger past the boiling point, his senses clogged with hatred for the cruel subhuman who sat slouched in his chair.

It would be so easy. Just one shot and we'd all be free, and Willow wouldn't hurt anymore. He thought of his mother, how she cowered and surrendered to his father's every demand. Her hollow eyes haunted him. His innocent little sister who had no right to feel and see the things she had at such a young age would soon be hurting as her big sister did now. "Bastard!" he spewed through clenched teeth.

Moss snorted and made unintelligible noises. His chin lay on his chest, a whiskey jug sat at his feet, empty. Thorny fumbled with the rifle, put the stock to his shoulder, took aim, and then brought it back down again. Murder was a hard thing.

"Olive'll be next sure as I don't do somethin'," he mumbled, and lifted the rifle's stock to his shoulder once again. He closed one eye and squinted with the other, drawing a bead on the cruel man's head. *Do it*, his mind screamed. *Do it! Do it! Do it!* He pulled the hammer back, his finger tightened on the trigger. *Squeeze it, get it over with.* His mind raced. He fought a bitter battle between good and evil, between right and wrong, between the surety of continued misery and the certainty of a better life for all.

He applied more pressure to the trigger. The bullet waited for the explosion that would propel it to its destination, sending a lost soul to the highest flames of hell.

The door flew open. Rose ran onto the porch, arms waving. She mouthed the words, "Stop! Don't do it!" Thorny's finger relaxed, the barrel pointed toward the ground in defeat. Moss grunted. His head rolled against his shoulder; his mouth opened exposing yellow teeth with tobacco stuck between them.

Rose walked up to her son. "No, son, don't let him make a killer out of you."

"He don't deserve to live. Look what he's done to Willow, what he's done to you. And you know what he'll do to Olive b'fore it's over with."

"The law'll put you in prison," Rose said softly.

"Ain't I in prison already?" Thorny looked deeply into his mother's eyes. "Hell, ain't we all in prison? How much worse can iron bars be than this?" He cradled the gun and disappeared into the woods.

❧

Bud finished his shift with the sheriff department, getting home just before dark. He herded the cows to the adjoining pasture where better grass waited.

"Like I said this morning, that boy's skeleton skinny. How those raggedy clothes stay on his body is a wonder in itself." Bud sat at the table with a glass of tea as he and Ellie talked about Thorny and Willow.

"I know the old man runs hooch whisky, got a still somewhere, or I suspect he does. So does the sheriff. Always has money to spend on the whores over at Harley's, from what I hear, anyhow."

Ellie put a finger on her lips. "Not so loud, the younguns might here you using that word."

"Probably nothing they ain't heard before. Anyway, from the talk I hear Branch always seems to have plenty of money and appears to eat good in the restaurants around town. From what people say he even cleans up and wears nice clothes like some darb from New York City. Of course I've never seen it myself and can't imagine him looking like anything but a mangy cur."

"All while his family does without," Ellie added. "And those bruises on Willow weren't caused by her falling down, either. You can't convince me that Branch isn't the one that put them there. He's out-and-out rotten. I knowed it the first time I laid eyes on him the night Lucas died. He's done it alright. You mark my word."

"My suspicion, too, and the sheriff's, but we can't prove it. When I went to the Branch place the other morning and Willow wouldn't come to the door, just stood back in the shadows, I felt something wasn't right then. And the mother, she's as skinny as Thorny, and bruises up, too. I ain't seen the baby, don't know what she looks like, but I can only imagine."

Ellie made a face. "She's probably starving, too, poor child."

Bud drained his glass. Ice jangled as he sat it down and refilled it with more sweet tea. "Funny thing, Willow's a little skinny, but not like Thorny and her momma, and she's always decked out in those fancy store-bought dresses. It's never made any sense to me. It's funny, though, how Branch always has money for himself and his needs, but nothing for his family, except for those fancy dresses he buys."

Ellie spoke up. "Speaking of those dresses, I heard Willow say to Maggie how she hates them, and that her deddy makes her wear them. Said she'd wear Maggie's dresses. And what about the strange thing she wrote on Maggie's cast? Something's bad business up there." Ellie reached for Bud's glass, took a sip of cold tea and touched the sweating glass to her cheek. "One thing's for sure, I'll be cooking more than usual. Thorny, or whoever it is taking the food, brings the dishes and pots back and always sets them on the shelf right below the water dipper. Clean, too."

"Providing it is Thorny, and I believe it is. Maybe we should put leftovers in syrup buckets. Make it more convenient for him to carry and you wouldn't have to worry about your bowls and such."

"Good idea, except they won't be leftovers, not really. Leftovers sound like something buzzards eat. I'll do it tonight."

"Don't say anything to the younguns about suspecting Branch to be Lucas' killer. I just wish we had hard proof, but all things point there."

Ellie's face turned red. "I suspected it was him all along. Sorry piece of trash! And I know I shouldn't say it, but that's what he is — trash! As much as I hate to admit it, Elvira's right. May God forgive me."

"No forgiveness necessary, Ellie. None at all."

"You ain't God."

"I ain't implying it. What I meant—"

"I know what you meant," Ellie said patting him on the arm. "Anyhow, he sure was quick to get Willow away from the church, and we've seen little of her since, and every time we do she looks bruised up, and she never looks happy. In fact I ain't never seen anybody as sad looking as that girl. Looks like she's gonna cry all the time, even when she's smiling."

"Yeah, and the boy's a mystery, too. Won't be seen in

public. Corbit and Fred seem to be the only two people around having any close dealings with him, except for Charlie Brewster, who buys all of his pelts, and the colored folk who buys the coons from him down in niggertown." Bud drained the glass of cold beverage again. "That hit the spot."

❧

Callie approached the bedroom she shared with Maggie. Anxiety weighed her down, as it did every time she entered. Her heart, heavy with remorse, seemed to scarcely beat as if bound by chains. Even the door intimidated her. Old Doc Morton could have nailed a sign on it that read, *Quarantined – scarlet fever*, and it could not have been more unapproachable. She had been dreading this all day, as she had every day since the accident, dreading Maggie's look of scorn and hurt, dreading seeing her turn away.

Callie's hand shook as she gripped the doorknob. She stood there holding on to it, building her courage to enter. Soft sobs filtered through the solid pine door like water seeping through cardboard. She shoved the door open, ran in, fell to her knees beside Maggie's bed and wailed, "I'm sorry I hurt you. Please don't hate me."

Maggie turned onto her left side, the white cast on her right arm lying against her side, a memorial to her suffering.

"Go away and leave me alone. You got what you wanted. You won't have to hear my banjer no more, but I guess you already know that."

Callie jumped up, ran to her bed, and buried her face in the soft down pillow. A quill poked through and stuck her on the cheek. She jerked back and looked at the feather sticking through the pillow case. She stared at it. A smile inched across her face. She looked over at Maggie and said, "I'm gonna get you that Gibson banjo."

Chapter 21
A Testament of Cruelty

Finally able to get out of bed, Maggie wandered about the house looking lost. She spent her days staring with longing eyes at the Montgomery Ward and Sears & Robuck catalogs at the one thing that would make her whole again. Everyone waited on her hand and foot, except Callie. She tried, though, but Maggie wouldn't have it. She wouldn't talk to her or even acknowledge her presents when she entered the room. Her eyes seemed to bore into Callie's soul. The guilt Callie felt grew like a volcano mountain on the verge of eruption.

The loss Maggie felt could not be put into words or even articulated in thought. The only expression she knew, she ever knew, came from her soul, deep within from a place only she could reach and understand. When she held a banjo in her hands it became a pump drawing feelings as if it were water deep down in the earth plunging to the surface with each pluck of a string. So she dreamed and longed, but knew she could not draw water from a dry well.

Bud and Callie gently rocked on the porch swing, the soft creaks accompanying each back and forth movement. A thought had been brewing in Callie's mind since the feather pricked her cheek. Her face lit up. "Deddy, can you take me to see Miz, Plank, Miz McCrackin, Miz Ward, and Miz

Vaughn, and maybe some other folks?"

"I guess so. How come?"

"I got an idea today," she said and whispered it in his ear so Maggie couldn't hear.

"Why, that's a good idea," Bud said, smiling from ear to ear. "We'll start out first thing in the morning." He pulled his daughter close and held her tight. "And I think I know those other folks we can see, too."

A waning moon crowned treetops with uneven halos and the countryside shimmered in a sedate glow. Tall cornstalks, leafy tobacco, and curled pea vines stood out like armies camping in the fields. The green of the watermelons glistened and the red hills soaked up the pastel beams as if bathing in them.

One place, seemingly the only place in Brush Creek not enjoying the contentment of a calm evening stood on the hill above the Kinser place. Inside the shack the stench of fear and loathing hung over the ceiling and clung to the walls. It lay over the floors and sparse furniture like a disease where all hope had rotted away and death awaited its curtain call.

"Who et the leftover stew!" No one uttered a syllable, or even moved. Moss glared with contempt at Rose. "I asked you a question, you stupid old woman. Who et the stew!"

"We — they were hungry." The kind gratuity from the Kinsers helped, but did nothing to alleviate hunger pains when Moss happened to be home lording over his imaginary kingdom. Rose could barely be heard as her voice quivered with fear in anticipation of what he would do.

"They was hungry? They... was... hung-ry?" His fist pounded the table. "I don't give a rat's ass if *they* was starvin' to death. *They* don't eat 'less I say so, an' you know it!" He reached across the table and backhanded Rose. She slammed against the wall, the print of his hand a red outline on her right cheek. She slumped to the floor.

"You leave her alone, you piece of shit!" Thorny threw himself into the big man's side, knocking him off balance. He rammed him again. Moss fell against the table grabbing a chair to break his fall. It skidded and turned sideways. He grasped for the edge of the table, too late. The chair flew out from under him sending him to the floor with a heavy thud. The force of the fall shook the house. Moss lay sprawled on his back, the chair landing beside him.

"You pig!" Thorny dove on top of the surprised man and landed a fist square on his mouth. Moss's lower lip split, blood oozed from the cut and trickled through his whiskers. He hit him again. "I'll kill you, you sum-bitch!" He pulled his arm back to strike him the third time.

Moss grabbed it with his left hand and swung with his right, landing a fist on Thorny's head just above his left ear. Thorny clattered against the toppled chair, landing halfway under the table. Moss kicked him on the shoulder, rolled over and pushed to his feet.

"Hit me, will ya!" Full of rage he dragged Thorny by the feet from underneath the table, gripped him by the straps of his overalls and pulled him off the floor. "I'll learn ya to lay a hand on me, boy!"

Moss struck a blow to Thorny's temple. He went limp. The raging bull hit him again, this time in the chest. He hit him again in the ribs, then let go. Unconscious, Thorny's body crumpled to the floor. He didn't move.

"Thorny!" Willow screamed. "You've kilt him!" She ran and fell to her knees. "Thorny! Oh, Thorny!"

Olive ran to her mother and cowered by her side. Moss glared at her and she buried her head in the folds of her mother's dress.

"He ain't dead, but he'll wish he was when he wakes up. He's lucky he ain't. Teach 'im to jump on me, the little bastard."

"You're the bastard!" Willow shouted as she cradled her

brother's head. "I hate you — we all hate you! I hope you—"

Moss grabbed her hair and snatched her across the floor. Thorny's head plunked against a loose plank as it slid from his sister's arms. "I know what you need, what you want. You want to be tamed, manhandled."

Willow walked backward on her heels to keep from having her hair pulled out. He suddenly let go. She fell to the floor. Too mad to cry she screamed, "Leave me alone! Leave us all alone! You ain't nothing but an animal. A stinkin' — dirty — animal!"

Moss smiled as he turned a wad of tobacco in his mouth. "Okay, girly, I'll leave you alone. He looked at Olive. "Com'ere, Olive baby, come to Deddy."

Willow stiffened with fear. "No! You leave her alone!" She jumped up and ran to her sister. Rose had already pulled her baby into her arms and curled over her. Willow, defiant, stood over her cowering mother and glared at Moss.

"Ooohh," Thorny groaned and tried to open his eyes.

Moss kicked him in the ribs. "You stay put!" Thorny's mouth flew open gasping for air.

Willow grabbed a tin cup and threw it. Moss batted it away and laughed.

"You think you can stop me from doin' your sister? Just watch me." He smacked the tobacco with yellowed teeth and grinned. "Maybe she'll like it as much as you do. Ain't too young to start learnin' her how to please a man."

"You leave her alone or I'll kill you myself!" Fire darted from Willow's eyes as she spoke with the venom of a rattler.

Like a cat, Moss reached out and grabbed Willow by the arm, flinging her over the table. She landed next to Thorny. Still gasping for air in short, ragged breaths, he tried to get up but couldn't, the pain too much. With several ribs broken and an egg-like knot bulging above his right temple, he barely remained conscious.

Willow looked upon his gaunt, pain-ridden face. "Oh,

Thorny, don't die," she pleaded. "Please don't leave me here alone. I'll help you get well, just don't die."

Moss laughed. "Be better if the little shit did."

"You baby killer!" Rose jumped to her feet with the agility of an antelope and ran toward her husband, her arms flailing. With fury and courage she had never felt before, she pounced on him scratching and screaming. "Leave be my children! You hear me?" She gouged him in an eye.

Moss bellowed, and threw hands over his eyes to keep from getting them scratched out.

"I'll kill you, you piece of hog shit!" Rose slapped, scratched and kicked, but Moss just stood there unmovable like a mountain. He grabbed both of her wrists and held them with one hand. The other came down with a sickening thud. She went limp.

Willow leaped to her feet, "No! Leave her alone!" Then, with resignation in her voice she said, "Please… I'll do anything you want, just leave them alone." She glanced at Olive curled up in the corner, her head covered with both arms, her slight body shaking. "I'll do what you want."

Moss spat. Brown spittle drenched Rose's thin, tattered dress. He grinned. "I was supposin' to give you somethin' purty I bought in town this mornin'. You'll like it."

He grabbed her by the arm and pulled her toward his bedroom. He kicked the door shut and pushed her onto the bed.

Willow saw a clear glass jug half full of mesh whisky. *Maybe it'll deaden me,* she thought. She pointed toward the jug. "Can I have some of that?"

"You want sour mash?" Moss laughed and reached for the jug. "Shore, go ahead, take a swig."

Without hesitating she turned the jug up and let the fiery liquid slip down her throat. It took her breath. She gasped for air and held her throat, coughed. She didn't care how it felt or how it tasted. She only cared about the effect it would have on her mind. *Maybe I'll pass out.* She took another swallow, and another, and another, until the jug slipped from her hands. Moss caught it.

"I see ye like it as much as ye do my pleasurin'." Moss laughed without humor. "Think I'll have a swaller m'self." He drained the jug and cast it. It rolled across the floor and clattered against the wall. He wallowed out of his dingy overalls.

The liquor deadened the pain and humiliation but did not eliminate it. It couldn't. Nothing could, except death. She smiled at the thought.

❧

The morning came early as it always did on a farm. A farmer worth his salt always beat the sun up. To be in bed when daylight arrived was considered shameful to men and women who had worked hard all of their lives. Water had to be drawn and hauled, cows fed and milked, milk cans spring-housed, and eggs gathered, all before breakfast. Those work ethics were instilled in the Kinser children from an early age. Callie and Corbit knew the routine and there were no exceptions, except for sickness, and only the bed-bound kind; even church had to wait on milking and feeding.

With Maggie, though, it had been different from the beginning. Corbit had always accepted it, but Callie never had — until the incident.

"Ready to go, Callie?" Bud donned his hat and smiled.

Callie untied her apron and tossed it on the back of a chair. "I'm ready."

"Hey, where're you going?" Corbit asked as he pushed the screen door open. It closed hitting the heel of his brogan; the door whiplashed and banged against the top door jam. "Ouch, confound it all! Can I go, too?"

"No!" Callie answered. "Me and Deddy're going to "see a man about a horse" and you can't go."

Corbit shot back, "I ain't asking you, smart mouth!"

"Calm down," Bud said. "I promised Callie just me and her would spend some time together this morning while I run some errands for the sheriff. We'll go another time."

Callie grinned like a possum. "Yeah, and you can finish my chores while I'm gone."

"I ain't gonna do it!" Corbit snapped.

"Don't get carried away, young lady. I didn't say you didn't have to do your chores, just put them off for a couple of hours until we get back." Callie's grin evaporated. "Come on, let's go, we'd better get to it if we're going to see everybody." He started the car. "Let's begin to commence to go," he said with a laugh.

Bud had informed Ellie of Callie's plan the night before. She approved, saying, "Looks like she's growing up."

"Yep, looks like it," he agreed.

"I'll have lunch ready by the time you get back," Ellie sang as they slammed the car doors shut a split second apart. "Be careful, you two."

Bud thought of something as pushed the clutch in and turned the ignition. The engine sputtered to life. "Oh, Corbit — let Kate out to pasture."

"Kate! But that ol' mule's gonna bite and kick me as sure I'm standing here. Why can't you do it?"

Bud drew his head back, his mouth tightening up. "Corbit—Ettis—Kinser , you just do as you're told young man! Come on, Callie, let's go."

It felt like cold water had been thrown in his face. He had just been called Ettis, by his own father, no less. "Everybody's against me today," he sulked, and threw his hat on the ground, but not before the car blanketed him with a cloud of dust.

The sky, cloudless and hazy, brought on an early heat. Farmers were working their fields. A wagon clattered over the dusty road, pulled by a single-collared sway-backed mare. The Ford sedan passed on the left leaving a trail of dust in its wake. As the car climbed Fox Hill Bud downshifted into second causing the engine to whine on the climb to the top.

"Seen Willow lately?" Bud asked.

"No, sir. I missed her when she came to see Maggie." She wanted to tell him about Willow's secret place, their long talk, and the encounter with Moss.

"I heard about the pie pan."

"It didn't make sense, the scattered pie, and all — until we saw the footprints."

"Footprints? Nobody mentioned footprints."

Callie wondered why she had left such an important thing out. "Big footprints all around where we found the pan."

"Moss's, you reckon?"

"I reckon. I think he got a-hold of the pie and tore it up for some reason."

Bud shook his head in agreement. "I think you're right. Why don't we stop and see for ourselves how they're doing? Maybe we'll get to see the youngest girl while we're there."

He paused before asking, "Has Willow ever said anything to you that seemed strange?"

"Like what?" Callie shifted in the seat and leaned back against the door.

"Oh, things like, why she hates wearing those pretty dresses, or things about her deddy, and such."

"She said she hates those dresses, says her deddy makes her wear them. Says her deddy ain't no good for nothing, too, but she won't say why." She looked at her father with questioning eyes. "How come Willow has so many nice dresses if they're so poor and all?"

"That's what I'd like to know, too. Have you noticed anything else, like bruises or cuts?"

"Well... I... maybe. I don't know."

Bud shifted into low gear and pulled the car to the side of the road just shy of the Branch shack. He pulled the emergency brake. "You don't know? Did you or didn't you? It's important, Callie."

She hesitated, glared at the floorboard, and fidgeted with a rip in the mohair seat. "I promised her I wouldn't tell."

"Listen, I understand you made a promise, and it's important to keep promises you make, but sometimes, if somebody might be in danger, it's okay to break that promise. Understand?"

"Yes, sir, I understand. But I promised, and she wouldn't trust me anymore if I did."

"You need to tell me what you know, Callie, for Willow's sake."

She flopped back in the seat. "Well… I've seen bruises on her arms and legs, and her eye was swolled real bad one time. Looked like a hen's fruit."

Bud pressed, "Has Willow ever said anything else about her deddy?"

"Only that he's a no-account, like Maggie said."

"Anything else?"

"She keeps saying things like, she's no good, and she's a sinner, and everything's her fault 'cause she's pretty." Callie thought. "And she keeps mentioning babies, but she shuts up when I ask her what she means."

"Babies? I recall her saying something about babies the night Lucas died. I hope it ain't what I'm thinkin' it is. That'd explain everything, though."

"What do you mean?"

Bud avoided the question. "What about Thorny, have you seen any bruises on him?"

"I've never even seen Thorny, except down at the creek when Miz Plank like to of blowed his head off. You could ask Corbit and Fred, though. They'd know."

Bud winced at the mention of Airy Mae's near miss. He nodded. "I will." He released the emergency brake and drove the remaining few yards to the Branch shack partially hidden in the shadows of the trees. He pulled into the yard and shut off the engine.

Moss stepped off the porch. He glared at Bud and spewed a brown stream leaving a long trail in the red dirt. He pulled out a plug of tobacco, opened his knife, sliced off a chunk and crammed it into his mouth. "Don't bother gittin' out, Kinser. You ain't got no bidness here, you, and thet little nosey gal of yourn."

Without hesitating Bud pushed the door open and stepped out of the car. "I'm a little concerned about your children, Branch."

Moss waved him off with a flip of his wrist, the knife still open. "My younguns and my old lady ain't none of your bidness. Now, you just turn around and git!"

Bud didn't flinch. "I'd put the knife away if I were you, Branch. And your children *are* my business if they're hurt, or hungry, and it appears they're both. I'm not talking to you as a neighbor right now, but as a lawman."

"The sheriff's done come here askin' a bunch of questions 'bout thet murder, and all, like I had somethin' to do with it. Well, I ain't! And the goings-on here are my matter. It ain't nothin' for you to be 'cerned about."

"I'm well aware of the sheriff's visit, and it's got nothing to do with why I'm here. I want to know why Willow's got bruises on her face and arms, and why Thorny looks like he's about to starve to death, and your wife, too. And speaking of Thorny, did you know he saved my youngest daughter's life? Well, he did, so I figure I owe him something for that."

"Ain't a man got a right to punish his younguns if they need it? Don't you punish yourn? And I don't know nothin' 'bout saving nobody." Moss added with venom, "You don't owe thet little no-account sum-bitch *nothin'*! Not one—

damn—thang !"

"Punishing is one thing, but beating and starving them is another, and I don't consider Thorny to be a no-account. I consider him a hero, at least in my eyes, and my familie's. Now, I want to see them — now!"

Bud stepped around Moss and walked toward the porch. Moss spat, splattering the back of Bud's brogans with brown goo.

Bud froze. He lifted his foot and looked at the back of his shoe. He frowned. His face turned red. He snapped around, took a measured step, and got right in Moss's face.

"Thorny's hurt Mr. Kinser. He needs help real bad." Rose stood behind the screen door where light and shadow mixed allowing only splotchy sketches of Rose's frail body to be seen. "Can't even stand up." Rose held on to the door jamb to keep from falling. The beating from Moss had taken a toll on her as well.

Ignoring Moss, Bud turned and hurried to the porch, bounded up the steps and yanked open the screen door. He paused, flinched. What he saw shocked him. One whole side of Rose's face had turned black and blue. Her left eye had completely swollen shut.

"Lord have mercy! You look like you need to see a doctor yourself. What happened to you, Mrs. Branch?" Bud gently turned her head to get a better look in the dim light. She almost fell. Bud caught her.

"Did your husband do this to you?"

Moss bellowed, "Done tole ye, Kinser. Ain't none of yore matter!"

Rose nodded toward Moss. "Drunk, beat up on Thorny. I ain't worried about me, but he's hurt bad, ribs swolled and he can hardly breathe."

Rose led him to a bedroom where Thorny lay on a ratty mattress on the bare floor, his face flushed with pain and fever. Willow sat by him with a wet cloth over his forehead.

Deep bruises pockmarked her face, arms, and legs, her hair was matted and her countenance a picture of worry and pain. Not the physical pain, but the debasing, life-draining, debilitating, soul-eating kind. She looked up at Bud as he entered the room and a flash of hope beamed in her green eyes.

Willow pleaded, "We've got to get him to a doctor, Mr. Kinser. I think his ribs are broke and something inside him is terrible wrong."

Tears ran down her face tracking a familiar path. Olive sat at the head of the mattress looking at her brother, rocking back and forth, sucking on two fingers. She backed against the wall when the strange man entered the room.

Bud said to Olive, "It's okay, sweetheart. I'm not going to hurt you. I'm here to help." He dropped down to his knees and felt the boy's forehead. Thorny mumbled something incoherent at his touch. "When did this happen?"

"Yesterday," Willow said. "Last night. He's been like this ever since, talking out of his head, and all. Got real hot last night and I've been keeping a wet rag on his face and forehead. Ain't got no Anacin to give him. Ain't got nothin'!"

Outside, Moss leaned one arm over the car while sticking his head in the driver's side window. "You and your deddy ain't nothin' but busybodies mindin' ever'body's bidness but yourn," he sneered. "I know what Willer's been tellin' you, but ain't none of it true. She's crazy, just like her momma is."

"She ain't crazy!" Callie shot back. "You're mean!"

"Back off, Branch," Bud said in a stern voice as he jumped off the side of the porch.

Moss yanked his head from inside the car, bumping it on the door. "Damn it all to hell," he hissed, rubbing his head. Bud strode toward the larger man.

"You're a nosy sum-bitch, ain'tcha, Kinser?"

"And you're a no-account woman and child beater," Bud seethed through clenched teeth. "And more besides.

I'm taking your boy to the doctor. Fact is, I'm taking all of them."

Moss snarled, "You ain't takin' them nowhere, Kinser. I got my rights!"

"I'm talking as the law right now, and I'm telling you what I'm going to do. So I'd advise you to stand aside." Bud's eyes bored into the other man's like a drill bit.

"Here, Deddy," Callie said, retrieving the gun and holster Bud always kept underneath the seat when he wasn't on duty.

"I don't need a gun to do what I intend to, Callie. Put it back."

Yellowed teeth continued to chew. The tobacco plug wallowed from one side of his mouth to the other. The giant mass of grimy flesh took a step backward, never taking his eyes off of Bud. Without batting an eye, Bud turned and walked back to the porch.

"It ain't over, Kinser, you can bet on it."

Bud held the door open, turned to face Moss. "You're right, Branch, it ain't!"

Callie scooted off the car seat and ran to join her father.

After a few minutes Bud returned with Thorny in his arms. "Mrs. Branch, you and Willow get in the back seat and I'll lay Thorny across your laps."

"Ain't got no right just because—"

"Shut up!" Bud snapped.

Moss's stained mouth clamped tight. Rage filled his face.

"Hey, Olive," Callie said in a gentle voice. "You can sit up front with me. I'll roll the glass down and you can look out the window. Okay?"

Olive glanced at her mother and then at Willow, her two fingers still in her mouth. Her round eyes were dull, almost void, her face filled with worry and confusion.

Willow smiled and touched Olive on the face. "It's all

right honey, you can ride up front with Callie. She's my friend, and she's nice."

Callie took Olive by the hand, gently pulling her into the car.

The gears ground into reverse and the Ford whined as it backed out onto the road. As it pulled away Rose looked back at her husband. A wicked grin crossed his face sending cascades of fear through her body.

Callie looked at her father with a profound look of respect, and of shock. She had never seen him be confrontational with anyone before, not like that. She swelled with pride and admiration. "I'll be John Brown," she whispered, and smiled.

Chapter 22

Just a Different Kind of Prison

Sheriff Vaughn joined them in the Emergency Room after getting a call from Bud. The sheriff listened intently, his mouth tight as Bud explained all that had transpired.

"Give the whole family a good checking over, will you, Doc?" Vaughn said. "Check both girls' privates. I'd appreciate it if you'd let me know what you find."

Doc Morton shook his head. "I expect it won't be good."

Thorny, as it turned out, had three broken ribs, a punctured lung, and a deep cut on his head. He also had a concussion. A surgeon had been called in.

"Hi, what's your name?" Doc Morton asked Olive. She hid behind her mother. "I bet you like ice cream."

Holding on to her mother's dress, Olive peeped around Rose's leg and shook her head in a shy yes motion.

"You do? Well, I'll tell you what. I have to check you out to make sure you're strong enough to eat all that ice cream. You have to be real strong to eat bowls full of chocolate, vanilla and strawberry ice cream, you know. Why don't you come over here and sit in my lap, sugar. Okay? After we finish, I'm going to ask another doctor to give you and your sister a very special examination. In fact, you and your sister can be examined together."

"It's all right, Olive," Rose said, taking her by the hand. She led her to Doc Morton, picked her up and put her in his lap.

He sat Olive in a chair next to him. "You're next, Mrs. Branch. Looks like you could use some ice cream, too." He retrieved a tongue depressor from a jar and turned to Olive. "Stick out your tongue and let me look at your throat."

Olive sat there.

"Stick out your tongue. You want some ice cream, don't you?"

Olive looked at Rose, and then at Willow.

Willow stroked her sister's hair. "It's all right, honey, he means for you to loll your looper."

Olive's tongue darted out and right back in again.

Doc Morton laughed. "You folks must be from the mountains. I forgot you people have your own language up there."

"Can I have a poke of ice cream to give to my brudder?" A tiny voice asked.

"Well, it won't be necessary, sweetheart. We're going to give your brother all the ice cream he can eat… and you, too. Now, loll your looper and hold it out."

☙❧

"What's going to happen to Willow and Thorny now, and Mrs. Branch, and Olive?" Callie asked.

"I don't know, but I guess it's really up to Mrs. Branch. She told the sheriff she's going back home because she didn't have nowhere else to go."

Callie's brow wrinkled, "Why, that don't make sense, at all. But at least Thorny's staying in the hospital until he gets well. I hope Sheriff Vaughn puts that mean ol' man in jail for what he done to him — to all of them."

"It ain't likely unless Mrs. Branch swears out a complaint against him." Bud patted Callie on the leg and smiled. "The sheriff's going to go and tell Moss the way it is, put the fear of God in him. He'll keep an eye out, and so will I from now on."

"You really told that mean ol' man what for, didn't you, Deddy?" Callie smiled at the thought.

They made stops while in town to see some people they knew, and others Bud had become acquainted with through his job. Afterwards they went out to the countryside, where they visited the Planks, McCrackens, Vaughns and other neighbors in and around Brush Creek. Flour sacks, remnants of cloth, mostly flawed leftovers from the cotton mill in Chattanooga, and spools of thread, mostly white, lay amongst piles of solid white and floral print cotton cloth on the back seat. A few dress patterns lay folded with names pinned to them with straight pins and measurements written in pencil along the shaded lines of the patterns.

"You did pretty good," Bud said, smiling at his elated daughter. "You've got enough work to keep you busy for a while."

"Yeah, and if I didn't have to do chores—"

"Whoa now, back up. I don't think that's part of the deal. Besides, your momma would skin both our heads if you mentioned anything about not doing chores. I expect Corbit would have something to say about that, too."

"Oh well, it was only a thought."

Bud smiled. "I'll tell you what, and this's between you and me, I'll help out on the sly, Gather the eggs, help stack dishes after dinner, little things like that so nobody'll notice. That should give you enough time to sew an extra piller case or apron."

Callie beamed. "Thanks, Deddy. I can't wait to see Maggie's face, to see her happy again, and have her not hate me anymore."

"She doesn't hate you, Callie. Like I said, she's just a little lost right now. She'll come around, you'll see."

A horse-drawn wagon hugged the side of the road. The old mare wore blinders to keep her focused on the road ahead. The farmer, an older man wearing a well-worn straw hat, sat on the wooden seat half asleep. Bud slowed down, shifting into second gear to prevent throwing dust in the face of the horse and driver.

Bud glimpsed at the hazy sky and wondered how his farmer neighbors without irrigation would make it through next year without a decent crop. Even those with irrigation or a spring found themselves limited as to the amount they could use. The lack of rain had depleted their ponds and irrigation would soon be impossible. Bud felt a surge of pride in Corbit for his idea to dam the spring. He noticed how the spring flowed much slower from its underground source lately. Even the well had been steadily dropping, the water now cloudy. An orphan cloud, white and fluffy, hung in the sky void of rain.

❧

"Momma, you can't go back, you know what he'll do." Willow pleaded with her mother while stroking Thorny's matted hair.

"The sheriff's gonna talk to him, tell him what for. Besides, we ain't got nowhere else to go." Rose's hands, once soft and beautiful, now gangly and wrinkled, pushed against her face in an expression of regret.

"We can go to Aunt Gertie's; she won't mind us staying there for a while."

Rose lowered her hands and placed them flat on her lap. "She's as bad off as we are, and besides she's in Brewton, Alabama. I don't know how we'd get there. Anyhow, things'll be different now. He has to change. The sheriff's gonna talk to him, tell him not to touch you or Thorny no more."

Willow spewed, "He ain't gonna change, and you know it! He's too damn mean — I'm sorry I swore, Momma."

"It's okay. I don't blame you one bit. I guess you've got a right to it." Rose's face, sullen yet determined repeated the same words she had time and time again. "He'll change this time. It's different now."

"What about Olive, Momma. Do you want her to go through what I have? You want her to have babies and have him make her bury them after he's kilt them?"

Rose's breath caught as if a stabbing pain had gone straight through her heart. "I won't let 'im."

Willow stood. "Like you didn't let him do me? Like you didn't stop him from killing those babies? You're gonna stop him? Is that what you're gonna do, Momma?"

Another pain shot arrow straight and deep within her soul. Rose wept.

Olive crawled into her lap and wiped a tear as it ran down her face. "Don't cry, Momma," she said her words unusually clear. Rose drew her into her bosom and held her tight.

Rose looked at Willow and said, "You and Thorny can go… and Olive. Go stay with the Kinser. They're nice people, be glad for you to stay for a while. After all, didn't Thorny save the little girl's life?"

"We can't burden them with all of us. Besides, Thorny won't go. You know how he is, not liking being around people, and all. And you know he won't leave you all alone with him. You know he won't."

"Your deddy won't bother me, not if you ain't there to…" Rose paused.

"If I ain't there to tempt him, is that what you mean? You always did say I had the devil in me because I was made pretty. You said yourself it's the reason he's he won't leave me alone. Ain't it so, Momma?"

"No — I mean … yes, it's what I said, but it ain't no ways true, it ain't your fault. I was only making excuses."

Willow lowered her voice. "I know I'm sinful for what

I done, Momma. I know I ain't fit and I know I gotta pay for it, but that sorry so-called man caused me to be filthy, and I know I can never be clean. I know I can't take back what I done to those babies. They died, taken away because I'm a heathen sinner."

"You ain't sinful, I am. I let you be soiled. Those babies dying ain't your fault, either." Rose buried her head in her hands and wept.

"Whatever you say, Momma, but I know the truth of it."

Olive, confused, looked from Willow to her mother, her eyes sad, her face cheerless.

Willow said to her mother, "I'm not leaving without you, and it ain't your fault neither. It's his!" She thought about the one thing haunting her day and night. *But I guess you're right about me. It's my fault he done what he did. And I caused them babies to die.*

Thorny stirred, groaned, and opened his eyes.

❧

"I've been doing chores all by myself," Corbit lamented. "Where've you been all day?"

"With Deddy," Callie said with a grin.

"I know that, doodoo head, but *where've* you been and how come you got all of that cloth, and thread, and stuff?"

"To sew stuff."

Corbit stepped in front of her. "You know what I mean, Callie. Dang-nabbit, you're making me plumb mad."

"And you know what? Deddy got in that mean ol' man's face and gave him what for."

"What mean ol' man? Come on Callie, tell me."

"Willow's deddy. He made him shut up and got Willow and Thorny, who's real bad hurt, Thorny, I mean, and took them to the hospital in Athens. He took their momma, and Olive, too."

"Why, you don't say!"

"Got right in his face. Told him to back off!"

Corbit got antsy. "Back off from what?

"Told him to shut up. Told him he's a no-account woman and child beater!"

"He didn't!"

"Yep! I tried to hand Deddy his gun, but he said he didn't need a gun to do what he needed to."

"Deddy said that? Really?"

"Yep, plum mean-like. Busted his chops good." Callie leaned toward Corbit's face. "Looked at him like a wolf. His eyes were steely gray, his fist all balled up—"

"Well, I'll say. He didn't!"

"Really 'cooking with gas', he was. You should've seen him. Marched right in and picked up Thorny in his arms and carried him out to the car."

"I declare!"

"Uh huh."

Corbit stomped his foot. "It ain't fair!"

"What ain't fair?"

"That I didn't get to see it, that's what!"

Callie, teasing, turned to walk off. Corbit grabbed her. "Wait, you gotta start from the beginning and tell me everything, and don't rag me either… please?"

❧

"I'll tell you what, Ellie, that's one no-account human if I ever saw one." Bud took a long drink of iced tea. "More of an animal than human. Like to of beat the boy to death because he tried to defend his mother."

Ellie twisted her apron. "I knowed all along he weren't worth the powder it'd take to blow his brains out!"

"I wouldn't waste a bullet on that bupkis. Not my bullet, no ways."

Ellie squinted as she asked, her voice low. "How bad are the rest of them?"

"Bruised up." Bud paused. "Maybe battered's the right word. Mrs. Branch's face looks like it'd been hit with a tire iron. And Willow's lip is split wide open. Both are bruised and swolled all over."

"Lord have mercy!" Ellie plopped down in a chair and sighed. She thought of the baby, flinched. "What about the little one?"

"Scared and confused, but otherwise seemed okay. Olive, the baby's name, she's the only one that didn't reap the rewards of his wrath, physically anyhow."

Ellie relaxed a little. "Thank the good Lord."

"They were all half-starved, though, except for Willow, and I think I know why."

"I hope it's not what I'm thinking, and what I've been suspecting all along."

Bud shook his head, "I'm afraid so, Ellie. I'm afraid so."

❧

"If I had my way, Branch, I'd put you under the jail." Sheriff Vaughn stood on the porch, looking down at Moss sitting in his chair spitting off the side of the porch.

"That boy of yours is hurt pretty bad from your beating." He paused for a few seconds and then said with dripping sarcasm, "I can tell from the look on your face you're *really* worried."

"It's what he gits for bein' a smart mouth and threatenin' to hit me. Fact is, he did hit me."

"Not hard enough, I'd say."

Moss leaned over and spat again. "Just tryin' to learn him a lesson, Sheriff, like any good deddy would do."

"I don't call beating your boy half to death being a good deddy, Branch. Don't look like he's eat in two weeks, either, or the rest of your family for that matter." The sheriff stepped down with one foot on the top step and the other on the porch. He put his arm across his leg and leaned in to Moss. "Looks like you've beat everybody but the baby, and I see you haven't gone without."

"What I do with my family is nobody's bidness but mine." He spat a brown glob splattering spider-legged on the bottom step. "Got a right to dis'pline my younguns, an' old lady, too, for as the matter goes."

"I didn't come here to argue, Branch. I'm saying you don't have the right to beat them half to death and then let them lie on the floor to die like your boy almost did. His ribs are broken, three of them, and has a punctured lung to boot. On top of it all his kidney is bruised, had six stitches in his head where you hit him, and he's weak and bone skinny from being starved. That ain't the half of it. He's still unconscience."

"You gonna 'rest me or not, Sheriff?"

"I reckon not, since Mrs. Branch won't swear out a warrant against you. I can't arrest you for being a sorry ass, but if I could I'd be hauling you off by the hair of your head in a manure wagon. Anyhow, that's not why I'm here, or at least not all of it. I want to ask you about Willow."

Moss stopped chewing. "What about 'er? She done gone and told lies about me agin?"

"She ain't said a thing, won't either as far as it goes. But I know something's going on that shouldn't, things not natural to humans. The doctor examined her and confirmed it."

"Like what, Sheriff. You got no right to 'cuse me—"

"Now you look here, I know you've been having your way with her. I just can't prove it."

Moss looked up and grinned. "Why, Sheriff, what zackly would make you say somethin' like thet? She ain't nothin' but a lying little whelp if she did say it. Probably a whore like her momma is."

"Ain't but one liar, and I'm looking at him. Like I said, she's been examined and there's proof she's been spoiled."

"And like I said, she ain't nothin' but a sharecropper. Ain't no tellin' who's been croppin' her field."

He snatched Moss out of the chair, rapped him in the mouth, back-slapped him, and shoved him back in the chair. "Damn you, you sorry bastard! That girl's no whore, she's a victim of your cruelty. That's what!"

Moss started to get up. "I'm gonna show you what for!"

"Come on, Branch. Get up!" the sheriff taunted. "Make a move toward me. It'd be my pleasure to blow your sorry ass to kingdom come! I'd really enjoy it." He placed his hand on the butt of his revolver.

Moss eased back into the chair, pushing against the slats.

"She's too damned ashamed to tell the truth, but when I find out I'll — oh, hell."

Calming down, Vaughn resumed his stance, and said. "Just tell me where your still is. I know you've got one back in the woods somewhere. Want to tell me where it is?"

"I ain't got no still! I'm a law-biden citizen."

Vaughn laughed. "Yeah, sure you are, Branch, sure you are. Tell me this, where're you getting the money to rent whores and buy steak dinners with, and buy those fancy cloths you deck out in like a darb? I know that's the only way they'll let you in the whorehouses. Want to explain it to me, Branch? Or maybe you just inherited the money from a rich uncle."

Moss spat. "Ain't none of yore concern where I git my money. Maybe I work for it."

The sheriff threw his head back and roared. "You haven't done an honest day's work in your sorry life, and you know it."

"Maybe, but you ain't got no right, law or no, to come 'round here sayin' things you got no proof of, callin' me names and hittin' me and such." His tongue pushed the used-up wad of tobacco from his cheek, puckered, and spat it out. Reaching into his pocket he pulled out a plug of Days Work, cut off a slice, and took it to his mouth with knife blade and thumb. His voice muffled by the unchewed cut, he mumbled, "Ain't got no still, an' ain't doin' thet gal, neither." He looked the sheriff in the eyes and grinned. "I'm busy, Sheriff, if you ain't got nothin' else."

"There's one more thing, Branch. Where did you say you were the night Mr. Ward got killed? Before you came high and mighty to claim Willow, that is?"

Anger flared. "I done tole you whare I was, and I done tole you I didn't have nothin' to do with no killin'!"

"Well, I'm not convinced of it yet. You having a 30-aught-6 Springfield, and all, the kind that blew Ward's head off. Not to mention it was your dog my deputies found tied up by the creek to throw my hounds off track."

"I don't know how the dog got there, she roams the woods all the time, anybody could've tied that 'ol hound up. 'Sides from that a lot of folks have a 30-aught-6, an' I done tole you plain and simple, it don't belong to me. It's the boy's gun."

"And those who do own one don't care if their daughters go to church, and they didn't happen to show up sudden, like you did, after Lucas Ward got killed." Vaughn stepped down and said, "I'll be watching you, Branch. And I promise you this — if you lay a hand on Thorny, or touch Willow, or any of them again, I won't need a warrant. I'll take care of you personal. You hear?"

☙❧

Everyone settled in to the never ending chores of farm life. Everyone except Maggie, who wandered around the house like a lost soul going from one room to the other carrying her music books, constantly on the verge of tears.

Callie had everything laid out on the table on the back porch: pin cushion full of straight pins, needles, spools of thread, and scissors. Bud and Corbit carried the Singer treadle sewing machine and sat it next to the table.

"Why're you taking in all of this sewing, Callie?" Corbit asked. "Looks like an awful lot of work for somebody as lazy as you are."

Callie smirked, "Very funny, Ettis."

"Hey, watch it!"

"It ain't fair!" The door slammed as Maggie limped onto the porch. "Why do you get to sew and have fun when I ain't got my banjer to play?" She burst into tears. "It just ain't fair!" The gash on her leg with the line of black stitches looked ghastly. The white arm cast with names of family and well-wishers had started to turn a dull gray. Willow's cryptic message a constant reminder of the truth it carried stood out from other well-wishers.

"I ain't got nothin', and it ain't fair that you do!"

Callie's countenance dropped, her smile disappeared, and a melancholy curtain fell over her. She stared at the sewing machine, but said nothing.

"Why don't you shut up and quit feeling sorry for yourself?" Corbit rebuked. "It's just an old banjo, a piece of wood with strings, and rawhide. You act like it was alive or something!"

"Leave her alone!" Callie demanded. Corbit wrenched his head around, surprised. "She's right. It ain't fair — but I'm going to make it up to you, Maggie. I promise."

"What's going on out here with all the ruckus?" Bud stepped onto the porch, took the dipper off the nail, plunged it into the water bucket, and took a swallow. "Got some real good news, Maggie."

She wiped her eyes and whimpered, "What is it?" Then her face lit up. "Am I gettin' a new banjer, Deddy, am I?" She held her breath.

"Well, no, but somebody's coming to town next month, somebody special you might want to see."

"Oh." Her lungs deflated. Her face took on the gloomy gus look again.

"It's that Scrubbs banjo picker you like so much. He and the Lost John Miller Band will be doing a show in Athens put on by the Chamber of Commerce. Thought you might want to go."

The light returned. "Earl Scruggs is coming *here?* Why, he ain't done it!" Maggie looked as though St. Peter had opened the gate and said, 'Enter.'

Bud emptied the dipper and hung it back on the nail. "He sure is, little Maggie."

"And I get to go watch him play?"

"Yep, but if you don't want to —"

"Oh, I do!" Scowling at Callie, she added, "But I wish I had my banjer to take with me."

Chapter 23
New Over-hauls

That Branch boy sure won't talk much," Sheriff Vaughn said.

Bud agreed. "He doesn't like being around folks at all. He gets where he'll talk to me somewhat, but I have to drag it out of him."

"I know what that slimy piece of unwashed chitlin' is doing to Willow, but she won't confirm it and neither will Thorny. Only because she doesn't want him to, I suspect. The momma won't either. I think they're too ashamed to say. All Thorny'd say is that he'd take care of things himself."

"I know," Bud said. "I had the same problem. And I am afraid Thorny may do just that — take care of things himself."

Vaughn waded up a piece of paper and made a three-pointer in the trash can. "That sorry sum-bitch ought to have his balls cut off and hung on a fence post the way we do hogs. Only thing is, I don't want to insult the hogs. Anyhow, be that as it may, I hope the boy don't do anything rash. But if he did I'd do everything possible to see that he walked."

"It's gonna be a chore all right for him to live up there with that old grizzly bear, especially after all that's happened."

Vaughn nodded, "I did ask Thorny if he'd like to stay with the Clyde Beck family and work on their farm. Talked to them a couple afternoons ago, explained the situation. They liked the idea. Clyde said he could use some help with the crops since his boy has gone off to UT in Knoxville."

"What did Thorny say, as if I don't already know?"

"Said he 'couldn't leave his sisters and momma alone with that sum-bitch,' his exact words." Vaughn shook his head, "Although I don't know what he can do to protect them—he just about got himself killed trying to this last go-round."

"A 30-aught can talk pretty loud," Bud said. "I wish we had enough proof to arrest Branch for Lucas's murder. It'd sure solve a lot."

"Me too, but we don't. And it would — solve the problem, I mean. All we have is a slug from a 30-aught 6 and a tied-up hound, and that's not enough. I know three or four people who own a 30-aught, me included." The sheriff stood and donned his hat. "The boy's being released to go home this morning. Told him I'd pick him up and take him home myself. He refused, said he'd rather walk."

"Why, it'd take him all day," Bud said. "He's been in the hospital nigh on to two weeks. He's still weak. He ain't able to walk that far."

Vaughn agreed. "What I told him, said I'd take him and for him not to argue."

"I'll take the boy, Joe, no need you going all the way out there when I have to pass his place anyhow. Besides, I want to impress on Branch's mind, again how we'll be keeping an eye on him. I've checked several times over the past couple of weeks and so far he's kept his hands off. He ain't bothered Willow, either, or so she says, although she's still not admitting he's done anything to start off."

The sheriff took his hat off and put it back on the nail.

"Okay, Bud, you do that. Oh, by the way, I've an idea where Branch's still might be."

"Back where we got the fourteen-pointer last year?" Bud lengthened his arms to illustrate the buck's rack.

"Yep, the very place."

"You're right it's a perfect place for a still. There's a big overhang, a partial cave and plenty of trees to disperse the smoke."

"Gonna try and find it." The sheriff smiled. "Want to go with us?"

"You bet I do. Want to see it for myself, help bust it up. I'll even bring my own ax." Bud smiled. "Yessir, that'd give me great pleasure, Joe. And if we're lucky, maybe Branch will be there to witness it. It'd be a fine day if we could lock up that sorry — well, you know."

Joe laughed. "Yeah, I know. Why we'll even take pictures for the paper."

❦

"I can walk it," Thorny insisted.

"Look, son, you've had a bad concussion and broke ribs to boot It's gonna take some time to completely heal. You're still too weak to walk that far right out of bed. Need to give yourself time to get your energy back. Besides, I'm going right past your place."

Thorny's eyes narrowed. "If he's laid his filthy hands on any of 'em, I'll kill the bastard graveyard dead!"

"Your momma says he hasn't. I've kept a check on her and your sisters since you've been in the hospital."

Thorny spat venom. "I *ain't* gonna take no more crap off that sum-bitch. Not ever! He ain't gonna hurt nobody again. I can promise you thet."

Bud warned, "I can imagine how you feel, son, but don't do anything you'll regret. He ain't worth going to prison over."

Thorny picked up his battered cap and slid it over a full head of tangled brown hair. Lowering his head he said in an almost inaudible voice, "It wouldn't be any different than it is now, 'cept I'd be behind bars."

Bud shook his head in solemn acknowledgement. "Let's go, Thorny, let's get out of this hospital."

Thorny picked up a paper sack with the worn-out overalls he had on the day he entered the hospital. "Tell Corbit thanks for the over-hauls." Both hands slid down the bib and rested on the pockets with two fingers lodging in the narrow watch pocket at the waist. "This's the first pair of over-hauls I've ever had without holes bigger than the pants. And thank you, Mr. Kinser, for what you've done for my family."

Bud placed a hand on Thorny's shoulder, "I'm proud I can help. For what you've done for Maggie, saving her life and all, I can't ever thank you enough."

Chapter 24
A Plain Dress for Willow

Callie rocked the treadle of the old Singer with a firm foot, the wheel spinning at a steady clip. She guided the needle around the cloth as it stitched together Tommie Sue's new dress.

"I can't wait to try on my new dress. It's gonna be so purty," Tommie Sue said as she sat down beside Callie.

"It won't be long before it'll be ready for you to try on."

"I wish I could sew like that. I'd have a hunnert dresses, one for every day of the week."

Callie smiled. "I think you'd have to change fourteen times a day if you had a hunnert dresses to wear in one week, Tommie Sue."

"And I would, too, and they'd all have flowers on them. I'd never, ever wear another croker sack dress. Not never!"

"This'll be number one. I've got two more to make and you're gonna have flowers on all three." Callie broke the thread and tied a knot. "There, it's all finished except for the hem. Come on up to my room and you can try it on."

"It sure is purty, Callie."

Surprised, both girls jumped. "I declare, Willow, it's you!" Callie cried. "I'll be John Brown if you didn't like to of skeered us half to death."

"I'm sorry. I didn't mean to skeer you."

"Oh, it's all right," Tommie Sue said. "We didn't jump too high, so you just skeered us a little bit."

"Yeah, it's okay. We just didn't see you come up," Callie said.

Tommie Sue gushed, "See the dress Callie made me. Ain't it purty? She's making me two more, and they're all gonna have flowers on them just like this one."

"Come on, Willow, she's about to try it on to see if it fits." All three clambered up the stairs, laughing and giggling.

Callie pushed the door open and all three excited girls rushed in at once. "Maggie," Callie said, surprised. "I didn't know you were in here."

Maggie sat in the corner with her music books spread out in front of her along with Montgomery Ward and Sears & Roebuck catalogues.

"Hi, Maggie," Tommie Sue said. "Your leg looks like it's about well, and I heard your cast'll be sawed off soon."

"Hi, Maggie," Willow sang. "I sure am glad you're doing better and all."

Maggie stood. "Not that taking this old cast off'll do any good. It ain't like I've got a banjer to play." Callie hung her head.

"Hi-de-ho, Willow, howdy, Tommie Sue," Maggie said as she walked out of the room.

"I'm sure you'll get another one some day. You just wait and see if you don't," Tommie Sue said as the door closed.

Willow noticed Callie's crestfallen look. "She'll be all right soon. She don't mean nothin' by it."

"She hates me worse than a skunk," Callie said in a low voice. "Worse than ten skunks."

Tommie Sue pulled her croker sack dress over her head and dropped it on the floor. "Let me see my new dress, Callie. I can't wait another minute to try it on."

Spirits seemed to lift in the room. Tommie Sue stuck her arms in the sleeves and worked the dress over her head.

"Wow, Tommie Sue, it's beautiful!" Willow cried. "I just love it."

Tommie Sue cooed and hugged herself. "It fits perfect, Callie, just like I knew it would." She turned around and around. "You're the best sewer in the whole wide world."

Willow hugged both of them. "I think it's just about the purtiest dress I ever did see."

Tommie Sue looked surprised. "This dress is pretty, for a flour sack dress and all, but it ain't like the beautiful store-bought dresses you're always wearing, and that one's real purty."

"I hate them! All of them! They ain't purty to me," Willow said with scorn. "I'd rather have your croker sack dress. I wouldn't be wearing this fancy dress, but it's all I have. Ain't got nothin' else."

Tommie Sue looked astonished, "I don't see why —"

"I've got a surprise for you, Willow," Callie said. She opened the closet door and lifted a dress off a wire hanger. "I made this for you. Of course I had to guess at the size and all."

Willow's eyes widened. "For me?"

"I hope you like it."

Willow's eyes filled with tears. "Like it? I love it!" She held it close to her body turning one way and then the other. "Oh, Callie, thank you!" She ran and threw her arms around her. Tommie Sue joined in.

Callie flashed a crooked smile. "I've never sewed a dress for anybody with such big boobs before, except for my momma, so I had a lot of guessing to do."

Willow blushed. "There ain't but one way to find out." Facing the wall she unbuttoned her blue "Dancer" dress and let it fall to the floor.

Tommie Sue gasped. Callie's eyes grew large with alarm. Scars lined Willow's back and buttocks. Before Tommie Sue could say anything Callie held her palm out and mouthed, *no* while shaking her head. Willow, too excited about her new dress didn't notice.

"Here, let me help." Callie lifted the new dress over Willow's head and slid it over her arms. The dress fell into place, a perfect fit. Blue asters with orange centers dotted the dress with a matching blue bow tied in front. The sleeves were edged with white lace matching the bottom border.

Willow's eyes moistened once again. "Oh, Callie, it's the most beautiful dress I've ever seen. I won't ever take it off. Thank you!"

Callie smiled. "You're welcome. But you'll have to take it off if you're going to wear this one." Callie pulled another dress out of the closet and slipped it off the hanger. It also had asters, except they were pink with orange eyes. A pink sash hung from each side. Willow took it, held it, and cried.

"Take this to your momma and Olive." Callie handed two more dresses to Willow. "I had to guess on their size, too, but I think they'll fit. Olive's was easy, and your momma doesn't have big boobs to worry about."

All three laughed, and they hugged again.

"Oh, I almost forgot, here's a shirt for Thorny. It ain't fancy, but I hope he likes it."

Willow's hands flew to her mouth. "Oh, Callie. He'll love it! He ain't never had a new shirt before."

Tommie Sue didn't mind all the attention on Willow's new dresses. Seeing Willow and Callie happy made her happy.

Chapter 25
Rattlesnake!

Sheriff Vaughn stood on the periphery of the Kinser farm prepared to lead Deputies Bud Kinser and Jimbo Seagraves up the trail to the back of the Branch place and then deep into the woods where he felt sure the still would be hidden. Each lawman carried a Savage Humpback 12-gauge shotgun in the folds of their arms and a double-edged ax honed to split hairs. At the request of the sheriff, *The Daily Post Athenian,* newly established, had been more than willing to send a reporter and photographer through the woods for a chance at a story sure to attract readers and new advertisement revenue.

The sheriff instructed, "Okay, boys, make sure your weapons are loaded."

Dry, hot weather had rattlesnakes crawling in search of water making snake boots standard fare for the five searchers. Wiping sweat from his brow the sheriff stepped into the lead and began the climb up and around Fox Hill with the *Athenian* fellows taking up the rear.

Just moments earlier, the morning dew had blanketed the land with moisture, but not enough to refresh crippled stalks and withered leaves of some of the farmers. The first rays of daybreak licked the remaining wetness from the countryside. The parked patrol car, hidden in a grove of cedar about a quarter mile from the Kinser place, was concealed from anyone passing by, including Moss Branch.

Bud thought of Moss's last name, Branch. The name immediately brought to mind images of a clean, clear, stream lined with trees and clover. The image changed with Branch, the man, who in real life was a raging torrent of cruelty and self-indulgence destroying his family with fists, words, and selfishness.

"So, Sheriff, you don't really know if there's a still or not?" asked the overweight senior, and only reporter, as he huffed up the trail.

"Oh, there's a still all right, Mr. — ah, sorry, forgot your name."

"McGregor, Silas McGregor."

"Well, Mr. McGregor, I'm just not sure exactly where it is, but I've a pretty good idea where it might be."

"How far back do you think it is?" The young photographer, called Flashy, wanted to know. Sweat ran down his flushed face and channeled down his neck. His shirt, already dark with perspiration, clung to his skin showing the outline of ribs on his slim, boyish frame.

Jimbo said with a grin, "Oh, a mile or two, I guess, counting all the twists and turns. Not too far at all. Just watch out for rattlers."

"What? You mean rattlesnakes?" Flashy's face turned pale.

Sheriff Vaughn pointed at their boots. "Why do you think you're wearing snake boots — to go to Sunday school? Probably some seven-footers in these woods as big around as your leg, I'd say."

"Don't worry, Sheriff," Jimbo said. "They've got a pen and camera to chunk at them. That should skeer them off."

Vaughn cleared his throat. "Just make sure you have your snake boots laced good and tight. This really is rattlesnake country, and like I said, there's some big-uns in these woods."

The late morning sun turned all five shirts dark with sweat as they made their way deeper into the woods. They worked their way around the side of Fox Hill near Willow's special place where the stream bubbled from underneath the boulder, the same stream where Willow and Callie had sat and talked.

Moonshining was not totally frowned on by the law, depending on the circumstances. The war and Great Depression had taken a toll on the nation, and the people of Brush Creek were no exception. Men came home scarred from war and found few jobs waiting. So the law tended to look the other way when otherwise good fathers and husbands did a little side business to feed their families and keep their farms out of foreclosure. They had sacrificed time, limbs, and sanity, so the least the law could do was look the other way — at least for a while. That's the way Sheriff Joe Vaughn saw it.

Moss did not fit into the sacrifice category. The only thing he had sacrificed had been his family. He was neither a good father or husband, nor anyone who resembled a man, but only an animal, cruel and vile, willing to deprive his family to satisfy his desires.

The deadly sound of a rattle filled the air.

Sheriff Vaughn held up his hand, his face showing alarm. "Rattler! Stay still!"

Flashy panicked. Turned, ran. He heard a thump. Felt a jolt as his leg went out from under him. He fell and rolled. The rattler coiled again. His tail and rattles pointed toward the sky, vibrating furiously. His head flattened readying for another strike.

"Stay where you are," Bud instructed in a calm voice. "Don't move."

The rattler's eyes, hard and unmoving, stared at Flashy.

It drew its head back, slow and steady. Its tongue flickered, tasting the air.

"Shoot 'im, somebody," Flashy pleaded, his voice filled with panic.

"Can't." said the sheriff. "It'd give us away."

On the verge of tears, he begged, "Please, Sheriff, do something."

Jimbo picked up a tree branch with dead leaves, worked his way to the side away from Flashy. Holding it out, he shook it. The snake struck. Jimbo threw the branch hitting the rattler. It crawled off into the underbrush.

"He's gone. You can get up." Jimbo reached and pulled Flashy to his feet.

"Oh! Shit fire that hurts!" Flashy limped over and leaned against a tree.

"That's a goodun," Jimbo said, pointing to two holes in Flashy's boot. "It was a good six-footer, I'd say. Not the fangs, the snake."

Bud inspected the fang marks. "I suspect you've got a sizable bruise on the calf of your leg. Going to be sore for a few days."

Sheriff Vaughn examined the boot, too. "Damned if he wasn't full of venom." Poison ran down the side of Flashy's boot. "Now you see why I insisted you wear snake boots?"

"I sure the hell do, and, damn, it's sore."

Silas McGregor eyed the damaged boot. "Yessir, that's gonna make a great story. Thanks, Flashy,"

"You ain't welcome!"

"You should've taken a picture while you weren't doing anything lying there on the ground. Would've been a great visual, really spiced up the story."

"I was too busy peeing my pants."

Everyone looked down.

Jimbo laughed. "You weren't kidding, were you, boy?"

"Hell no! Ain't ashamed to admit it, either."

They walked on in silence. Everyone seemed skittish, eyes darting from side to side with every step.

Vaughn held up his hand. Everyone froze and listened for the warning rattle, but heard none. He pointed down into a little valley.

Below the rock overhang Willow sat on the shallow bank of the spring, feet dangling in the water, a faraway look in her eyes. She wore the dress with blue asters with orange eyes. Then, as if an alarm sounded, she glanced up and saw the five men standing, some with shotguns and axes. She snatched her feet from the water and scooted against a tree, terrified.

Bud stepped forward and said, "It's okay, Willow, it's me, Bud Kinser, and the sheriff. Don't be frightened."

Willow relaxed. Bud laid down his gun and ax, then rounded the outcrop, and slipped down into the little peaceful valley where Willow anxiously awaited. "Hi, Willow, I didn't expect to see you here." He stepped over the narrow stream and squatted down beside her.

Willow smiled, "You're looking for the still, ain'tcha?"

Bud took a handkerchief from his hip pocket, tipped his hat back, and wiped the sweat from his brow. "Uh huh, do you have any idea where it is?"

Willow pointed in the direction of the cave. "Not exactly, but I know it's back yonder someplace. I followed him one morning, for a while anyhow, until I lost my nerve and turned around. I got afraid he might catch me. I wanted to find out where he had it so I could go back and tear it up when he was passed out drunk. I wanted to demolish it into a million pieces. I had planned to hide so I could see his face when he found it."

"I'm glad you didn't take the chance." Bud lowered his voice. "Has he hurt you?"

"No. Not since you took Thorny to the hospital, and the sheriff came out and had words with him. And you."

Willow hesitated. "He threatens me and Thorny — all of us, when he's drunk, but we don't say nothin', just let him go on about how he's gonna show us what for, and how he's gonna beat the hell out of you." Willow looked down and said, "I'm sorry."

"You don't have to be," Bud assured her.

"Anyway, says he's gonna beat the fire out of you when he gets the chance."

"Real fine, that he's not hurting you, I mean, and don't worry about the other. How about Thorny, is he okay?"

"Says he's gonna kill 'im if he messes with us again." She looked at Bud with pleading eyes. "I don't want him to, not that I care about that no-account so-called deddy. I don't want my brother to go to prison."

"I don't either and that goes for the sheriff, also. He's a good boy, Thorny is, and brave, too."

"Thank you for saying so, and thank you for the food, Mr. Kinser. We ain't hungry no more, and everybody's gaining some weight. Olive sure is happy, especially when Miz Kinser sends a cobbler." Willow smiled. "She calls it a gobbler."

Bud chuckled, "You're welcome, and anything else you need I just need to know what it is."

"Deddy, uh, Moss, left this morning. I think Thursday's one of his delivering days, at least that's how I have it figured."

"Any special reason why?"

"He always gets back late, if at all—and he don't," she looked away, "he don't mess with me no more. I guess there's no need to hide it, it's plain enough."

"I know where the old man keeps his still!" Thorny stepped out from behind a tree. "I know where it's hid, and I'll lead you there."

Chapter 26
Turnip Pot

Willow stood. "I'm going, too!"

"No, you ain't!" Thorny snapped.

She snapped back, "Yes, I am! I've got a right to see that old still busted up after all he's done to me!" She stopped and looked at Bud. Thorny looked away.

"I know you do." Bud laid his hands gently on her shoulders. "But Thorny's right. There might be trouble, and I don't want you to get hurt. Besides, if Moss is there, he might see you, and I don't want to give him an excuse."

"I don't care if he sees me or not!" Willow folded her arms and tapped her foot. "Besides, he'll see Thorny, too. What's the difference?"

"I kin take care of myself," Thorny said.

Bud looked from Thorny to Willow. "We've got to find the still, Willow, and we need Thorny to show us where it is. Your brother'll be enough for us to worry about without having to worry about you, too."

She sat back down on the edge of the spring, placed her feet in the slow-running stream. Water swooshed around her ankles causing tiny whirlpools to form and spin off downstream. The soft gurgle of the stream always offered her comfort and peace—but not today. Now she wanted to be rid of it, at least for a while.

She wanted to see Moss's source of joy eliminated, totally destroyed. She wanted to see how he looked when the axes went to work. She craved to see the anger on his face, to see his body quake with rage as he watched the still being chopped to pieces, or better yet, when *he* chopped it to pieces. She knew it to be common practice to have the owner do the handiwork. She smiled at the thought.

She looked at Bud. "I'll stay, but I won't like it."

Thorny led the way. Soon they were following a well-worn path, first around the rim of the hill not too far from the Branch shack, and then down the side deeper into the woods. The Athenians wiped sweat from their brows. The out-of-shape reporter, huffing and groaning with each step, struggled to keep up. The young slim photographer took the trail with ease. Constantly on the lookout for snakes, he jumped at every snapped twig.

Sheriff Vaughn said to the struggling newspaperman in a low voice, "Mr. McGregor, I know this is a hard walk for you, but you'll have to be a little quieter or we're going to give ourselves away."

McGregor huffed, "I'm sorry, Sheriff. I'll try and suffer a little quieter from now on."

"You're doing real good, son," Vaughn said to the young photographer. "A little skittish, maybe, but you're doing all right."

Jimbo asked, "Is Flashy your real name? I suspect it ain't."

"It's what they call me at the paper because of the flashbulbs I use in my camera. My real name's Tim."

"Why don't you stay here and rest, Mr. McGregor," Bud urged. "Sit under the shade of the old oak over yonder and take a breather. You're going to have a heat stroke if you don't cool off."

McGregor wheezed, relief showed in his face. "That's a good idea. I think I will. I'll catch up with you later, boys."

The other four waved and disappeared into the woods.

☙❧

Callie continued her sewing. Three people stopped by to drop off patterns and material for dresses to be made for their daughters. People in town had seen her work and were eager to hire her services. They were amazed to see her intricate needlework and lace trim turn plain flour sacks into fashionable Sears & Roebuck dresses.

"Looky, Momma, at how much money I've made already, and I'm just getting started. It won't be long before I'll have enough to buy—"

The screen door screeched open. Maggie stomped out onto the porch. She stood for a minute and finally said with a scowl, "I'm sure glad you're having fun sewing and all, seeing you don't have my banjer to listen to, and not be bothered by all the noise."

Callie stopped working the treadle. The needle came to a slow stop. "I ain't having fun, Maggie, I'm working."

Maggie snapped, her voice rising, "No, you ain't! You're having fun while I'm miserable and all broke and cut up. It ain't fair, that's what!"

Ellie interrupted, "Now, Maggie, that's no way to talk. Callie's sorry for what she's done and you ought to be a little more forgiving."

"Well, I ain't gonna, and she can't sew worth a dog turd, neither! I hope you stick a needle in your eyes so you'll go blind and you can't see to sew no more!"

"Maggie! Stop that! You ought to be ashamed of yourself!"

"Well, I do, Momma. I hope she sticks a needle right in her eye. Maybe then she'll know how I feel." She reached, grabbed the cloth and yanked. The needle bent as the cloth pulled away from the feed dog of the machine tearing a long gash in the cloth. She leaned over and spat in Callie's face.

Callie said nothing as the spittle ran down her check.

"There! You deserve it, and I'm not sorry, neither. That's for the dishwater you poured on me, for all the nasty things you said to me, and for my broke arm, and for my broke banjer!"

Ellie glared at Maggie, astonished beyond words. She had never seen Maggie that way before, and never expected to. She took her apron and wiped off Callie's face, then turned to face Maggie. "You ought to be ashamed! Spitting on somebody's the worst thing a person can do. Now, you say you're sorry."

"No! I won't! And I ain't sorry!"

"Go over to the worsh pan and wet that new bar of soap, have a big taste of it. Maybe that'll temper your words. When you're through with that you can go cut a switch and bring it to me."

"But, Momma, she—"

"Don't 'but' me! Do as I say or I'll do it for you and there won't be much soap left to worsh your little toe with, and I promise I'll cut the limberest hickory switch I can find. Now go!"

Callie pleaded, "Don't make her put the soap in her mouth. And don't whup her, neither. She's right."

"No, she ain't right, and she's going to get a good lather on that bar before she sticks it in her mouth. It needs a good worshing and it's going to get it, too! After that she's going to do a dance and I'm calling it." Ellie pointed toward the wash pan. "Now get!"

∾∾

"There it is, just where I expected it to be," the sheriff said, shining his flashlight into the cave.

"I want to help bust it up," Thorny insisted. "There won't be nary a thing left when I get through with it."

"You're welcome to my ax," Bud said.

Jimbo pointed. "Well, looky there. He's started to set up a Submarine still. I guess this old turnip pot just don't turn out enough to meet his customer's demands."

"Both stills are a good fifty feet in. This cave's a perfect place for a stillhouse," the sheriff said while scanning the cavern with his light.

"Looks like he's got several barrels fermenting," Bud said, kicking one of the barrels.

Jimbo inspected the inventory. "He's got sacks of corn piled high as the roof and about five hundred pounds of sugar to boot, I'd say."

"I don't see any beading oil," Vaughn said.

"Beading oil? What's that?" Flashy asked as he snapped a picture of the turnip pot.

Bud explained, "Beading oil's usually kerosene that's dropped into the whiskey to make it bubble. It's used to make low-quality whiskey look like the high-quality stuff."

"Don't use it," Thorny said. "He takes pride in his whiskey. He don't doctor it up. That's why he gets so much business. He makes it strong. I've heard him brag about it many a times. Says he don't puke it, neither. I guess that's about the onliest thing he can do good — make good whiskey, that is."

"Puke? You mean they puke in it sometimes?" Flashy said with a big frown.

"It means he don't boil it over and run it into the copper tubing," the sheriff explained. "To make good whiskey you have to keep the temperature in the pot even. If you get it too hot it'll boil over, and it could scorch."

Thorny threw the ax over his shoulder. "Can I start busting it up now?"

"Right after Flashy gets all the pictures of the still he wants," the sheriff said. "And of course he'll want to take pictures of us busting it up."

Bud had a thought. "Maybe it'd be a good idea if

Flashy didn't take pictures of Thorny. It might mean trouble for him."

Thorny started to object. Vaughn held up his hand. "I think Bud's right. But don't worry. After he gets pictures of me and the boys taking a few swings at the still you can go at it all you want."

"It's too bad we didn't catch Branch in the act," Jimbo said.

"Well, this ought to put him out of business for a while anyway," Bud said.

Vaughn glanced at the still. "He left his copper worm. That's unusual because it's the hardest thing to come by. Shiners usually take it with them in case the still gets discovered and busted up. Having it makes it easier to get started again."

Flashy lowered his camera. "What the heck's a worm?"

Bud laughed. "A worm's the copper coil used to condense the alcohol. It sets in a bath of water. You take that box over there next to the Submarine still, it's called a flake. The coil sets right in there."

Jimbo continued, "See the hole in the bottom of the flake, and the piece of copper sticking out of the end of the box on the turnip still? It's called the money piece. The alcohol drips out and into a jug or wooden box. That's how it's collected."

"You take the Submarine still," Bud said, pointing to the newer still with wooden sides and curved ends. "See how big it is? It can produce ten times the shine this old turnip top can."

"How come it's called a turnip top?" Flashy wanted to know.

Pointing at the still Bud explained, "See how it's shaped? It looks like a turnip with a root."

Vaughn interrupted, "That's enough still talk. We'd better get to it."

Flashy took plenty of pictures of the sheriff and his deputies welding their axes busting open barrels of prime mesh and taking swings at the two stills.

"That's going to look good in the paper," Vaughn said.

"It just might get you a few votes," Jimbo said with a laugh, "Especially with the church ladies."

"Yeah, but it might lose you a few, too," Bud said. "Shine's hallowed stuff to a lot of folks around these parts."

Another flash exploded. Flashy said, "I wish Mr. McGregor could see this."

"I thought he'd catch up by now," said Jimbo.

"Now can I?" Thorny asked.

"Here you are," Bud said handing him his ax. "Have at it, but be careful and don't let the blade bounce back on your leg. I've honed it down pretty good just for this occasion."

⊱⋅⊰

Two people stood motionless watching the scene play out. A happy smile crossed one face. The other, standing unnoticed in the bushes, had a twisted scow on his.

Like a cat sneaking up on a bird a hand reached out and covered Willow's mouth. It stifled a scream.

"Havin' fun watchin' them destroy my still, little bitch?" Moss's rank breath bathed Willow's ear. Her eyes grew large with fear.

"Wait until I git a-hold of that sorry bastard. He'll wish he'd never been borned."

Willow tried to break free. Bearlike hands held her like a steel trap. "An' I got somethin' special for you, bitch." Moss backed up with Willow in his grasp pulling her into the brush. They disappeared without so much as a broken twig or the rustle of dry leaves carpeting the forest floor.

⊱⋅⊰

Callie, broken-hearted, listened as the hickory switch slapped Maggie's bare legs. She grimaced as her cries carried throughout the house and onto the back porch. "All of this is my fault." Callie sobbed as she heard light footsteps going in circles and heavier ones following.

Callie couldn't take it. She jumped from her chair and ran into the house. "Stop it!" Leave her alone! Please — it ain't her fault, Momma. Don't whup her no more."

The switch hung in midair. Maggie stopped dancing. The limber switch dropped to the floor. "Go to your room," Ellie said to Maggie. She looked at Callie, whose eyes were wet and red.

"It'll be all right, Momma. She'll be her old self again after she gets another banjo. I ain't never going to let anything happen to her ever again. Not never!"

Chapter 27
Free at Last

Sheriff Vaughn inspected the ruined stills, the splintered barrels, and the wasted corn and sugar. "That should do it. There isn't anything to salvage out of this mess. Let's head on back."

"I hope Mr. McGregor's okay," Flashy said. "I figured he'd want to be here to see this for himself, but I guess he's just too winded."

"The old man was pretty give-out," Jimbo said. "He's prob'ly asleep in the shade of that big oak."

"I'd give anything to see the look on that ol' sum-bitch's face when he sees his still busted in a million pieces," Thorny said with a smile.

Bud warned, "You just watch that he doesn't take it out on you and your family."

"I'll kill that sorry sum bitch if he lays one hand on airy one of them!" Thorny barked,

Vaughn warned, "Now, son, you come to us and let the law handle it."

"Listen to the sheriff, Thorny, for your own good. Come and get me," Bud said.

Thorny looked evenly at Bud, "I ain't gonna wait until he kills somebody."

The men said nothing as Thorny stepped into the trail leading away from the busted stills.

A few minutes later they came to the place where they had left McGregor. He lay stretched out on the ground.

"See, I told you he'd be asleep," Jimbo said.

Bud noticed blood on McGregor's head. "He's bleeding!" Everyone rushed over to see.

"He's dead, ain't he?" Thorny asked. "The bastard's done kilt him!"

"We don't know that for sure," Bud said.

The sheriff went down on one knee and felt the prone man's pulse. "He's not dead, but he's hurt bad. We'll have to carry him out of here."

Because of McGregor's dead weight, and he being a big man, too, it had taken over an hour to get back to the hidden cruiser. Vaughn, Bud, and Jimbo laid McGregor on the back seat to take him to the hospital. Flashy rode in the back seat with his partner, his head in his lap.

Thorny helped carry the hurt reporter part way before deciding to go home. He knew his family would be in danger if Moss had watched his still being destroyed, and he felt certain he had. He wouldn't just take it out on him, Thorny knew, he would beat the first person he came to. He would show no mercy. He quickened his pace.

Thorny thought of Willow, and what Moss would do to her. Even Olive might feel his wrath.

He ran.

Agonizing thoughts zipped through Thorny's head as he dashed around rocks and trees. His breathing became labored. His throat felt like fire. The thought of his family being in danger, though, gave him the adrenalin boost needed to make the climb. His ribs, not completely healed, throbbed, his injured lung burned.

His imagination ran wild as he saw in his mind's eye Moss slapping his mother until she passed out — or died. He imagined Willow, beaten and bloody, lying underneath Moss, her body withering under his weight. He felt guilty he hadn't stopped it before now. He would have, he told himself, if not for his mother's pleading. And then he thought of Olive.

His throat felt like the opening to hell. He wanted to stop, fall to the ground, to breathe again without pain. He wanted to, but knew he couldn't. He could not risk it.

Thorny stumbled over the rise and saw the shack. Just a few more steps and he could quench the heat in his throat and ease the pain in his chest and side.

Something happened. A sound not heard in months echoed over the countryside.

Thunder shook the earth in gentle waves as it rolled from far away. It rumbled louder as it gathered speed like a locomotive rushing downhill. The tsunami of sound ended in a crescendo of crashes, splitting the sky with fire, shaking windows, spooking livestock, and making babies howl with fright.

Thorny slowed down at the unusual sound, one he hardly recognized it had been so long since he had heard it. Glancing toward the sky, he noticed the black clouds gathering. More thunder rolled. The sky split apart with forks of lightning. A few drops of rain tapped his face, and then a few more. It felt like the balm of Gilead, soothing, cool, and refreshing.

He sprinted for the back porch. His rifle remained firmly in his grip. The door swung open, hitting the wall with a slap. He rushed in. The torn screen flapped and the door almost came off its hinges. As his eyes adjusted to the dark, he saw something on the floor. He stopped dead still.

Rose lay on the floor, the bottom of her left eye flayed open—the gash wide. Blood poured down her face. Her lips puffed out, making her swollen face look like something from a circus sideshow. Her breaths came in ragged pulls. Olive sat next to her, fingers in her mouth, fear in her eyes.

"Momma!" Thorny shouted as he fell to his knees. He

took her head in his arms. Rose tried to open her swollen eyes.

"Willow… help her. Don't let him…" She passed out. Her head flopped to one side. He heard a commotion in Willow's room.

Moss slapped the girl again She fell against the wall and slid to the floor. "So you liked watchin' my still git busted up! He picked her up and hit her again with a sickening thud. Willow crumpled like paper.

He grabbed her up from the dirty floor. "You like this dress thet little noisy gal made, do ya?" He grabbed it by the sleeves and yanked. "This time there won't be no purty store bought dress!" Moss unbuckled his overalls. They fell to the floor.

Thorny raised his rifle, aimed. A shot rang out. Moss fell forward, his body landing on the side of the bed. He swayed, stayed suspended for a few seconds, and then slipped to the floor. He didn't move.

A car skidded to a stop in the yard. Doors opened. Feet trampled across the yard, up the steps, and over the porch. Bud Kinser and Sheriff Vaughn burst through the door, their weapons drawn.

Thorny turned, lowered his rifle, and let it fall to the floor with a clatter. He fell to his knees.

Rose lay prostrate on the floor with Moss's rifle lying across her chest, the barrel emitting wisps of smoke. She had come to and somehow had summoned the strength to pull up from the floor, stagger to the door, lift the rifle, and pull the trigger. Thorny never fired.

Willow ran, grabbed Olive, and held her tight. Thorny cradled his mother's head in his arms. She managed to open her eyes enough to see through the narrow slits.

Sheriff Vaughn checked Moss for a pulse. He found none.

"We're free at last," Thorny said as he wept.

Thunder burst the sky wide open and the rain came down.

Chapter 28
Pretty Rags

The death of Willow's tormentor did nothing to alleviate the shame she felt. The heavy burden of perceived sin weighed her down. *Them babies. It's my fault they were borned, and my fault they died. It's my sins that caused it.*

Her heart ached with sorrow, sorrow she could no longer bear. She thought of the two babies, as she did every day. She dreamed about them often. In her dreams they were pleading to let them live, to nestle in her arms. The boy had light blond hair and the girl's hair had a red tint. She pictured her with silky auburn hair like hers, snuggled in her arms and smiling. The boy would grow up to be strong and kind, like Thorny." I'll never know," she cried out in anguish.

Moss had snatched them straight from her womb, put a pillow over their faces, and made Willow watch as he denied them breath, using the same pillow she laid her head on. He then handed them to her and forced her to bury them in a plain grave. "Whatcha git for havin' younguns," he had said.

She had no pine box, not even a cardboard box to lay them in. Both times she had begged for a blanket even a rag to wrap their tiny bodies in, but Moss would not allow it. The dirt would be their only covering and the grave their earthly home.

Cotton bark tea had since become her drink of choice, drunk from a bitter cup.

The rain danced rhythmically on the tin roof of the old shack for the second day. Leaks abounded. What should have been a calming sound to the ear drove Willow to the periphery of insanity. Each drop represented pain, each flash of lightning a stab to the heart.

She bolted from her bed, grabbed an armload of her pretty dresses, and ran for the door. The prettiest dress, the ones she cherished, the remaining one Callie's hands had fashioned, hung on a rusted hanger, alone. She had on the dress Moss had ripped, holding it together with pins.

❧

The Kinsers sat on the porch watching it rain. Maggie observed, as raindrops splattered in the dirt, how each left its mark as it encountered the earth. She listened to the magical sound of rain on the tin roof, imagining each drop a single note adding to the others to form melodies, soothing lullabies led by the hand of God.

"You were right, Ellie, all it took was a little faith, and you provided most of it, too." Bud said, patting Ellie's hand as they sat side by side on the porch swing.

"I'd almost forgotten how rain sounds on a tin roof, how relaxing it is." Ellie yawned. "I slept as tight as a hibernating bear last night."

Callie set her sight on Fox Hill and sighed. "I wish Willow and Thorny had come to stay with us. I don't like them up there alone in that old shack. I bet it's raining inside as much as it is outside."

"No doubt," Bud agreed. "Thorny flat refused to come and Willow, well, she wouldn't go without him. I wish she'd gone to the hospital like her momma, at least to be checked out. Insisted she'd be all right. But at least they're together. And I expect Rose'll be laid up in the hospital bed for a few days."

Ellie chuckled. "Airy Mae's plumb tickled to take care of Olive. Said having a little one to take care of quit giving her the urge to rock Fred and put a diaper on his bottom."

Callie paced back and forth. "What's got you frettin'?" Corbit asked. "You're about to worry a furrow in the floor."

"I'm worried about Willow. She's sick. Not the head cold kind of sick. She's just — you know, head sick. Something's awful wrong with her thinking. She talked real crazy like, mumbled things I couldn't understand when I saw her this morning. She had a funny look on her face, like she was somewhere far off and couldn't find her way back."

"I am too," Bud said to Ellie in as low a voice as possible to keep the children from hearing it. "She seemed just like Callie said. And it ain't no wonder, either, with all she's been through. Her life's been pure hell on earth. When Thorny told me about them babies, and how she had to bury them, my heart about broke in two. I can't imagine what it has done to the poor girl."

⊱⋅⊰

Willow bolted from the house. The wet clay stuck to her bare feet as she navigated the narrow lane in the dark. She slipped, fell, and slid on her back. The dresses remained tucked in her arms. She rolled to her knees. Pushing to her feet she slipped and fell again. The rain came down in sheets, and her tears matched the rain in intensity. Wet and muddy hair fell over her eyes as she clambered to her feet once again.

⊱⋅⊰

Bud assured Callie, "Don't worry, I'll check on them tomorrow morning, make sure they're all right and see they have something to eat. I'm sure things will be better for them now that Moss is dead and gone."

Ellie agreed. "Yes, but the damage's already done to those younguns. It'll be hard for them to overcome everything that's happened, especially Willow."

"The sheriff plans to get in touch with Rose's sister, see if she can take them in. Once they get away from that miserable hovel maybe things'll change. Any life's got to be better than the one they had."

"What about Rose killing Lucas? What's the sheriff gonna do about that? Will she stand trial?" Ellie wanted to know.

"Since Rose was aiming at Moss and not at Lucas, it's considered an accident. She might face manslaughter charges, depending on the DA, but the sheriff don't think she will, considering all she's been through with Moss. The fact of the matter is she didn't have to admit she did it. Nobody would've ever known. The fact that she did, though, should help her. Joe's going to do all he can to convince the DA not to press charges."

"That poor woman's had to live with it all this time," Ellie remarked.

"She wanted to say something, but was afraid she'd go to prison and leave the kids, especially Olive, alone."

∂•∂

Lightning lit up the sky, outlining the shack at the top of the hill, while a ghost-like figure made its way through the woods and rain.

Willow stumbled toward the place where she and Thorny had sat and found comfort in each other's pain, where they had talked and dreamed of something better.

The images of her lost children flipped maddeningly through her mind like pages of a book fluttering in the wind, only the book had no ending. As soon as the wind had turned the last page, it reversed direction and howled the other way until the first page of the first chapter stared back at her, forcing her to speed-read it again, and again.

She wanted to write the final chapter, to be done with it. She wanted to record the last period and close the book. It would be the last "amen!"

She stood on the rock overhang facing the valley below. Streaks of lightning revealed the Kinser farm and cattle lowing in the pasture, seemingly oblivious to the rain. The waters of the Brush flowed along, growing strong again as it captured each raindrop. Looking toward the Kinser house she imagined the faint images of a family weathering the storm together. She glanced toward the shack but could only see the fury of the storm, the one in her head that had tossed her family to and fro battering it to tiny pieces.

Willow sat underneath the lone tree that stood on the precipice of the overhang, a stoic sentinel guarding the valley. She took each dress and tore it into rags. *Now they really are pretty*, she mused. She took strips of each dress, tied them together and fashioned a rope. She threw the remnants in the air, the wind catching and whirling them away.

Her babies waited for their mother. She would go to them, wrap them in her arms, let them suckle at her breast, feel their warmth and love. She would give them life… again. She would live, too, for the first time.

Tying the dress-rope around her waist, Willow climbed to the lowest limb sprawling ten feet above the ground. The limb shook from the wind as if it were weeping, inconsolable. Reaching the bough, she tied the pretty rags around it, tied the other end around her neck, and jumped.

"No!" Thorny shouted, and grabbed her legs just before the rag-rope became taut.

⌘

"Ain't it exciting!" Callie gushed.

"It sure is," Bud agreed. "How about it, Maggie. You excited?"

Maggie hunched her shoulders. "I guess so." The cast, now off of her arm, left it white and shrunken. Her other wounds had healed as well, only the long scar down her leg remained.

Ellie looked surprised. "You *guess* so? Why, I would've thought you'd be beside yourself with Earl Scruggs coming to town and all."

Maggie looked at Callie and frowned. "I want to see him, and all, but I don't have a banjer to play, so it won't be as much fun."

Corbit couldn't hold it in. "Ain't you going to give it to her, Callie?"

Maggie looked around the living room. Everyone had a Cheshire cat grin. Callie left the room with a bounce in her step and a few minutes later came back with a brightly wrapped package. "Here, Maggie, this is for you. I hope you like it."

"Yeah, it cost $27… $27.45 with shipping," Corbit bragged.

"Hush, Corbit," his mother admonished. "It ain't polite to tell what you paid for a gift, or in this case, what Callie paid."

Maggie took the huge package and set it on her lap. She stared at it for a full minute, carefully outlining the shape of the package with her finger.

"Well, open it!" Corbit said, excitement oozing from every pore.

Maggie's hands trembled as she tore off the paper. Corbit and Bud held on to each end to prevent the gift from sliding off her lap.

A black case came into view. Maggie threw her hands to her mouth. She bounced in her chair. Bud and Corbit held onto the case.

"Go ahead, open it up," Callie said, standing on her toes and pressing her fingers together to form a tepee.

Maggie unlatched the case and opened it. She gasped, held her breath. Shaky hands reached in and lovingly removed a brand-new Gibson Mastertone banjo.

"Just like Earl Scruggs plays," Callie said, her smile filling the room.

Bud took the case and laid it on the floor. Maggie admired the beautifully scrolled neck and the maple body of amber and smooth gloss lacquer. On the very top of the neck white letters in cursive spelled *Gibson*.

"Callie bought it for you with the sewing money she made" Corbit spurted.

Maggie looked at Callie through teary eyes. She sprang the few feet separating them and threw her arms around her, the banjo draping across Callie's back. Both sisters cried. Atonement had been made and forgiveness granted.

"Aw, cut it out and play your new banjo," Corbit begged.

"Like Corbit said, it's just like that Scrubbs feller plays," Bud interjected.

Maggie laced the strap around her neck and placed brand-new picks on her fingers and thumb. She fretted the neck and strummed the taut strings. "Needs tuning," she said. Slightly turning the four pearl-white tuning keys at the top, and the fifth string tuning peg lower on the neck, she plucked the strings until they blended to form the right pitch. Everyone watched as she prepared. For the first time Callie noticed how professionally Maggie handled her instrument, how she listened with her head cocked, and the intent look on her face.

"Oh, I'll be John Brown," Callie whispered.

Maggie's fingers moved like lightning as she played "She'll Be Coming Round the Mountain." Afterwards, and without any hesitation, she transitioned into Bill Monroe's "Muleskinner Blues."

Wearing the plain dress Callie had made, Willow sat quietly in a straight-back chair smiling and looking on in wonder as the Kinser family shared joy and happiness in one another's company. She watched as two girls became sisters again, and marveled as their parent's eyes glowed with pride instead of the hate and fear she was used to seeing.

"Come on, Willow," Corbit said rather boldly as he took her hand. "Let's dance the Hucklebuck."

"Oh, no, you're not!" Ellie grabbed Corbit's arm. "That ain't a proper dance for younguns." She pulled them to the center of the room, Bud moved furniture against the wall, took Callie's hand and joined them in a square.

Bud winked at his wife. "Momma's right, I think a good old-fashioned square dance will do just fine,"

"I ain't never danced before," Willow said.

"Oh, it's plumb easy," Corbit assured her. "Just do what we do."

Maggie fretted the strings with her left hand while her right hand played "Poor Polly" with flawless rolls. She did a string bender by tweaking a tuning key first one way, and then the other creating a wavy twang. The dancers joined arms and circled, did the dosey-doe meeting right shoulders and back to back. Next they did the see-saw around left shoulders, peeled the banana, and executed the slide as Bud called out instructions.

Outside the air had been scrubbed clean and fresh from the rain. The crops were green and the Brush flowed with new water, high and rising.

"We'd better go if we're to make Earl Scrubbs's show," Bud said, a little out of breath.

Maggie laughed. "No, Deddy, it's Scruggs. S-C-R-U-double G- S. Not scrubbs, silly."

"Well, whatever his name is, we'd better go or we'll miss the show."

A crowd gathered around a flatbed International truck on East Washington Avenue in downtown Athens. Kids raced around playing and having the time of their lives while men stood and smoked Prince Albert and talked about the rain and saved crops. The ladies talked and cooed over babies.

Most people were dressed in farm clothes, but a few were dressed in their Sunday best for the occasion. Callie noticed several ladies wearing the dresses she had made, and a baby wore a blue bonnet trimmed in white lace she had just finished yesterday.

A man with a red flannel shirt climbed on top of the flatbed and stood in front of the microphone. He tapped it and spoke. Immediately it squealed like a pig. Kids held their ears and grimaced.

The announcer tapped the microphone again. "Testing, testing," he said. The squealing slowly abated as someone adjusted the sound.

"Ladies and gentlemen, on behalf of the city of Athens and your Chamber of Commerce, I am pleased to present Lost John Miller, featuring Earl Scruggs and his famous banjo." Everyone burst out in applause. Maggie could hardly contain herself.

After about fifteen minutes of picking and singing, John Miller stepped up to the microphone. "Well, neighbors, it's an honor to be with you here in Athens today. I hope you're enjoying the music so far." Applause whistles and hoots cut the air. "I want to bring up our banjo picker. You all know who I'm talking about. Come on up, Earl!"

Another round of appreciation was rendered by the large crowd. Maggie slapped her hands together, hopping around like a rabbit. Her banjo lay across her stomache in the playing position as if she would join in if asked.

After Scruggs played several tunes with his long series of defining staccato notes, he said, "I can see you all like good pickin' and sangin', so I have a special surprise for you here this evening. We have a young lady in the audience that, so I'm told, can pick a banjo like a whirlwind. Her stage name is Little Maggie. Make welcome your own Maggie Kinser. Come on up, Little Maggie!"

The crowd went wild. Bud, Ellie and Corbit looked

at Maggie in total shock. Callie had a jack-o'-lantern grin. Maggie couldn't believe what she had heard. She looked at the famous man and then at the hand-slapping crowd.

"Well, go on up, Little Maggie, everybody's waiting on you," Callie said.

Maggie, still speechless, worked her way through the crowd to the flatbed. She climbed the portable steps on the back side of the truck bed and walked onto the stage. Her eyes were saucer- sized. The crowd applauded even louder. Whistles could be heard over the clapping hands and cheering of the hometown crowd.

"What do you wanna play first, Little Maggie?" Scruggs said.

Maggie Kinser, future star of the Grand Ole Opry — transformed from Maggie the farm girl into a person only she knew existed, someone reborn — realized dreams in this moment in time were as real and as important as Callie's dresses and pillow cases, or Corbit's dam. *I, Little Maggie, have something to offer, too*, she thought.

Maggie stepped up to the microphone, conceived, born and raised for this moment. "I'm gonna start out with one of yourn, Mr. Scruggs, if that's okay." He smiled and gave a thumbs up.

Her fingers went to work. She stood poised, proud and professional. She played her part, stepped back from the microphone at the right time so the fiddler could step up to play his part, and the guitar player, his. Maggie had learned the routine from other acts when the Chamber would bring them to town. The mandolin took its turn and then gave way to Scruggs' galloping banjo. Maggie closed with the last refrain.

The Kinser family stood in awe. This was not the Maggie they knew, the timid, somewhat lazy, and very awkward Maggie Kinser. This was a new person recently born, new to the world, a bright star in a galaxy of musical excellence known as Little Maggie.

"Rocky Top" gave way to "Clinch Mountain Backstep," "Carolina Boogie," "Cluck Ol' Hen" and a couple of other tunes before Little Maggie reluctantly yielded the stage to Lost John Miller and Earl Scruggs. The applause began as soon as she picked the last note. The world disappeared. At that moment she had become the star she had always envisioned. The applause went on for an eternity. She could hear it, but it sounded far-off and dreamy. To keep it forever Maggie captured it and put it away in a special room in her brain where it would remain to be recalled at will.

Scruggs stepped up to the microphone. "Well now, it sounds like Athens loves you, Little Maggie, and I have a feeling everybody that hears you from now on will love you, too." The crowd broke out into loud applause and whistles. The musician continued, "Lost John wants to know, Little Maggie, if you'd do him a favor and play with us on the Grand Ole Opry next month. Would you do that?"

Maggie's hands flew to her mouth. She gasped and dropped down to her knees. Her hands covered her face. The surprise drew the breath right out of her.

Ellie gasped and flung her arms around Bud. Corbit jabbed his arm into the air and shouted, "Hot-diggity-dog! Maggie's gonna be famous!"

Willow joined in the celebratory applause as she watched the Kinser family share their joy. Again she stood amazed at how happy a family could be.

Callie smiled. Not expecting an answer, she had sent a letter to WNOX in care of Earl Scruggs, telling him about Maggie, her brush with death, and her love for the banjo. After a week he'd replied with an invitation for her to join him on stage.

Maggie leaped to her feet and hugged Earl Scruggs with all her strength. "I'll have to ask my momma and deddy, Mr. Scruggs, but I'm sure they'll let me."

Scruggs leaned into the microphone. "Well, how about

it, Mr. and Mrs. Kinser, can Little Maggie play the Opry?"

Bud, Ellie, Corbit, Callie, and Willow yelled their approval as one voice. They held on to one another and danced in a circle while the crowd offered their boisterous approval once again.

On the ride home Maggie beamed at Callie. She beamed back. The pride Bud and Ellie felt for Maggie was immense, but the pride they felt for Callie was immeasurable.

"I don't care if you call me Ettis," Corbit whispered to Callie.

Callie shot back, "That ain't fair!" Corbit just grinned as he realized he had won the contest.

"Can we do Family Funnies Monday night?" Willow suddenly asked. "And can we play Clothespins in a Bottle, bake cookies, and do the Hucklebuck?" She paused. "Well, maybe a square dance?"

Sleep did not come easily for the Kinser household. Excitement raced through their veins, but when it did come, it came with peaceful dreams.

Early sunlight sneaked through the windows, but did not catch anyone sleeping. Chores were being performed long before the sun's rays glowed above the horizon.

After breakfast Corbit, Callie, Willow, but not Maggie, went off to finish the chores. They had already planned to spend the afternoon cooling off in the creek. In the meantime Maggie had to practice for her debut on the Opry. Earl Scruggs had given her a list of songs for her to practice. This time Callie didn't mind. In the coming days she and Corbit, Willow, Fred, and Tommie Sue would be Maggie's attentive audience providing loud applause and standing ovations.

⊱⊰

Willow waved goodbye to her mother and Olive as they found their seats on an Alabama-bound Greyhound. "Bye, Momma, bye, Olive. I'll see you soon."

Olive crawled into her mother's lap and waved back. "You promise?"

"I promise," Willow said as the driver grabbed the handle and pulled the door closed. She watched until the bus shifted into high gear and disappeared into the future.

⤞⤝

Lost John Miller and Earl Scruggs picked up Maggie on their way to Nashville and the Opry.

Saturday night found the Kinsers and Willow huddled around the Philco listening to "The Lone Ranger" while waiting for the Opry to come on. Bud adjusted the dial to try and tune out some of the static.

"Ladies and gentlemen welcome to WSM, and the… Grand… Ole… Op-ry!" The Kinsers joined in the applause. Clapping with them, Willow watched the Kinsers enjoying every moment. She had only imagined what it would feel like being a part of a happy family.

After Minnie Pearl and Grandpa Jones completed their act, Mother Maybelle Carter and the Carter Family sang "Keep on the Sunny Side," "Will the Circle Be Unbroken," and closed with their signature tune, "Wildwood Flower."

The tall and gangly Mother Maybelle stepped up to the microphone and said in her southwestern Virginia twang, "Thank ye ever'body. And now I'd like to introduce a young lady, 'a *banjer* picker,' in her own words, that got her inspiration from another *banjer* picker named Earl Scruggs, who's with us here tonight. Her name is Little Maggie Kinser from Brush Creek, Tennessee." The Opry crowd responded with a polite applause.

Maggie looked out from behind the stage. She couldn't believe she actually stood in the Ryman Auditorium with some of the biggest stars in country music. *The Grand Ole Opry,* she thought with wonder, *I'm about to play my banjer on the Opry!* Her eyes moistened when she heard her name.

Roy Acuff put his arm around her and said, "Welcome to the Opry, Little Maggie. I've heard some mighty fine things about you from Earl and John. Don't be nervous, you'll do just fine." Grandpa Jones, Minnie Pearl, String Bean, and the rest of the Opry cast all made it a point to stop and offer encouragement to the budding star.

Mother Maybelle continued, "Welcome to the stage of The Grand Ole Opry, Little Maggie — come on out and show ol' Earl how to *really* play a banjo."

The crowd broke out in applause. To Maggie it sounded like thunder. The Kinsers, Willow included, gave a standing ovation.

Ellie twisted her apron into a pretzel. "Oh, my, I'm so nervous. I hope she don't mess up and get embarrassed and all."

Callie laughed. "Oh, don't worry about that. She might get nervous picking up a hen's egg, but not her banjo."

Corbit agreed. "Yeah, she lives and breathes by her banjo. Forgetting a note would be like forgetting to breathe. It just comes natural."

During Maggie's ten minutes on stage all of her dreams melded into one and became a reality. She transformed from a backward farm girl to a star. She became a household word, a Favorite Daughter to Brush Creek, and someone with worth to herself. She soared to the heavens and stood on the moon as everyone on earth looked up.

><

"This letter came today," Ellie said handing it to Bud. "It's from Thorny."

Bud read the letter:

Deer Mr. and Mrs. Kinser,

I just wanted to rite and thank you for what you done for my fammily. I owe you more than I could ever say or do. I'm glad I took Sherif Vaughn's advice and joined the army. I like it here at Ft. Campbell. Boot camp is hard, but not as hard as what the old man put me through. I hope Willow is doing ok, tell her that I'll rite her directly. Tell Maggie that I herd her on the radio when she played on the Opry. Mother Maybelle and Earl Scruggs shur bragged on her a lot. Nobody here at camp believes that I knowed her. Tell her hi and that I'm glad she didn't drownt. Tell Callie and Corbit hi, to. Tell Corbit I want to play him and Fred in a game of marbles agin one day. Tell Mrs. Kinser that she is the best cook in Tenessee.

Your friend,
Robert
(PS. Robert is my real name)

Brush Creek still flowed from the mountains of yesterday through the fields of today, and the hollows and hills of tomorrow. Family Funnies, games, and warm cookies with a real family full of love and respect gave Willow a piece of life she had always envisioned. The dreams of her babies still haunted her. Guilt riddled her mind, her grief real and deep. Her father having his way with her still filled her with deep and abiding shame. She had borne Thorny's pain as Moss beat him, and witnessed the haunting eyes of their mother and sister as they endured his physical and mental abuse.

Her countenance lifted, however, every time she thought of the tenderness in her brother's eyes and the softness in his voice the many times he had given her comfort at the very place he had saved her. Because of him, and the new life her mother and Olive now enjoyed, and the goodness of a family in Brush Creek, she would be able to endure it, and eventually, with the help of God whom she now sought, could overcome it.

Willow packed her new wardrobe Callie had sewn for her in a worn-out suitcase of Ellie's. The ride to the bus station was both happy and sad. She would see her family again. Rose had a job as a seamstress in a local shop in Brewton, Alabama. She and Olive now lived in a small rental house, a house for the first time they could call home. Thorny, home on leave from the Army, had a new life, not a thorn-in-the-side nothing, but a man named Robert.

The sad part came with leaving her Brush Creek family. They had learned from each other, had grown stronger together. She would miss them, but would always love them. They were her salvation, the people who, in spite of the rocky beginning in a church with fire on the roof, had pointed the way to a better life.

∂∾∽

The summer of 1945 was at an end, the nights and early mornings were cooler, the days shorter. The rain had transformed the surroundings from a drab and dusty brown to a luxuriant green, everything seemed refreshed, the earth, the people, even the birds seemed happier, their trills seemingly more lively than during the harsh dry spell. The rains continued throughout the rest of the summer washing away all signs of a drought. The Brush was back to its normal level with Old Man Oak still guarding its banks as it waited patiently for the next rope swinging reveler.

Callie, Corbit, and this time, Maggie, made the early morning climb to the top of the *Hill* as due sparkled in the rising sunlight and sunbeams fairie danced on the ripples of Brush Creek far below.

"I can't believe school's starting tomorrow," Corbit said, his countenance reflecting melancholy. His summer had been a mixture of extreme sadness and joy, but something was now missing from his youth that, he knew, was gone forever.

"Yeah, me either," Callie agreed. She too felt the emptiness of innocence lost to a world both hard and beautiful,

Callie and Corbit wanted to make the trek up the Hill normally reserved for the first day of summer vacation, not to celebrate the beginning of summer, but the ending—the summer that had changed each of their lives, and the lives of those that had lived in a shack on top of another hill underneath the shade of guilt, shame, and hopelessness.

More than anything they wanted to be with Maggie to watch the sunrise over the smokyblue mountains eastward, to sit with her in the damp grass, to share in the scent of fall flowers as it wrapped them in their varied flavors of delight. Each of them had changed, emerged from their cocoon to become a butterfly in their own right, their lives had morphed from youthful innocence to something more profound. They had grown together, became older and wiser. Together they looked over the farmland, the forest, the dewy hillsides, and watched as Brush Creek flowed from the past and on to the future.

"Play something, Maggie," Callie said as she plopped down on moist grass and leaned back on elbows, her legs bent at the knees.

"Yeah, play the song Earl asked you to play on the Opry next week," Corbit said with a yawn, arms stretched out to greet the sun.

Without a word Maggie propped her foot on a rock and celebrated with a song the new beginning with her siblings. She knew what her calling had been from the beginning; she just didn't know it would come so quickly. Still she devoted most of her time to perfecting her craft, but not all of it. She did chores, maybe not as many as she should, but she performed them with a little less distain now.

When she finished with her usual flair Maggie said, "This sure is nice."

"We wanted you to see, too. We wanted you to be a part of it. Corbit, well, he always wanted you to come, but I — well, you know," Callie said with a sheepish grin.

Maggie beamed. "Do you think things will ever change?"

"How is that?" Corbit asked.

"You know, climbing this hill, doing things together and all?"

Corbit didn't have to think about it. "Yeah, things'll change, just like it did this summer. Just look at us. Hey, look at you. You're not the same ol' Little Maggie. Not by a long shot. None of us are the same, I guess. Our whole lives have changed in different ways."

"Oh, but some things won't never change, will they?" Maggie asked with apprehension.

"Doing things together has been the bestest thing about this summer. It's been the most wonderfulness time of my life!"

Callie pushed up on her elbows, her shadow following. "Really? Even better than playin' on the Opry?"

"Yeah, better. Maybe as good as watching Willow and Thorny be happy." Maggie looked from Callie to Corbit. "Playing on the Opry's fun and all, a dream really, but learning to swim and fish has been the goodest time."

Callie thought about how wrong she had been and how much better it was now having Maggie around. She smiled as she sniffed the air, "I smell bacon."

"And coffee," Corbit said. "I can hear it plurping in the pot!"

"Race ya!" Maggie cried, and scampered like a rabbit, her banjo resting on her back.

"No fair!" Callie and Corbit wailed together. "Wait for us!"

They ran past saplings that had grown a little taller while measuring the days from summer to fall. They jumped over rocks and swooshed around old trees that had watched time pass for ions. In a dead heat they smashed through the edge of the forest into the open yard. All three stopped short of the house, stood there, inhaled slowly and deeply.

"That sure is a nice smell," Callie said, her eyes closed.

"Yeah, it smells like a song," Maggie sang, strumming her banjo.

"Yep, and home," Corbit finished.

Together they trotted toward breakfast carrying with them something much more profound than they had known at the beginning of the summer. Things had changed, and would change again. Like Brush Creek life would alter its course over time.

Author Notes

I wanted to write a story about my mother, Callie Sliger Miller, my Uncle Corbit Sliger, and my Aunt Maggie Beebe who grew up in Athens, McMinn County, Tennessee, in the farming community of Brush Creek. They grew up in the 1920s, but I moved it to the 1940s. I found it more convenient because I was born in the latter part of that era. It just seemed more comfortable to me. My grandmother Sliger's maiden name was Kinser. I liked the easy flow of the name so I used it for my characters in the place of Sliger. It also distanced me from the family, which made it easier for me to write.

My grandmother's first name was Maggie. She named her youngest daughter Maggie, so I changed my grandmother's name to Ellie to avoid confusion. Maggie, the daughter, was also known as Mag Ellen and Maggie Ellen. I started off using Maggie Ellen, but it got my simple mind confused very quickly. Growing up I heard Meg Ellen pronounced Mag-gallon, leaving out the "E", so I always thought that was her name. I wondered why she was named after a measure of liquid.

My mother is still living at this writing. She will be 102 on September 11, 2014. Uncle Corbit passed at the age of 100 and still mowed his own grass. Aunt Maggie had lived until the age of 82 having passed on in 1999. She raised a large family on her own in the projects of Chattanooga. Not an easy task.

The sibling rivalry was real. My mother still talks about how Maggie always managed to get out of work. She would say (and still does), "All she ever wanted to do was sit around and strum that ol' banjo while I did all of the work." Maggie was the youngest, after all.

My friend Jimmy Redmon and I were playing around on our Walkie Talkies saying things that were not nice when the preacher of the local Church of God interrupted us. He admonished us for the crude lauguage and then invited us to his church for a revival. We accepted. Reverend Powell sat us on the stand with him making us feel special. As the hymn singing got underway a woman burst through the door and shouted, "There's fire dancing on the roof!" Reverend Powell, seeing that as a sign, marched to the pulpit and proclaimed the fire on the roof to be the Holy Ghost. And that is how I came up with Lottie Finch and the Holy Ghost roof fire. I believed it then, and I believe it now.

Mama always wanted to own a house but could never afford one. My father, Conlin Miller, never made over $400 a month in his life. It was all he could do to buy beans and keep a roof over our heads, let alone buy a house. After Daddy died she said, "Well, I guess I'll never have a home of my own."

I was determined that she would. Mama paid her house off with the money she made as a seamstress in her new home. She was as good at sewing as I depicted in the book.

Uncle Corbit really did dam the spring and save the crops during the drought. He said that you could hear the cornstalks pop and straighten up as soon as the water hit the roots. He was also an inventor and a machinist who helped modify the bomb bay for the Enola Gay that dropped the first atomic bomb. He was also a jeweler and jewelry store owner. His store is still in downtown Athens and is now owned by his son, Gene.

When Uncle Corbit was 100 years old his wife, my aunt Hazel, herself in her late 90s, had to be put into a nursing home. He would ride the bus to the nursing home every day and stay until she had her evening meal. In Tennessee we call it "supper." He would then catch the bus back home and tend to his chores. His children would have a meal waiting for him.

When Uncle Corbit fell ill and had to be hospitalized, he asked to be put in the nursing home next to his wife. Their beds were placed side by side. They would hold hands, and that is how he died. He was 100 years and four months old. Aunt Hazel never knew because of the state of her mind, but she still talked about him until the very end a few months later. Now that's a love story!

Maggie played the *banjer,* as she called it. She loved music. The murder in the one-room school, used as a church, actually happened. They never found out who did it. Willow and Thorny came from the inner workings of my imagination.

Callie lived with Linda and me for almost four years, a daunting task to say the least. My mother has always been independent and self-sufficient, so having to be helped did not come easy for her. My sister, Sylvia, and her husband, Alfred Mobley, are now taking care of her. It has been a privilege for the four of us.

When I was very young and still living in Tennessee I remember hearing someone say that a boy had fallen into the creek into a bed of Cottonmouth Water Moccasins. When he was found the snakes were still attached to his body. They mentioned how swollen he was from the poison. That's where I got the idea of Minner and the moccasins.

McMinn County was not a pleasant place in the 1940s. The sheriff's department was funded through fines, which opened the door to false arrest, mostly for traffic violations and public drunkenness. The sheriff used it liberally. Elections were won by secret ballot counts and forged ballots. The poll-watchers were beaten; voters were intimidated and brutalized, even shot if they refused to vote for those who ran the political machine. The FBI and the Department of Justice refused to intervene, and had for years.

Finally the people had had enough. The returning veterans from WWII decided to nominate some of their own for office, including sheriff. Paul Cantrell had been sheriff three times since 1936. When he was elected to the State Senate, his Chief Deputy, Pat Mansfield, was elected in his place. When Cantrell left the senate in 1946, he again ran for sheriff. The vets had just fought a war in Europe and the South Pacific to preserve the freedom to vote their conscience and to live in peace. They were not about to let those freedoms be taken away in their own county.

After the polls closed on August 2, 1946, deputies confiscated ballot boxes and took them to the sheriff's office to be counted under lock and key. The veterans decided to fight back. They armed themselves by scouring the county for weapons and even raiding the armory. By 8 p.m., a group of former GIs and other locals headed for the jail to get the ballot boxes. They occupied the high ground facing the jail but left the back door unguarded to give the jail's defenders an easy way out.

They were fired on from the jail and two ex-GIs were wounded. The vets fired back and one person inside the jail was badly wounded. Finally the vets pushed the issue and threw some dynamite damaging the front porch of the jail. The deputies gave up and Cantrell disappeared into the night. Law and order was restored and the citizens of McMinn County enjoyed free and open elections. This incident has come to be known as the Battle of Athens.

My grandfather, Bud Sliger, was a deputy in the 1920s. My mother remembers him going to work on a mule.

About the Author

Ron Miller is the author of "Horse Bones, 12 Tales of Secrets, Ghosts, and Legends", for middle readers, stories from his growing up years in his home town of Lake City, a small town in north central Florida. "Callie Kinser of Brush Creek" is his first novel reflecting his Tennessee roots. He loves the South, its traditions, people and history, so his stories reflect the Southern way of life. Ron is also the owner and publisher of the newly established Antebellum Press showcasing Southern fiction.

Ron has also written numerous newspaper and magazine articles featuring best-selling and award-winning authors and other stories rich in community interest.

He lives with his wife, Linda, in Yulee, Florida, and together they have a Brady Bunch family of nine children and twenty grandchildren. He says to his youngest son, Chris, "When are you gonna get married and have me some grandyoungins?"